Home Before the Leaves Fall

Home Before the Leaves Fall

N. L. Collier

Matador
9 Priory Business Park,
Wistow Road, Kibworth Beauchamp,
Leicestershire. LE8 0RX
Tel: 0116 279 2299
Email: books@troubador.co.uk
Web: www.troubador.co.uk/matador
Twitter: @matadorbooks

ISBN 978 1788039 055

British Library Cataloguing in Publication Data.
A catalogue record for this book is available from the British Library.

Printed on FSC accredited paper
Printed and bound in Great Britain by 4edge Limited
Typeset in 11.5pt Aldine401 BT by Troubador Publishing Ltd, Leicester, UK

Matador is an imprint of Troubador Publishing Ltd

"For all flesh is as grass, and all the glory of man is as the flowers of the grass…" (Brahms, A German Requiem)
To the fallen of the Great War

„Denn alles Fleisch es ist wie Gras, und alle Herrlichkeit des Menschen wie des Grases Blumen…" (Brahms, Ein deutsches Requiem)
Den Gefallenen des Großen Krieges

I

"Mama, Papa, I... I've got something to tell you." I could hear the tension in my voice. *Steady, Franz. This is nothing to how you're going to feel.*

"What is it, dear?" Mama looked at me expectantly, her tone indulgent.

Papa remained behind the newspaper. "I suppose you need more money. God knows what you do with it. I hope you're not spending it on fast living."

God, not that again. I didn't get through half what some of the other students spent.

"No, Papa. I won't need your money for a while –" I took a deep breath. "I'm going to Heidelberg today, to meet Karl, and we're going to volunteer."

Papa folded the newspaper and put it carefully on the table.

'Glorious advance of our troops into Belgium!' shouted the headline. *That's where I want to be. Not stuck in lectures while everyone else gets all the action, all the glory.*

"Franz, I really don't want you to do this," Papa said gravely. "You don't know what it's going to be like."

Neither do you. You've never fought either. I didn't say it. The temperature would rise fast enough without my saying things like that. Papa always started by saying he didn't want me to do something, and finished by laying down the law.

"You're only nineteen. You're far too young. Let the Army fight – God knows it's big enough."

"I'll have to go next year anyway."

"The war will be over by then. Enjoy the rest of the summer holiday and go back to Heidelberg. There's no sense at all in breaking off your studies when you've only just started."

"Your father's right, Franz," said Mama. "There's no need for you to go."

Her eyes rested on my face. Stay at home, they said. Stay at home where you're safe.

Stay at home and let other men risk their lives... *What sort of man would that make me?*

I shook my head. "I have to go. I can't sit at home while all my friends go off to fight."

"While your *friend* goes off to fight, you mean," Papa said. "This is all his idea, isn't it?"

"No," I said rather defensively. "It's just as much my idea. I sent him a cable, just like the one he sent me."

"You did what?" He was beginning to sound impatient. "What has got into you?"

He paused, and then continued, his voice starting to rise.

"Why on earth did you have to get mixed up with someone like him, with a Junker of all people? Let him go and fight if he wants to – that's all the Prussians are any good for. They've got us into this mess and they can get us out again – and they can do it without your help. I'm not having you maimed or killed for that strutting buffoon in Berlin!"

"Josef!" Mama didn't share Papa's politics. "You shouldn't talk about the Kaiser like that!"

He ignored her. "Use some sense, Franz. You've got your whole life in front of you – why do you want to throw it away?"

"I don't. I'm not going to. But I am going to volunteer. I'm going to meet Karl, and we're joining up together."

"You'll do no such thing." He'd lowered his voice again, but it held a familiar note of finality. *I have spoken, and you will do as you are told.*

He picked up the newspaper, as if the conversation were over.

This is how it's always been, ever since I can remember. You expect me to obey, and I always have. I've never had any choice.

If I give in this time I will still be a child, not a man. I took a deep breath.

"Papa, I'm going. I have to. If I don't I'll despise myself for ever."

He stared at me, his face thunderous. "Why can't you just do as you're damn well told?! You have to bloody argue, every time! You're becoming completely impossible!"

It's no use, I thought with a rising sense of elation. *This time you can't make me do what you want. I'm old enough to enlist, and that's what I'm going to do.*

My bag was already packed.

"I'll be off, then," I said casually. "I can just make the next train."

The anger in Papa's eyes faded suddenly as he realised that the only way to stop me would be to lock me in the house.

Mama started to cry. "Franz, please don't do this. You're our only son—"

"There's no point talking to him, Grete. The fool won't listen to reason."

Resignation mixed with the anger in his voice. He'd lost, for the first time, and he knew it.

I left the room quickly, went upstairs and picked up my bag.

My sister Johanna came in from the garden just as I came back down.

"How did it go?" she asked.

"They tried to stop me but they didn't succeed!"

She flung her arms round me. "I can't wait to tell Liese! My brother the hero! Do be careful, won't you?"

"I'll do my best. Look, I've got to go – er, Papa's furious."

"Oh, God. What, really spitting?"

"'Fraid so. Bye then, Sis. Sorry to leave you to face the music."

She stood watching me until I'd turned the corner of the street, as if she felt that she might not see me again. For a moment I almost felt uncomfortable, but the feeling disappeared under the August sun.

I walked briskly to the station. *I'll soon be marching instead, in field-grey with my pack and rifle...*

My victory over my father felt like the advance guard of victories to come. *The French won't get their revenge for 1870. We'll smash them, just as we did then, and we'll be home before the leaves fall, as the Kaiser said, and I'll be a hero.*

Maybe I'll win the Iron Cross – now that would be something! The girls will all fall over me, and maybe I'll have a couple of scars to show them – nothing serious, just enough for a bit of extra attention. Just enough to make them think I'm someone special.

The atmosphere was electric, even in our small town, and the newspapers were full of the departure of our armies. There was an illustrated special, its front page covered with photographs of smiling soldiers with flowers in their rifles, of the women of Berlin marching beside their men. *That'll be me soon, marching off to war while girls cheer and blow kisses.*

I'm going to make history.

It was intoxicating and I could hardly feel the pavement beneath my feet. Forty years of peace had left Europe dull and stale and dirty. We were going to sweep all that away and the world would emerge brighter and cleaner. Our fathers led dull, safe lives, but my generation was singled out for glory.

We'll soon be entering Paris in triumph, flags flying, bands playing. Germany will be safe, the French and the Russians defeated, our future assured, and I'll have helped to bring that about. They'll write about us for generations, and maybe my name will be in the history books.

I didn't stop to think what war really was. I could shoot, of course, and I knew that the targets would be men instead of paper or animals, but the reality of that was beyond my imagination.

They'll be shooting back, there'll be bullets and shells coming at me – but I couldn't take that seriously. Death was something that happened to other people.

It'll be good to see Karl again, I thought, as the train pulled out of the station, *and even better to go off to war together.* I'd found myself missing him almost as soon as I'd got home, even though we'd only known each other for a couple of months.

We'd met during that first week when we freshmen all felt very new and uncertain. I'd noticed him at once, partly because he was tall and broad-shouldered, but more because he didn't seem to care what anyone thought of him and I wished I could be like that.

I wanted to talk to him, but had no idea how to start the conversation. The strange thing was that I felt as if I'd met him somewhere before. It was impossible, but the illusion was there all the same, and once or twice when our eyes met I thought he shared it.

At the end of the first week of term, I found myself sitting next to him in a lecture. It was on some intricate legal point and the delivery was less than exciting.

"God, I'm bored."

He muttered it, but enough of us heard him and there was a ripple of suppressed laughter. I was slightly shocked – it wasn't the thing to say in a lecture by such an eminent professor. I wasn't honest enough to admit that I was bored rigid as well.

Finally the professor droned to a halt.

Karl turned to me. "Jesus, I need a coffee after that."

"So do I."

"I don't know why I agreed to this," he said. "There must be an easier way of keeping Pa off my back."

"Don't you want to be a lawyer?" I asked, surprised.

"No. Absolutely not. Do you?"

"Well, yes… So, er… what do you want to do, then?"

"Be a pianist – you know, professionally."

It was the last answer I'd been expecting.

"Look, I'm giving a recital on Monday evening. Beethoven and Chopin. You're very welcome, if you'd like to come. Of course if you're busy it doesn't matter."

His manner was rather diffident, as if he didn't expect me to want to listen to him. *Anyone who thinks you're arrogant should have heard you just now*, I thought.

"Yes, I'd like that," I said, and he wrote down the details for me.

I went to the recital, out of curiosity and because I wanted to get to know him. I wasn't really expecting him to be any good. Papa always called the Prussian nobility 'cultureless boneheads', and the words stuck in my mind.

It's just prejudice and hatred of an old enemy. You've come to university to get an open mind, so just go and listen.

The audience was rather larger than I'd expected at a recital by some unknown student, and when Karl started to play I understood why.

He began with Beethoven's Appassionata Sonata. I knew how difficult it was because I'd heard Johanna wrestling with it, but in his hands it came alive. The passages she stumbled over cascaded out, powerful and spellbinding, and the music swept me away so that I had a sense of shock when it finished.

After the interval he played Chopin's Funeral March Sonata. The march itself was raw, searing grief. The hairs on my forearms stood on end and my throat tightened. *How do you do it?* I wondered as I left the hall. *How do you play like that, with so much feeling?*

I went backstage, reality returning slowly. The room was so noisy and crowded that I nearly left, wanting to hear the last echoes of the Chopin, but I had to talk to him. He was in high spirits from the music and the applause, his eyes alight.

"Did you enjoy it?" he asked.

"It was superb," I said truthfully. "But why in God's name are you studying law and not music?"

He sighed. "Family. We go into the Army or the civil service, and the eldest son – which thank God I'm not – has the joy of running the farm. I'm stuck till I'm twenty-one – then I'll be off to the Paris Conservatoire or the Royal Academy."

I was still there long after everyone else had gone. In the end the caretaker threw us out and we went back to his room, where we carried on drinking champagne and talking. The illusion of having met before was getting stronger.

"So tell me about your family," I said.

"Well, Pa was a major in the First Foot Guards but now he's a farmer in Brandenburg. My sister Elisabeth is the eldest of us – she got married in '10 and lives in England with her husband and my two little nephews, and I've got two older brothers: Friedrich, who's a Guards officer as well, and Johann, or rather Johnny, who's at Göttingen."

"Studying law?"

He laughed. "In between duels and drinking contests. You'd like him, Franz. He's good fun."

He hadn't mentioned his mother. I didn't like to ask. *She must be dead – or maybe she ran away and there was a scandal.*

"My mother died," he said quietly. "Cancer. Two years ago."

"I'm sorry." *Now I understand the Chopin.*

"You must come and stay," he said. "Pa's what you'd expect, but I'll try and fix it so Friedrich or Johnny is there."

"Thanks. I'd love to."

"Your glass is empty, Franz. That won't do."

I woke up on the floor the next afternoon with a splitting head. From then on we were inseparable.

We rented a flat together, as it would be cheaper than two sets of rooms. We weren't short of money, but we did want to have as much fun as possible. And it would be our own little household, where we could do as we pleased.

We found a light, airy apartment with two bedrooms and a living room. Karl took down the landlord's dull landscape and hung a nude over the fireplace instead.

She was a beauty, with brown hair tied up in a blue ribbon and wonderful creamy skin. She reclined on a chaise longue, her right arm draped over the back, her right leg bent while her left foot trailed on the floor. She had a lovely figure, full but not too plump, and her parted lips invited a kiss.

"Very nice," said Kurt with appreciation.

"Yes," Otto agreed. "Pity her legs aren't a bit further apart, though."

"Oh, I don't know," said Anton. "Best to use your imagination a bit, don't you think?"

Karl opened a bottle of champagne. "Welcome to our new home!"

"So where are the girls?" asked Otto.

"Ah, well," Karl began.

"There aren't any!" Kurt said gleefully. "He's got us here under false pretences!"

"Didn't old Prof Lippmann say something about that the other day?" asked Anton.

"Misrepresentation," said Otto.

"They'll be here at ten," Karl finished.

"Don't believe you!" Anton retorted.

Ten came and went, and there were no girls.

"See – I told you!" Kurt said, pointing at the clock. "False pretences!"

The doorbell rang. Karl smiled.

"I'll get it," I said.

I opened the door and my jaw dropped. Five lovely young women were standing there.

"Aren't you going to ask us in?" said a dark-haired one.

"Yes, er... of course... er—"

"Come in, Anna, ladies!" Karl called out. "The party's in here!"

So that's Anna, I thought as the dark girl embraced Karl.

"I eat my words," Kurt said.

"I'd rather eat her," Otto muttered with a gesture at one of Anna's friends.

I realised I was blushing furiously. I didn't want any of them to know I was a virgin.

Karl had guessed, though – my reaction to the pictures in his room had given me away. He had six beautiful pen and ink drawings, four of a man with a girl, and two of two girls together.

"Where on earth did you get those?" I'd asked, staring at them with more than a flicker of interest.

"Johnny drew them."

"I didn't know he was an artist."

A very good artist, I thought as I looked more closely. But what a subject! I'd never seen pictures like those before and I felt myself reddening. The faces weren't distinct, but I couldn't help wondering...

The party broke up some time after midnight. Our friends escorted three of the girls home – or wherever – and Karl and Anna went to bed. That left me in the living room with Inge.

She sat beside me on the sofa, her leg pressed against mine, and gestured up at the nude.

"Quite pretty," she said, and then murmured in my ear, "but only paint on canvas."

9

Her tongue flicked over my earlobe, and her hand landed softly on my thigh and made its way upwards.

"Let's go to my room," I managed to say.

She closed the door behind us and unpinned her hair. It fell to her waist, blonde and shimmering. Her dress dropped to the floor, followed by one garment after another until she stood there naked. I threw my clothes off and we tumbled onto the bed.

"I've got a rehearsal," she said in the morning. "I'll have to go."

"Come back tonight."

"Tomorrow – I need some sleep or I'll be falling over my feet."

I joined Karl for a late breakfast. Anna had gone as well.

He raised an eyebrow. "Which one was that?"

"Inge," I said, and a satisfied grin spread itself slowly across my face.

So much for that, I thought, gazing out of the train window. *Still, it was good while it lasted.*

She stayed at the flat quite often, usually arriving after the performance and leaving some time the next day. One Saturday after she'd left I couldn't be bothered to get dressed, and lay on the living room floor in my dressing gown, smoking a cigarette and enjoying the afterglow.

I really should be studying…

I forced myself to pick up a book, and I'd been reading for about two minutes when the doorbell rang.

Who the hell is that? Perhaps Inge's forgotten something. Or perhaps it's the landlord.

I got up reluctantly and went to the front door. I opened it wide – and stood transfixed with horror, trying to pretend I was pleased to see my parents.

The problems ran through my mind in swift, appalling succession. They didn't approve of my smoking and my cigarette was still burning in the ashtray. The nude still hung over the fireplace. And they would expect to be shown round the flat, which raised the question of Karl's pictures – and far worse, of Karl himself, who was in bed with Anna. Beside all that, the empty bottles in the kitchen were insignificant.

"Er… hello Mama, Papa… er, come in and hang your coats up. I'll just tidy up a bit."

I hurried back into the living room, hid the nude behind the sofa and hung the landlord's boring picture in her place. I was only just in time, and it was swinging slightly as they entered the room.

"So this is your new apartment," Mama said. "You've done very well. It's very nice. Where's your friend?"

"Oh, Karl's in bed with a stinking cold, so I'm afraid he won't be coming out to meet you. And I can't really show you his room."

Not very gallant, describing Anna as a stinking cold, but it was all I could think of.

"Oh dear. I hope you won't catch it."

"How are your studies going?" asked Papa, picking up a book.

"All right, thanks. There was something I wanted to ask you."

There was a muffled giggle. Mama looked at me sharply.

"That's… er… that's the girl next door."

"It sounded closer than that," she said suspiciously.

"The walls aren't very thick. Look, why don't we go out. There's a nice café round the corner. I'll just get dressed."

Papa gave me a disapproving look. He regarded late rising as a form of degeneracy.

I got dressed as fast as I could and got them out of the flat. I got a moderate grilling for smoking and being lazy – but my hair fairly stood on end when I thought of their reaction if they'd seen Karl and Anna.

And suppose they'd turned up in the morning? Or just as Inge was leaving? I knew I hadn't fooled them, but they didn't have anything concrete to go on. All they had were suspicions.

The train stopped again, jerking me back to the present, and I smiled. *That's going to seem very tame after a bit of action.*

It took me about three weeks to realise that Inge had someone else, someone older and richer who gave her nice presents. When I found out I said some very harsh things and sent her on her way.

"Why?" Karl asked in bemusement.

"I didn't like being second fiddle. I don't know how you put up with Anna."

He shrugged. "She's a good fuck and I never get bored – never quite know what's coming next!"

That was an understatement. Anna was half-Spanish and temperamental to go with it. She slept with whom she pleased, but for some unfathomable reason she made a fuss about Karl's casual encounters. I heard her shouting at him once because she'd caught him in one of the actors' dressing rooms with the wardrobe mistress.

"And why were you going in there in your dressing gown?" he asked, more amused than angry.

She lost her temper and started screaming at him in a mixture of Spanish and German. I went out and left them to it, and by the time I came home they were in bed, the row apparently forgotten.

I couldn't help being envious, though, and rather regretted throwing Inge over.

"You don't want to be too fussy, Franz – if a girl's a good fuck then just accept whatever goes with it," he said. "You're not going to marry her and she's not going to marry you."

"Do you have to be so bloody crude?" I snapped.

He just grinned and fetched me another beer.

"Farm boy," he said. "We're all like that... Tell you what, come home with me this weekend. You can meet Pa and maybe Friedrich or Johnny, and enjoy some clean country living – and if one of the farm girls takes a fancy to you, then so much the better!"

The journey took longer than I'd expected and we had to cross Berlin. I'd never been to the capital and I wanted to linger.

"Let's come for a weekend next term," Karl said. "You wouldn't believe the fun a fellow can have here."

"Papa did warn me about it," I said, laughing.

"Oh, he doesn't know the half of it. I could tell you – but I shan't!"

Brandenburg was far lovelier than I'd imagined – the train chuffed slowly past fields and woodland, and lake after lake sparkling blue in the June sunlight.

We got out at a tiny station in the middle of nowhere and were met by a hulking middle-aged farmhand in work-worn corduroy, leaning against a wagon. A battered straw hat shaded his eyes and he tipped it with one finger but didn't take it off.

"Hello, Pa!" Karl said, and I almost dropped my bag in astonishment.

"Good afternoon, Herr Major," I said politely, finding I was looking up. He was bigger than Karl and rather imposing.

A pair of grey eyes appraised me coolly and a large hand shook mine with a grip just on the civilised side of crushing.

Not someone you'd mess with, I thought, feeling somewhat overawed.

"Well, get in," he said, and we climbed into the back of the wagon and sat in the hay.

I'd been expecting grand people who lived in style. What I found was a plain, rather austere manor house on a working farm, where everyone rolled his sleeves up and got his hands dirty. The nobility in my part of Germany lived in a far more exalted fashion.

Karl's Pa made mine seem easy-going. Once or twice he gave me a cold stare that made me quite uneasy and there was some sort of undercurrent between him and Karl that I didn't understand. I was very glad Friedrich had leave for the weekend.

"Shame Johnny couldn't make it," Karl said, "but his duelling society has an away match. Can't remember where."

"Let's hope he gives more than he gets this time!" Friedrich said, and they both laughed.

The Major grunted. "Sometimes wonder why I waste my money."

The train stopped and I looked out of the window. Not quite there yet.

The last weekend of term I took Karl home. I had misgivings about it but I owed him the hospitality. I did hope Papa would try to bury his prejudices and see Karl as my friend rather than as a member of the class he hated most, but that was more than a bit naïve of me.

To be fair to Papa I think he was prepared to make an effort. The trouble was that Johanna took one look at Karl and liked what she saw, and every time their eyes met she blushed.

Papa didn't like it at all. He was clearly worried that his daughter's virtue was at risk. I knew it wasn't, but there was no way of saying so without making things even worse.

Added to that, he didn't think Karl was suitable company for me. He guessed that Karl had led me astray and the result was a 'man-to-man chat' which was even more embarrassing than usual, full of veiled hints about dirty women and terrible diseases.

Why can't you just say what you mean? You've never told me anything useful about protecting myself. It's just as well Karl has, otherwise I really would be in danger of catching something.

That's all in the past now, I thought as I got off the train. The next couple of months will be *really* exciting.

Half the population of Heidelberg seemed to be out on the streets. Our usual café was crammed with excited, chattering students and I squeezed in with some difficulty.

I wonder if Karl's here yet... It's going to be impossible to get a table – but we won't be staying long.

"Franz! *Franz* – over here!" He was waving to me from a table by the window.

"How are you?"

He looked very well, his face brown and his hair bleached almost blond by the sun, but there was something I couldn't read in his eyes, something like disquiet.

"Fine. And you?"

"Yes, fine. Shall we go?"

"Sit down first and have a coffee."

"But –"

He laughed. "The war'll wait another half hour. Enjoy a cake and a cup of decent coffee while you can."

"All right."

The atmosphere was vibrant, festive. We were all setting off on the same great adventure.

"So it's war!" I said.

"Yes, it's war," he said, very soberly.

"You don't seem very happy."

"Happy? Franz, what is there to be happy about?"

"Well –"

I didn't have an answer. The war was so obviously wonderful and exciting that I hadn't really thought about it. Karl's face was grave and his eyes were hard and more grey than blue as he waited for my reply.

"Have you any idea what war means?" he asked.

"Well, no, I suppose not, but... I thought you felt the same about it as me. I don't understand what you're doing here if you don't."

He sighed. "I'm here because there's nothing else I can do. But don't give me any of that crap about what a glorious adventure it's going to be. I've had enough of that from Kurt."

"He's here as well?"

"Of course – it's his big chance, isn't it? His parents can hardly object to his joining the Army now. He's gone to find Otto and Anton. I said we'd see them in the queue." His tone was flat and matter-of-fact.

"Don't you want to go, then?"

He put another cigarette in the holder and lit it. "Look, a lot of my ancestors died on this battlefield or that, including my namesake, who was only seventeen, and I've listened to stories about the war of 1870 from my uncle Heinrich and from old Henning ever since I can remember. You remember Henning?"

"Yes." Henning was the Leussows' butler.

"You know we lost fifty thousand men at Metz alone? Do you know what fifty thousand men looks like, let alone fifty thousand casualties? And that was only our side. The French lost thousands as well."

"But this isn't the same," I said stupidly.

"Of course it is. War isn't a glorious adventure. It's a failure of civilisation. It's a disgusting, bloody business."

His words cast a cloud over my mood.

I laughed. It came out rather forcedly. "God, you're gloomy today! Are you scared or something?"

"Not yet! But we will be. We will be. Oh, don't misunderstand, I'm going to volunteer. But I'm doing it with my eyes open."

For the first time I felt a flicker of doubt. "Do... do you think we won't come back, then?"

He shrugged. "Possibly. It's not worth thinking about."

He finished his coffee and stood up. "Well, let's go and sign ourselves away."

"You know," I said as we walked out into the bright sunshine, "my parents blame you for dragging me into the war, and I'm the one who's full of enthusiasm while you're spouting gloom and doom."

"Realism, you mean. Did you have much trouble with them?"

"Papa's livid. I… well, I suppose I walked out, really. Mama was in tears…" Suddenly I felt quite guilty. Suppose I don't go home again? "I don't suppose you had any problems."

He laughed. "With *my* family? Pa rushed off to Berlin as soon as we mobilised and he's on General von Grimnitz's staff. Friedrich's probably in Belgium now – his regiment was one of the first to go – and Johnny's volunteering in Göttingen. So that's all four of us carrying on the glorious Leussow tradition. I just hope there'll still be four of us at the end of it."

For a moment I couldn't catch my breath, as if Death had stepped closer. Karl had almost shown me that the golden immortality of youth was only an illusion.

How can you be so calm about it? I wondered. *But you're right – we will be scared and some of us will be killed. It might even be me.* For a moment my enthusiasm dimmed. *Perhaps Papa was right. I don't really know what I'm getting into – but it's too late and I wouldn't go back home even for a million marks.*

"Franz! Karl!" Kurt, Anton and Otto were running towards us.

Otto leapt on me and Anton leapt on him, and we landed on the pavement and rolled over.

"You'll have to do better than that when it's the Frenchies!" Kurt said.

A couple of mature men looked at us and shook their heads. We didn't care. *We're off to fight for you,* I thought.

A duelling society swaggered past us, arms linked, singing

at the top of their voices, caps askew above their scarred faces. They sounded as if they'd been at the beer.

"Look at those louts!" one of the older men said to the other.

"Don't be so hard on them, Konrad," he replied. "They're going to enlist. That's where all the students are going."

"Oh, well – that's different." He turned to us. "Are you going to enlist as well?"

"Yes, we are!" we chorused.

"Good for you, boys!" he said, and clapped Anton on the shoulder. "Oh, how I envy you! It's such an honour to fight for the Fatherland. But I'm too old, you see!"

"Bloody hypocrite," Karl said as the men walked away. "You could almost hear the relief in his voice."

"Why would anyone be relieved?" asked Otto.

"Anyone would think you were scared!" Kurt said to Karl.

"Not yet. But we will be. Oh, what's the use! No one's going to listen to me!" he said with a laugh.

"What are you going to join?" Kurt asked him.

"The infantry."

So were we all.

"I'd have thought you'd have gone for the cavalry," Otto said to Karl. "Don't most of your family?"

"No – it's usually the infantry. My great-uncle Heinrich was a cavalryman, though… Had to shoot his horse at Gravelotte. He said its guts were hanging out."

We were suddenly silent. If that could happen to a horse…

"I just hope I don't come back like Uncle Heinrich," he went on. "In a wheelchair with a broken back."

"I didn't meet him," I said.

"No, he died in '11." He gave a short laugh. "You wouldn't have liked him – he was a cantankerous, drunken old bastard. Drank himself to death in the end… He got hit at Metz. He was only twenty and that was it – couldn't walk, no women, nothing.

He told me he went off to war with his head full of crap about glory and he did come home with the Iron Cross – but he paid for it."

We looked at each other and it was as if a shadow had passed across the sun.

I thought of the portraits of Karl's ancestors that lined the walls of his home, all the men in uniform. A lot of them got killed, he said…

"How did your parents take it?" I asked Kurt. I wanted to change the subject.

"They were all right, actually. They both feel I should do my duty, and Papa said something about it 'making a man of me'." He rolled his eyes and then laughed. "He still expects me to finish my degree afterwards and then join him in the bank, though. If I'd told him I plan to spend the rest of my life in the Army there'd have been one hell of a row and I didn't want to cause that much trouble, not when I was just leaving. How about yours?"

I told them.

"Well, your pater's a socialist, isn't he, and they don't believe in war," Otto said. His freckled face creased into a grin. "Mine don't even know yet. I was hiking in the Bavarian Alps with my brothers when we heard what had happened. I tell you what, the Bavarians may be a bit odd but the girls down there! Whew! You should see them!

"Anyway, my three oldest brothers rejoined their regiments at once, Dieter went back to Freiburg to join up with his corps brothers, and here I am – and the poor old parents know nothing about it! I mean, they'll find out, though, when they get the photo of me in uniform."

"I think that's really mean of you," said Anton. "Mama was really upset. She's going to be on her own now. I don't have any brothers or sisters, you know, so if anything happens to me, that's it." He sounded worried. "I really feel I shouldn't have left her but what was I to do? She's a widow, you know – I mean, she's got gentleman friends, but that's not the same thing as a husband, is it?"

Karl and I avoided each other's eyes. Anton's mother had come to visit him in the second half of term. She was a striking woman in her thirties, very expensively dressed, very sophisticated, with something in her eyes that made me feel rather hot.

Karl seemed a little uncomfortable when they were introduced but she smiled and said, "We met at a party in Berlin a year or so ago, didn't we?"

"Ah, yes, that's it. I knew I'd met you somewhere before – I just couldn't quite remember where."

"I didn't know you knew Frau Döpfner," I said to him later.

"Only in the biblical sense," he replied. "She's one of the most expensive tarts in Berlin. When I was in the last year of school, ten of us pooled our money and then drew lots for who was to be the lucky fellow."

"And you won!"

"No, I didn't. Part of the deal was that the winner had to tell the rest of us all about it – and I mean *all* about it, nothing left out – and after hearing all that, I saved up for six months and then went to see her myself."

"Was she worth it?"

"Actually, no. It's like food, I think. Once you pay a certain amount for a meal, I think that's a sort of optimum. You *can* pay more but you don't get a proportionate increase in pleasure. I think it's the same with tarts. I wouldn't go a second time."

Tart or not, she obviously adored Anton, as he did her, and I couldn't help feeling rather sorry for her, left on her own. *She's probably crying her eyes out, just like my mother. I wonder if he knows what she does for a living, where all his money comes from.*

"You know what the Kaiser said," I told him. "'Home before the leaves fall'. She'll have you back in time for Christmas and you'll have lots of exciting stories to tell her."

"Yes, I expect so," he said, but there was a note of uncertainty in his voice.

The entire university seemed to be joining up and the queue stretched out of sight ahead of us. It was late in the evening before our turn came.

A jaded sergeant sat at a table covered with papers.

"Name?" he asked, without looking at Karl.

"Eckhardt von Leussow, Karl Friedrich August."

The sergeant looked up wearily. "Just yer name, laddie, not yer bleedin' pedigree."

"Von Leussow, Karl."

"That's better. That'll fit on the page. Age?"

"Nineteen."

I was next, and the sergeant gave me a suspicious look. "And I suppose you're Thingummy von Whatnot as well."

"Becker, Franz Ludwig."

"Quite sure? No pedigree?"

"No."

"Where've all these blue bloods come from, then?"

"The university." Fully a fifth of my fellow students were noble.

"Goin' to do something useful for a change instead of carvin' each other's faces up?"

"I hope so." It wasn't worth trying to explain that I didn't belong to a duelling corps.

Behind me it went on. "Meyer, Kurt… nineteen… Döpfner, Anton… nineteen… Kramer, Otto… nineteen… Schrupp…"

They had more volunteers than they could take and they weren't going to need us for a couple of weeks. I don't know what I'd been expecting but I suddenly felt very flat.

We were all tired and hungry.

"Let's drop our things at the flat and go and get something to eat," Karl said. "With a bit of luck Anna might be at the theatre."

She was, and she kissed Karl passionately, in front of us all. *What a contrast you two make – North and South embracing, fair and dark, strong and slender.*

She turned to us.

"It's lovely to see you," she said. "But not because of this." She gazed at Karl. "Have you done it?"

She could speak perfect German but offstage she affected a strong Spanish accent. I wasn't sure if I liked it or not. I could never tell when she was acting and when she was being genuine, and I don't think Karl could either.

"Yes, we have."

"May God bring you all home safely. I shall pray for you every night."

There were tears in her eyes and I swear they were real. She held onto Karl as if she would never let him go.

"Don't get dramatic, Anna. We've had a long day. Are any of your friends free?"

"I'll ask."

She managed to find three friends who agreed to come out with us. That meant one of us would have no companion and I'm ashamed to say that we drew lots while we waited at the stage door, before we'd even seen the girls.

Kurt lost but didn't seem to mind. "There's nothing to say the rest of you will get anywhere, after all!"

He was right. I didn't have any luck and I lay in bed trying not to think what Karl and Anna were doing, and wishing I hadn't been so quick to give Inge the push.

I'd better go home, I thought in the morning, *say goodbye properly.* I felt rather guilty about the way I'd left. Suppose the

Army had wanted me straight away? I'd have been off to war without seeing my family again.

"Do you want to come with me?" I asked Karl.

"Thanks, but I don't think it would be a good idea," he said. "I think I'd be persona non grata – and besides, I've got a hot woman here and it might be my last chance!"

I wish you wouldn't keep going on about getting killed. You might like thinking about it but I don't.

My parents and my sister were very pleased to see me, and Papa bent over backwards to be nice to me. He even managed to keep his politics to himself, though he couldn't resist pointing out that our violation of Belgian neutrality was illegal and immoral and that it had caused the English to declare war on us as well.

"Do you understand what that means?" he asked. "Now we have their Royal Navy against us as well. They might not have much of an army but at sea they're a force to be reckoned with—" He stopped himself suddenly. "But I'm sure the war will be over quickly, before they can do much."

You need to believe that, I realised. *You need to believe I'll be home soon.*

They treated me like royalty, to the point where it began to feel like a feast for the condemned. There was a continuous unspoken undercurrent of "we might never see you again", which made me very uncomfortable. Everyone seemed to be focussed on the one thing I wanted to ignore.

I was beginning to realise what I'd done and that it was far too late to change my mind. I had signed my name. I belonged to the Army and it was just a question of when they would want me.

At the same time I was impatient to be off and time began to drag. *If they don't send for me soon it'll be too late and I'll miss all the action. It would be frightfully boring to do the training and then go back to Heidelberg without fighting.*

After a fortnight my papers arrived and so did a telegram

from Karl. We were going to be together. Even Papa seemed pleased.

"At least you'll be with someone you know," he said, and then took me into his study for the usual lecture on virtue and chastity, this time full of warnings about the immorality of French women.

I had great difficulty not laughing, because he really believed that I was still a virgin and likely to remain one, and because he seemed to know less about sex than I did – or else he was completely incapable of talking about it.

There was a long queue again, this time for the medical examination. There was no sign of my friends anywhere. I was almost desperate to find Karl, because if we could stick together through training then there was a chance of our being kept together when we went to war. I didn't want to be surrounded by strangers.

I passed, and was told to report to a school a couple of kilometres away, which had been requisitioned to accommodate the overflow.

If I don't find him soon we'll be split up...

A hand descended on my shoulder and I jumped.

"Keep your eyes open, Franz!" Karl said.

"Where did you spring from?" I asked.

"I had my medical an hour or so ago and I guessed you'd be later than me so I waited."

"Where are the others?"

"Waiting at the school gates – or rather, just round the corner. I told them not to go in without us."

They weren't there.

"Maybe we should wait," I said.

"Not a good idea," Karl replied. He indicated a stern-looking sergeant heading towards us. "He's Field Police and you don't want to get across him. Let's just go in and we'll find them later."

The school was being transformed into a barracks. Most of the classrooms were full of iron bunks and the assembly hall had become the dining hall, while the playing fields served as the parade ground.

There still wasn't enough room for us all and quite a lot of men were billeted with local families. We found out the next day that Otto was one of them.

"They spoil me rotten," he said. "I've got my own room – I mean, I've got a nice soft bed and proper linen, and I share their bathroom."

I couldn't believe what I was hearing and contrasted it unhappily with my hard bunk and scratchy blanket. I hadn't been able to sleep at all.

"Lucky bugger," I said. "You should see what we have to sleep on."

"Don't envy him too much," Karl said to me later. "Sleeping rough will be a lot easier for us. He's going to find a muddy ditch really unpleasant, whereas we'll think it's nice and soft!"

Later that day we had our hair cut, or rather had our heads practically shaved. We looked at each other and laughed.

Karl ran his hand over his head. "Oh, if Pa could see me now – it would make his day!"

"At least I've got rid of my ginger thatch," said Otto.

"You've still got ginger eyebrows," Kurt said.

"And eyelashes," I added.

"Oh, piss off, all of you! Anton looks just like a baby."

And he did, with his round, boyish face no longer framed by dark curls.

"Or a cherub," Karl said.

"Cherub?" said Otto. "Disciple of Beelzebub, more like."

I had to laugh when I looked in the mirror, but at the same time I felt a bit more like a soldier and Otto said much the same thing.

All I need now is a smart field-grey uniform, I thought, but there weren't any for us. Instead I was given a dreadful old blue thing, which had been washed so many times that it had faded to a dingy nondescript hue. No one else's was any better. And we had no rifles. Those would come later, we were told, and in the meantime we began learning rifle drill with broom handles.

Nothing in my life had prepared me for the Army. I'd always slept in a feather bed in my own room, with fine bedlinen. My bunk was rock-hard and for the first couple of nights I was kept awake by the snores of the others. After that I was so tired that I fell asleep the moment my head touched the thin pillow. Papa would have smiled in spite of himself to see his lazy son getting up so early and working so hard.

We did physical training and drill, and exercised on the 'parade ground' until we were sick of it and the lush grass had all been worn away. We had to learn the Prussian parade march – the goose-step – and saluting and a thousand things that seemed to have no relevance at all to war.

I got most of it wrong to begin with and my ears rang from being shouted at by the NCOs. My only consolation was that Otto and Anton were even worse than I was.

Karl, on the other hand, knew most of it already.

"How do you know all this stuff?" I asked him. "I'm still working out what half the orders mean."

"Didn't you play soldiers when you were a boy?"

"Well, yes, of course, but it was just running round in the woods and pretending to shoot each other. You didn't do drill as a kid, did you?"

He laughed. "Friedrich went to cadet school when Johnny was eight and I was seven. When he came home in the holidays we were only too happy to dress up in miniature uniforms, and yes, we did drill. I mean, we ran around pretending to shoot each other as well but Friedrich was always in command. He got a bit too bossy once and we mutinied and threw him in the lake. Shows the importance of keeping the respect of your men, Pa told him."

"There's one or two here who could do with being reminded of that... I don't think I'll ever get it right."

"Oh, you will. It just takes a bit of practice."

The hard physical work was not the only shock, nor the worst one. The obedience demanded by my father was nothing compared to that required by the Army. Yes, I'd always had to do as he'd said, but at the same time he'd encouraged me to have an open, inquiring mind. Once I'd told him I wanted to be a lawyer, he'd discussed his cases with me.

"Look at it from every angle," he'd said. "Don't just accept what you're told."

My short time at Heidelberg had reinforced that attitude and now I had to shed it. If you'd said 'intellectual freedom' to our NCOs they'd have thought you were blaspheming.

"Bloody hell," Anton said one evening as we queued for dinner, "I think I should have sent my brain home with my clothes."

"It is a bit much sometimes," Otto agreed, "but it's just at the beginning. That's what my brothers said. Later they do want you to think. I mean, you have to know what to do if the officer gets killed."

"Yes, but you still have to obey, don't you?" I said.

"What do you expect?" Kurt asked. "Without discipline you don't have an army, just a rabble."

"You're just looking forward to giving the orders!" Otto said.

"All in good time," Kurt replied. "'Learn to obey—'"

"'That you may learn to command'," Karl finished with him.

"I'm buggered if I want to do either!" said Anton.

"Shouldn't have joined up, then, should you?" Alfred said, and Anton gave him a punch on the arm.

"Too bloody late, isn't it?" he replied.

Alfred Friedemann had the bunk above Anton's in our room. He was a medical student from Berlin and his scarred face showed how he'd spent his time.

"I did study as well," he said when Karl compared him to Johnny.

"So why've you joined up here?" I asked.

"I was on holiday here with one of my corps brothers – we came here a year or so back to visit one of your societies and we decided to come back for a proper look round."

"Instead of just fighting duels and drinking," said Karl.

"Exactly – the scenery's stunning but we didn't see much of it before. Anyway, being as we were here we got on with volunteering."

"So where've they put your chum, then?" asked Otto.

"Failed the medical. Something wrong with his heart, so he's gone home to see a specialist."

Kurt grinned. "'Something wrong with his heart?' That's a bit vague from a medical student!"

Alfred pulled a face. "It's what he said to me – he's reading philosophy. Bugger all use to anyone if you ask me."

"So why aren't you in the Medical Service?" asked Anton.

Alfred clamped a hand over Anton's mouth.

"Shut the fuck up before someone hears you!" he whispered urgently. "That's the last place I want to be – I'm after the best fight of my life and I don't want some bastard stopping me!"

Karl gave him a rather doubting look and then shrugged.

"Didn't you believe him?" I asked him later.

"With a face like that? I believe him, all right – but he might get more than he's bargained for."

Karl stood the iron discipline without even seeming to notice it and I realised that the Major must have raised his sons to follow him into the Army. Once, after I'd been shouted at for about the fiftieth time in one day, I had a good old grouse to him. He smiled and shook his head.

"Franz, Franz, it's no use talking about individuality. The Prussian Army's not the least bit interested in Franz Becker or Karl Leussow – all it wants is two more soldiers in anonymous grey. The only freedom we've got left now is in here." He tapped his head. "Now you understand why I refused to go to cadet school."

"It's the *German* Army," I said with a stab of irritation.

He just smiled again and I knew what he meant. We were at war, so Prussia commanded – and as if to underline the point the reservists who had joined us said they were "with the Prussians" rather than "in the Army".

The reservists made up about a third of our number. They were men with families, who saw the war as a grim necessity. All had served their years a decade or so earlier, and they wanted to get the business over quickly and get home to their children and their jobs.

Their opinion of us was quite plain.

"Wet behind the ears, the whole bloody lot of you," said Weiss.

"What sort of stupid cunt actually *wants* to get his bollocks shot off?" added Kienle.

Zeller grinned at them and then at us.

"*We* don't need to worry," he said. "The silly sods will get shot before us!"

"So don't you want to fight, then?" Otto asked.

"I want to finish those fucking Frenchies off and get home," Weiss replied. "What's my missus supposed to do, on her own with the smithy?"

"Of course I wants to fight," Zeller said indignantly, "but only as much as I has to."

"Right fucking mess, the whole business," said Kempff. "Still, if the Frenchies and the Russkis and the Tommies want war they can have it."

"And we'll make them regret it," Weiss agreed. "But you lot of young fools have to become soldiers first and you've got a bloody long way to go."

"Yes," said Zeller. "You has to learn: never volunteer."

The others agreed but none of us saw it that way.

"You should be grateful," Kurt said. "Every time we step forward you get let off!"

"Well, there is that," Kienle agreed grudgingly.

Kempff looked at Anton, who was trying to get the mud off his tunic. We'd had a long afternoon of "Forward! Down! Up!" and we were completely filthy – and everything had to be immaculate before we went on parade yet again.

"Not like that, you daft young bugger," he said. "You'll only drive the dirt in further. Give it here... Look, this is what you do..."

"Smoke, anyone?" offered Anton.

"Cheers, mate," said Weiss, and there was a chorus of "Don't mind if I do".

"I'll stick to mine, thanks," Karl said, and got one of his favourite black cigarettes out of his silver case, put it in the holder and lit it with his silver lighter.

"I can't get over you doing that," Zeller said. "Fucking poncey object, that holder."

Karl just smiled through a cloud of strong smoke.

"Bloody poncey case and lighter, too," said Weiss. "Let's have a look, then."

Karl handed him the lighter.

"Christ," Weiss said, "it's solid silver."

He turned it over and saw the Leussow arms engraved on it.

"Fuck me," he said. "This on the case as well?"

"What do you expect from a bleeding 'von', anyway?" asked Kempff.

"Aren't you worried about them getting nicked?" Otto asked.

Karl just looked at him.

No, I thought, *you're not quite as big as the Major, but not far off, and I saw today how strong you are. No one in his right mind would nick something of yours – you'd put his teeth down his throat.*

"Wonder how much longer we'll be here," said Alfred.

"And will it be East or West?" asked Kurt.

"I want to go East," Karl said; "throw those fucking Russians out of East Prussia. My uncle and his family have had to leave."

"They've always been the same," Alfred said. "Raping everyone in sight."

"Oh, come on," said Otto. "Surely that's just propaganda."

"Yes," I agreed. "No one really rapes and pillages any more."

Karl and Alfred just looked at us.

"Every Prussian knows what the Russkis are like," Alfred said.

"That's for sure," Zeller chipped in. "Look what they did in the Seven Years' War."

Otto and I looked at each other. Both our states had fought against Prussia in that war and we didn't want to mention it.

Karl started laughing.

"What's so funny?" Alfred asked.

"Our dear friends wouldn't know what their old ally got up to," Karl said. "Franz being from Württemberg and Otto from Saxony."

"Oh, right!" said Alfred. "Foreigners! Well, I suppose we're all German now!"

"Sod the East," Kurt said. "Well, that is, of course the Russians have to be sent packing – but I want to go West. That's where the war will really be won."

"That's where your best opportunities for glory are, you mean," Otto retorted. "I don't care where it is – I just want to get there before it finishes without us."

"I'm with Leussow," said Kienle. "My family's had to leave home because of those bloody Russians as well."

"Yes," I said, "but the French haven't forgiven us for 1870 and they want Alsace and Lorraine back."

"What do you mean, back?" Anton said. "They were German until Louis XIV pinched them."

"And now they've got the English to help them," said Karl. "It seems to me that we've made too many enemies and now we have to deal with them all at once. If we fail we've had it."

"Do you think so?" Otto asked.

"I don't think a defeated Germany could expect any mercy from the Allies," Karl answered. "Think how much we're likely to show them when we win."

"Karl's right," said Alfred. "We're fighting for our survival. We're surrounded by enemies who want to destroy us and we have to finish them first."

Gefreiter Dittrich's voice cut through our chatter.

"You useless lot! You're on parade in fifteen minutes and you're gossiping like a load of old whores! I want you all spotless, or God help you! Leussow! You're to report to Major Fessler at seven sharp!"

What the hell's that about? I wondered. *Why on earth does the Commandant want to see Karl?*

I asked him later.

"Don't ask," he said with disgust. "He remembered hearing me give a recital in Berlin."

"So?"

"They've got guests in the mess tomorrow night and he thought it might be nice to have some music. I don't want to do it, I can tell you – I haven't touched a piano for nearly a month, as you know." He sighed. "Well, I expect I can keep them happy. It's not as if they want the Transcendental Variations."

The following night he crept into the room very late and shook me awake.

"Karl, for God's sake!" I whispered. "Why can't you just go to bed?"

"Oh, well, if you don't want to know where we're going…"

Suddenly I was wide awake.

"Where?"

"Antwerp."

"How do you know that?"

"I heard them talking about it. They probably thought I couldn't play and listen at the same time."

"Shut the fuck up, will you? Some of us want to sleep!"

Antwerp. The West, after all. I was secretly relieved at not having to face the Russians. There was something barbaric about them and part of me shrank from the thought of Cossacks with lances and sabres.

Frenchmen with bayonets will be just as lethal – the abyss opened at my feet and I recoiled. It had all seemed so easy under the August sun, but lying awake in the dark I was suddenly filled with dread, with a sense that Death was waiting for me.

You're going to die sometime, I told myself, *and it's better to go when you're young and healthy, and for a cause. Who wants to drag on into a crippled old age?*

But I wanted, so much, to live. *Please God, when the order comes to advance, please don't let me fail!*

You won't. The others will be with you and you'll be fine. And by then you'll have finished your training and you'll know what to do. They won't send you to the Front until you're ready.

Finally I fell asleep but had one bad dream after another. *It'll be all right*, I thought in the daylight. *I'll get through it all right.*

A couple of days later we had yet another afternoon lecture and I took my place with no enthusiasm because I knew my mind would wander. I did try to pay attention to all the instruction in case I missed something vital, but all too often without success.

Old Fessler made his portly way into the room, followed by a tall, powerfully-built Leutnant with his right arm in a sling. Karl gave an audible gasp of astonishment and I just stopped myself echoing him.

What on earth is Friedrich doing here? I wondered.

Karl and I had arrived at the Leussow house on the Friday of that weekend – which already seemed to be in another world – and Friedrich had come home on leave the next day. We were out riding and he caught up with us on one of the dirt roads on the estate, a big, solid man on a black stallion that must have measured seventeen hands and that carried his weight easily.

What struck me first was how like Karl he was. They both had the same light-brown hair, shining reddish gold in the bright sunlight, and the same rather narrow grey-blue eyes. It wasn't long before I saw the differences.

Friedrich was Karl's senior by only three years but it seemed like a lot more. He had a calm, reserved dignity and it was almost impossible to get him to talk about himself, and yet his quiet presence was imposing. It was partly his size – he was the same height as his father and almost as broad – but more the force and determination that lay beneath his modest, courteous manner.

You'll go a long way, I thought. *A very long way.*

Major von Leussow's gaze softened slightly when it rested on him and I realised that he loved his eldest son deeply, though I couldn't imagine him admitting it. It was strange to see affection in the Major's hard grey eyes – every time he looked at me I felt he was finding fault.

That afternoon, as Friedrich waited for Fessler to finish his ponderous introduction, I saw that he'd changed. I couldn't define it at first – something in his eyes or about the set of his mouth?

After a couple of minutes I realised what it was: he'd faced the test and passed it. This wasn't just Karl's brother or a man in a smart uniform. This was a real soldier, who'd recently been in action. We'd never seen anyone like that before. The last war had finished forty-three years earlier and the men who'd fought it were old and grey.

He spoke confidently and fluently, without notes, about the war as he'd seen it. We were all riveted to every word. It was the first really interesting talk we'd had.

Later Karl was bombarded with questions. He fended them off, not very graciously.

"What's wrong?" I asked when we had a quiet moment.

"Pa could have told me Friedrich had copped it. He is my brother."

"He must be busy. Perhaps he thought you'd see it in the casualty lists."

It didn't sound convincing, even to me. *He should have told you*, I thought.

"Perhaps he thought Friedrich would tell you himself," I added.

That was crap – both his brothers were terrible correspondents. Karl had had one letter from each of them at university and one from Johnny since we'd enlisted.

He shrugged. "Who knows?"

"Where did it happen?"

"On the Sambre." He seemed to realise how abrupt he was being and after a moment he continued, "Old Fessler left us alone for an hour, bless him, so we could talk properly. I managed to call him 'Herr Leutnant' in public but I don't think I could have kept it up without slipping and saying 'du' by mistake."

"So what happened to his arm?"

"Got broken by a French bullet. He says it was clean enough and he thinks it's healing all right, but he broke that arm in a riding accident last year and the doctors are a bit unhappy with it. That's why he's here – he's got a hospital appointment in town, orthopaedic specialist. He came to see me, and Fessler roped him into giving that talk."

He sighed.

"He said it's driving him mad. He feels perfectly all right and he just wants to get back. He's always been the same – years ago he broke his leg and Pa locked him in his room because he'd caught him riding with it still in plaster."

"Why?"

"He was bored. Pa said he admired Friedrich's spirit but he didn't want another bloody great doctor's bill."

There was a note of anxiety in his voice that he didn't quite manage to hide.

You're worried about him, I thought, realising suddenly that it was with good reason. *Friedrich didn't tell us how he'd been wounded and he didn't mention anyone being killed. He just spoke about 'casualties'.*

My imagination couldn't connect a dry little word with the reality of death and injury.

The next morning we had first-aid training, which went into unwelcome detail. *Some of us will be those casualties*, I thought. I looked at the others and wondered who, and whether they would be badly injured. *Some of us will be killed* – but I still couldn't believe that anything like that could happen to me.

II

Bit by bit we received our equipment, and by the end of September all of us had smart new field-grey uniforms with red piping, and stiff boots which gave us blisters and which we spent hours trying to soften.

"You just have to break them in," Kienle said.

"I think they're breaking me in," Otto replied.

"Keep rubbing the Vaseline in," said Kempff. "Does the trick eventually."

Alfred raised one eyebrow at that but whatever the thought was he kept it to himself.

"Ah yes," Karl said. "Where would we be without Vaseline?"

Alfred gave him a glance that I really didn't understand. For a moment I felt excluded and slightly pissed off.

Kurt started laughing. "Does come in handy when you fancy going in the back way!"

Going in the—? Oh. I see. I felt myself going scarlet because I'd never done that or even thought about it.

"That's for sure!" Zeller was laughing as well and we all joined in.

Presumably you all have, then, or else you're bluffing like me.

"At least we look like soldiers now," Anton said, changing the subject.

"More appearance than substance!" Zeller said with a laugh.

We looked even more like soldiers when we were issued with our rifles, early in October. These caused a bit of a problem. All the NCOs were older men who had been recalled from retirement and only Unteroffizier Betzing had ever even seen a Model 98 rifle. None of them had actually used one and apparently it was different to the Model 88, though I wasn't quite sure how.

A couple of days later Fessler announced to us that we would soon be on our way to Belgium. We erupted into cheers, completely drowning the efforts of the NCOs to silence us. At last! It was all we could do not to jump for joy.

Once again Karl didn't seem to share our enthusiasm.

"Don't you want to go?" Otto asked him.

"Of course – but think about it. We haven't even been on the firing range yet. We've only had our rifles a few days. All we've done so far is drill and saluting, and a bit about attack and defence. That's not going to be much use, is it?"

We looked at each other. He had a point.

"I've never fired a gun in my life," said Anton.

"Neither have I," Otto said.

Karl stared at his hands and I had the feeling he didn't want to look at either of them. There was an awkward silence.

"Well, we're not going just yet," Kurt said. "I expect they'll put that right in the next couple of days."

Sure enough, that afternoon we marched to the range. I did reasonably well and so did Kurt and Anton, but poor Otto only got one round into the target.

Karl was frighteningly accurate.

Alfred put a good face on it but he was obviously a bit pissed off. He'd been comfortably ahead until Karl took his turn.

"Very good shooting, Leussow," said old Betzing. "Very nicely done."

It was the first time I'd seen anything like approval in his eyes.

"I knew you could shoot," I said later, "but I didn't realise you were that good."

"You make it look so easy," Anton said.

"Yes," agreed Otto. "I'm glad you're on our side!"

"I've had a lot of practice," Karl replied, and there was a sort of shadow in his voice.

"Well, tell us, then," said Kurt. "Do you shoot for Brandenburg or something?"

Karl laughed. "Oh, God, no, nothing so glamorous. No… Pa made me go hunting as soon as I was big enough. I hated it – the animals are so beautiful when they're alive and then when you see them dead, they're just…" He broke off, gazing into space, and then continued, "I don't understand how anyone can enjoy killing. It's completely beyond me."

Anton looked at him, rather puzzled. "But if you hate hunting, why did you do it?"

"It wasn't optional. Pa was always watching, so I decided all I could do was inflict as little pain as possible. So I practised."

"Karl, if you hate killing animals, how are you going to…? I mean…" Kurt didn't know how to finish the sentence.

Karl's eyes were grey, and colder than I had ever seen them.

"I've never seen a stag with a bayonet," he said with a hard tone that I'd never heard before, and that made me rather uncomfortable.

The reality of what we were going to have to do crystallised. *Will I be able to do it? It's easy making holes in a target but how will I feel when I have to shoot a man?*

You have to kill them to stop them killing you, Franz. It's as simple as that.

"At least you'll be some use," Otto said. "I'll just miss."

Karl clapped him on the shoulder. "Oh, don't worry – if you miss the fellow you're aiming at you'll get the one beside him! You'll be fine when you've had a bit more practice."

Over the next couple of days the new regiment began to take shape. The five of us plus Alfred were lucky enough to be put in the same platoon under Leutnant Hartmann. He was the same age as us and had been commissioned in haste from the military academy at Lichterfelde, like all the junior officers.

Our company commander, Hauptmann von Schürmann, was at the other end of the scale, having returned from retirement like the NCOs. There was no one available to lead us apart from the very young and inexperienced, and the ancient. We'd assumed that all the older men would be staying at the training camp and it was a surprise to find that they would be taking us into battle.

"I hope they're more familiar with their weapons than some of the fellows here," Karl muttered to me, "or life could be just a bit too interesting."

"I expect we'll all get a bit more practice," I said. "You might not need it but the rest of us do."

But the next day we were told that we would be leaving for Belgium in three days' time, as part of a completely new army. To my joy its commander was Duke Albrecht of Württemberg.

"Where?" asked Zeller, deadpan.

"Some funny place in the south," Alfred answered with a grin at me.

"Where all the best people come from, of course!" I said.

"Bloody hell," said Zeller, "I hope he's got more wits about him than you has!"

"Your hope is in vain." Karl pointed to a notice on the wall. "Have you seen what he's said?"

We gathered round to read it.

"Fucking hell," said Weiss. "What a load of crap."

'Do their duty with the old German courage and loyalty, to the last breath … every officer and every man is ready to give his last drop of blood…'

"You won't see him giving his last drop of blood," Kienle said.

"No," agreed Kempff. "That's for us to do."

"It's the Frenchies who I want to give their last drop of blood," Kurt said.

"And the fucking Russkis," added Alfred.

"I'll second that," Karl agreed.

"And the Tommies," said Weiss. "Fucking turncoats, they are. Been on our side for God knows how long and now they've turned on us."

"You just can't trust 'em," Zeller said.

There was a chorus of agreement but Karl said nothing. Fortunately no one seemed to notice.

It must be rough, I thought suddenly, *knowing that your brother-in-law is on the other side.*

I'd hoped for leave before we departed for the Front but there wasn't time. The pace of our training was suddenly stepped up and I began to have a faint idea how little I knew. *It'll be all right,* I told myself. *They won't send us to fight until we're ready.*

Two days before we were due to leave, we finally got our packs, our 'monkeys' as the reservists called them.

"Why?" asked Anton.

"Because it's hairy and sits on your back," said Zeller.

"And weighs a fucking ton," Kempff added.

He wasn't wrong. I was horrified by the amount that had to go in it, and by the weight of the thing. The thought of carrying it for hour after hour was not pleasant. It was going to be a very different matter from a weekend hike with just some spare clothes on my back.

We marched fifteen kilometres that afternoon with a full load, and my back and shoulders were aching well before halfway. *Perhaps we won't have to march far. This is the twentieth century. Perhaps they'll take us in trucks.*

"Jesus," said Otto, "I didn't realise I was going to be a bloody packhorse."

"Now you're beginning to find out what soldiering's really

like," Kienle said. "You wait till you've done that three days running."

"And on iron rations," added Weiss.

"Or nothing," said Zeller. "You has to remember – you only eats the iron rations if the officer says so. Don't matter how hungry you gets."

"We'll get used to it," Kurt said.

Kienle laughed. "No chance – you'll all get killed in no time!"

"Yeah," Zeller agreed, "no idea how to take cover, any of you!" He looked at Karl. "Except you, Mr Hunter. You knows how to vanish, all right."

"Cheers," Karl replied. "Creeping round the woods might come in handy, after all!"

"But how are we going to fight carrying all that?" Anton asked.

The reservists burst out laughing.

"We knew fuck all when we started," Kempff said to the others, a shade reproachfully. "You don't," he said to us. "You just carry the assault pack."

And that was still bloody heavy. Ammunition, iron rations, coat, mess tin, water bottle… The only consolation was that the Belgians and the Tommies would be just as heavily laden.

"I'm never going to make any of this look neat," Otto said. He'd almost got his coat rolled when his hand slipped and it unwound itself and landed at his feet. "I'm just not co-ordinated."

"Do it like this," Kienle said, taking it from him.

"I don't know," Weiss said, looking at Otto. "Can't shoot, can't roll his coat, can't march in step – no hope for him at all!"

"It ain't him I wants there to be hope for!" Zeller said, and we all laughed.

On the last day we got our spiked helmets and their field-grey covers with the regiment's number in red.

"Now we all look like bloody Prussians!" said Otto.

"Can't take a joke, you shouldn't have joined!" Alfred retorted.

"Shame we have to cover up that nice eagle," Karl said.

"Why do we?" Anton asked.

Kienle and Weiss just looked at each other.

"Because it would catch the sun and show the enemy where we are," Karl said patiently.

I looked at the inscription before I put the cover on: 'With God for King and Fatherland'.

"Don't know why they always drag God into it," said Alfred.

"Don't you believe, then?" I asked.

He shook his head. "But if you want to believe God's with us, be my guest."

That was on our belt buckles: 'God with us'. I did find it a comforting thought, even if going to confession had always been a bit wearisome, and I'd attended Mass every Sunday so far along with Weiss and Kempff, while Karl and the other heathens went to the Lutheran service.

"Right, boys – kit inspection." Feldwebel Braun's voice carried easily, without his having to shout.

Years of practice, I thought. Braun was about forty-five, the same height as me but at least as broad as Karl's Pa. His nose had been thoroughly broken at some point and he was the sort of man you just obeyed automatically. Not doing as Braun said would never have occurred to any of us.

Otto held his breath as Braun went through his kit but this time, at last, it was all in order.

Braun raised his eyebrows. "Well done, Kramer, you're learning!"

"Phew," Otto said after Braun had left. "I really thought the Gorilla was going to find something wrong again."

"Only reason he didn't was cos Kienle helped you," Zeller said. "Reckon you owes him a beer."

"Reckon I do," Otto said.

"And for fuck's sake don't let Braun hear you calling him the Gorilla," said Alfred.

Otto gave a mock shudder. "No chance!"

To our astonishment the six of us got a pass that evening, for the first time. We were sick of army food and decided to treat ourselves to the best meal that we could find. Our last chance to have dinner on china with a tablecloth under it, before setting off to war...

Tomorrow we'll be on our way, I thought. *There's no way back now, even if I wanted one.*

"Well, I know where I'm going before dinner," Karl said. "There must be a decent whorehouse or two."

Anton looked at him with something close to disgust. "You don't do that, do you?"

He doesn't know about his mother – or does he?

"Well, I prefer not paying but in the circumstances I don't think that's an option."

There was no time to get to Heidelberg to meet up with Anna and her friends, and by the time they were free we'd be back in barracks.

"You can count me out," I said. "The idea's completely revolting."

"Might be your last chance," Karl said. "You wouldn't want to die without ever fucking again, now, would you?"

Do you have to sound like a farmhand? And do you have to talk about death like that?

"Come on," he said. "It'll do you good after all these weeks of abstinence – well, not *quite* abstinence, perhaps, but that's no substitute for the real thing, is it?"

I felt myself blushing. Karl had the top half of our bunk and

44

neither of us could move without the other feeling it. *Everyone does it. It's nothing to be ashamed of. And Karl's right. The real thing's much better.*

"All right," I said, "but I'm not going to do it again."

Karl laughed. "Bet you ten marks you do! Anton?"

"I don't know…"

"Come with us and have a drink. You can always change your mind."

Kurt and Otto didn't need persuading. Either they had done it before or they were thinking the same as Karl.

"What about you, Alfred?" asked Kurt.

"No, thanks." Alfred wrinkled his nose.

"Don't be such a prude!"

"I'm not – it's just not my idea of fun."

Karl grinned at him and raised an eyebrow. "Oh well, fair enough. See you later, then."

The knocking shop looked quite presentable but we were turned away.

"Officers only," said the sergeant outside. "Yours is down that street there."

It looked rather dingy and we all hesitated.

"Well, I suppose this is what we'll have to get used to," Karl said with resignation. "But a fellow could get more than he bargained for in a place like this."

We had to push our way in. There were two rooms on the ground floor, both crammed with soldiers, and the air was thick with cigarette and cigar smoke, beer and sweat.

"Bloody hell," Kurt muttered. "You have to be desperate to come to a dump like this."

"We are," I said.

It was nothing like I'd imagined a house of joy would be. There was a fat madam taking cash and keeping some sort of order, but no sign of any girls.

"Where are the girls?" Anton asked, his round face creasing with uncertainty.

"They're probably so ugly she keeps them hidden," said Otto. "I don't think we get a choice here. I think it's just whoever's free."

"Needs must," Karl said. "Let's have a beer while we're waiting, anyway."

When my turn came I was glad I'd had a couple of beers. The girl was plain and clearly rather tired, and if I hadn't been spurred on by the thought that it really might be my last chance I wouldn't have given her a second glance.

Afterwards I felt dirty and ashamed and, feeling I should make some sort of amends, I gave her almost as much as the fat bitch downstairs had charged me. She was absurdly grateful and I fled.

Karl's lost that bet, I thought as I hurried down the rough staircase. *There's no way I'm ever doing that again, even if the war lasts ten years.*

The others were waiting for me, apart from Anton. All I wanted was to get out of the place and into the fresh air. I didn't want to hang around for anyone.

"Anton's only just gone up," Kurt said. "He changed his mind."

"Look, I'm going to wait outside," I said. "The air's a bit thick in here."

"I'll come out with you," said Karl, and the two of us shoved our way through the corridor towards the door.

We were stopped by a medic with a needleless syringe in his hand.

"Antiseptic injection," he said. "You don't leave till you've had one."

"Where?" I asked. *How do you give someone an injection without a needle?*

He rolled his eyes. "Into your prick, of course, you stupid sod. Stop you getting a dose."

"We used condoms," Karl said.

"Yeah, and my best girl shits flowers," said the medic. "Get it out."

Karl shrugged and produced his used condom from his handkerchief.

"Extract of tart on the outside and extract of me on the inside," he said. "You can have a look if you like."

The medic took it in one rubber-gloved hand and examined it. "Yeah, all right mate, I'm convinced."

He handed it back and turned to me.

"Same here," I said, handing him the evidence.

"All right, you can go."

The night air was cool and refreshing but I felt filthy. We leaned against the wall in the shadows.

"I hope you enjoyed that, being as it was your idea," I said. "You've really corrupted me now, you bastard. Inge was one matter, but this!"

"Have a cigarette, Franz." He held out his silver case to me and as I took one he said softly, "I had no idea it was going to be as sordid as that. So no, I didn't enjoy it much – it was marginally better than wanking, but that's all – and I just hope my rubber friend's stopped me catching anything nasty."

"Likewise," I said grumpily.

"Look, I understand – I feel dirty, too, but come to Berlin with me when we get leave and I'll make it up to you... Oh, bugger it, my lighter's run out."

"It's all right, I've got mine here somewhere... I'm not paying again, Karl. I don't care how luxurious the place is. It's too commercial."

"You won't have to. I know a couple of dancers who are really good fun – and it won't cost you a penny. We can have a bloody good time."

His hand rested on mine as I lit his cigarette.

"Forgive me?"

His voice was light and good-humoured but in the flare of the flame his eyes held a softness that surprised me. Our hands remained together a moment longer than was necessary, the gentle pressure of his fingers matching his expression.

My anger evaporated. *Of course I forgive you. How could I do anything else?*

"It's a deal," I said quietly.

"Hey, Karl, what was yours like?" The voice was loud, coarse, and slightly drunk.

Karl started, and it was as if some sort of spell had been broken.

"Fucking 'orrible!" came the reply from a short man who half ran across the road to where his friends were waiting.

"About the same as mine, then!" Karl said, and I heard rather than saw the grin.

I took a deep drag on the fag he'd given me and almost choked. "Bloody hell, Karl, how can you smoke these?"

"Practice! Amazing what you can get used to, as I'm sure we'll find out… I wonder how much longer Anton's going to be – we'll be late back at this rate."

The door opened again and the other three came out. They turned away from us and Karl ran up behind them, leapt on Kurt and wrestled him to the ground. They rolled over and over in the dirt, coming to rest with Karl lying on his back and Kurt sitting astride him, both laughing.

"You're a fucking sight better looking than the tart I've just had!" Kurt said, holding Karl's shoulders down against the road.

"I should bloody well hope I am!" Karl replied with mock indignation. "I wish I could say the same about you!"

"Had the only beautiful girl in the knocking shop, then?"

"Of course! Come on, get off me and we'll go and get something to eat. We've just about got time."

It was only just. We wasted more time trying to find Alfred, and we hadn't finished eating when the café started to empty.

Otto glanced at his watch. "Shit! We're going to be late!"

Kurt shrugged. "They won't lock us up, will they? We're off to the Front tomorrow."

"Are you sure?" asked Anton.

"Yes – be a good way of skiving otherwise, wouldn't it?"

"We'd still get punished, though," I said. "And I'd rather not be. I don't want that in my book."

We ran all the way back and as we turned the corner we heard the bugle sounding tattoo. We just made it before the gate closed.

"Good evening, chaps?" Alfred asked.

"I just hope that wasn't my last ever fuck," said Kurt.

"And that the next one will be free," I added.

"You can dream!" said Alfred.

But my dreams were rather darker – I woke twice with a feeling of profound disquiet but unable to remember the details, and lay staring at the ceiling and listening to the others snoring.

I wonder where I'll sleep tomorrow. And how long it will be before I see Germany again, and my parents and Johanna?

The next morning the band played as we marched to the station, one stirring Prussian march after another. My heart lifted to the fanfares of 'The Great Elector's Cavalry' and of 'The Glory of Prussia' and, finally, as we reached the station, to Frederick the Great's exuberant victory march, the 'Hohenfriedberger'.

Suddenly I was marching through the Brandenburg Gate in a huge triumphal parade, a vast crowd of people cheering the homecoming heroes... Germany's victory and my own survival seemed inevitable, and it didn't occur to me that there might not be such a parade or that I might not be alive to take part in it.

"They could have played something other than Prussian marches," Otto grumbled to me at the station.

"The Devil has all the best tunes!" Kurt replied cheerfully.

We sang one soldiers' song after another in the train, all the grim ones, cheerfully roaring out that there was no more beautiful death than in battle.

"Give that fucking singing a rest, will you!" Weiss grumbled when we paused for breath. "You might all want to be killed but I'm fucked if I do!"

We looked at him in astonishment. *We don't either*, I thought suddenly. I just hadn't thought what the words really meant. Whistling in the dark, singing about death like that, I suppose...

There was silence until we crossed the Rhine.

As the train began to puff across the bridge, Kempff picked up his mouth organ and began to play 'The Watch on the Rhine', and in two seconds flat the whole carriage was singing.

"Dear Fatherland, be reassured, Fast stands and true the Watch... the Watch on the Rhine... And while one drop of blood still glows... No enemy will tread your shore..."

The river sparkled in the early autumn sun and what had been a youthful adventure suddenly became a sacred duty. I was going to war, not because it would be wonderful and exciting but to defend my country against its enemies. *If I die, it will be* for *something*, I thought as the song died away. *We all have to die some time but I will be giving my life for Germany. No more beautiful death...*

Everyone was silent for several minutes and I wondered how many of the others were sharing my thoughts.

When we crossed the Belgian border everyone cheered and clapped and stamped until the windows and doors shook.

Nearly there. Soon we'll be in Antwerp, where it'll be quiet, and we'll get some more training before we go into battle. For a start I need to get used to carrying my pack and all my equipment, and most of us could do with going on the firing range a few more times. And none of us really knows what to do when we attack, or how to prepare a defensive position.

It began to get dark.

"I don't know about you," I said to Karl, "but I'm getting bloody hungry."

"So am I. I'd have thought they'd have fed us by now."

"Maybe there'll be something when we get off the train."

"Whenever that may be."

Alfred produced a box from his pack. "Anyone like a cake? My dear old Ma made them."

"I've got some chocolate," said Anton, and we all pooled what we had and managed to dull our hunger a little.

The train rumbled on into the twilight. Leutnant Hartmann came to talk to us again, as he had at intervals during the journey. He was very conscientious and seemed genuinely concerned for our welfare and I began to think that we were fortunate in being under him.

"Nice bloke," Otto said after he'd gone.

Kienle looked at him as if he'd taken leave of his senses. "He's an officer."

Weiss snorted. "If you can call him that – I could be his father."

Zeller laughed. "Fucks a lot of ladies, does you?"

"Two of my brothers are officers," Otto said. "And so's one of Karl's, after all."

"Yeah, well, he is a bleeding Junker," said Kempff with a grin. "What do you expect?"

"Can't help it," Karl said cheerfully.

"So why aren't you wearing nice shiny epaulettes?" Weiss asked him.

"Didn't fancy getting killed at twenty," Karl said. "But it seems fate has caught up with me!"

"But you are going to go for a commission, aren't you?" Alfred asked him.

"Not fucking likely! Soon as the war's over I'm back to my piano – whatever Pa might say."

"But you are, aren't you?" Anton said to Kurt. "Going for the officer's career path?"

"If this goes on long enough, yes."

Kienle looked at him. "So you want to be an officer, then?"

Kurt nodded. "It's not what my parents want, though."

"Someone's got some sense, then!" Weiss said.

"So d'you live in a big fancy house, then?" Kempff asked Karl. "And sit round all day talking posh?"

"Not bloody likely. Ever tried growing rye in sand? It's fucking hard work and pays bugger all."

"Sand?" Kempff repeated incredulously.

"Yeah," said Zeller. "Brandenburg's just sand. You can see it in Berlin when they digs – just sand."

Kempff shook his head. "Rather you than me, mate," he said to Karl.

It was pitch-dark outside. I tried to sleep but found it almost impossible. I was too cramped to get comfortable and my hunger overrode my tiredness.

I jolted awake as we stopped and realised I'd been asleep.

"Where are we?" I asked Karl.

He peered out into the night. "God knows."

Gefreiter Dittrich came back into the carriage. "There's said to be tea, boys."

"That's something," said Kurt, "but I'm fucking hungry."

"You young fellows are always hungry," said Kienle.

There wasn't any food – or any tea either.

"Bugger that for a joke," Kempff grumbled as we climbed back on board.

Eventually the sun rose on another fine day. A couple

of hours later the train stopped at Gent and we all got out, stretching our stiff bodies.

My pack felt twice as heavy as it had when we left.

"I think my monkey's expecting," I said.

"Shouldn't have fucked it, then, should you!" said Zeller.

"Christ, I don't want to see the offspring!" Kurt said.

"It might have legs of its own," said Anton. "And I wish mine did!"

It was a relief to be out in the fresh air and at long last there was food. It wasn't hot but we were all far too hungry to care.

That's better, I thought. *I feel ready for the rest of the journey to Antwerp.*

It was not to be.

We fell in to be addressed by our ancient battalion commander, Major Grabowski, who was actually sitting on a fine bay horse like some apparition from the century before. Unfortunately his voice didn't carry that well and I missed nearly everything he said.

The only part I heard was "Ypres" and "fighting".

He rode off. I was dying to ask Karl if he'd heard.

"Well, boys," said Schürmann. "In case you didn't hear, we're going to Ypres, where our troops are engaged in heavy fighting against the French and the English…"

My stomach turned over and I actually felt sick. *This is what you wanted and it's no good quailing now you're about to get it.*

I glanced at Karl. His face was impassive, but when his eyes met mine I saw that they held both disquiet and determination.

It's too soon, I thought, and it was as if he answered, yes, much too soon.

Alfred was obviously full of enthusiasm and Kurt looked resolute, but there was apprehension in Anton's eyes. I couldn't see Otto's face but I doubted he'd be happy facing the enemy when he still couldn't shoot straight.

"Well, the sooner it's over the sooner I gets home," Zeller said, which just about summed it up.

We formed up and began marching along the autumn road towards Ypres and whatever might be waiting for us. It wasn't three months since we'd volunteered and we'd had all of six weeks' 'training'. Too soon, my boots said. Too soon, too soon…

We marched on and on, kilometre after endless kilometre, often tramping through villages where the inhabitants stood sullenly beside the road, watching us pass. The contrast to the cheering German crowds couldn't have been greater.

"God, they really don't want us, do they?" Anton said during a break.

"Would you?" Karl asked.

"It can't be helped," said Kurt. "We have to go through Belgium to beat the French. There's no point attacking across the border where they expect it."

"No, General!" I said.

"They're in the way and that's that," said Kienle.

"Yeah," Zeller agreed. "Should've given us free passage like we asked for."

"Then we wouldn't have to worry about being shot," Anton said.

It's not right, I thought. In the last village we'd seen bullet holes in the wall of the village hall, where some men suspected of being irregulars had been shot out of hand.

"Well, they shouldn't shoot at us," said Weiss.

"Too right," Kempff agreed.

You can't just shoot people without a proper trial – but at the same time the thought of being killed by some unseen gunman made my hair stand on end, and I found myself looking at the men in the villages and wondering if they had rifles in their bedrooms…

By the end of the first day my back and feet were sore and

my monkey was pulling on my shoulders for all it was worth.

"Only five more kilometres, chaps," said Leutnant Hartmann. "Then we're in quarters for the night."

He stretched, picked up his haversack and put it on.

I looked at it with envy. *Maybe I will go for a commission. He's not carrying anything like as much as us.*

"Wonder where 'quarters' will be?" Otto asked.

"Dreaming of the farmer's daughter, is you?" Zeller said with a wink, and as we moved off again he began to sing.

"Ten thousand men, Set off upon manoeuvres…"

We all joined in. *At least this song's not about death,* I thought as the farmer rejected the penniless officer's bid for his beautiful daughter's hand. At least I presumed he was an officer – the farmer called him 'Horseman', and the only horseman I'd seen was Grabowski.

I started laughing.

"What's so funny?" Karl asked.

"I was just imagining old Grabowski after the farmer's daughter!"

Kurt laughed as well. "Don't know what he'd do with her at his age!"

'Quarters' was indeed on a farm but there was no sign of any daughter, beautiful or otherwise. Not that she'd have been interested in sweaty, dust-caked enemy soldiers.

All I was interested in was food and sleep. *Bloody hell,* I thought, as I joined the dinner queue – *I've never been so fucking hungry and weary in my life. And this is only the beginning.*

"Rum outfit, this," Zeller said. "We hasn't even got a proper goulash cannon."

There was a sort of stove on the back of a wagon instead of a field cooker, but the stew was hot and I didn't care where it had come from.

The straw in the barn was quite soft and I fell asleep at once –

but something woke me in the middle of the night. The ground seemed to be trembling and there was a faint intermittent rumbling. I wondered briefly what it was but my eyes closed again before I found an answer.

"Did you hear the guns?" Kurt asked in the morning.

"Is that what it was?" asked Anton.

"Nah," said Zeller. "Too much bleeding imagination, you lot."

There were more holes in the walls in the next village. *That's not right*, I thought again. *You can't just put someone against a wall on a suspicion. We're supposed to be a civilised nation.*

I didn't understand then that war is anything but civilised.

My pack got heavier and heavier until it felt like a lead weight, and after a few more hours I decided to get rid of everything I could. During my fortnight at home Mama had knitted me a sweater, and the autumn sun still shone warmly.

I hesitated, guilty at the thought of throwing it away.

"You're not getting rid of that?" Karl asked as I put it down at the roadside.

"I don't want to. It's just everything's getting so heavy."

"Look, if you really don't want it I'll take it – though I don't suppose it'll fit me."

"Try it on – it's a bit big for me anyway."

The sweater fitted Karl perfectly.

"You might as well keep it," I said.

"Thanks very much. Just let me know when you want it back."

The side of the road was littered with discarded clothes. We'd received presents from all over Germany: scarves and gloves, chocolate and cigars, and so on, and we felt even more overwhelmed by people's generosity now that we had to carry it all.

Kurt, like Karl, kept what warm things he had.

"We'll need them later," he said. "It may be nice and sunny now but it'll be cold and frosty soon enough."

"But we'll be home before winter," Anton said.

It's already October, I didn't say.

That night there were no quarters and we slept in the open fields beside the road. We were very hungry as well as tired and there was no sign of our cooker.

"Bleeding rubbish show, this," Zeller grumbled.

"I don't know what's gone wrong," said Leutnant Hartmann. "Braun, take a couple of chaps and see if you can find out."

Weiss and another fellow went with him. While they were gone Schürmann came and spoke to each one of us.

"They tell me the cooker's on its way," he said. "With a bit of luck it won't take much longer."

It never arrived. Braun and the other two came back none the wiser.

"We only got a couple of kilometres," said Weiss. "The road's all clogged up."

"Yeah," said the other man, "four more kilometres for fuck all."

Smoking dulled my hunger a little.

"Try one of mine," Karl said. "Bit stronger."

"I'll stick to my own, thanks. I don't know how you can smoke those things."

"You just need more practice."

He took one of his black cigarettes and put it carefully in his elegant black holder.

"Leussow, that poncey holder belongs in a whore's boudoir," said Dittrich.

"I know, Corporal – it'll be just right in the fleshpots of Paris! And I'll even let you borrow it when we get there!"

Dittrich just snorted.

Our progress the next day was painfully slow. The road

was crammed with traffic and we spent more time stationary than moving. My feet didn't mind one bit and neither did my shoulders.

"The war'll be over by the time we get there," said Alfred.

"With a bit of luck," Weiss said.

An hour later it started raining and didn't stop. The road turned to mud and it stuck like glue to our boots. Every time we stopped, my feet sank in and it was a real effort to pull them out again.

We were all soaked to the skin.

"Hope we finds somewhere dry to sleep," said Zeller.

"Yeah – like a feather bed with a girl!" Kienle said with a grin, and we all laughed.

We stopped for the night at a farm and again there was no sign of the cooker. It was probably still stuck in the traffic.

"Bugger this for a joke," said Kempff. "I'm fucking frozen."

Schürmann had a brief conference with the other company commanders and Grabowski. One of the captains took his cap off and I was shocked to see that his hair was almost completely white. A few minutes later he walked away, with the stiff gait of an old man.

"How in God's name can he march?" I asked Karl.

Karl shrugged. "Schürmann may be older than Pa but he seems to be the youngest of this lot."

"Never mind marching," said Weiss. "How the fuck is he going to fight?"

Schürmann had come within earshot and we shut up. He had a quiet word with Hartmann, who came over to us.

"Right, chaps – I need three volunteers to go and get provisions from the farmer."

Karl stepped forward.

"I can speak Low German, sir," he said, "and I think it's rather similar to Flemish."

I joined him, if only because we went everywhere together, and Otto came with us.

Karl looked dubiously at the farmhouse as we approached it.

"I don't know how much luck we'll have. This place looks dirt poor."

He was right. We returned empty-handed.

The farmer had insisted he had nothing, and the place was so rundown and dingy that it wasn't hard to believe him.

The night was cold and the rain still hadn't stopped. There wasn't any shelter for us and we huddled together on straw spread on the mud. The dampness soaked into my bones, even through the waterproof tent quarter.

The lack of food made it even worse. It felt as if the fire inside me had gone right out.

"You'd better have your sweater back," Karl said.

"No, it's all right. You keep it."

"You're shivering."

That was true, and I couldn't hide it because we were so close together.

"Look, you've never been in our house in the winter," he said. "It's always bloody freezing. I'm used to the cold."

"Thanks. And thanks for stopping me throwing it away."

You had more sense than I did, I thought as I put it on, *and you've probably got more sense than me about the war as well.*

The next morning Braun said, "I'm going to see that farmer. Who's coming with me?"

I didn't want to try again. Dittrich stood up and so, unusually, did Weiss, Kempff and Kienle. I suspected their stomachs were hurting. Mine certainly was.

Karl offered his services as translator again.

Braun shook his head. "They'll understand."

"I'll bet they will," Otto muttered. "No one's going to argue with the Gorilla."

Half an hour later the five of them came back with a few loaves of bread and some chickens. The farmer's wife stood at the open door of the farmhouse, crying.

"That's probably all they had to last the rest of the month," Karl said.

"They must be hiding something," said Alfred.

"If they've got anything to hide," Karl replied.

"Some blokes from Third Company was in the barn and they said there was fuck all there," said Zeller. "The blokes before us must have taken it all."

It's theft, I thought. *We've taken just about everything they had, and all we're going to get is a slice of bread each and a mouthful of meat. Our own people should be feeding us. We shouldn't have to steal.*

Is this what war is? Murder and theft?

A few hours later there was a definite rumbling in the distance.

"Now do you believe me?" I said to Zeller.

"Yeah, mate. Even if you was making it up before!"

"We must be getting pretty close now," Kempff said.

It really is the guns, I thought.

Karl cocked his head and listened. The sound rolled like distant thunder, booming, swelling and abating. It was as if there were something electric in the air, and everyone's eyes shone with excited anticipation.

The traffic clogged solid. We were so close to the battle but progress was almost impossible and it became difficult not to get separated.

"It's going to take us another week to get there," Kurt grumbled.

Kempff laughed. "It can take the rest of the fucking year!"

"Just so long as it stops fucking raining," said Zeller.

"We can't get any wetter than we are now," said Alfred.

"I'm fucking starving as well," Weiss said to general agreement.

But there was no food again, and even Braun's best efforts produced nothing.

"Well, I'm having one of those," said Kienle, pointing to a pile of raw turnips in the field by the road.

"Fuck it, so am I," said Zeller.

"You'll get the shits," Karl warned them.

"I'll take my chances," said a man from Leutnant Wetzel's platoon. "I'm fucking starving."

"Will they really give us the runs?" Anton asked Karl.

"Yes. It's better to be hungry."

Sure enough, a few hours later Zeller leapt up, ran into the field and pulled his trousers down.

"Oh, fuck!" he shouted. "Nearly shit myself!"

"Bit early for that!" Kempff shouted back.

Ten minutes later Kienle did exactly the same and so did several of the others. I was very glad I'd taken Karl's advice. It would be terrible to miss the battle just for a bad stomach.

The afflicted had to make several more dashes into the field and the rest of us laughed at them.

"It's just fucking liquid," Kienle grumbled.

"Yes, we saw!" said Weiss.

I used to be shy about going for a crap in front of other blokes, I thought, *and now I don't give a – shit? Amazing what you can get used to.*

The next day we fought our way through the congealing traffic again. We'd been told we had to be in Poelcapelle by dark, though quite how we were going to make it was anybody's guess.

At about twelve we got completely stuck. We stood in the road and waited and waited but nothing moved, and an hour or so later we all fell out to wait in the fields, while Major Grabowski cantered off to find out what was happening.

I wasn't at all sorry to get the weight off my feet. They were hurting more and more and I had a place on my right heel that felt almost raw. My back and shoulders ached as well, and the thought of putting my monkey back on and marching God knows how much further was not pleasant.

"I wonder how long we'll be stuck here," Kurt said.

"God knows," Karl answered, "I expect—"

There was a sound like dry twigs crackling in the fire and we all looked at each other nervously.

"Don't worry," said Kempff. "That's not coming anywhere near us."

"Steady, boys," Braun said. "There's no need to get worried till I do."

That's all right, then. We're not under fire yet – but we will be, today or tomorrow, and how will I behave?

The rifle fire was followed by powerful explosions a few kilometres ahead, and huge plumes of smoke and earth flew up. We could hear the enemy artillery firing quite clearly and then ours opened up in response.

"Someone's getting it," Alfred said cheerfully. "That'll be us soon."

I imagined flying shards of hot metal – *Stop. You'll have to do it, Franz, and there's no point thinking too hard about it or you'll be useless. Just keep a grip on yourself. You'll be all right.*

The exchange of fire stopped as abruptly as it had started. There was almost continuous shelling in the distance, but nothing more close by.

A couple of hours later the traffic unclogged itself and we began to move. After a kilometre or so a group of wounded came the other way, bloodstained and roughly bandaged. Some walked unaided, others supported each other, and there were a couple of stretcher cases inert under their blankets. A few were clearly in pain, and although I felt sympathetic I couldn't believe it could ever happen to me. I couldn't imagine what it would feel like.

Maybe like breaking my arm when I fell out of that tree? But I was a little kid then and I can't remember it hurting, just that I wanted to scratch under the plaster and couldn't. And there were compensations: I didn't have to write anything in school for weeks, and Mama made a fuss of me and bought me a chocolate ice cream in the park.

I wonder if I'll get chocolate ice cream back in Germany if I get wounded and sent home. And maybe the girls will make a fuss of me and go to bed with me...

Several hours later we reached the spot the enemy had shelled. There were several craters in the road and next to it, and a couple of dead horses – and a dead German, crumpled like a rag doll.

He was face down, one leg at an unnatural angle, his uniform soaked with blood. I'd seen my grandmother laid out in her coffin, her eyes peacefully closed and her hair braided, but he didn't even look like a man any more.

Is that what I'll be, just a shapeless lump? But it was impossible to believe that I could end up like that.

We all stared at him as we passed. Kurt and Zeller looked with frank curiosity, but Anton went very pale and turned away quickly.

Karl scowled blackly at the dead horses.

"Pa sent all ours to the Army," he said quietly to me.

"What – all of them?"

"Yes... Even Black King – the stallion you saw Friedrich riding."

"But if your stallion's gone..." *You don't have a stud any more*, I didn't want to say.

"Oh, no doubt we'll get compensation," he said distantly. "And Pa was breeding for the dragoons anyway, but..." He sighed.

But you don't want your beautiful horses to end up like that. I remembered him showing me round the stables and the pastures, his love for the animals obvious. *No,* I thought, *if they were mine I wouldn't want them here either.*

Another small group of wounded appeared and we made way for them. The fact that other men had been killed and injured only added to my feeling of immortality.

We'll be fighting soon and we'll show the Tommies and the Frenchies what we can do!

From the looks we exchanged I could tell that the others felt as I did, and we sang as we marched, our voices ringing out strongly. Karl's gloom seemed to vanish after a while and he seemed just as exhilarated as the rest of us, his eyes blue and bright.

We never did make it to Poelcapelle. We reached the village but we couldn't get in because everyone else had got there first. The road was overflowing with vehicles, horses, guns and men, all trying to move and failing, in a cacophony of orders and curses. God alone knows what it must have been like in the village itself.

We camped in the mud, in what remained of the gardens and vegetable patches, and Schürmann gave us the wonderful news that we were to attack the English the next day, to take Langemarck.

At last! He left it to Leutnant Hartmann to give us the details but I think Hartmann had too much respect for our intelligence, because he said rather a lot and Kempff had to ask him to repeat half of it.

"I wish it weren't the English," Karl said to me.

"No, quite…"

"It's not just Henry – my brother-in-law – but at least half a dozen of my cousins as well."

There wasn't anything I could say to that. No one wants to fight his own relatives. *What will you do if you come face to face with one of them?*

It struck me suddenly that the war was really quite absurd, and for a moment I wondered why we were there.

"At least we've still got our Company Commander," said Otto. "The First and Third have both lost theirs."

"Lost how?" asked Anton.

"Sick, apparently," Otto said. "One of them's that white-haired fellow."

"Well, he shouldn't have been here anyway," said Kienle. "Poor old bugger could hardly walk, never mind fighting."

"We'll have to see if ours can fight," Kempff said. "He's old enough to be my dad."

"And my grandpa!" said Kurt. "But he seems fit enough."

Kempff just grunted.

Yet again there was no food. We were all soaking wet and bloody starving, and the cold penetrated our bones.

I'm not sure I could eat this evening anyway... The anticipation and apprehension were almost tangible and we could hear the guns clearly.

"Think you can make your assault pack up properly this time, Kramer?" asked Braun.

"Yes, Sergeant Major," Otto said.

Dittrich gave him a very expressive look but Otto did make a decent fist of it.

"Where are we leaving the big packs, Sergeant Major?" asked Kempff.

"In the barn, over there."

"Hope no one nicks nothing," Zeller said as we deposited them.

"You haven't been dumb enough to leave anything valuable?" said Weiss.

"Look," said Zeller, "I may look thick but I'm not that fucking stupid!"

"It'll all be here," Kienle said.

But will we? No one said it but it was in everyone's eyes. *Best not thought about.*

The six of us sat together, smoking and talking and checking our equipment. The rain got into everything and keeping the rust out was an unending battle. Karl was humming softly to himself, and I listened and recognised snatches of the Emperor Concerto.

You played that just before the end of term, I thought, looking at his large, capable hands with their broad, strong fingers. Suddenly I was back in the concert hall, that glorious music soaring.

I wonder whether Karl will ever play that again – but of course he will.

My friends were just as immortal as I was.

"Sorry, Anton, what did you say?"

"One of the older chaps asked me if I'd made a will. I haven't. I wondered if you had."

"A will?" Wills were something to be studied at university. Wills were made by old or wealthy people. "I haven't got anything to leave."

"You must have something."

"Just my clothes and books, and my savings account, and I suppose those will go to my family anyway."

"Karl," I said.

"Mm?"

"What happens if one of us dies without making a will?"

He looked up, surprised. "We haven't studied that yet."

"Yes, I know, but I thought you might know something about it. I mean, what would happen to your savings, and so on?"

"What a bloody gloomy conversation! I imagine it would all go back into the family melting pot. I don't really mind who gets anything of mine."

He went back to cleaning his rifle with an air of closing his part of the conversation. The firelight caught his almost Slavic cheekbones, casting his eyes into shadow, and it seemed to me that his face had gone very still.

Is your resigned attitude to death more assumed than real, or are you worried about your brothers?

Either way, I didn't care for the way his face looked with the bones highlighted and the eye sockets darkened. I'd had enough of the conversation as well.

"You don't want to worry about that, anyway," I told Anton. "We'll be all right."

He gave me a look which said very plainly, We can't *all* be all right, but said nothing more.

"Well, that's my bride nice and happy!" Zeller said, patting his rifle. "Just how a girl needs to be – nice and clean on the inside with a good bit of lube!"

"And ready for action!" Karl said with a grin.

"No animals in your barrel today, then?" Weiss said to Otto, and we all laughed.

"You're never going to let me forget that, are you?" Otto said with mock hurt.

"No – being as it was fucking nigh impossible to keep my face straight at the time!" Weiss retorted.

"Even the Gorilla smiled," said Kurt.

"Nah," said Zeller, "you was imagining that!"

"It was only a tiny spider," Otto said. "I don't know why Schürmann made a fuss about it."

Kienle wrinkled his nose. "'Kramer, there's an *animal* in your barrel'," he said in a perfect imitation of Schürmann's accent.

"That's why you keep missing," Alfred said. "The menagerie in your rifle!"

"Oh, shut up!" said Otto.

"Let's have a look!" said Weiss, taking it from him. "Bloody hell, there *is* a spider… and a mouse… and even a bloody cat!"

We all laughed far harder than the banter really merited and I realised how tightly my nerves – and everyone else's – were strung.

Hartmann came round and spoke to every one of us, and once again I was impressed by his awareness of his responsibility.

"He reminds me of Friedrich," Karl said after he'd gone.

"Yes, I was thinking that too." *But he hasn't got Friedrich's experience or his maturity. He's barely older than we are.* "Karl – tomorrow –" I wasn't sure what I wanted to say. Tomorrow was not something to talk about.

"Tomorrow?" He laughed and continued in English.

I hadn't expected him to change languages and I had to ask him to repeat what he'd said.

"'Tomorrow? Why, tomorrow I may be Myself with yesterday's seven thousand years'."

My English isn't that good and I had to think about what he'd said.

"You should read Omar Khayyam some time," he said. "Eat, drink and be merry, for tomorrow we die."

How can you be so calm about it? The abyss opened before me again with a sickening lurch in my stomach and I recoiled from it. Karl seemed to have looked over the edge, seen what was there and accepted it.

"Not *quite* tomorrow, I hope," said Otto. "I've got ambitions to be a great-grandfather."

"Do you want to be old and senile?" Alfred countered. "I'd much rather go with my boots on."

I don't want to go at all. Not for a long time, anyway.

"Better get some sleep, boys," said Braun. "Big day tomorrow."

I tried to sleep but I couldn't. My mind was full of the next day. *Men are dying there, where the shells are falling* – but I couldn't imagine it. Death was just a word. And tomorrow? *Tomorrow we will conquer. And if I die – what better way to go?*

But my mind wouldn't rest and the time dragged interminably. I was nervous. No, that's not true. I was scared. I was scared of failing my friends more than anything, scared that my legs would refuse to carry me, that I would be seen to be a coward.

Will I be alive this time tomorrow? The abyss opened in front of me again and I looked away from it. *Not yet, God, please not yet. My life's only beginning.*

I was ashamed of being scared. *Some hero you are, lying here shivering and telling yourself it's the cold.*

I turned over yet again, trying not to disturb Karl who I thought must be asleep. Then I felt a hand on my shoulder. In the dim, intermittent light I saw his eyes looking into mine, and his hand gave a gentle squeeze as if to say, Yes, I know. His presence was immensely comforting and I moved a bit closer to him.

It'll be all right. We'll go forward shoulder to shoulder... Suddenly I had the absurd but reassuring idea that nothing could happen to me as long as Karl was beside me.

Suddenly he was shaking me awake. For a moment I couldn't work out where I was – then reality came back and my heart beat faster.

It was time to go.

The night was alive with gunfire, the mist lit weirdly by the flashes of the artillery. My nerves were on edge, as if their ends were outside my skin. My hands were sweating despite the cold but my mouth was dry. My stomach was tight and I couldn't get my breath properly. I tried to relax and breathe normally but it was impossible.

We shuffled forward in the darkness, not sure where we were going or how to get there.

We stopped.

"Which way, sir?" Braun asked Hartmann.

He looked round uncertainly. There was no sign of the rest of the Company. Somehow we'd got separated.

From somewhere ahead we heard voices singing the Prussian national anthem, 'Hail to Thee in the Victor's Laurels', then the crackle of rifle fire. The singing stopped abruptly and then the voices switched to 'The Watch on the Rhine'. This time there were no shots.

Alfred started laughing. "I reckon we've found our comrades, sir!"

"Yes, Friedemann, I reckon we have!"

We headed towards the singing.

"Why in God's name were the silly buggers singing our anthem?" Karl said. "Don't they realise it's the same tune as 'God Save the King'?"

"They do now!" said Dittrich.

"I wonder how much further it is?" said Anton nervously.

"You can't be finding that heavy?!" Kempff said.

"No…"

The assault pack did feel much lighter than the monkey, and the contrast underlined that tonight was different. *Tomorrow – or rather today – I'll find out what I'm really made of…*

I wasn't sure I wanted to know.

A couple of minutes later we found Leutnant Wetzel and his platoon.

"Oh, jolly good," said Hartmann. "We're in the right place, then."

Wetzel laughed. "That's if we are!"

We were, and after about half an hour we were directed to a ditch.

"Langemarck's over there," Hartmann said, pointing into the mist. "About five hundred metres away. We're scheduled for ten in the morning."

"At least we'll be able to see by then," Braun said after he'd gone. "Better make yourselves as comfortable as possible."

He posted sentries and the rest of us settled down on the muddy ground.

I peered at my watch. I was just able to make out the luminous hands and then I wished I hadn't. It was four in the morning, and we had six hours to just sit and wait and listen to the sporadic shelling – and try not to think about what was to come.

It was like exam nerves multiplied a thousandfold and I was sharply aware that I'd never been really afraid in my life. Fear of failure rose in me again. *For God's sake, if I feel like this now, how will I feel when we attack?*

In one of the flashes I saw a shape ahead and to the left. My heart leapt and my stomach turned over. I grabbed Karl's arm and shouted into his ear.

"There's someone out there!"

"Where?"

"There – look!"

The pause was agonisingly long. The shape hadn't moved. I was aware of Karl staring silently into the mist.

He put his mouth to my ear. "It's a tree, you idiot!"

Oh, Christ, so it is. I can even see part of a splintered branch. Silly arse, being scared of a tree!

The time dragged endlessly. I just wanted it to be over. I'd written to my family the previous evening, and now I realised how thoughtless my letter had been and I wished I could take it back. I'd written with careless enthusiasm that we would soon be going into action, and now I understood that those words would settle like ice round Mama's heart until she heard that I was safe.

If I was safe… My stomach was tying itself in knots and I felt sick, my hunger forgotten. I remembered Kempff saying that it didn't matter there not being any food, that it was better not to eat before a battle in case you got a stomach wound. We knew he'd never fought, any more than we had, and we didn't believe him.

In those hours of waiting, filled with the crashes of the exploding shells, I wondered if he wasn't right.

Not that it makes any difference. My stomach couldn't be emptier. If it does get sliced open—

Shut up, Franz. The last thing you need is to dwell on what could happen to you.

Damn it, I'm not going to be scared. When ten o'clock comes I'll stand up confidently and go forward with the others. I won't fail.

III

The day dawned cold and grey in the lingering mist. The others' eyes held the same mixture of fear and resolution that I felt.

Anton looked very pale but determined. *We shouldn't have poked fun at him about wills* – but I didn't want to raise that subject. It was best left until afterwards.

Karl was smoking casually but his eyes were grey and very steady and seemed to be fixed on something beyond this world, as if he didn't expect to survive. I didn't like that expression at all. It was too resigned.

He turned and smiled at me, and once again I felt I would be safe if I stayed with him.

Kurt and Otto were off to my left, too far away to be seen, and Alfred was beyond them.

"Penny for them, Franz?" Karl asked.

"I wonder if Alfred's still looking forward to a good fight."

He laughed. "Probably!"

I felt braver now I could see my friends' faces. *For Christ's sake, let's get on with it!* I thought, and was surprised at myself. I was stiff and cramped and cold, and the tension in me was desperate for release.

The English were shelling harder and the ditch was too shallow to give us much protection. The scream and burst of each shell had us pressing ourselves into the earth but they kept missing us.

The fellows somewhere off to our left were not so fortunate, and screams and shouts of "Medics!" reached us faintly. Poor bastards...

I could almost feel the hot sharp metal slicing into my own flesh and when I looked at Anton I could see him thinking the same.

If it happens, it happens. There's no point worrying...

Time slowed until the hands of my watch seemed to be stuck, and I gave up looking at the bloody thing.

How much longer, for fuck's sake?

In one of the quieter intervals I heard someone close by muttering, "Ave Maria, gratia plena..."

If I come through this, God, I'll be a better Catholic. Spare me and I'll be at Mass every Sunday...

And give up booze and fornication?

I hesitated.

"Karl."

"What?"

"If you could make a pact with God that if you survived you'd give up booze and women, what would you say?"

He burst out laughing. "I'd say tell the Devil I'm on my way! Or ask Thor to make room in Valhalla!"

I laughed as well. "Looks like I'll be with you, then!"

"Ten minutes, boys," said Hartmann.

My stomach turned over and I was almost sick. *Ten minutes might be all the life I have left.*

Karl's face was calm, his eyes far away. He lit another cigarette with careful precision and blew out a huge cloud of smoke.

"You still shitting yourself, Zeller?" Kienle called out.

"Speak for yourself!"

"You will be soon!" Weiss said cheerfully.

I hope to Christ I don't...

How long can ten fucking minutes last?

"Fix bayonets!"

My hands shook so badly I almost dropped the bloody thing. Fumble, fumble...

Karl was perfectly steady. *What the fuck are you made of?* I wanted to ask him.

"Slow down," he said quietly. "You've got plenty of time."

Time – time had clotted and I wished my insides would. Sweat was pouring down my back in spite of the chilly air.

We took off our spiked helmets and put our students' caps on instead. We'd brought them all the way from our universities for this day.

The buglers sounded the charge.

Hartmann stood up and swept his arm forward. "GO!"

"GO!" bellowed Gefreiter Dittrich.

I was so cramped I could hardly get up. My knees were like jelly and my stomach was curdling. Anton was on my right shoulder and Karl on my left, their solidity reassuring. We strode forward together and my nerves disappeared.

"Deutschland, Deutschland, über alles, Über alles in der Welt..."

We were singing at the tops of our voices, singing to drown out the guns. We wanted everyone to hear us: the English, and everyone from Switzerland to the sea.

This was the culmination of my life, the reason for my birth. I was exultant, triumphant. Shells crashed and bullets flew around us, the air sang with flying metal, but nothing could touch me. I was immortal, invulnerable.

I realised, without understanding, that Hartmann no longer led us. Then there was a gap on my right...

The singing grew fainter and stopped, and the air was filled with groans and cries and the fury of the guns. I looked to my right and could see almost no one standing.

Only Karl and I seemed to be left, in a cloud of acrid yellow smoke so thick I could hardly breathe. Our steps faltered and we looked at each other. There was no sign of Dittrich or Braun. They'd vanished like the others.

Where are the English? And where is everyone?

"What do—" I began.

The smoke blew away abruptly and we stood in the open. The entire English army seemed to open up at us and in the same instant Karl flung his arm round my shoulders and threw me to the ground, so hard that the breath left my body and for a moment I thought I'd been hit. We lay there stock-still, not daring to move. God knows how they'd missed us.

If Karl hadn't thrown me to the ground I'd be dead. And Karl? He was lying so still beside me, so horribly still.

"Are you all right?" I croaked.

"I think so." *Thank God.* "And you?"

"Yes – at least I think so."

I realised that no one had passed us. The explosions and rifle fire merged with the cries of pain and shouts for help into a hellish cacophony.

Not far away someone started screaming. The sound cut right through me. I went cold inside with horror as I realised that that could so easily have been me, *could be me, at any moment.* My head whirled in panic.

Karl's hand tightened on my arm. "Keep still, you idiot!"

I hadn't even been aware of moving. I remembered with astonishment the bold, foolish fellow I'd been only a few minutes before.

Immortal youth! *Bloody idiot.*

There was, for some inexplicable reason, a lull. Karl raised himself cautiously and dropped down smartly as his cap flew off.

"Well?"

"No one."

No one? "What do we do?"

"Stay here until dark." He paused. "If they counter-attack we'll have to shoot as many as we can before they reach us."

I wasn't sure I could shoot anyone. I was petrified and the feeling intensified when I understood what Karl had said.

If the English counter-attacked we were dead. It was as simple as that. If we survived that long.

Karl's mind seemed to be working with enviable, cold-blooded clarity, while mine spun in a frenzy and I sweated and shook with fear. It was all I could do to lie still. Every sense was screaming at me to run like hell, but I knew that would be suicide.

How right we'd been to be worried about our lack of training, and how shockingly unprepared we'd been for the reality. I'd imagined some fine, glorious advance, sweeping unstoppably over the enemy positions, not that short, brutal action.

I was on a narrow ledge above a vast drop, a ledge which was slowly crumbling and which would soon cast me into the void. I prayed as I'd never prayed before and I wished I'd gone to confession.

The bugles sounded the advance again and again – "potato soup, potato soup, the whole day long potato soup, and no meat" – and each time the English fire rose to a shattering, deafening pitch. A small group passed us and we started to get up and follow them but they were mown down before my appalled eyes.

In the intervals between the attacks we could hear our comrades crying desperately for help. The man behind us to our right was still screaming and shrieking, "Mama! *Mama!*"

I wished I were deaf.

The intensity of terror faded slowly to apathy and in the end I lay there in a mood of resignation. I was stiff and cold from lying on the wet earth, and I was both burning with thirst and dying for a piss.

If I have to wait much longer I'll wet myself, and I know what everyone will think. I'm damned if I'll appear like that.

I managed to wriggle a bit to one side and roll slightly off my belly without getting shot, then made a bit of a scrape in the ground and pissed with immense relief.

I wriggled back. I didn't want to lie on the pissed-on place.

"No one would be able to tell," Karl said in my ear. "We're covered in mud anyway."

I realised he'd done the same. "All the same, I don't want to smell of it."

"Better than shit!" he said with a short laugh.

I did need a shit as well but that would have to wait.

The mist was closing in again. *Good*, I thought, *that'll hide us from the Tommies* – but it was rising gently into the air.

Strange. Very strange.

Finally darkness fell. I sat up cautiously and picked up my water bottle – and the bloody thing was empty. There was a hole in it.

"Take his," Karl said, pointing to a man who stared blankly at the sky, his uniform dark with blood.

I poured water into my throat. My body suddenly felt completely alien and I couldn't understand why its survival had been so important.

I was almost afraid to speak, though no one could have heard me through the howling.

"Which way do we go?" I whispered into Karl's ear.

That strange mist was rising all around and the visibility was poor. The darkness was lit only by the intermittent shelling and I had lost my bearings.

"This way, I think."

We started to crawl back. My legs were so stiff they would

hardly move. Karl got to his knees and then stood up cautiously. Nothing happened.

All around us men lay crumpled and shapeless. Here and there a dim shape dragged itself slowly back towards our lines.

"Who was screaming?" I asked. The man had stopped shortly before dark, exhausted or dead or unconscious.

"I have no idea."

There was a shell-hole, still smoking, parts of men scattered around it – a boot with half a leg still sticking out of it, part of a head, a torso ripped open and naked – and there was the noise. *Dear God, the noise.*

Hell cannot be worse than this.

In the now-dark, now-luminous mist I could hardly see where I was going. I tripped over a body and fell headlong and landed on another. I got up, my hands and face wet, the sharp smell of blood catching in my throat. I wiped my face with my sleeves, my stomach turning.

Someone nearby began to whimper. It was a hideous sound, barely even human, and my back hairs prickled. It was hard to tell exactly where it was coming from and we almost fell over the man before we realised we'd found him, curled on his side on the damp ground.

We knelt beside him, and I took hold of his shoulders with trembling hands and started to turn him over. He gave a horrible choking, gurgling cry that went right through me, and the most awful stench filled my nose and mouth. I retched.

What in God's name can smell like that? He was rigid and trembling in my arms, and that ghastly whimpering chilled me to the core.

"He must have got it in the belly," Karl said. "If only we had more light!"

As if in response someone sent up a flare which lit the mist to blinding brilliance. We froze. When my eyes readjusted I could see the man's face but it was so contorted that at first I didn't recognise him.

"Anton!" I gasped. "Oh, Jesus!"

His intestines were spilling out over the ground in gleaming loops and his hands were locked across his belly, trying to hold them in. Bile rose in my throat and I swallowed desperately. I couldn't be sick over Anton.

The flare burned out and we were plunged, dazzled, into darkness. I didn't care if I never saw again. I had seen more in those few seconds of light than I had ever wanted to see.

My numb, shocked brain was slow to register that Anton was limp and silent in my arms.

"Anton," I said uncertainly. "Anton."

Karl's hand moved across my arm to Anton's throat, to feel for the pulse.

"He's dead," he said, his voice sad and awed.

I still knelt there stupidly. *He can't be dead.*

"We've got to get back," said Karl.

"We can't just leave him here."

Karl squeezed my arm. "There's nothing more we can do for him. We have to help the living. Come on."

I laid Anton carefully on the ground, wondering why I was being so gentle when he couldn't feel anything. *All the care in the world won't make any difference now. The poor sod's dead.*

We moved on hesitantly. A way off to our right someone must have lit a fire. The mist flamed suddenly with a brilliant orange glare and we dropped to the ground again. Sounds of heavy fighting reached us but we couldn't tell who was attacking whom.

Please God, don't let them counter-attack, not now! Sweat broke out all over me again and I felt myself trembling.

All I saw when I looked up were dim figures struggling slowly back. We got up cautiously and no one shot at us.

After a few metres we found a Leutnant lying on his back, his epaulettes gleaming faintly. His face was smashed to a pulp and one arm was missing. His other hand rested on his chest, a gold ring shining in the orange light.

Karl bent down for a closer look, took hold of the hand and turned it slightly.

"It's Hartmann."

"Are you sure?"

"Yes – it's his ring. Look."

I didn't want to look at him. I remembered the conscientious, dutiful young man he'd been and I didn't want that mutilated corpse to be the last I knew of him.

Karl tried to take the ring off, to send it back to his family. "It's bloody stuck…"

"Help me, for God's sake, *help me!*"

For a moment I was too afraid to look.

"My legs – it's too far…"

The voice, though plaintive and agonised, was familiar.

"It's Kempff, isn't it?" Karl asked me.

"I think so."

"Who's that?" Kempff called out, fear in his voice.

"Becker and Leussow," Karl answered. "What's wrong with your legs?"

"Broken – both of them. Thank God you're here!"

"I'll have to cut your boots off," Karl said. "I'll try not to hurt you – don't move."

But Kempff screamed as soon as Karl touched him and then lay frighteningly still – *Oh God, not you as well!* – but the pulse was still beating fast in his throat.

"He's passed out," I said.

"That makes it easier."

Kempff's legs were a mass of blood and torn flesh. The right leg was worse by far, the shin-bone apparently smashed.

"Hold his leg up for me, Franz, so I can get round it… I hope I get this right – I've never dealt with a broken leg before."

"You've done this sort of thing before? When, for God's sake?"

"Only on the horses. Pa used to let me help, when they had a cut or something… Bugger it, two of these aren't going to be enough."

He got out one of his own field dressings and used that as well. At least they'd managed to issue us with those.

"That'll do," he said. He got up, lifted Kempff as if he weighed nothing and put him carefully over his shoulder.

I didn't realise you were that strong, I thought. *Kempff must be my size, at least. At least you're not carrying me back. At least I'm still in one piece, though God knows how.*

"Can I help?" I asked.

"No, it's all right, thanks. You could bring his rifle, though."

"This mist is really odd," I said. "The way it's rising like that…"

"Yes, isn't it?"

More and more small groups were stumbling over the rough ground in the semi-darkness, many carrying others or supporting them. The mist was thickening to fog and I was afraid of getting lost and walking straight into the English.

"Oh, fuck, I'll never make it," one man said in despair.

"It's all right," I said, taking hold of his arm. "I've got you."

"Cheers, mate."

I put his arm over my shoulders and staggered as he leaned on me, my boots slipping in the mud. *Don't drop the poor bugger, Franz, for God's sake!*

Houses loomed ahead of us and the ground was suddenly smoother beneath my feet. I knew then what a pitifully small distance we'd covered. We'd got nowhere near the enemy.

"Halt!"

I barely even heard.

"Stop or I shoot!"

Karl grabbed my belt. "Franz, *stop!*"

"Password!"

I couldn't speak, couldn't find my voice, never mind remember the bloody password. I was shaking from head to foot, with cold and reaction.

Karl answered for us. "Where's the aid post?" he asked.

The sentry peered at me. "Christ, mate, you look bad! Keep on down this road – it's not much further."

"Thanks."

I turned to Karl. "Do – do you want some help, now – now we're on the road?" I stammered.

"No thanks, it's easier just to keep going – Jesus, Franz, your face!"

"What's wrong with it?"

"It's covered in blood."

Why? Am I injured? I rubbed my face and then remembered the corpse I'd fallen on.

"It – it's not mine. I fell on someone, remember?"

"Thank God for that. You had me worried there."

Eventually we reached the aid post. There was a big queue of men sitting or lying on the ground outside and dozens more straggled towards it.

Most were shocked and silent, but a boy who must have joined up from school was calling for his mother, over and over. *Anton,* I thought – *it must have been Anton who screamed all afternoon...*

There are so many here, so many, and these are just some of those who've managed to get back. There must be thousands still lying out there.

"Cheers, mate," the man I was helping said again. "I can make it now."

I released him, and grabbed him again as he almost collapsed.

Karl caught one of the orderlies as he hurried past. "Where shall we put these fellows?"

He took one look at me and said, "Sit over here, mate. You'll have a bit of a wait –"

"I'm all right. It's this fellow."

"You sure? Your face—"

"*It's not mine!*" There was something close to hysteria in my voice.

"All right, all right. No need to shout." He took hold of the man I was supporting. "Come and sit down, mate. We'll have a look at you when we can."

"Cheers, mate," he said again.

"This fellow's legs are broken," Karl said.

"Oh, right. Put him there, by that wall, with the stretchers."

Karl found a space and laid Kempff down carefully. He was still unconscious.

"God knows how long it'll be before they see to him," Karl muttered. "They must be working flat out."

I was beginning, just beginning, to understand what a disaster the day had been.

"We'd better report back," Karl said.

"Where to?"

"Where we started from this morning, I suppose – if we can find it."

We lapsed into silence. I was still trembling and I felt sick. Karl had been so cool and self-possessed that I wondered whether he had any emotions at all or whether they'd been bred out of him.

Somehow we found our way back to the ditch we'd left that morning. At first I didn't recognise it.

My God, is it even the same day? It feels as if an entire century has passed.

I want to go home. All I want to do is go home. Why in God's name did I let myself in for this?

Feldwebel Braun was sitting by a ruined wall. *He can't be all that's left. There can't be just Braun and us. Someone else must have survived.*

The light flickered on his greying hair and the lines in his face. There was no emotion in that face at all – it was still and hard, the eyes impassive.

"Well, that's two more," he said. I heard his words with relief. Two more. "Did you see anyone else?"

"Leutnant Hartmann's dead, Sergeant Major," said Karl.

"You sure?"

"Yes. I recognised his ring. I couldn't get it off, though." Braun's face changed a fraction as Karl's words sank in. "And we left Kempff at the dressing station with two broken legs."

"Anton D-Döpfner's d-dead." The words stuck as I tried to say them. All I could see was Anton's intestines spilling out.

I shivered and moved closer to the fire. Braun looked at my face.

"Becker, what the bloody hell are you doing here? You should have got that seen to."

"It's not mine – not mine," I said, remembering that my face was covered in blood.

"All right. Have some of this. And clean yourself up – you look horrible."

I was expecting water or tea and the strong spirit stung my throat. I coughed and my eyes watered, but it settled inside me with a warm glow that made me feel a little steadier.

I handed the flask back and he passed it to Karl. His hand shook as he drank and I realised he was every bit as shocked as I was. He was just better at dealing with it.

"We're to dig a trench fifty metres forward from here," said Braun. "I've pinched some spades from the sheds around here

– being as we weren't issued with any – and I've got everyone digging. D'you reckon you can find the right place?"

"Yes, Sergeant Major," said Karl.

I hope you can because I'm damned if I could. If you get it wrong we'll probably both get shot. I was so disorientated that left to myself I would have ended up God knows where.

We got there fairly quickly, and Gefreiter Fischer set us to digging. The trench was just a shallow ditch and we dug with all our energy.

The English spurred us on by shelling us sporadically. They hadn't quite got the range but it was still nerve-racking. I was desperately tired and I wanted to sleep but the urge to live was stronger, and if we were going to face an English attack I wanted a deeper trench – especially if they were going to put up a bombardment like ours.

Alfred was there, unscathed and digging like mad. I was so relieved to see him.

"Are you enjoying 'the best fight of your life'?" I asked when we paused for breath.

"That wasn't really a fight, was it? We never even saw the enemy. The buggers just shot the crap out of us. I'll feel a lot happier when we get the chance to have a shot at them – and after today I can't wait to shoot the fuckers."

I thought of Anton and Hartmann and part of me agreed with him but a larger part was too shattered to find the energy to fight. I was completely empty of everything.

Pull yourself together, Franz. That was only the beginning and God knows when it'll end.

The wind brought the pitiful cries of those who still lay on the battlefield. The sound made me shiver and I wished I could blot it out. *God, do we have to listen to that all night?*

I imagined lying out there in pain with the cold wind blowing round me, calling for help which never came, growing weaker as my blood drained into the earth. *Please, dear God, don't let that happen to me!* I felt cold inside, right through to my heart, although I was hot from digging, and my teeth chattered. I wished I were deaf.

Karl stopped digging and looked out into the mist.

"Bastards." He hissed the word between his teeth. "Fucking *bastards.*"

We bent our backs to digging faster. The soil was wet and heavy and my back and shoulders were beginning to ache, and I was so fucking tired.

Some time later Kurt and a few of the others returned with – unbelievably – hot food. *At long fucking last!*

I could have done with this yesterday evening, I thought, suddenly absolutely ravenous. I began devouring it like a starving man and was surprised by how quickly I started to feel better.

"Have you seen Otto?" Kurt asked.

Otto had been his closest friend since the beginning of our university days.

"One moment he was beside me," he said, "and the next he'd just – gone."

There was bewildered incomprehension in his voice, mixed with concern that he failed to hide.

You wanted to be a soldier and now you're just as far out of your depth as I am.

"We haven't seen him," said Karl quietly.

"I expect he'll turn up soon," I said. It didn't sound at all convincing.

"I just hope he isn't – out there…" Kurt's voice trailed away, then he said, "What about Anton?"

"He's dead," Karl said.

I saw Anton as he'd looked in the light of the flare and the stink of torn intestines filled my throat. My stomach turned over. The stew turned to dust in my mouth and I couldn't swallow it. I sat very still, trying not to be sick.

"You have this," I said to Karl when I could speak. "I'm not hungry any more."

"Franz, you'd better eat some more," he said. "You haven't eaten half of it."

I shook my head.

His hand was like iron on my arm. "We'll have to fight tomorrow, and the day after, and the day after that. They've been bloody hopeless at feeding us so far and with us being in action it'll be even worse. They might not be able to get food to us for days. You're a bloody fool if you don't eat now, while you've got the chance."

"It's just that I keep seeing—"

"So do I. But we can't let ourselves."

I forced down half of the rest and couldn't manage any more.

"Here," I said to Kurt.

"Thanks."

I hadn't realised how thirsty I was until Kienle came up with water, and then I couldn't get enough of it.

"Better wash your face," Karl said, "or you'll have Braun on your back."

I'd forgotten about the blood on my face. It had dried and I had to rub hard to get it off. Someone's blood, some poor bastard's blood. I'd been walking around half the night with someone's blood on my face and I'd forgotten all about it. How could I forget something like that?

We picked up our spades again and dug and dug, desperation urging us on. Sweat ran down me in spite of the chill and the seams of my uniform chafed.

I'd never worked like that in my life. My back was killing me, my hands were blistered and my muscles ached ferociously, but I was only too aware that the hours of darkness were nearly over.

It won't be only your back that's 'killing you' if you don't keep at it – it'll be the English and it'll be for real.

Braun didn't seem unhappy with the results.

"Have you seen any of our officers?" Kurt asked me.

"Not alive, no. What about you?"

He shook his head. "It's just Braun being in charge made me wonder if any of them are left."

"Thinking of promotion already, is you?" Zeller asked. "They'll have to kill a lot more before they gets to you!"

"It's still one less!" Weiss said.

"And they won't get to you at all if you carries on like today," Zeller said. "That was fucking stupid, what you lot did."

"Yes, I think we know," said Alfred.

That's for sure, I thought. *How many more days like that can we take before we're all dead?*

In the intermittently glowing mist the others looked insubstantial and I had the sudden illusion that we were all ghosts. *But you're not, Franz – you're only too alive, with all the potential for suffering that life holds.*

I tried to ignore the cries from the fields beyond. There was no time to go and fetch them, and all I could do was pray that they'd be picked up soon and that I wouldn't end up like that myself.

Schürmann turned up about an hour before dawn.

"Thank fuck for that," Karl muttered to me.

I just nodded, very relieved that he was still alive and that he'd come back to us. If anyone could get us through, he could.

In the uncertain light I noticed that his left sleeve had been cut off at the elbow and his wrist was bandaged. It seemed to be splinted as well but I couldn't be certain.

You're an old man and you've come back to us with a wrist

that's probably broken. You don't have to be here. You could have been on your way home.

His voice was perfectly steady and gave no indication of the pain he must have been feeling. His presence was reassuring, his voice heartening. I almost felt safe with him and Braun there – until he told us that we were to attack again in a few hours' time.

The surge of nausea was so powerful that it nearly overcame me. This time I knew exactly what I was facing. I didn't know how I was still alive, and I couldn't see how I was going to survive another attack like that one.

You won't. It's as simple as that. And if you do survive tomorrow, you probably won't survive the day after. It's over. It's just a question of when.

The finality of it was too much. I wished with all my heart that I could go back to the beginning of August and listen to my father's advice instead of rejecting it.

"Get some rest while it's quiet, boys," Schürmann said. "There's tea and rum on the way."

I put my spade down and suddenly realised how fucking tired I was.

I sat beside Karl on the damp earth. "Karl."

"Mm?"

"You were right."

He turned to me, amusement in his eyes as the mist flared luminously. "What about?"

"War."

"Ah. Well, I can't say being right gives me any pleasure. In fact, I'd really rather have been wrong – but there it is."

The tea and rum was almost cold by the time it reached us but the alcohol put fresh life into me. And there was bread and sausage, and I made myself eat because I knew I needed it.

The time dragged unbearably, until finally the mist began to lighten. *This is it. The last dawn I will ever see.*

Please God, let it be quick. I don't want to end up like Anton or like those poor bastards we can still hear.

I couldn't stop myself shaking.

"Franz, are you all right?" Karl said in my ear.

"I'm bloody frozen." That was true, but I was thoroughly scared as well.

He put his arm round my shoulders. "Whatever happens, I won't leave you."

"You might have to. If I get hit, you'll have to go on."

"Then I'll come back for you as soon as I can. I won't abandon you, I promise, not while I'm alive."

"Nor I you."

I turned slightly towards him and returned his embrace. I'd never thought there could be such strength and comfort in someone's arms. *It'll be all right. We'll live together or die together. Either way I won't be alone.*

We waited and waited. *They've changed their minds. In a minute Schürmann will tell us it's off…*

Of course he didn't. An hour or so later the bugles blew and my shaking legs did their best to carry me forward.

We were met once again with bullets and shells but nowhere near as many as the day before, and I felt a glimmer of hope. *We might do it, we might just get there.*

We stumbled over the dead, and the wounded who still lay there called out to us but we couldn't stop for them. A hand brushed my ankle but hadn't the strength to hold onto it. I felt nothing: no pity, no regret that I couldn't help him, nothing at all. I was unable to feel anything.

Men were falling around me but not at the frightful rate of the day before. Braun was still going, so was Schürmann. Karl and Alfred were still with me. And at last we could see the English positions, about a hundred metres ahead.

It was a hundred metres too far. Their fire suddenly increased in intensity. Bullets sang past my ears, something tugged at my sleeve—

"After me!" yelled Schürmann, and we ran into the remains of a farm building.

From what was left of the first floor we could see not just the enemy positions but the English soldiers. There they were at last, the bastards!

We knelt beneath the windowsills. Karl, Alfred and the others began firing at once. Schürmann had picked up a rifle at some point and was banging away, apparently untroubled by his wrist.

I took aim at one of the Englishmen and was suddenly paralysed by what I was about to do.

I'd recited the Ten Commandments over and over as a child. *Thou shalt not kill… but they're firing at our people – and look how fast they're doing it. They killed Anton and Hartmann, and if you don't kill them they'll kill you.*

I steadied myself and fired, and the man fell. And another, and another. Soon they ceased to be men, became just targets, and I found myself cursing when I missed. At last we were fighting back, instead of being helpless victims.

None of our fellows were getting anywhere near the English. Like us, they got to a couple of hundred metres away and then were felled, or turned and ran back. Our artillery wasn't making much impression and I realised we were being rather useful.

We can't keep it up all day, though – we'll run out of ammunition –

I barely heard the scream of an approaching shell. The farmhouse rocked in the crash of the explosion, dirt and stone chips flying everywhere.

"The bastards are shelling us!" shouted Alfred.

The shell was swiftly followed by another and it landed even closer. Our safe little refuge was becoming hazardous.

"Wait a minute!" Braun yelled. He listened intently as the next shell howled towards us. "They're ours!"

No! They can't be. Our own people can't be trying to kill us!

Schürmann nodded. "I agree. And they're just about getting the range. Time to leave, boys."

There was only one way we could go. There were only about twenty of us and there was no way we were going to storm the English positions.

"Becker and Schäfer, stay with me. Braun, you go first with the others. We'll keep their heads down as much as we can, then we'll follow."

Karl and I looked at each other but there was nothing we could say. I shot as accurately as I could, feeling that every round was helping him to safety.

I was so concerned about him and about being separated that I didn't realise how much more dangerous our own departure was going to be. Suddenly the artillery fire increased in intensity, one screaming burst after another.

"Theirs too, now!" Schürmann shouted. I could barely hear him over the shattering racket. "Time to go!"

I took a deep breath as we left the farmhouse, before plunging into the maelstrom of metal. It felt as if every shell, every bullet was aimed at me personally.

We ran as if all the devils of hell were on our heels. Schäfer was out in front, Schürmann was beside me, and I was amazed that an old man could run that fast.

We won't catch Schäfer, though – he's trying for the Olympics...

The shells screamed and crashed. Schäfer's head flew off his body. Somehow it took a few more steps, blood spurting from the neck, before he collapsed in front of us.

Faster, faster – we stumbled, gasping for breath. Not much further – my legs burned and my lungs were bursting. My vision blurred, sweat running into my eyes.

If Karl's lying here somewhere I'll never see him.

Suddenly the English shrapnel fire stepped up. *Oh God, they're going to attack! Faster –*

I was alone.

I turned round. Schürmann was struggling to rise to his feet. I ran back towards him.

He waved me away.

"No, Becker! Go on!"

As I reached him he shouted again, "*Becker, leave me! GO!*"

How could I leave him? He'd come back to us when he didn't have to and I couldn't abandon him.

"Sorry, sir," I said.

I put his right arm round my shoulders, held him firmly round the waist and together we stumbled across the heavy clay.

Bullets from our own trenches cracked past.

"Don't shoot! Germans!" I yelled as loud as I could, though God knows why I thought anyone would hear me.

Schürmann was still wearing his spiked helmet and maybe someone saw it in spite of the smoke, because they stopped firing and by some miracle we reached a shallow trench and tumbled thankfully into it.

"Well done!" someone shouted, thumping me on the back.

We lay dragging air in, my breath sobbing in my throat.

"Becker – next time – you do as you're – bloody well – told!"

"Yes, sir." *Ungrateful bugger. You'd probably be dead if I'd left you.*

My vision began to clear but I could see no one I recognised. *Where are they? Where's Karl? Where is he?*

"Not sure who this lot are," Schürmann said, looking around. He sat up and turned, looking, like me, for a familiar face.

His left sleeve was torn near the shoulder. The grey cloth was soaked with blood and it was running down his arm.

"You're bleeding, sir."

He turned back towards me. "Am I?"

"Yes, sir – your left arm."

He looked at his bandaged wrist and I think he was about to contradict me when he saw the fresh blood. He stared at it in surprise.

That must have been why you stumbled.

"I'll have to cut your sleeve, sir," I said.

"Just rip it out of the armhole and do the same with my shirt."

There was a nasty gash through the muscle, right at the top of his arm, and it was rather awkward to bandage. I hadn't patched anyone up for real before and I was afraid of hurting him.

"Pull it tighter, man! I won't break!"

"You all right, there?" called a voice from the left.

"Yes, fine thanks," Schürmann called back. "It's Gebel, isn't it? Third Company?"

"Oh, hello Schürmann! Didn't recognise you. All a bit mucky, aren't we? Your lot are off to the right somewhere, I think."

"Jolly good."

Gebel waved a hip flask. "Haven't got much but you're welcome to join me. Medicinal, of course."

"Of course," said Schürmann. He turned to me. "Thanks, Becker – and thank you for coming back for me."

Not such an ungrateful bugger after all, I thought, wondering why he'd been so cross with me for helping him. He scrabbled the couple of metres to Gebel and the two of them were soon deep in conversation.

Gebel's men were the same mix of students and reservists as our lot. The faces around me were weary, just as mine must have been, and none of us felt inclined to chat.

The day wore on slowly. No orders reached us and there was no question of going anywhere, not in daylight.

Reaction set in and I sat there trembling. I was starving hungry and suddenly dog-tired and I closed my eyes for a moment. Shells burst all around, Schäfer's head went flying – I woke with a start and spent the rest of the afternoon in a sort of half-trance, dozing and dreaming and waking and thinking.

I desperately needed to sleep but couldn't, and my mind went over and over the last two days. I fired again and again at the Englishmen and watched them fall, but still the enormity of what I'd done failed to register. In the intervals of being fully awake I worried about Karl and prayed that he was safely with the others and not lying out on the field.

Night brought freedom to move.

"Go and see who you can find," Schürmann said to me. "And when you've found them come and fetch me. There's no sense both of us blundering about the place."

His voice was strained and I realised he was in quite a lot of pain. *You'll have to go back now, and then who'll lead us?*

The trench was narrow and far too crowded for me to move along in it. *I hope I don't get shot*, I thought as I climbed out. The mist was closing in again and the darkness was almost total in between the occasional explosions. It was hard to see who everyone was and where I was going. It would be only too easy for someone to mistake me for an Englishman, especially without a spiked helmet.

I saw one lying on the ground and picked it up. It had the right number on it and a good coating of mud but happily that was all.

Which way to go? Right first. That was what Gebel had said.

"Fourth Company?" I asked again and again but all I heard in reply was "No mate", or "Not here".

They must be somewhere. Perhaps they're all dead. Perhaps Karl and Alfred and the others are dead or dying...

There must have been thousands of men lying out there and the sound of them was frightful. *Someone must do something – we can't just leave them all to die.*

The mist was getting thicker and I was afraid of losing my way.

"Fourth Company?"

"Here," said a familiar voice. "Who's that?"

"Becker." I almost fell into the trench right on top of Kienle and Kurt.

"We thought you'd had it," Kurt said.

"I thought you had. Where's Karl?" I was afraid of the answer.

"Just over there."

Thank God. Oh, thank God!

I climbed out again, and as I did so I heard Karl call out, "Franz!" and then he was standing in front of me.

He wrapped his arms round me and squeezed so hard I couldn't breathe. *You're here*, I thought. *You're here and you're safe.* Neither of us spoke. There was nothing to say.

He released me and said, "Alfred was just saying that if you didn't hurry you'd miss the rum and we agreed that that would never do."

"There's rum?"

"Yes, but no food – to our utter astonishment, of course."

"I have to go and fetch Schürmann first," I said. "Keep some for both of us. I think he'll need it – he's been hit again."

"Do you need a hand?"

"No, I think he can walk."

I turned and began heading back towards where I'd left Schürmann.

"And where do you think you're going?" The voice had a hard, grating edge that was really rather unpleasant. It didn't occur to me that the man was speaking to me.

"Stop that man!"

Gefreiter Fischer caught hold of my arm. "He means you, Becker."

I turned round and found myself face to face with a small, wiry man. In the flickering light I just recognised him as Leutnant Krypke, one of the other platoon commanders. Like Hartmann he was a hastily commissioned cadet, but unlike Hartmann he had a bit of a reputation.

"Don't you pay attention when an officer speaks to you?"

I stood to attention as if I were on the parade ground. It felt rather ridiculous.

"I do apologise, Herr Leutnant. I didn't realise Herr Leutnant was speaking to me."

"What's your name?" he demanded, in the same tone.

"Becker, sir."

"And where were you sloping off to?"

"I was going to fetch Hauptmann von Schürmann, sir."

"Oh, yes? And where might he be?" It was plain that he didn't believe me.

I felt myself starting to get warm. "Over that way—"

"I don't suppose you can be more specific?" he interrupted sarcastically.

You stupid bastard. "I left him with some men from Third Company—"

"I don't much care for your tone, Becker," said Krypke. "You can stay here and work on this trench."

I opened my mouth to protest. Out of the corner of my eye I saw Fischer shaking his head, and realised there was no point arguing.

I'll have to wait until no one's looking and then slip away. Schürmann will kill me if I don't get back to him soon.

"No point arguing," Fischer said quietly after Krypke had gone. "Especially not with him. Now, what's this about Schürmann?"

I told him and he said, "Right. Off you go and get him. Don't worry about Krypke. I'll deal with him."

Retracing my steps in the thickening fog wasn't easy but thankfully not much was happening. Maybe everyone was exhausted by the past days or maybe the artillery on both sides was running low on shells – I didn't much care which.

It took me a good hour to find Schürmann. He was still chatting with Gebel, who he'd obviously known for some time.

"Ah, Becker. Any luck?"

"Yes, sir." I told him who I'd found and roughly where they were.

"Good," he said and turned to Gebel. "Well, I'll stand you dinner once we're out of this."

"I'll hold you to it! May you be shot in the neck and stomach!"

Just like the fucking theatre. Break a leg...

Schürmann's left arm was in a sling and I offered him my hand to help him out of the trench.

"I can manage," he said rather testily, and scrambled out unaided.

We groped our way through the darkness and the eerily flaming mist. He was following me and to his irritation I kept turning round to make sure he was still there.

After about the fourth time he could contain himself no longer.

"Keep going, man! Don't keep stopping like some bloody woman on a shopping trip!"

And so I reached what remained of the Fourth Company a little way ahead of him. And of course the first man I met was Leutnant Krypke, whose anger was all too obvious.

"I told you quite explicitly to stay here! Where the devil have you been?"

"Sir, I went to fetch—"

"Hauptmann von Schürmann. A likely story. I won't have shirking, Becker—"

"Krypke, what is this about?" Schürmann's voice would have cut through steel.

Krypke opened his mouth and closed it again.

"I – er – I told Becker to stay here, sir," he said rather lamely.

"Didn't he tell you he had orders from me?"

"No, sir."

You lying bastard.

"I expect to hear no more of this," Schürmann said coldly, and walked past Krypke as if he didn't exist.

Krypke glared at me. *I hope I don't have too much to do with you,* I thought. *You'll have it in for me now.*

Karl had saved rum for us, and Schürmann seemed as grateful for it as I was. It reduced my hunger a little and helped to ward off the chill of the night, and it probably blunted his pain.

I told Karl and Kurt about my run-in with Krypke.

"Ah yes," said Karl. "A thoroughly unpleasant character. With a bit of luck we won't have much to do with him."

"What happens now?" I asked.

"God knows. Probably more of the same."

"Is this what you imagined?"

Karl stopped digging for a moment. "Something like it, I suppose. At least we managed to shoot back this time."

"Yes," said Kurt. "It was making my blood boil, just being shot at all the time by men we couldn't even see."

It didn't matter, poor old Otto not being able to hit anything. He never got the chance.

"Any news of Otto?" I hardly liked to ask.

Kurt just shook his head.

Anton, I thought, seeing him again for the thousandth time. *And that beautiful, expensive woman who will soon be crying her* eyes out because the only person who really loved her and who never judged her is dead.

"Alfred's missing," Kurt said.

"And so's Zeller," added Kienle.

And what of me and my family? My poor mother. She'll cry too...

Stop it, Franz. You're not dead. You've survived this far. Today you evened the score a little. Who knows what will happen tomorrow? Perhaps we'll take their positions after all.

You have to believe you'll survive.

We dug and dug, and waited for our orders for the next day. I was famished, and so tired I could hardly stay awake. My grubby uniform clung to my sweaty skin, my eyes were full of grit and my hands were sore. I'd escaped death by the narrowest of margins and I had no idea how many men I'd shot.

So this is what I volunteered for. This is what seemed so fine and glorious.

Out in the darkness men groaned and called for help, only too audible in the relative quiet. I knew the medics were out there, but there were nowhere near enough of them to cope with the carnage of the past two days.

Sometime in the early hours of the morning Braun stood beside us.

"Any volunteers to go and fetch some of that lot in?"

"I'll go, Sergeant Major," Karl said at once.

"And me," said Kurt.

"Me too," Lange and I said together.

"Right," said Braun. "That's all I can let go just now. Leussow, you're in charge. Keep your wits about you and come straight back if there's any sign of trouble. Anyone you pick up, just bring him back here. You're to be back by four. Got that?"

Karl repeated the orders back and then turned to us.

"Right. Four of us, two groups of two. Franz, you stay with

me, and it's probably best if the four of us stay as close together as we can."

God knows what we'll find – but at least we're doing something, and it can't be worse than Anton.

My back hairs prickled as we picked our way out into the eerie darkness. It was a scene from Hell: the swirling mist lit by the occasional flares and flashes, ghostly figures creeping about, all accompanied by the cries of the tormented and the random detonations of the shrapnel shells.

In no time we found a fellow trying to drag himself back towards our lines.

"Help me!" he called out to us, his voice dry and cracking. "Help me, for God's sake!"

"It's all right," Karl said. "We've come to get you."

He started crying, actually crying. "Thank God! I thought – I can't – two days –"

Poor sod. You must have thought you were going to die here.

"Where are you hit?" I asked.

"Stomach."

I hardly dared look, afraid I'd see guts falling out again – but he'd managed to patch himself up. The dressing was stuck fast.

"We'll leave this," Karl said. "Don't want you to start bleeding. Sorry, but we're going to hurt you. Franz, take his feet, would you?"

He sat the man up, apparently oblivious to his cry of pain, and linked his hands under the fellow's arms. We stumbled with him over the uneven ground, barely able to see where we were going. He bit back another groan and then to my relief he passed out.

We left him in the trench and went back for another, passing Kurt and Lange on the way. After five I lost count. After four hours of carrying them my legs and back were aching, but it didn't matter.

"I wish we didn't have to hurt them," I said to Karl.

"So do I – but what can we do?"

Alfred was back, to our relief. The medics had given him a bag of dressings and he was working non-stop, his hands and sleeves covered in blood.

"It's nearly four," Karl said as we went out again. "This will have to be the last one."

We'd made such a small difference. There were still hundreds of men lying on the cold ground, hoping someone would get to them in time.

Perhaps in the end you don't care. Perhaps you're so weak nothing matters.

"Well done, all of you," said Schürmann, "and you too, Friedemann. It's a great help having you around."

"Thank you, sir."

He went on to tell us that another attack was planned for nine o'clock.

I can't do it. I can't do that again. I'm fucking exhausted and running on empty, and I just can't face having the crap shot out of us again.

None of us wanted to look at each other. Karl was staring at his hands, his fingernails suddenly of absorbing interest.

I barely heard the rest of Schürmann's words. I was too busy trying to convince myself that I might survive, that we might even reach our objective this time.

The wait was interminable. *These are probably my last hours,* I thought as I lit yet another cigarette. *Please God, let it be quick.*

There were so few of us left. All the little groups of mates were broken up, and Lange and Krebs had attached themselves to Weiss and Kienle.

The company now consisted of two platoons, one under Krypke and the other under Leutnant Kittelmann. Braun was there, of course – the Gorilla seemed indestructible – but

Dittrich was still missing. Unteroffizier Rombach, whom we barely knew, had a bandage round his head but insisted it was just a cut.

"With a bit of luck they'll shoot at that and not at me," Kurt said with a grin.

"Optimist!" said Alfred.

"If I weren't an optimist I wouldn't be here," Kurt replied, and there was no answer to that.

Time congealed again and I didn't mind in the least. *No point wishing away the last bit of my life... though I'd far rather spend it clean and well-fed and in bed with a pretty girl.*

The only small consolation was that we were allowed to eat one day's iron rations. Stone cold, of course, and as Kurt said, not exactly gourmet, but who cared?

"Any ideas how to make coffee with cold water?" asked Alfred.

"What water?" Kienle replied.

The lack of water was far worse than the lack of food. We'd picked up as many bottles as we could when we'd gone out, but a lot of them were holed and we were all thirsty.

"Maybe they'll send someone back for it tonight," Kurt said.

"There's your optimism again!" said Alfred.

"On two counts," Karl said with a grin. "One, that you'll be alive, and two, that there'll be water!"

"Well, if I'm not then it won't matter!" Kurt retorted.

Tonight was too far away to contemplate. *Strange, this succession of days where I see the dawn but have no idea whether I'll see darkness fall... It used to be guaranteed, in that other life.*

"The attack's been cancelled," Braun said just after half past eight.

Thank fuck for that.

"Someone's had some bloody sense at last," Karl muttered to me. "Perhaps now they'll arrange a proper bombardment and get the Regulars to finish the job."

Half an hour later the bugles blew on our left and a grey mass leapt from the earth and surged forward.

"What the fuck are they doing?" Kurt exclaimed.

"Lange! *Lange!*" shouted Schürmann. "Run back to Battalion and find out what the hell's going on!"

They didn't get the message, I thought, *and now the poor bastards are going in with no artillery support at all...*

There was nothing we could do. We watched helplessly as they fell in dozens.

"Jesus," Alfred said. "Oh, Jesus Christ."

The remnants came running or crawling back towards us. *That could have been us, so easily. What in God's name happened to the messenger?*

It was over an hour before Lange came back, having got lost several times.

"Our orders were correct, sir," he reported to Schürmann. "They're sending fresh runners to the other companies."

Why bother? It's too fucking late.

Schürmann posted extra sentries and the rest of us tried to get some rest. I was worn out but my nerves were on edge and I couldn't forget those poor sods getting mown down right in front of us like that.

Who knew when we'd be ordered forward again?

The morning dragged on. During the night the trench had been deepened somewhat, so we could move around a bit. That meant we saw more of Krypke than we really wanted to, but Schürmann came and spoke to all of us frequently.

I'd follow you to Hell and back, I thought, and then had to laugh. *I've certainly followed you to Hell, but back? Who knows?*

Alfred looked at Schürmann's hand and frowned. "Would

you like me to have a look at your wrist, sir?" he asked cautiously.

Schürmann gave him a rather straight look.

"It's just that your hand's rather swollen, sir. I think the bandages may be too tight."

"Well, yes, thank you, Friedemann."

"I could look at your arm as well, sir, if you like. I won't be able to do much but it should help until you go back."

"I'm not going back," Schürmann said.

Alfred opened his mouth, but clearly realised it was better to say nothing and shut it again.

Schürmann's wrist was a mess. Even I could see it was getting infected. He gritted his teeth as Alfred changed the dressing, sweat standing out on his forehead.

"You should go back, sir," Alfred said quietly. "This is only going to get worse."

To my surprise Schürmann's only reaction was to shake his head.

"Thank you, Friedemann," he said after a moment. "But that's quite out of the question."

He sat silently while Alfred dealt with his arm, thanked him again, then got up and moved away.

Kurt said softly, "He won't leave us."

"No," said Alfred. "But if he doesn't he'll lose his hand. That arm's not too good either."

The words were hardly out of his mouth when the enemy began shelling us. They hadn't quite got the range and most of the shrapnel shells burst behind us but we knew what it meant: they were about to attack.

In a flash we were lining the edge of the trench, waiting. I tried not to duck as the shells flew overhead. I could hear them going past, and prayed they'd continue to do so.

"We'll know they're coming when it stops!" Braun yelled. "This lot know what they're doing."

The bombardment went on and on for eternity. Then it stopped, quite abruptly. My stomach turned over. *They'll be coming now, with fixed bayonets, long and sharp, ready to slice me open...*

"Here they come!"

Running figures emerging from the smoke, red trousers – the French! *Jesus, so close!*

"Fire!"

My heart was pounding, my hands shaking. *Get a grip, Franz, you mustn't miss.* I made a huge effort and steadied myself, chose a Frenchman and fired – and to my intense relief he fell. *One less to stick his bayonet in me, two less, three, four, five. Reload – quickly, Franz, quickly – don't drop the clip, you stupid bastard – they're still coming!*

We won't be able to hold them – the remaining Frenchmen turned and ran back.

We waited but no more came. I sagged against the earth. We'd managed to repel them and we were all still alive.

They didn't attack again. Towards evening it began to rain, a fine rain at first that became steadily heavier until it was pouring down, and the howling of the wind almost blotted out the cries of the Frenchmen. The earth turned to mud around us, and as we dug the bottom of the trench started to fill with water.

Soon we were bailing, with whatever we could use, but it made no difference. The water welled up as fast as we could pour it out.

"Pity we can't drink it," Lange said. "I'm fucking parched."

Shortly after midnight a carrying party appeared, with water bottles, iron rations and ammunition.

"See?" Kurt said gleefully. "It pays to be an optimist!"

"You can say that once we're out of here," Karl replied with a grin. "I'm not betting on anything!"

"No rum," said Kienle glumly.

"Shut up and drink your water!" Alfred retorted.

"Drink your own bloody water!" said Kienle, and we all laughed.

Dawn revealed grey, scudding clouds and a dismal landscape of mud. All I wanted to do was get dry, have a nice hot bath and get into a soft, warm bed. In the cold, grey light I could see that the others were weary, haggard and unshaven, and I realised I must look the same.

Schürmann looked worse than any of us. His face was flushed and his eyes glittered with fever, and he couldn't quite hide the pain.

About halfway through the morning Braun said quietly to Karl, "Leussow, go and find Major Grabowski or any other senior officer."

"Higher than a captain, you mean, Sergeant Major?"

"That's it."

Karl came back some time later.

"Grabowski's ordered Schürmann out of the line," he said. "I'm to take him back after dark. In the meantime, Alfred, he'd like to see you again."

Best for him to go back, I thought – *but not for us. I feel so much safer with him here.*

I knew he couldn't actually protect me but he stayed so calm, no matter what was going on, and I did know I could trust him.

To my surprise and relief nothing more happened. I didn't know why and I didn't care. I was just relieved when darkness fell without our having to stagger across the mud while the other lot shot at us, and without them coming to kill us either.

Karl left us after dark and it was several hours before he came back. Schürmann's departure seemed to have left Krypke in charge. He kept us all hard at work all night and asked several times whether or not Karl was back. He came to check up again just as Karl returned.

"Ah, Leussow," he said in that sarcastic tone of his, "good of you to join us. Nice stroll, was it?"

"No, sir," Karl said expressionlessly. "Rather hard work, in fact."

"Well, now you're here, you can do some proper work. I want this trench dry."

"Stupid bugger," Karl said after he'd gone. "Anyone with half an eye can see we've reached the water table."

"What's that mean?" asked Kurt.

"It means we'll have wet feet until we find somewhere higher up – and being as this is Belgium we've bugger all chance of that."

The following day we had to attack again, and the day after that, and the next day the French attacked us. By sheer good fortune I stayed alive, and so did Karl, Kurt and Alfred.

Darkness fell that last day on a tattered group of exhausted men. The Fourth Company existed in name alone, as did the First Battalion, and the Regiment. The Fourth Army was being destroyed.

I had all but given up hope of ever leaving that place – and then, quite unexpectedly, we received the wonderful, glorious news that we were to be relieved, that we were going back into rest.

At about midnight the relief arrived. They were as we had once been, young and eager and with no idea at all of what awaited them. We fidgeted while our few remaining officers handed over to their full complement, and then turned our aching backs on the front line and plodded rearwards.

We retrieved our monkeys at the farm, leaving a huge pile of packs without owners. Each one represented a man who was dead or wounded or missing, and I didn't want to think how many there were.

Krypke and Kittelmann had a brief conference.

"Yes, I agree," Krypke said, his tone only fractionally less abrasive than the one he used with us. *You're going to be popular*, I thought.

Kittelmann summoned a couple of fellows whom I didn't know, and a minute later they left and the rest of us fell out and sat down.

"If I sit here for long I'll fall asleep," Alfred said.

"Me too," said Lange.

"Fag?" Karl held out his silver cigarette case.

"Thanks," said Weiss and took one.

We all did. The strong tobacco was just right, and revived me a little.

After about two hours a wagon appeared and we loaded the orphaned packs onto it and trudged along behind. My monkey felt as if it had doubled in weight in the days since I'd seen it last.

"I wish we could ride in a bloody wagon," Kienle grumbled.

But of course there was no chance of that. Our legs had to carry us on through the night.

After an hour or so we halted by a field kitchen and had the first really good meal we'd had since leaving Germany. It made the slog to our new quarters a little less weary.

Much later, sore-footed and almost asleep on our feet, we reached a farm where we were directed to a barn. The floor was spread with fresh straw, and we took our kit off and collapsed onto it. I removed my boots, realising suddenly that I'd been wearing them solidly for over a week. My socks were moulded to my feet and I hadn't the energy to peel them off.

I lay down and was instantly asleep.

IV

Inge stood before me naked, and unpinned her hair. It fell down in thick waves, over her breasts and down to her hips. I pulled her towards me, felt her soft, warm flesh against mine, ran my hands down her back to her buttocks. I wanted her so much. I was lying on my back on my bed and she was sitting astride my waist, brushing her hair across my face, to and fro…

"Stop it!" I laughed, and tried to lift her hips to lower her down onto me. She wouldn't budge. The tickling continued and I couldn't escape it.

I could hear laughter, *male* laughter. Why? My eyes began to open and I wasn't in my bedroom. Where the hell was I?

Kurt's face came slowly into focus. The sod was sitting on me, tickling my face with a wisp of straw.

I yelled and pushed him off. "You bastard! *You lousy fucking bastard!* You ruined my dream!"

More laughter.

"Good one, was it?" Karl asked.

"Yes, it bloody was. I was in bed with Inge and she was sitting on top of me and we were just about to, well, you know – and then I find it's you ugly bastards playing silly games."

Karl burst out laughing. "Hey, Kurt! You nearly lost your virginity!"

I blushed scarlet. They both laughed even harder and after a bit I saw the funny side myself.

I stretched and rubbed my eyes and looked round the barn. *We came here last night*, I thought, *after we were relieved*.

"What time is it?"

"Midday," Karl answered.

"Bollocks." I squinted at my watch. "Bloody hell, so it is!"

"Would I lie to you?" he asked with mock offence.

"There's a rumour of a bath later," said Kurt, "and clean clothes."

"And we're free till two," Karl added, "so if you move your lazy arse, we can have a bit of a look around."

"Where's Alfred?"

He shrugged. "No idea. He woke up a couple of hours ago and buggered off by himself."

The farm was shabby and neglected. A few pigs and chickens scratched about and an old man passed us, his eyes fixed on the ground. The farmhouse was large but rather ramshackle and we weren't allowed near it. Officers only.

"Bit of a tip, this," Karl said. "Could be bloody good if someone spent some money on it, though. Look at the soil."

I didn't know anything about soil but had to agree the farm wasn't up to much. The only other farm I'd really seen was the Leussow estate and there couldn't have been a greater contrast.

Three black-clad women passed us, without a glance in our direction. Two were old but the middle one was young and slim, and to our starved eyes unbelievably beautiful.

We turned as one as she went by, captivated by the swing of her hips under her long dress.

"God, I want a fuck!" Karl voiced all our thoughts, but the coarseness of the expression grated.

"Why do you always have to sound like a bloody farmhand?" I said.

He looked at me in surprise. "But, Franz, I *am* a farmhand."

I shook my head. "Oh no, you're not. I know the truth. You're – what's your pedigree again? Ah, yes: Karl. Friedrich. August. Eckhardt. Von. Leussow!"

He laughed. "I'm still a farmhand, fancy name or not. You've stayed with us, Franz. You've seen how we work. We're glorified peasants... And what do you want me to say, anyway? All I want right now is to get into bed with some willing girl and give her a good shafting – and in my book that's a fuck. And don't tell me you don't want the same."

"Well... yes, I do. I just wish you wouldn't call a spade a bloody shovel."

"I'm nowhere near as crude as Pa."

I couldn't argue with that – I'd heard the Major swearing at one of his labourers. Even Braun's vocabulary wasn't that colourful.

"Lange said there's a knocking shop in the village," Kurt said. "We might be able to get passes. Mind you, I'd rather have that slim little thing."

"Fat chance," Karl retorted. "You saw those two old dragons guarding her honour."

"I don't want to go anywhere near a girl until I've had a good bath," I said.

"Nor do I," agreed Kurt.

Our uniforms were stiff with mud and other men's blood, and our hands were filthy. My friends' faces were caked with grime and lined with fatigue in spite of a good night's sleep, and mine must have been exactly the same.

We didn't know how likely a bath really was, so we washed our faces and shaved in the horse trough and felt a fraction more human – in one respect at least. The past few days returned to me as disjointed images that rose up in my mind and then faded away, disturbing and somehow unreal. It was hard to believe that any of it had actually happened.

The cooker had reached us, and there was stew with potatoes, and hot coffee. And best of all there were extra portions.

"Just underlines how many of us have copped it," Alfred said as the cook dolloped another ladleful into our mess tins.

"I'm trying for thirds," said Kienle. "I'm still fucking starving."

"Nah, mate," the cook said. "'Sempty. 'Ave a look."

Kienle peered in, shrugged, and came back to us.

"Well?" asked Weiss.

"Empty, like he said."

"Oh well – two portions was better than fuck all."

At two o'clock we assembled in a field and the NCOs called out the numbers of the companies. We found Braun easily enough, Krypke and Kittelmann standing beside him. Gradually the chaos sorted itself into order, apart from a small group who clearly belonged somewhere else.

Braun called the roll, his face and voice expressionless.

"Gefreiter Dittrich?"

Silence.

"War Volunteer Döpfner?"

Anton's intestines spilled onto the ground in the light of the flare – my throat closed up.

"Dead, Sergeant Major," Karl called out.

Thanks.

So many names were met by silence or by a call that the man was dead or wounded.

"Reservist Kempff?"

"Wounded, Sergeant Major," I said.

"War Volunteer Kramer?"

"Wounded, Sergeant Major. Got it in the thigh." I didn't recognise the voice.

"You sure?"

"Yeah. Me and Klose picked him up."

"Thank God for that," Kurt breathed. My relief was almost as great as his. Otto was safe.

"Reservist Schäfer?"

"Dead, Sergeant Major," I said. Schäfer's head flew off his body, blood spurting from his neck…

"Reservist Zeller?"

Silence.

I felt the soft rain on my face, my living face, and was so glad to be alive. Even the dingy autumn landscape looked beautiful. The battle was like some ghastly nightmare – but we could hear the guns and I knew I was awake.

We'll have to go back to that – that carnage – before long. The thought made me feel ill. *Perhaps I'll pay for a girl, after all. Only eighty-three left, out of two hundred odd. How many will come back next time?*

After roll call we marched to a brewery, where some of the vats had been converted into baths.

"A brewery," said Alfred. "Just imagine – a litre of cool, golden beer topped with white foam—"

"And a pretty girl on your knee," said Kurt.

"Oh, shut up!" *No point thinking about things we can't have,* I wanted to add but didn't.

It was utterly wonderful to shed my filthy uniform and to peel my shirt and socks off. I shivered in the sharp air, the breeze clean and fresh on my bare skin. The bathwater was lukewarm and we bathed in groups, laughing and splashing each other and throwing the soap around. It was glorious, and so was the feeling of clean clothes.

It doesn't take much to make me happy now. A girl and a good meal and I'll be in heaven.

The road into the village was just mud and so was the main street. The houses were grubby and the whole place looked as though it needed a good scrub. The brothel wasn't any better and the queue outside made it even less appealing.

"What do you think?" I asked.

Karl hesitated. "I don't know... I thought I was desperate but now I'm not so sure. Let's have something to eat and think about it."

There was a small café, crammed full of soldiers. It was just as dirty as the rest of the place and the service was very slow.

Eventually we got a bottle of wine and a couple of plates of eggs and chips. The wine was watered and vinegary but at least the food was good, even if the portions were rather small.

"If the knocking shop's as bad a deal as this I don't want to know," Karl said.

"Everything's so dirty. What if the girls are dirty as well? I don't want to catch anything."

"No, neither do I."

We had another bottle of wine, in the vain hope that it might make us slightly drunk, smoked a few cigarettes, and left. It wasn't the evening I'd had in mind at all and I felt flat and depressed.

That's probably that. They'll soon send us back and I'll be lucky to come back out again. Reaction to the past few days set in and I began to feel sick and shaky.

Get a grip, Franz. It's only just begun. You're going to have to do it all again and again, and it's no use being yellow.

It was still raining, but only lightly, and neither of us was in a hurry to get back. We sauntered slowly along the muddy road. In the distance we could see Ypres burning, and the bombardment was clearly audible.

"How long do you think it'll be before they send us back?" I asked.

"God knows. They'll have to reinforce us first – but no doubt there are plenty more eager, willing youths in Germany." There was a touch of bitterness in his voice. "Though if they send them in the way they did us, there won't be."

It wasn't right, I thought for the first time. *None of us knew what we were doing.*

"Eighty-three." I was thinking out loud and I wished I hadn't.

"Yes, I know…" He linked his arm through mine. "But look at it this way. We've got a bit of experience now. The new fellows won't have. We've got a better chance of surviving than them."

"Do you think so?"

"Yes. Look, Franz, there's no point worrying about the future – or anything else, for that matter. Just be happy now and enjoy not having to fight for a few days."

We carried on in silence. There was something very companionable about strolling together like that and I was almost sorry when we arrived back at the farm.

"Hail to the conquerors of the fleshpots of Belgium!" Kurt called out cheerfully as we walked into the barn, still arm in arm.

"Sorry to disappoint you," Karl said, "but a quick reconnaissance showed that an attack would have been foolhardy."

"He means the brothel was a filthy old dump," I added.

Alfred looked up at us and smiled, and there was something in his expression that I couldn't quite read.

"Someone's had some sense, then," he said, but I had the feeling he wasn't really saying what he meant. God alone knew what was in his mind. There were times when I felt that Alfred didn't see things quite the same way as the rest of us.

"So I might as well not bother," said Lange.

Karl shrugged. "Up to you. Depends how much of a chance you want to take."

"Well, if I do get the pox I won't live to die of it," he said, and got up and left.

The rest of us just looked at each other. *That's a chance I don't want to take*, I thought, *even with my rubber friend.*

I couldn't sleep that night. My exhaustion had worn off and my mind went over and over the battle. Every time I closed my eyes the things I'd seen and done appeared, so vividly that I wondered whether I was dreaming or hallucinating.

I aimed at the Englishmen and the Frenchmen again, fired and saw them fall, and the enormity of what I had done came home to me. *You had to do it, especially the Frenchies. They were coming to kill you. What were you supposed to do – get skewered?*

And the Tommies were shooting at your comrades – and you can't be sure you actually shot any of them, anyway. Everyone else was firing too. Someone else might have chosen the same target… but that was dodging the issue.

Men are dead by my hand, I thought, feeling sick and ashamed. *It's not as if I did it with any reluctance, either, once I got over the initial hesitation. What does that make me?*

A soldier, Franz. That's what it makes you.

I turned over and tried again to go to sleep – and then woke with a horrible jolt, soaked in sweat, my heart pounding. I must have been dreaming but I couldn't remember the details. *Probably better not to…*

The barn was dark and filled with snoring. Someone muttered in his sleep. Karl stirred restlessly and I wondered if he was awake. I wanted to talk, but at the same time I knew it was impossible. I would never be able to frame the words.

I'm going to have to do it all again. Face death again, kill again, watch the others die again, until either the war ends or I get killed or badly wounded. There's no way out now.

I saw Anton again as he'd looked in the light of the flare. *That could be me next time.* I tried to push the thought away but it wouldn't leave me and I curled up on my side shaking, trying to banish the sick terror that filled me.

Please, dear God, don't do that to me. If I have to die then please let it be quick.

I lay staring into the darkness of the barn. I was dying for a fag but I didn't dare smoke in there, and I was afraid of disturbing the others if I got up to go outside. Time dragged, and I was grateful for the dawn.

It was Sunday. I went to confession and to Mass. The priest was very kind and reassured me that I had only been doing my duty. He seemed certain that men killed in battle went straight to Heaven but I couldn't quite believe it.

Karl went to the Lutheran service, though I had no idea whether he went out of gratitude for still being alive or because he felt as guilty as I did. A couple of times I thought of asking him but I didn't think I'd get an answer.

In the afternoon there was a mass funeral for the men who'd died in the dressing stations, conducted by both padres and the rabbi. So many shapeless forms in shrouds, laid together in a pit, without the dignity of a coffin or a cross. Only the officers got those.

The rain fell gently as we sang the soldiers' lament, 'I had a Comrade'. I'd always thought the song sentimental but now I knew what it was to watch men die.

We fell out in silence. I couldn't help thinking about all those who still lay out on the battlefield and who would have no grave for a long time, if at all.

The post came and I was glad of the distraction. I had a large parcel from home and letters from all my family, judging from which they hadn't received the one I'd written just before Langemarck.

I should write back at once; they'll be worried sick about me – but I didn't know what to write. *I'll do it later*, I thought, and shared out the cake Mama had sent me, with what remained of our platoon.

Karl tried to refuse. "Franz, it's very kind of you, but I'm never going to be able to reciprocate."

"Just take me to see those dancers when we get some leave."

"It's a deal! You won't regret it, I can tell you."

That assumes we ever get there… I didn't want to say that.

"Who were your letters from?" I asked instead.

"One's from Pa and the other from Friedrich – he's been given temporary command of a company *and* they've given him the Iron Cross, Second Class."

His eyes glowed with pride but there was disquiet in them.

"That's terrific!" I said.

"Bloody excellent," said Kurt. "He's doing really well."

"You'll be promoted before long," Karl said to him. "And we'll all have to call you Herr Leutnant."

"And stand to attention," said Alfred.

"Oh, rot! You'll be promoted before me!" Kurt said to Karl.

"I'll bet you five marks I'm not," said Karl.

"Done."

"Any news of Johnny?" I wasn't sure if I should ask.

Karl shook his head. "No, but he's always been a lazy bugger when it comes to writing letters. The war'll be over before I hear from him."

He spoke with assumed nonchalance, which did nothing to hide his anxiety.

I don't envy you having two brothers caught up in this, especially when they're far away and you can't see what's happening to them – though that's probably better. Who wants to see his brother carved up like Anton?

"Do you think we should write to Anton's mother?" I asked.

Karl looked at me. "What on earth could we say? They'll write her an official letter. Let's just leave it at that."

I'd better write to my own family.

'Dear Mama, Papa and Johanna,' I began, and had no idea

what to write next. *Just tell them you're safe. That's all they want to know. Don't tell them what happened.*

I wasn't sure whether to mention any of the others or not. *If I tell them that Karl and Kurt are all right, they'll wonder what happened to Otto and Anton. Each man who quietly disappears from my letters will only worry my mother more. Best to leave them all out for now.*

Kurt was sitting staring into space, his writing pad on his thigh.

"Difficult, isn't it?" I said.

"Fucking impossible."

"What is?" asked Karl.

"Writing to our families," I replied.

He looked at me, astonished.

"It's all right for you," said Kurt. "Yours are all soldiers. Our parents are worrying themselves to a frazzle."

"I appreciate that," Karl said slowly. "But isn't it better to tell them the truth?"

"How can we?" I asked. "Your brothers know what happens to men in battle. My parents have never seen anyone get killed, or... or die like... like Anton. They can't imagine it."

"I think you have to credit them with some imagination – I mean, don't give them all the details but I'd tell them we had several days of hard fighting. They'll get that from the papers anyway."

He had a point. I kept the letter brief and factual, stressing that I was in good health. *That's the most important thing anyway,* I thought.

I hadn't finished writing when Rombach appeared.

"There's a load of monkeys that need going through," he said.

We looked at each other.

"If you all do two each it'll get done nice and quick," he went on. "Put the contents in three piles: Army issue, personal effects, and stuff like chocolate and tobacco. Army kit gets re-issued, personal effects get sent home, and the last lot of stuff gets shared out. And no nicking stuff."

"Not that anyone would know," Weiss said as we started the dismal job.

"How would you feel if someone nicked your stuff?" asked a theology student whose name I couldn't remember.

Weiss looked at him as if he had two heads. "Wouldn't fucking care, would I? I'd be fucking dead."

"You might be in hospital."

Weiss shrugged again. "Tough luck, isn't it?"

"Well, it's between you and your conscience," said the other. *Breuning; that was it.*

"What's one of them?" Weiss asked with a laugh.

What indeed?

"Nicking someone's stuff's not the same thing as shooting Frenchies," Alfred said.

"Quite," said Karl firmly, and gave Weiss a look that should have frozen his blood.

"All right, all right! Never said I was going to, did I?"

The contents of the first monkey I opened were depressing beyond words. There were several letters addressed in a very feminine hand, tied together with ribbon, and I recognised the name as one of the dead.

She won't see him again… There was also half a box of chocolates and another of cigars, gifts from her or from someone else who had loved him and who would soon learn that he was dead.

And French and English parents will hear that their sons are dead, because I shot them.

Close your mind, Franz, and just get on with it. Letters to go home, chocolates and cigars for the rest of us, Army kit for re-issue.

We had quite a party with the booze and food of those who were gone. *Next time, someone will be enjoying whatever Mama sends me – and good luck to them.*

We were reinforced and reorganised. To my dismay we were put into Krypke's platoon.

"Pity we're stuck with him rather than being under Kittelmann," Alfred said. "He's a decent sort of chap."

"He's still an officer," said Weiss. "And if you ask me, Denzer won't last five minutes – he's almost old enough to be *my* dad, never mind yours."

Hauptmann Denzer had taken over as Company Commander. He was about the same age as Schürmann but overweight and florid, and didn't inspire the same confidence.

"You're probably right," said Alfred. "Blood pressure must be sky high."

Our new comrades were mostly as we had been: young and naïve and enthusiastic. We tried to warn them what was waiting for them but they wouldn't listen. The fact that they were needed so soon should have told them something, but they all suffered from the delusion that nothing could happen to them.

Three days later we marched back up towards the front line. The new fellows swaggered along, singing cheerfully, while we were filled with grim foreboding.

I looked at the autumn trees. The leaves were falling, and thousands would never go home.

The Front was almost exactly where we'd left it and the men we relieved were haggard and exhausted, their eyes bleak.

They've been fighting for nearly a week and they've got nowhere. I could see the thought in the others' faces. *What chance have we of doing any better?*

All we can do is fight as hard as we can. All I can do is fight for Germany until the end, however it may come.

And fight we did, in one desperate, futile attack after another, across open ground swept by enemy fire, with little or no artillery support. It seemed our generals believed that machine-guns and artillery could be overcome by sheer weight of flesh, that any position could be taken if enough men were thrown at it.

The reinforcements behaved just as we had, and they fell by the score. The dead lay in pitiful grey bundles and the wounded looked at us with hurt, bewildered eyes. It did not take long for the eyes of the survivors to lose their innocence.

Those were days drenched in blood, days we endured in fear and exhaustion, desperate men in a sodden, lethal world of mud and flying metal.

Weiss had been right about Denzer – he collapsed and died on our third day in.

"Heart attack," said Alfred. "Not surprising, really – overweight man that age, all this stress and running about. Bound to happen."

Kittelmann got a shell splinter in his head. I bandaged him with shaking hands, shocked by his white stillness and by the stream of blood pouring from him. I thought he would die before dark but the stretcher-bearers carried him away, motionless beneath a muddy blanket. He hadn't regained consciousness and I doubted he ever would.

When Krypke was wounded as well I realised we'd lost all our original officers. Braun the indestructible was still there, acting as Company Commander.

Alfred got it in the leg and had to go back. Weiss got blown to fragments by a direct hit, and Lange was shot dead right beside me. I almost gave up hope of surviving, and so, I think, did the others. Karl smoked one black fag after another, and before every attack had that faraway, resigned look in his eyes.

In the end I was too tired to care what happened to me. I just wanted to sleep, to take off my heavy, muddy boots, lie down somewhere warm and dry, and sleep for weeks.

After an eternity we were relieved and our remnants were withdrawn east. As we left the front line I turned for a last look at it.

The mist was rising from the fields again.

"That looks really odd," I said to Karl. "I mean, mist normally just hangs there."

Bauer, who'd been studying physics, was standing beside us.

"That means it's warmer," he said. "Warm air rises."

"But how can it be warmer?" asked Kienle.

We looked at each other, mystified.

"I couldn't give a shit," Kurt said, and we turned to leave.

We marched in silence. I was beyond feeling anything and there was little point rejoicing at being spared when the reprieve was so temporary.

Once again our losses were dreadful, but Karl had been right: most of the dead and missing were from the new men. Those of us whose second time it was had done rather better. *Maybe there is a scrap of hope...*

We were withdrawn far enough for the battle to be barely audible. Around us was the tranquillity of autumn instead of mud and corpses, and the air was empty of shells and bullets. We could almost believe that the war really was just a nightmare.

The village was larger and cleaner than the last one. The café was better and the brothel had a less unwholesome appearance.

I still didn't like the idea of paying. I craved warmth and intimacy – we all did – but all we could have was a few minutes with a tired whore.

I wonder if I'll ever know what it is to fall in love, I thought as we left.

"You owe me ten marks," Karl said.

"What? How?"

"You remember, before we left Germany, you said you'd never pay again, and I bet you ten marks that you would. Time to pay up, Franz! – though maybe I should let you off after all those nice things you've given me."

"No, no, a bet's a bet." I dug out my wallet and found it was empty. "I'll have to pay you later. I've got nothing left."

He shook his head sadly. "Spent it all on booze and loose women. What will become of you, Becker?"

"The same as you, I expect! – though Hell can't be big enough to hold all of us."

I slept badly and woke with the dawn. I couldn't get back to sleep and I lay thinking, wishing I could stop.

Karl was fast asleep, curled on his side facing me. His fine fair hair fell across his forehead, giving him an almost childlike appearance.

You had more sense than to want to get into this, I thought. *You never complain, but I bet you'd far rather be lying in bed with some beautiful girl, making slow, rapturous love…*

I sighed. *I could do with that myself but there's bugger all chance of it until this business is over, and then I'll have to find someone. If I hadn't given Inge the push, perhaps she'd be waiting for me.*

You mean the way Anna's waiting for Karl? He hasn't even had one letter from her. So much for praying for us every day. More like out of sight, out of mind.

Karl opened his eyes, blinked a couple of times, and smiled.

"Penny for them, Franz?" he asked softly.

"I was thinking about Inge and –" I broke off, not sure whether I should mention Anna. "And I was thinking about the Turkish baths."

"Mm – wouldn't that be wonderful!" He stretched lazily. "All that lovely steam, and a good scrub and a massage – heaven! You know, when I get leave I think that's the first thing I'll do – or rather, the second!"

I wasn't too sure about the massage. I'd tried it once and

found it faintly embarrassing. Karl had loved it and I'd almost expected him to start purring.

"I might just join you," I said, scratching. "It'd be good to be clean, and not have lice."

"Indeed."

Bloody lice! In one of the lulls in the fighting I'd realised I was itching and then that something was crawling over my ribs – and then that it wasn't alone.

I pulled my shirt out of my trousers, ran my hand over my side, and caught hold of something small and hard.

It was a louse.

"Oh, fucking hell!" I exclaimed.

"What?" asked Kienle.

"Look."

He laughed. "You mean you've only got one?!"

Karl was laughing as well.

"It's not funny," I said. "I feel like a bloody tramp."

"We are tramps," Karl said. "Of no fixed abode, carrying all we possess on our backs – we might as well be verminous!"

Since then, of course, the little bastards had multiplied and I was trying not to hate them, because getting rid of them was impossible. We'd had a bath and been deloused and given clean uniforms, only to find ourselves being bitten a few hours later as the eggs in the seams hatched out.

We were reinforced and reorganised once again. Oberleutnant Sauer, our new Company Commander, was actually on the active list. Clearly someone had realised that we needed officers who were neither ancient nor barely out of school.

For the time being we were spared Krypke's sarcasm but we knew he'd soon be back. In the meantime we had Officer Cadet Rippel as our temporary Platoon Commander, and were very thankful that Braun was really in charge.

Among the new arrivals was a small, wiry Bavarian called Peter Thoma, who we'd known slightly at the training camp. He'd broken his ankle in the first couple of weeks and had had to stay behind when the rest of us left for Belgium, and seemed determined to make up for lost time. He was full of what he'd do when we met the enemy again.

Kienle told him he was talking shit, and the rest of us either took the piss or got up and left.

I think he realised he was becoming unpopular but he didn't seem to understand why.

"Of course," he said loudly one day, "it's the Prussians who've fucked it all up. They think they're so bloody clever, and they can't manage to beat the English, or even the French."

We all looked at Karl, who shrugged slightly and carried on trying to clean his fingernails.

"I don't see the problem," he said to me later. "I've got nothing against Bavarians and I really don't understand why some of them hate us so much. But if he's got a problem with me, then it's his problem, not mine."

Irritating as he was, Peter was preferable to Horn.

Horn was from Essen, and claimed to have knifed a man in a street fight. Kurt reckoned he'd probably be a useful bloke in battle, but I wasn't so sure. He was a short-tempered bastard and didn't take kindly to being given orders – though even he did as Braun said, without hesitating, as if he knew he'd met his match.

The only reason to look forward to Krypke's return was to see how he and Horn would get on.

We couldn't be bothered to make friends with the new volunteers. There was a gap between us that no words could bridge. They asked us about the war, about fighting, and we couldn't answer. I tried, but the words stuck in my throat. They would have to find out for themselves.

We must have seemed distant and unfriendly, but we knew what a few days in action would do to both their numbers and their bright-eyed eagerness.

"It's not as if we'll know them long," Kurt said, and I couldn't disagree.

We were soon sent back up the line again. All I felt was grim determination mixed with a vague hope that I might survive. Nothing remained of the youth who had set off with such enthusiasm such a short time before.

I'll be really lucky to come back this time, I thought as we marched up through the autumn rain.

To my utter astonishment and relief the battle had fizzled out. We were no nearer Ypres than when we'd first arrived.

We could see the ancient town still smouldering in the distance. *It took centuries to build, and weeks to destroy – and for what?*

"What I really don't understand," I said one day, "is how the fuck it came to this."

Breuning shrugged.

"Neither do I," said Bauer. "'Fraid I don't really understand anything beyond physics."

"Nor I much beyond the piano," Karl said.

"The Prussians fucked up," said Peter. "They were doing all the diplomacy and they fucked it up. We ended up with enemies all around, and it didn't have to be like that."

"You're probably right," Karl said.

Peter's jaw just dropped.

"Well, however it happened we're stuck till the spring," said Breuning.

The ground was completely waterlogged – someone said the Belgians had opened the dykes and flooded it on purpose – and we all had the feeling that Breuning was right, especially as we had to work every night improving the trenches.

We couldn't dig any deeper as the water filled the holes at once, so we built up walls from sandbags, earth, wattle, boards – anything that would give us cover. Every couple of metres they made a right-angled turn so blast and bullets couldn't go far. Seen from above they had the shape of medieval battlements, as I found out much, much later.

"This is starting to look permanent," Karl said one morning.

"Yes, isn't it?" was all I had the energy to say.

I've never fancied being nocturnal, I thought as I crawled into a small hole in the side of the trench and tried to sleep.

A couple of nights later a carrying party brought huge rolls of evil-looking barbed wire and stakes to fasten it to.

"This is looking even more permanent," Karl muttered to me.

"Hope we don't have to hammer the stakes in," said Breuning.

"Of course we has to hammer them in," Horn said. "Ain't you ever done any fencing?" He looked at the wire. "Same as the stuff they use on prison walls."

"Yeah, but this time it's to keep them out and not you in!" said Peter.

Horn looked at him. "Not stupid enough to get caught, was I?"

We crept out of the trench, our boots slurping in the mud. Five minutes later I wondered why we'd bothered being quiet. The sledgehammer struck the first stake with a loud, reverberating clang.

A flare went up and we froze in its brilliant light. *Anton*, I thought, trying not to see torn intestines in shining loops...

Karl swung the hammer again and there was another clang as it hit.

"Can't you do that quietly?" I hissed.

"Of course I fucking can't."

"Muffle it with a sandbag," suggested Horn.

"Let's put the screw pickets in instead," said Breuning.

Another flare went up – and then we heard an identical clang from the other side of No Man's Land.

Breuning laughed under his breath. Karl swung the hammer again and hit the stake good and hard.

"This is an easy job," he said. "Only three whacks per stake and it's in nice and firm."

"Just what we all like," said Horn. "In nice and firm!"

The wire was vicious, hand-shredding stuff. In the morning I found my hands were cut in several places, and they fucking hurt. The others' were just the same.

Rippel looked at them with concern. "Braun, we'd better send out a fresh party tonight."

"My thoughts exactly, sir."

"Make sure you clean those out thoroughly," Rippel said to us with fatherly concern. That made us smile, as he was even younger than us.

"Bleedin' 'ell," said Horn after he'd gone. "Never thought I'd have a sprog givin' me orders."

"He means well," said Kurt.

"Yeah, well, I'd rather have a proper officer."

"You will have when Krypke gets back," I said, somehow keeping my face straight.

Karl was very careful to clean his hands, but since he'd been hammering they'd suffered a good bit less. He wrapped his handkerchief carefully round his left hand, which had one quite long cut.

"Being a bit precious, aren't we?" taunted Peter.

"If you heard him play the piano you'd know why," Kurt said.

"We'll have to find one when we get into rest," Peter said. "I've never heard a pig play the piano before, let alone a Prussian pig."

Karl just lit another fag and ignored him.

131

The days dragged themselves out. From the terror of battle we'd passed to numbing tedium, to long dull days and nights filled with work.

At least No Man's Land was silent – but when I looked through the periscope at the wasteland of mud and shell-holes I wondered how many men had drowned when the water had risen. It wasn't something I wanted to think about.

The young volunteers were disappointed that there was no fighting.

"Off their fucking heads," I said to Karl.

"You'd have been the same a few weeks ago."

I knew he was right but it was already difficult to remember how I'd been. I looked at the fresh faces of the new boys and I felt a hundred years old.

Is it really less than a month since Anton died in my arms? It seems like half a century.

It was boring, though, and there was little to do during the day except try to sleep in one of the cubbyholes in the side of the trench. I couldn't do more than doze – there were always men barging past or I'd be disturbed for my turn as sentry.

And at night, when I really did want to sleep, we had to work. The only good thing about being stuck in one place was that the supply problems got sorted out, and we received food and tea and rum every night. It was never quite hot by the time it reached us but at least it was there.

After a week we went back into support.

"At least we can stop being bloody nocturnal," Bauer said.

He was wrong. We had to provide the carrying parties that went up to the front line every night with food, water, rum, and everything else.

It was back-breaking work, stumbling over bad ground in near-darkness loaded up like a mule with ammunition boxes, rolls of wire and God knows what.

"Jesus," said Breuning as we set out one night, "I'd rather carry two monkeys than this bloody lot!"

Müller lost his footing and dropped the rum jar. Most of the contents gurgled out into the mud before he could right it again, and when we got to the front line they cursed him all the way from Berlin to Paris. It was a frosty night and they'd obviously been looking forward to a nice warming slug of rum. If it had been me I don't think I'd have had the nerve to face them.

After a few days of that we went back into rest, to everyone's huge relief.

"The sooner the war gets going properly again the better," Kurt said.

He said something else but I was already falling asleep.

My family sent me another, embarrassingly large, parcel and so many letters that I got teased about my huge number of girlfriends and bombarded with requests for introductions.

"Even if I did have a harem I wouldn't share them with you lot!" I said, but no one believed me and there was no point trying to deny it.

Karl, unusually, had two letters. As the laughter about my 'harem' finally died down he opened one of them, and a minute later said quietly, "Oh, God."

Kurt and I looked at each other.

"What's happened?" Kurt asked cautiously.

"It's from Friedrich. He says the Guards attacked the English on 11th November—"

"They'll have shown the Tommies what fighting is!" Kurt interrupted, and then looked embarrassed.

If the Guards had succeeded we wouldn't be stuck in the same old ditches...

"So what happened?" I asked. *At least Friedrich's all right.*

"They didn't break through. He doesn't say much more... The thing is, he's in hospital. He, er... he's lost his right eye."

"Oh, shit. Karl, I'm really sorry. Give him my best wishes, won't you?"

How stupid that sounds. What use are good wishes?

I looked at Karl's beautiful blue-grey eyes and remembered that Friedrich's were – had been – almost the same.

He was a handsome man but now he's disfigured. I wonder how much of a mess they've made of him.

"Thanks, I will." He opened the other letter. "This one's from Pa. He might say a bit more… Not really, just that it's only a facial injury and he'll be going to a special clinic in Düsseldorf – Good Lord! They've given him the Iron Cross, First Class! Friedrich, that is, not Pa."

"That's bloody good going," Kurt said with a touch of envy. "Two medals and the war's not four months old."

And two wounds as well… He's paying for the glory, just as their uncle did. The Major's a bit cold, though, writing 'only a facial injury' when his son's been half-blinded – but then I thought of some of the things I'd seen and realised he was right. And half-blind's better than dead.

I looked at Karl and saw the concern in his face. *At least one of your brothers is safe in Germany now – and he could be out of it for good, though I can't imagine Friedrich being happy with an honourable escape from fighting. He's a soldier by profession and I know how proud he is of his regiment.*

When I was in Brandenburg I'd mentioned the film I'd seen two years previously, of the big annual review on the Tempelhof Fields in Berlin.

Friedrich's face had lit with one of his rare smiles.

"I remember the cameramen being there. I was rather nervous – I'd been commissioned not long before and it was a very big event for me."

Karl had left the room and come back with a framed photograph. It was a still from the film, and he'd pointed out

Friedrich to me. It was just as I'd remembered: the Guards marching past the Kaiser in the parade march, moving in perfect unison.

Papa didn't like that film at all, I remembered – *in fact he muttered something very scathing.*

I'd admired the Guards' precision and I'd said so to Friedrich, which had made him smile again. I hadn't realised then how difficult it was to achieve. They must have drilled and drilled until they were sick of it, but the result was magnificent.

I could understand his pride in being part of that, and I knew he accepted the consequences.

Karl handed me Friedrich's letter. One paragraph jumped out.

'I was appalled to hear that you've already been in action. I don't know how much training you had but I do know it can't have been enough. Remember that enthusiasm is no substitute for knowledge and don't do anything stupid '

Friedrich wouldn't have written that unless he meant it. He's a professional soldier and he thinks it wasn't right. Why did they use us so soon?

"Hey, I've got one from Otto!" said Kurt jubilantly.

Karl looked up.

"What's he say?" I asked.

"He's in hospital in Dresden. His left thigh's broken and he's already had two operations."

"He'll be out of it for a bit, then," said Kienle.

"Listen to this," Kurt said. "'The hospital's really nice and some of the nurses are really pretty. And the local girls come in and talk to us and make a fuss of us.' Lucky bastard!"

"Almost worth getting your leg broken," said Bauer.

"That's for sure," said Kienle. "Get out of this fucking place."

"Yes, but two operations," I said. "It must be a complicated break – and I'll bet it hurts."

"Bloody hell," Kurt said. "The next bit's fucking stupid: 'All the talk here is of the Murder of the Children, meaning us. It's so patronising. We're not children. We volunteered as men and we fought like men. We knew what we were letting ourselves in for. As soon as my leg is better I'll be back with you and we'll show them what we're made of.' What a load of shit! As he says, we're not children."

We were in terms of military experience, I thought but didn't say – *and how the hell were we supposed to take positions the Guards couldn't?* I was beginning to understand that we'd been cynically exploited, and 'Murder of the Children' didn't sound ridiculous at all.

"Otto seems to be as belligerent as ever," I said to Karl later.

"Well, he got knocked over right at the beginning, didn't he? So I don't suppose he saw what happened and he certainly didn't have all the rest of it. He can say we fought like men if he likes, but the fact is he didn't fight at all – not his fault, I know, but there it is."

"And with a bit of luck it'll be over before he has to," I said. "Quite."

At the beginning of December we were in rest, on a lonely farm where there was nothing much to do. Karl and I were playing cards with Alfred, who'd returned the day before, the same as ever apart from a bit of a limp.

"Why do I always lose?" he grumbled cheerfully as I dealt another hand.

"Well, you know what they say," Karl said: "lucky at cards, unlucky in love!"

"You could have fooled me," Alfred replied.

"Come to the house of joy with us and see what you find!"

We all knew he wouldn't go near the place.

"You're fucking joking!" Alfred said. "You might all want to catch the pox but I'm buggered if I do."

"Leussow!"

Karl started violently and dropped his cards, then his face broke into a wide grin.

"Scarface! Come in! How did you know we were here?"

"Our Leutnant told me. He's got a brother out here as well and so he got me a pass."

"That was decent of him – everyone, this is Johnny, my next oldest brother. Johnny, these are: Franz Becker—"

"So *you're* Franz Becker," Johnny interrupted.

"Why? What's he said about me?"

Johnny laughed. "Wouldn't you like to know?"

"And, to continue the introductions," Karl said with mock severity, "Kurt Meyer and Alfred Friedemann."

That's a lot of scars, I thought, looking at Johnny's face.

He sat down, looked round and sniffed. "Didn't this used to be a pigsty?"

"Correct," said Karl, "and there are the dispossessed swine!"

The pigs did resent being thrown out and kept trying to move back in. We'd scrubbed the place thoroughly and they seemed to think it was for their benefit. There was still a smell of pig shit, but it was dry and quite warm when we were all in there together.

"I can understand this being appropriate for a Prussian pig," said Johnny, "but why are these gentlemen suffering as well?"

"Guilt by association," Karl said.

"Ah, Pa's favourite principle." He grinned at us. "He used to beat us all, regardless of who was at fault – on the basis that we must all have had some part in it."

"He was usually right!"

Johnny must take after their mother, I thought. His eyes were bluer than Karl's and rounder, and his hair was slightly redder.

I was counting his scars when he said, "Haven't you noticed?"

"Noticed what?" asked Karl.

"This one's new," Johnny replied, tracing his finger along his cheek.

Karl stared at him. "You never were any good at arithmetic, were you? Look, if you've got one apple and you're given another, that's a one hundred per cent increase and very noticeable. If you have ten apples and you're given one more, that's only a ten per cent increase and you can be forgiven for missing it."

"And what's all that supposed to mean?" Johnny asked.

Karl rolled his eyes. "How in God's name am I supposed to notice another scar on your face? You look like Frankenstein's monster."

Johnny looked at us with an expression of mock hurt.

"One day," he said, "my baby brother" – Karl snorted – "will understand that the duel is an honourable institution and that these are honourable scars."

"And one day," said Karl, "this foolish youth" – Johnny snorted – "will learn to use a sabre, then he might inflict a few cuts instead of receiving them. When in God's name did you find time for that?"

"Between signing up and being called for. We went to Berlin and had a meeting with the – oh, no point giving you the name, it won't mean anything to you – some like-minded fellows from the Humboldt University. We won, anyway."

"Well, they're crap," said Alfred. "At least they were when we fought them. Which corps are you in?"

Johnny told him.

"Oh, right," Alfred said with a note of respect in his voice. "Surprised we haven't met."

Johnny grinned. "We can put that right after the war!"

Karl just shook his head and turned to me. "Can you imagine anything more pointless than getting pissed and fighting duels?"

"Bollocks!" Alfred retorted.

"The contacts are useful," Johnny said. "Look how well the Kaiser's corps brothers have done."

"Oh, you've got a royal prince in yours now, have you? The only contacts you make are steel against flesh and the floor when you're drunk."

"I enjoy it."

"Ah, yes," Karl said. "My brother's passion for duelling is exceeded only by his lack of ability—"

"Karl, that's crap! I give more than I get!"

Karl got up and sat behind his brother, one leg either side of him. He took hold of Johnny's head and turned the left side of his face towards us.

"You see this?" he said, pointing to one of the scars. "This one's mine."

"No, it's not. It's the one beneath it."

"Does it matter?"

Alfred started laughing. Kurt and I looked at each other, unsure if they'd had a genuine quarrel or if they'd just been fooling about.

"You see, I grew up in this one's shadow," Karl said cheerfully, his hands on Johnny's shoulders. "He's a year older than me, was always bigger than me – though he isn't now – and started doing everything – well, perhaps not *quite* everything – a year earlier than I did. When I was learning to use a foil, there he was, with a year's head start, insisting we practise together, just so he could show off, the bastard—"

"Oh, come on! Fritze was away at cadet school – who else was I going to practise with?"

"... and Pa was carping about my piano lessons, saying I'd

turn into a pansy. I got pissed off with the pair of them. It took a couple of years of hard work—"

"Three. It was three years before you were as good as me."

"Three, then. Who cares? And you've never got near me since."

"So tell us about the scar," said Kurt.

"Well," Karl said, "Johnny went off to university and I was still at school. He came home from his first term with his first scars, very full of himself. The next term I went to visit him and he started ribbing me in front of his corps brothers, saying I might think I could handle a sabre but it would be a different matter if I knew I could get hurt. I couldn't let that pass, could I? So we settled the matter the next day."

"What did your father say?" I asked, trying to imagine how my own father would react to something like that.

"He just laughed," said Johnny. "Said he wished he'd been there to see it, and it served me right for winding you up."

"Well, it did!" said Karl.

"I'll get you back one day, though, spoil those lovely looks!"

"No, you won't! Does it ever occur to you that you'd fight better without the hangover?"

"Oh, bollocks!" Johnny said. Then he asked, "Have you heard about Fritze?"

"Yes. Scarred faces are the fashion in our family now, aren't they? I'm quite the odd one out..." Karl paused, suddenly serious. "Shall we go for a walk? I'll show you the exotic sights."

"See you chaps in a bit," said Johnny, getting up.

"My father would have killed me if I'd done that to Heinz," said Kurt. Kurt's brother, six years his senior, was a doctor in Hannover.

"Why?" asked Alfred, clearly bemused.

"Well, apart from anything else, Heinz was forbidden from fighting duels on pain of having the money cut off."

That was completely beyond Alfred. "Why, for God's sake? What's wrong with it?"

"I wouldn't expect *you* to understand, not with a face like that... Papa thinks it's a waste of time and money, and a stupid fashion—"

"*Stupid fashion!*" Alfred exclaimed indignantly. "What utter rot! It teaches you a lot about yourself, believe you me, and it sharpens your reactions, and out here that's a distinct advantage."

I left them to their argument and wandered off in search of a quiet spot. I had the idea of keeping a diary, and sat down to write about the past few weeks in the hope that writing about what had happened would help me deal with it.

It was extraordinarily difficult. I sat there, the images going round and round in my mind, but my hand was reluctant to write. There was something terrible about the words on the paper: they acquired strength and validity of their own, and what might have been mere imagination became concrete truth.

I was so appalled by what I'd written that I almost stopped, but I forced myself to continue. *You must record it all, Franz, so no one can lie about what happened here. People will say how fine and glorious it was and you must be able to tell them the truth.*

After a couple of hours I'd had enough. I put my notebook and pencil in my pocket and headed back to the pigsty.

On the way I bumped into Alfred. He didn't seem pleased to see me and I couldn't work out why. He tried to hide it with bonhomie which rang completely false, and then said, "I expect Karl will be back by now."

"Yes, I should think so. It's almost time for supper."

He looked as if he wanted to say something else but then changed his mind. The result was a rather embarrassing silence, which I had no idea how to break.

What on earth is wrong? I wondered, and decided that Alfred was probably more affected by his experiences than he wanted to admit. *We're entitled to be a bit strange after all that*, I thought.

Karl was back, unusually subdued. For much of the evening he smoked and stared into space, and once or twice when I spoke to him he was too lost in thought to hear.

Bloody dull evening this is going to be.

"Fancy a game of skat?" I said to Peter and Horn.

"Yeah, all right."

Horn won again, for about the fourth time. It made me very suspicious but I wasn't about to open my big mouth. Best not to play too often, and then only for very small stakes.

The day we went back into the line the weather turned miserably cold and wet. Walking along the trench was like wading down a shallow river and we sank in over our knees. The mud had a nasty, sucking quality to it, and it was difficult to pull our feet back out.

"Oh, fuck!" exclaimed Flechsig in disgust. "I've lost my fucking boot!"

He stood on the fire step on one leg, pointing at the mud in the bottom of the trench, his other foot waving in the air in a muddy sock.

"Don't worry," Alfred said. "We'll get it out for you."

He started digging, but the mud just oozed back in and half-filled the hole again almost at once.

"God, this is fucking bottomless," he said after a few minutes.

Karl and I both dug as well but there was no sign of the boot. The mud had just swallowed it.

"What's all this about?" asked Rippel.

"My boot came off in the mud, sir," said Flechsig, "and it's completely lost."

"It can't have just vanished," Rippel said.

"Well, we can't find it, sir," said Karl.

"There's no bottom," Alfred said.

Rippel poked the mud with his cane. It went right in and he almost followed it.

"Better put your spare on," he said to Flechsig, "and we'll get you another once we're out of the line."

Fuck this for a joke. We're living in a bloody swamp, and it's still bloody raining.

Later I stood shivering on sentry duty, with icy rain trickling down my neck.

I really have had enough of this.

"You wonder if we'll ever be dry again," I said to Karl later.

"What's 'dry' mean?"

"It's something civilians have," said Alfred, "along with 'warm'."

"Can't take a joke, you shouldn't have joined!" Kurt said.

"You can stick your joke up your arse!" retorted Müller.

"Along with the mud," Bauer added.

"You'd need a fucking funnel for that," said Kienle.

The rum kept the cold out but its effect was very temporary. *Sod this – I want to go home.* No one said it but I could see the same thought in everyone's eyes.

It rained for three solid days, and the water rose and rose until it was nearly waist deep. We bailed as fast as we could but we couldn't keep up with it.

"We'll see Noah floating past in his bleeding ark soon," said Braun.

Alfred, on sentry duty, turned round abruptly. "The English! They're getting out of their trenches!"

"Go and fetch Oberleutnant Sauer," Braun said to Kurt, and then climbed up beside Alfred. "What are they doing?"

"I'm not too sure, Sergeant Major... They're just standing around in their wire. Now some of them are sitting down."

Braun poked his head over the top. "Bloody hell, you're right."

He stood watching for a couple of minutes then climbed out of the trench. We all held our breath but nothing happened.

He turned round.

"Leussow, you speak English, don't you? Come up here and ask them what's going on."

Karl climbed up beside him. "What's going on?" he called out.

"We're flooded out!" came the reply. "If you need to get out as well we won't shoot."

Karl translated.

"We might have to," said Sauer, and a few hours later that was exactly what happened.

Both sides stayed within their wire and there was no further conversation. We just stared at each other.

So that's the enemy.

It was the first chance I'd had to look at them properly. They looked like us, wet and miserable. They were even the same colour as us, their uniforms just as coated with Flanders mud as ours. I could see no difference at all between us and them apart from the headgear.

What the fuck are we all doing here?

No Man's Land was utterly desolate, a wasteland of mud and water, pockmarked with shell-holes and scattered with the rotting remains of the dead. *We should go out and pick them up, now there's an informal truce – but any movement beyond our wire will be seen as hostile.*

It would be a horrible job anyway. They've been there for weeks. It's only the cold that keeps the smell down.

The relief could not come soon enough, and a very bedraggled group handed over to the next lucky fellows.

The rain ran down my neck all the way back and when we

got to our quarters I took my boots off and poured water out of them. We all did.

Alfred laughed. "The Bible's wrong about Hell. It's not fire and brimstone – it's rain and mud!"

"And there was I thinking that if I cop it I'll be out of this," Kurt said.

"If those silly buggers would make peace we could all go home for Christmas," said Kienle.

Christmas will be very sad in a lot of homes this year, I thought, *but hopefully not in mine.*

"We can but hope," Karl said quietly.

V

Krypke came back in the middle of December.

"If he thinks we're going to get the trenches dry he's in for a dose of reality," Karl muttered to me. "He might as well try to dry the ocean."

He did seem to realise the water had won but he was just as sarcastic and abrasive as ever. At times there was such an edge on his voice that I wondered if he took it out and sharpened it. His tone was only marginally more agreeable when he spoke to Sauer. It was obviously the way he thought an officer should speak.

Peter Thoma only ever referred to him as 'The Prussian Pig'.

Karl winced slightly but said, "In his case I have to agree. Fellows like him get the rest of us a bad name."

"You don't need him to get you a bad name," Peter replied. "And you all sound the same."

"Actually we don't."

"There you are, listen to you. 'Actually, we don't'."

Everyone burst out laughing and I don't think Karl realised we weren't laughing at him but at Peter. He had a rather thick Bavarian accent and his attempt to mimic Karl's voice was quite ridiculous.

Karl shrugged. "Suit yourself." I could see him trying not to get annoyed.

"Peter, don't bother going on stage," I said. "That was awful."

Karl's face cleared slightly.

"Just cos he's got a bloody plum in his mouth—" Peter said.

"Krypke hasn't got a plum," said Alfred. "He's got a fucking grinding wheel."

"The bastard gives you a harder time than any of us," I said to Karl. "I think he's jealous."

"Bollocks."

"He does, though," Kurt said. "If you ask me, it's cos you're what he wants to be but isn't. He's twice as sharp with you."

That was true. Krypke's glass-cutting tone acquired an extra sharpness when he was talking to Karl, and he obviously had a massive sense of inferiority.

There was only one man to whom Krypke spoke less harshly, and that was Braun. Krypke spoke to him once in his usual manner and once only. Braun looked at Krypke much as a large dog regards a small yappy one, and Krypke, to our astonishment, treated Braun with respect from that moment on.

Horn couldn't stand Krypke. I think he really began to hate him. From what Horn said about his past we gathered he'd been important in his underworld, and he was not used to being spoken to in such a fashion.

"'F anyone'd taken that tone with me, I'd've fuckin' carved 'im," he said once. "Dunno 'ow you lot stand it."

"Neither do I," said Karl. "He's an arsehole, simple as that. Still, we shan't be stuck with him forever."

"I'll fuckin' get 'im one day."

"Don't bother. It's not worth it."

"Prison's better than this shit-heap any day."

"They'd probably shoot you."

Horn looked at Karl. "D'you reckon?"

"If you kill him, yes. And if you don't then it's not worth the effort because he'll just come back."

"You've got a point," Horn said reluctantly.

"Let the Tommies do it," said Karl.

I think Horn recognised the logic of that, but still he often struggled to keep his temper.

"It would be rather good if he did kill him," Kurt said to me later. "Then we'd be rid of both of them."

"Not going to happen, unfortunately," I replied. "Horn's hot-headed but he's not stupid."

Krypke was not the only source of discontent. From the routine of front line, support and rest, it seemed we were going to be in the line over Christmas. We'd hoped to spend the festival in rest, preferably somewhere warm and comfortable where we could have a proper celebration.

"That really is the fucking limit," said Müller, "spending Christmas in some fucking hole."

"It's not where any of us wants to be," Rippel agreed. He had, of course, lost his temporary command of the platoon and was back in an officer cadet's usual position, acting as sergeant. "But we'll just have to make the best of it."

"We can have our own party, with Christmas trees," said Kurt.

"And where the fuck are we going to get those?" demanded Kienle.

"That copse half a kilometre away... If Sauer gives us permission, we could fetch a couple of small trees."

"That's a very good idea, Meyer," said Rippel. "Tell you what, I'll ask him."

Sauer did agree, and we set off for the line the day before Christmas Eve, with quite a few small trees.

Absurd, really, I thought, *that we're prepared to lug these through the mud along with all the other stuff we have to carry.*

The post had come the day before and we were overwhelmed by the generosity of the German people. The entire nation had put their hands in their pockets, and every man had a parcel.

They'd sent us warm scarves, gloves and sweaters, cigarettes, chocolates... Many of the parcels contained letters wishing us well, and we were deeply touched by the kindness of strangers whom we were never likely to meet.

There was even a present for each of us from the Kaiser: a box of cigars with the inscription 'Christmas in the Field 1914'.

Most of us had parcels from home as well. Even Karl had one from the Major, who'd sent him a box of cigars and a bottle of brandy, which he promised to share with us.

We were so burdened with all this goodwill it was a wonder we could march at all.

"Lucky bastards," Bauer said to the men we were relieving.

They just laughed, as well they might.

"You could always stay here and lend a hand with the wiring," said Alfred.

"Fuck off!" came the cheerful reply.

"And a very Merry Christmas to you too!" Kurt said.

At least the weather had dried out. It was bitterly cold and the mud was frozen hard and covered with a layer of snow. Christmas Eve was a glorious day that turned into a crisp and unusually quiet night.

We were all quiet as well, our thoughts far from the front line.

Back home my parents and sister will be decorating the tree. Mama and Johanna will be in the kitchen now, helping Klara prepare the meal. Later everyone will go to midnight Mass, and then when they get home they'll hand out the presents.

I wish I were there. I wish I'd been able to buy them all something nice.

Everyone had the same absent look in his eyes. The arrival of the food cheered us up a bit, and to our delighted astonishment a barrel of wine came with it, from Hauptmann von Schürmann's vineyards beside the Rhine. He wished the Fourth Company a very Merry Christmas, said the message, and was with us in spirit.

"Well," said Sauer, "we'd better tap this now. Braun!"

Braun did the honours and we all had half a mug full.

"Merry Christmas, everyone!" said Sauer, raising his mug.

"Merry Christmas, sir!"

It was months since I'd drunk good German wine.

"Riesling," said Alfred, "and bloody good too."

"It is," Karl agreed, "but then their stuff always has been jolly good."

"Who is he, anyway?" asked Peter.

"He was our Company Commander when we first came out here," I answered. "Bloody good bloke, got hit twice and didn't leave us till Grabowski sent him back."

I looked at the faces around me and realised with a shock how few of them had been there then. *I'm bloody lucky to be here at all*, I thought.

"Penny for them, Franz?" Karl asked.

"I was just thinking that Christmas with you lot is better than none at all!"

He laughed. "We'll have a better one next year."

"You are such an optimist!" said Kienle.

After supper we fastened the candles to our Christmas trees and lit them. The trench filled with points of light, barely flickering in the still, cold air. We sat in small groups and shared out cakes, sweets, and cigars, and it actually began to feel like Christmas.

"Let's put the trees on the parapet so the Tommies can see them," said Alfred.

"Don't be bloody stupid," Flechsig said. "They'll blast them to pieces."

"Let's just see," Alfred replied.

He picked up one of the trees and set it carefully on the

parapet. Nothing happened and after a few minutes Karl put another beside it. In no time at all the parapet was shimmering with tiny flames.

The Tommies still didn't shoot at them, and cautiously we raised our heads and looked out into No Man's Land.

"Stille Nacht, Heilige Nacht…" someone began to sing, and we all joined in, a rough chorus ringing out in the silence.

I thought again of my family, saw them gathered round the tree, and I missed them more than I would have believed possible.

Will I ever have another Christmas at home? When the fighting starts again I'll probably be killed. They'll have next Christmas without me.

Remember me, when you sing carols and give out the presents. There was such a lump in my throat that I could hardly finish the song. I looked at the others in the candlelight and it seemed to me that some of their eyes were rather brighter than usual.

The last note of the carol died into silence. There was a pause and then, from the trenches opposite, the Tommies began to sing.

"Silent night, Holy night…"

"God, they sing the same song as us!" Peter exclaimed, astonished.

"Shut up and listen," said Kurt firmly.

When they finished the carol a voice called out, "Your turn, Fritz!"

Krypke, of all people, got up on the parapet and turned to us. "Oh come, all ye faithful," he said.

We all began to sing, in Latin or German depending on what variety of Christian we were, and the English joined in halfway through the first line with their words.

Why in God's name do we have to kill each other? What for?

"Merry Christmas, Fritz!" they shouted at the end.

"Merry Christmas, Tommy!" we replied.

"See you in the morning!" called out a voice opposite.

See you in the... Is he fucking mad?

"I should get down, sir," Braun said to Krypke. "They might change their minds."

"I don't think they will," Krypke replied, but he did get down.

"Pity they didn't," muttered Karl as Krypke rounded the traverse.

"Oh, come on," said Kurt. "Goodwill to all men and all that!"

Peter looked at him. "There is a limit…"

"Hey, Fritz," yelled an English voice. "You got booze over there?"

"Certainly have!" Karl shouted back. "And fags! How about you?"

"You bet! You got women?"

"What do you think?!"

"Was worth a try!"

Karl translated and we all laughed. As we enjoyed our sweets and presents I imagined the Tommies eating their stew and bread and jam, just like us, and drinking rum and whisky, and smoking cigarettes or pipes.

It doesn't make sense, I thought. *We're just the same, and left to ourselves we'd all have a party together. It's the generals and the politicians who fuck things up.*

It made even less sense the following morning. It dawned bright, clear, and fucking cold. I had the last hour on sentry duty before the dawn stand-to, and I thought my feet were going to freeze to the fire step.

After we stood down Karl and Alfred got a brew going. Breuning was on sentry duty, and I'd just lit a fag to go with my coffee when he shouted, "Sir! *Sir!* The Tommies are getting out of their trenches!"

"What?" said Sauer, and got up beside him.

"Don't shoot!" shouted a voice from No Man's Land. "We've got Christmas presents for you!"

"Exploding ones, no doubt," said Müller.

To our amazement Sauer got his handkerchief out of his pocket, unfolded it and waved it in the air, then climbed out of the trench.

We were all on the fire step in an instant, rifles in our hands.

"Bloody hell!" said Peter.

I don't think the rest of us could actually speak. There was a line of Tommies wandering casually across the mud towards us, apparently unarmed. In front of them was an officer with three stars on his sleeves and, like Sauer, he was waving his handkerchief.

"Well, bugger me!" said Alfred.

Karl caught my eye behind his back and raised an eyebrow, and I almost laughed.

Sauer and the English Captain met halfway between the two sets of wire and shook hands. Then Sauer turned round.

"Come on, chaps!" he called out. "And Leussow, come here, would you?"

I stayed close to Karl. I still wasn't sure it wasn't some sort of trick.

"Would you translate?" Sauer asked him. "My English is rather basic."

"Certainly, sir. What would you like me to say?"

Sauer seemed a bit lost for words. The Tommy said, "We wanted to wish you all a very merry Christmas."

"Thank you, sir," Karl said in English. "And a very merry Christmas to all of you. Shall I introduce our officers?"

"Yes, do."

The Captain was accompanied by a second lieutenant who looked even younger than Rippel. The two of them looked at each other for a moment and then Rippel said in fluent English,

"I don't suppose you know my brother? He was studying at Oxford."

"Sorry," said the Tommy. "I was at Eton."

"Oh – well, then, you might know my cousin…" The two of them wandered off, chatting away.

Karl was looking at Captain Fortescue rather thoughtfully.

"I say, sir…" he began, and broke off.

"Yes, what is it?" Fortescue asked.

"Well, the thing is – I realise I can't ask you anyone's whereabouts, but if you should come across Major Lord Bartlett, please would you tell him that Karl von Leussow was alive and well when we met?"

Fortescue looked rather taken aback. "Er…"

"The thing is, sir, he's my cousin and my brother-in-law. My sister's husband, that is."

"Is he, by Jove? Well, there are a lot of families in that position. I don't know the gentleman but if I should encounter him, I shall certainly give him the message."

"Thank you, sir – I appreciate that very much."

Suddenly there was shouting, in English and German, and cheering. The three of us turned quickly.

Someone had produced a football. In no time coats were laid down as goalposts but, instead of starting to play, both sides surveyed the terrain uncertainly.

"Worst pitch I've ever seen," said Horn.

Apart from being full of craters, the ground was scattered with the remains of the dead. Not far from me a skull looked emptily from a spiked helmet and ribs protruded from the rags of his uniform.

"Leussow!" Sauer called out, and the two of us joined the officers.

"I think we should bury our dead," Fortescue was saying.

Karl translated.

"I agree," said Sauer. "We can do that first, then get the game going."

Fortescue called out to his men, and he and Sauer explained in turn what was to happen.

The ground was far too hard to dig, so we deposited the dead carefully in the deepest shell-holes. The task was just as ghastly as I'd feared – most were so decomposed that they fell apart as we tried to pick them up.

Some Christmas this is. Thank God it's cold.

At least we were able to get their tags. *That's the end of hope for so many families*, I thought – *but is it better to know the man's dead or to cling to the idea that he might come home?*

We managed to shovel some earth over them and then we assembled beside the holes, Tommies on one side and us on the other, and our chaplains took it in turns to read the burial services. The Tommies' bugler played the Last Post, and we sang 'I had a Comrade'.

Afterwards one of the Tommies asked Karl what the song was about.

"It's a fellow telling how his best mate got hit and died at his feet in the middle of the fighting," Karl said.

"Ah, right," said the Tommy. "Well, we all know what that's like."

"Indeed we do."

But you don't, I thought as I looked at Karl, *and neither do I – and I hope I never find out. I hope I never have to sing that for you.*

Everyone was looking at Fortescue and Sauer.

"Game on, I think!" said Fortescue, and blew his whistle.

They won three–two, the bastards.

Sauer said something to Flechsig, who nipped back into our trench and reappeared with a bottle of brandy.

"For you all, Herr Hauptmann," Sauer said to Fortescue.

"Thank you – we'll enjoy it."

"'Scuse me, Fritz," one of the Tommies said to me. "Don't feel like swapping that nice helmet for my shoulder flash, do you?"

His accent was a bit baffling but I understood the gestures.

"Yes, all right."

"Has it got an eagle on it?"

"Of course." I took my helmet off, removed the cover and handed it to him.

"That's really nice. Thanks," he said, and gave me the little curved piece of fabric with the name of his regiment on it.

Everyone was swapping bits of kit, chocolate, smokes, God knows what, and talking as best we could.

They really are just the same as us.

What would happen if we all put our weapons down and went home?

The sun was touching the horizon.

"Well, it's been lovely to meet you all," Fortescue said to Sauer, holding out his hand.

And so we all shook hands and, bizarrely, wished each other a Happy New Year, and went back to our trenches.

When the carrying party brought the food we told them what had happened. They stared at us in disbelief.

"Nah, mate, you don't expect us to believe that," said one.

"I took photos," said Bauer. "I'll show you once they're developed."

"And I've got this," I said, showing him the shoulder flash.

Kurt had buttons and Alfred had one of their peaked caps. Müller had a tin of tobacco and Kienle had a bottle of Scotch whisky.

"Oh. Well, shuts me up."

"God moves in mysterious ways," said Breuning.

You still believe that?

The next day it was business as usual. Bauer put his head above the parapet and lowered it smartly to the crack of a bullet fired deliberately high. The message was clear: stay in your trenches and keep your heads down.

"You could almost think you'd dreamed the whole thing," Karl said.

"Yes," said Rippel. "It really was quite extraordinary."

Bloody stupid, I thought. *The date's changed and so the war's resumed, even though we all know how similar we are.*

Fucking politicians, sending decent blokes like us to die while they sit in their nice warm offices and tell more lies. The whole bloody lot of them should be put up against the nearest wall.

I laughed at myself. *Some of Papa's socialism's taken root in me, after all – I could almost believe that the war really is the fault of the capitalists and their lackey governments, except I don't think I believe anything any more.*

The last shaky remnants of my Catholic faith had died. Christ had come and gone and the war continued.

Two days later the Tommies put up a sign reading, 'We're leaving now. Happy New Year.'

"Nice of them to warn us," said Braun. "We'd better expect more trouble from the next lot."

More trouble was exactly what we got. Our wiring party was shot at and then some bastard Tommy threw a jam-tin bomb among them.

Flechsig and Müller came back dragging Schmidt between them, soaked in blood. Alfred ripped his tunic open.

"Jesus," he said.

Nails and shards of metal were sticking out of Schmidt's torso.

"Bloody hell, that's a bit of a mess," said Klose, the more experienced of the Company medics.

"You are not joking," Alfred said. "Not even sure where to start."

I turned away. There was nothing I could do for him and I really didn't want to see any more than I had to.

"Bit of a contrast," said Karl.

"They're all bastards really," Peter said. "Fucking treacherous lot."

Karl just shrugged.

"Hardly," said Rippel. "This isn't the same lot."

"It's all Perfidious Albion," replied Peter.

Does he know Karl's part-English? I wondered, *or does he just dislike the Tommies?*

"It's all shit," I said, to general agreement.

At least we were out of the line for New Year's Eve, though we were in support. By the time we'd carried food, ammunition and Christ knows what else up to the boys, there wasn't much time for a party, but we still managed a bit of a piss-up before hitting the straw.

The temperature in the barn was well below zero. Karl and I huddled under the same blanket, close together for warmth. Almost everyone slept in pairs – it was the only way of not being kept awake by the cold.

Let's hope 1915 brings victory, I thought as I drifted off to sleep.

A couple of weeks later there was a rumour that an attack was planned for the Kaiser's birthday.

"Fucking ridiculous," said Kurt.

"I agree." Karl sounded disgusted. "That's no reason to stage an attack. What's it supposed to achieve, anyway?"

"Fuckin' stupid, getting killed just to give 'is bleedin' Majesty a birthday present," said Horn. "Can't 'e just give 'imself another gong?"

"What d'you reckon, Sergeant Major?" Karl asked Braun.

"I reckon you lot talk too much. We do as we're told and that's that."

He got up and walked away.

"You never can tell what he's thinking," Karl said, "but I'd bet he agrees with us."

"He's mad if he doesn't," I said.

It was the most stupid thing I'd ever heard, thought up by some twit of a staff officer, miles away, with no idea at all what it would mean for the men involved. *I'd like to get hold of some of those idiots and show them what it's really about. Then they might not be so quick to throw our lives away.*

No one was sorry when we heard that it was all hot air. The new rumour – which we didn't believe either – was that the Kaiser would be behind our part of the Front on the crucial day and that there'd be a big parade in his honour. That sounded much better than a pointless attack but we still didn't think it would happen anywhere near us.

All the same we were curious and rather excited

"He doesn't look that special," Karl said with a shrug. "You'll be disappointed."

"Have you met him, then?" asked Kurt.

"No, though Pa has, but I've seen him in Berlin a couple of times. He looks… well, like someone's uncle, really. Quite ordinary, apart from all the decorations."

I didn't believe it, and when one of the cooks told me I was to receive the Iron Cross, Second Class, I believed that even less.

"You'll get it from the Kaiser himself," Alfred said enviously.

"Bollocks! Of course I won't. I won't be getting the bloody thing at all. I've done nothing to deserve it. It's all a load of crap. And if I were going to get it they'd have told me officially. I wouldn't get it from the cook."

"They hear everything," said Rippel. "It's probably true."

The following day I was summoned by Sauer.

"Well, Becker," he said, "I've got some excellent news for you. You've been awarded the Iron Cross, Second Class, for rescuing a wounded officer under heavy fire."

"Me, sir?" I said incredulously, unable to remember doing anything of the kind.

Sauer smiled. "Yes, you, Becker. Congratulations. We're all very proud of you."

"Thank you, sir." I saluted and left the Company command post, more than a bit bemused.

"What was that about?" Karl asked.

"They've mixed me up with someone else," I said. "They're giving me the Iron Cross, Second Class, 'for rescuing a wounded officer under fire'. I didn't do anything of the kind."

Karl rolled his eyes. "It's for going back for Schürmann, you idiot."

"But I didn't even know he'd been hit."

"You knew about his wrist, though," said Alfred.

"Yes – but he'd already got that."

"And you knew he'd gone down," Kurt said. "You must have realised he'd caught it again."

"No, I just thought he'd stumbled. It was really hard to run in the mud and he's an old man... It's bloody daft, this. I don't deserve it."

"Well, you can't argue," Karl said. "It's an award from the Kaiser, so shut up and be proud of yourself. You're the first of us to get a gong – and now we're all going to have to try to catch up with you!"

The Kaiser's visit never happened and I received my gong from Major Grabowski instead, which was far less glamorous. I was very proud to wear the black and white ribbon through my buttonhole but I felt a complete fraud. All I'd done was help someone I liked and admired – and surely that's what anyone would do.

I wasn't sure whether to tell my family. I didn't want Mama to think I'd been taking risks.

They'll see the ribbon when I go home on leave anyway, I thought, *so I might as well tell them now.* To my surprise I received a congratulatory letter from Papa, who seemed to feel I'd achieved something at long last. It was most peculiar.

God alone knows when I will get leave, though. I was dying to go home, just for a few days, and I knew the others felt the same.

"You'd think they'd let some of us go, now we're up to full strength," grumbled Kienle. "I want to see my missus and the kids."

"Best not to think at all," Bauer said, and of course he was right.

The reinforcements were a mixed crowd, mostly artisans and workmen.

"What's the country supposed to do without blokes like that?" asked Bauer.

"I suppose they must be calling everyone up now," I said.

"Doubt it," Kurt said. "When you think in peacetime they can't take all the men available, there must be hundreds of thousands they haven't called up yet. The war'll be over long before we run out of men."

Once again we weren't bothered about making friends with the new fellows. We knew they wouldn't be around for long. They probably thought we were snooty but we couldn't be bothered to explain – and the explanation wasn't something they'd have wanted to hear.

The one man who did become part of our little group was a huge Hamburg docker nicknamed Tiny. He took to Karl at once, probably because they had a similar attitude to sex and a belief that nothing really mattered.

Useful thinking for a soldier, that – wish I could manage it.

To my surprise Tiny was something of a philosopher and very widely read. I'd never had much to do with men like him until I joined the Army, and it hadn't occurred to me that a labourer could be an intellectual.

"You've read more books than I have," Kurt said to him one day.

"That's cos you're 'educated' and I'm not!" Tiny answered. "See, I know a bit about a lot of things, while you know a lot about a few things – and most of those are no bloody use!"

Kurt laughed. "You're not wrong there!"

The days were getting longer again and we were pulled out of the line to train for a big Spring Offensive. We didn't mind that at all until we discovered how hard we had to work, and then we grumbled and groused. *No chance at all of leave now*, I thought discontentedly. *Maybe in the summer…*

If I get to the fucking summer.

After a couple of days my attitude changed. At last we were getting proper training, including dummy attacks and practice on the firing range.

"This is what we should have had before we came out here," Kurt said one evening. "I thought they'd sent us here a bit undertrained but I hadn't realised just how much."

"Yes," was all I said.

How different it might have been. How many men might still be alive if the top brass hadn't been in such an unholy rush… and Ypres might even have been taken and we might have been on our way to Paris.

It's no use, Franz. The world doesn't run on 'might have beens'.

"You knew, didn't you, Karl?" I asked.

"Yes – that is, I had some idea…"

The second time we went to the range Major Grabowski turned up, accompanied by an officer none of us recognised.

They both watched with interest, especially when Karl was shooting.

They conferred for a few minutes and after we'd all finished Braun told Karl he was to shoot again.

Karl looked a bit puzzled. "Wasn't that good enough, Sergeant Major?"

"Perfect – but the officers want to see you do it again."

If they think it was luck they're wrong, I thought. Everyone was watching this time, wondering what was going on.

Braun came back again. "Four hundred metres this time, Leussow."

And then it was six hundred, and then they wanted to talk to him. The rest of us were dismissed, and while I was consumed with curiosity I wasn't sorry to leave. The day was grey and cold and I was looking forward to warming up.

"What the fuck was all that about?" Kurt asked me.

I don't know why you're asking me. "Buggered if I know."

Karl wasn't long.

"What did they want?" Alfred asked him.

He laughed and it sounded a little false.

"Some bigwig's organising a shooting competition and they want me to represent the Regiment. I ask you! We're getting ready for a proper shooting contest, and that's all some crimson-collared bastard can think about! God alone knows when they plan to hold it – or who'll still be alive to take part in it."

"I think it's a really good idea," Alfred said. "Give everyone something else to think about for a day. They didn't mention a date, I suppose?"

"No. Said they'd let me know. You're down for first reserve, by the way, in case I can't make it."

There was something in Karl's eyes that I couldn't quite read, a sort of shadow, and I couldn't understand why. Surely he should be pleased to be selected for something like that? Or maybe he was thinking about the coming offensive.

"So what was it really about?" I asked him quietly over a beer and a fag in the Soldiers' Home.

He sighed. "They wanted to know if I've used a telescopic sight and if I've got one at home that I could have sent here."

"And have you?" *Why do they want that?*

"Yes – Pa gave me a very nice Zeiss four-power one for my birthday some years ago, together with a new hunting rifle."

I laughed. "I sometimes wonder if your Pa actually knows you."

He laughed as well, rather wryly. "So do I!"

"So what have they got in mind?"

"Some of the Regular regiments are finding the sights very useful – you can see much better in poor light and identify officers more easily. And of course the accuracy at long range is better."

"That would be dead handy when they're attacking. You'd be able to knock their officers over the moment they leave the trench. It's a bloody good idea."

Karl sighed again. "That's not all of it, not by a long way. They're sniping all the time when they're in the front line. Keeping the enemy scared and bumping off the officers when they can."

"What – in cold blood?" *That's going too far. Shooting someone who's coming to kill you is one thing but killing someone just because you can is another matter. That's bloody close to murder.*

"Yes, 'fraid so."

"So what did you say?" *I'm not sure I want to hear the answer.*

"I asked if I could think about it. They said it's volunteers only but it would be a valuable contribution, blah, blah."

"So presumably the Tommies are doing this as well?"

"They don't seem to be, not yet." He laughed. "Probably goes against their idea of sportsmanship!"

"War isn't a game."

"No. Indeed not."

There's no way Karl will agree to that, I thought as we wandered back to the barn. *He's like me – he only kills when he has to.*

The next day I was astonished to see Hauptmann von Schürmann.

I thought your war was over. Most men of your age sit safely at home – and should you be back here at all after those injuries?

He seemed to have made a full recovery and it was a couple of days before I noticed his left wrist was locked solid. I didn't mention it to the others.

It's his choice – though if I were given such a good excuse for not coming back I'd take it. I'd be out of here like a shot – just a bullet through my leg on the first day, get picked up quickly, and then off to hospital and home for a few weeks.

That would be bloody wonderful. I could lie in bed and read about the war, perfectly safe and clean and dry and louse-free... I stopped myself quickly. *Be careful what you pray for, Franz, because you might get it and it might be a lot worse than that. You don't want to go home minus a leg, do you?*

A couple of days later I was summoned to the Company office again.

"What, another gong already?" said Alfred.

"No – more like they found out who nicked that meat!" Bauer said.

"Shut up about the fucking meat, you cunt!" Kienle hissed.

"What meat?" I asked innocently.

"Quite," said Kienle.

"They'd have to find the evidence!" Karl said, and we all laughed.

I must have done something wrong, I thought as I knocked, but Schürmann was smoking his pipe with a half-smile on his face.

"Ah, Becker," he said. "As you're well aware, we've lost a lot of junior officers in the past few months and, well, we need replacements. Have you thought of applying for the officer's career path?"

"Me, sir?" *Christ, is that all I ever say in here?*

"Yes. You're just the sort of fellow we want. Good education, quite a bit of experience now."

"I… er… I haven't any plans in that direction, sir. I just volunteered for the war."

"Think it over and let me know if you change your mind. Friedemann and Meyer have put their names down and we really could do with you as well."

"Thank you, sir."

"And would you send Leussow along, please?"

"Of course, sir."

I left feeling flattered but unwilling. *The last thing I want is to become an officer and a prime target.*

"So what did you say?" asked Kurt.

"I said no – Karl, he wants to see you."

Karl looked at me and raised an eyebrow. "I suppose this is about going for a commission."

"That's right."

He laughed. "He'll be wasting his breath! If I'd wanted to do that I'd have listened to Pa and gone to cadet school."

Karl came back very quickly.

Alfred gave him a curious look. "So why don't you want to be an officer?"

"Because as soon as this shit is over I'm off to the Paris Conservatoire."

"They won't have you," said Kurt. "Filthy Boche!"

"Prussian pig," added Peter. "Even worse."

"Or wherever they'll have me," Karl said. "I'm fucked if I'm going to be an officer like my brothers."

"I thought Johnny was a war volunteer," I said.

"He was – but he's on an officer's course now."

"One of you's got some sense, then," said Alfred.

Karl shook his head. "Who are the first blokes to get knocked over? The junior officers."

"Except Krypke," Peter said. "I've had enough of him."

"So has everyone," said Tiny. He looked at Karl and me. "Buggered if I understand why you don't want to be officers, though. If they gave me the chance I'd jump at it – but I'll never get further than sergeant."

"I'd be happy with sergeant," I said.

"Fuck promotion," said Müller. "I just want to get home alive."

"Exactly," Karl agreed.

They're both right, I thought. *Here we are, worrying about what rank we do or don't want, and we're building up to one hell of a battle and a lot of us won't come out the other side.*

Everyone's tempers were beginning to fray. We all just wanted to get on with it.

Peter's foolish bravado really started to grate.

We'll all see how you behave when the day comes – and until then you can keep your fucking mouth shut.

But for some reason he kept trying to wind Karl up.

One day Kurt said something about Karl's fluent English, and I said, "Well, you have to learn it from childhood to speak like that."

"How did that happen, then?" Peter asked.

"My mother was half-English," Karl replied.

Peter stared at him. "What, you're a quarter English?"

"That's right."

"How do we know you're not a spy?" Peter demanded.

"Oh, shut up, Peter," said Kurt. "Karl's loyalty's not in question."

"The Kaiser's half-English," said Breuning. "Which is twice as much as Karl."

Peter wouldn't let it go. "But you must have relatives over there. What are you going to do if you meet one of them? I mean, how are you going to shoot or bayonet your own cousins?"

Karl got up and walked away, his face black.

"What would you do?" I said to Peter.

"Wouldn't happen. All my people are Bavarian, always have been. No funny blood in our family. Why's he walked off, anyway? Just proves something's not right."

"If I were you, I'd leave Karl alone," Alfred said. "You're always on at him about something and one day he'll lose his temper."

"So what if he does?"

Alfred shrugged. "The rest of us will watch with interest."

Peter didn't listen, and kept on with his baiting. Karl did his best not to respond but the final straw was when Peter started talking about homosexuality in Berlin.

"Of course, their precious Guards regiments are riddled with queers," he said. "I've heard that some of the privates walk the streets on their evenings off – and as for the officers!"

"My father and my eldest brother are both Guards officers," Karl said quietly, "and I can assure you neither of them is queer."

"Bet they are," Peter answered. "How do you know what your brother gets up to? Bet he likes bending some fellow over—"

Karl got to his feet. "Shut your fucking mouth!"

"Make me, then, you Prussian pig!"

"Get up!"

Peter leapt to his feet. They squared up to each other and a split second later Karl's fist connected with Peter's jaw with an audible thud. Peter staggered and fell, and then clambered to his feet. He was foolish enough to come back for more. The second blow knocked him to the ground and he lay motionless.

"Jesus, Karl, you've killed him," Kurt said.

"Bollocks. It'd take more than that."

Alfred knelt beside Peter and we waited with increasing anxiety.

"What's this I see, Leussow?" Krypke's voice sliced through the silence, even sharper than usual. We all sprang to attention. "Fine gentleman like you using his fists? What *is* the world coming to?"

Peter stirred, looked blearily at Krypke and slurred, "Filthy Prussian pig."

Krypke went crimson. I could see Karl's lips twitching and I daren't meet his eyes. None of us could look at each other.

"Do you know who you're speaking to?" Krypke demanded.

"No, sir, he doesn't," Alfred said hastily. "He's concussed."

Krypke looked disbelieving. "Leussow, why did you hit him?"

"I don't remember, sir."

"Don't be ridiculous! I want an answer."

Peter sat up and said slowly and clearly, "Because I called him a—"

"Shut up, Peter," said Alfred.

"What? What did you call him? Friedemann, you keep quiet."

"I called him a Pru—"

"Nothing, sir," Karl said loudly. "It was just a silly remark but I took offence."

Krypke wasn't fooled. He knew perfectly well what Peter had been about to say.

"Leussow, you go to Schürmann, now! You too, Becker, as a witness. Friedemann, take Thoma to the MO – and Thoma…"

"Sir?"

"If I hear you using that phrase in my hearing I shall take it you mean me and you'll be on a charge. Understand?"

"Yes, sir."

"If the cap fits," someone said loudly.

Krypke spun round. "Who said that?"

Silence. Krypke glared at us all and left. As soon as he was out of earshot we all burst out laughing. Even Peter was laughing, and I realised he'd known Krypke was there and had taken advantage of the bang on the head to have a dig at him.

"Come on, then," said Alfred, and pulled Peter to his feet.

"Hey – not so rough!" Peter protested. "My face bloody hurts!"

"Don't say I didn't warn you," Alfred retorted unsympathetically. "You got what you deserve – so shut the fuck up."

Karl turned to me. "Oh well, time to face the music."

"He had it coming," I said.

"Let's hope Schürmann shares your opinion – oh what the hell, it was worth whatever they give me!"

Schürmann listened impassively as Krypke gave his evidence. He hadn't heard the quarrel; he'd arrived just in time to see Leussow hitting Thoma.

"Well, Becker?" Schürmann asked me.

"Leussow and Thoma fell out, sir, and it got a bit acrimonious and Leussow hit him."

"Is that it?"

"Yes, sir."

"Leussow, what happened?"

"It was just as Becker says, sir."

He looked at us both. "Braun?"

"Sir?"

"Thoma's Bavarian, isn't he?"

"Yes, sir."

"Leussow, the ancient feud between your respective states is of no interest to me," said Schürmann. "What does interest me is the maintenance of discipline. This is an army, not a rabble, and I don't expect any repetition of this incident. What have you to say for yourself?"

"Nothing, sir."

"Dismiss!"

As the door closed behind us we heard Schürmann's voice quite clearly. "Krypke, don't you ever bother me with trivia like that again! Next time…"

"With a bit of luck that's me off the list of potential officers," Karl said cheerfully. "Though Schürmann didn't ask for my Army book, so it might not be recorded."

"Pity it was Krypke who turned up," I said. "Braun wouldn't have taken it so far."

"Krypke's an arsehole."

"That's for sure… Talking of arseholes, I wonder how much damage you did to Peter."

"Not enough."

Karl was right. Peter's face was bruised and swollen, but no one believed him when he said he thought his jawbone was cracked.

"Eating fucking hurts," he grumbled.

"Well, you won't be able to finish that, then, will you?" said Müller. "Best give it to me."

He reached for Peter's mess tin.

Peter pulled it away hastily. "Get your hands off! I'm all right!"

"Didn't know this was Lourdes, did you?" Alfred said loudly.

Peter just muttered something, and shovelled the rest of his food down before Müller could snatch it.

"You don't insult your mate's brother," Tiny said. "If you'd said that about my brother I'd have fucking killed you."

"The thought did occur," said Karl.

Peter glared at him.

"Perhaps you'll use a bit more sense in future," Kurt said to Peter.

"Why's everyone having a go at me?"

"Because you was well out of order," Müller said. "And if you say crap like that about my brother, you'll get my fist too."

There was a murmur of agreement and Peter got up and left.

"Too full of himself, that one," Müller said.

"He won't know what's hit him when we meet the Tommies," said Kurt.

Nor will any of the new men. Let's just hope they can all do it…

A few days later the Company had to fall in for a lecture. Schürmann was accompanied by a weedy little officer with spectacles, who looked quite unwarlike.

Not the sort of fellow you'd want to be in a tight corner with.

"This is Leutnant Pulkowski, of the Pioneers," said Schürmann, "and he's come to introduce us to a new weapon."

Everyone suddenly paid attention. *Well*, I thought, *he might not look like a soldier but the Pioneers are clever buggers.* The spring thaw had left the trenches waterlogged again, and they'd managed to put a drainage system in the front line that let the water run down the hill to the Tommies.

I hope they've invented something that'll win the war quickly.

"I've come to talk to you about chlorine gas," he began. "It's highly poisonous, and the intention is that it will clear the enemy trenches of all resistance – every man who breathes it in will be either dead or incapacitated."

We looked at each other. Karl frowned slightly, clearly thinking the same as me – *won't it kill us as well?*

Pulkowski went on to explain that the gas would be released when the wind was blowing towards the enemy positions. It was heavier than air and so would sink into their trenches.

But the front line twists and turns – and how long will it be before those trenches are safe for us?

He produced a cloth pad with string ties.

"As protection against the gas you'll wear these masks," he said, and went on to explain how it worked.

And how the fuck do we breathe in that? Has he ever run across open ground under fire? No, of course he bloody hasn't – and nor has the wanker who came up with that.

I didn't like the sound of it at all. It seemed to me that we were guinea pigs in a huge and very nasty experiment. When I glanced at the others I saw disquiet in all their faces.

"Any questions?" asked Pulkowski.

Half the Company put their hands up, including all the platoon commanders.

"Oberleutnant Sauer?" said Schürmann.

"How easy is it to breathe with the mask on?" Sauer asked. About two dozen hands went down.

"It does restrict breathing somewhat, but you'll be able to train with them and get accustomed to the feeling."

"Leutnant Krypke?" said Schürmann.

"What do we wet it with?" More hands went down.

"There'll be special fluid but if that runs out you can use whatever you like."

"Leutnant Meisner?"

"How long does the gas take to dissipate?" Most of the remaining hands went down.

"That varies with the atmospheric conditions – how strong the wind is, for example."

"Feldwebel Braun?"

"How do we know when it's safe to take the mask off, sir?"

"The gas is slightly green in colour, white when it's dense. If you can see gas, keep the masks on. If the air looks clear, lift the mask and have a sniff. The odour is very distinctive."

How much of a sniff will kill me?

"Officer Cadet Rippel?"

"What happens if we do breathe some in, sir?"

"That depends on how much. A lethal dose destroys lung tissue, less will cause damage proportionate to the amount ingested. The medics will have oxygen available to treat gas casualties."

Sounds like another way for our own side to kill us...

"Fucking great," muttered Bauer.

"Thank you, Pulkowski," said Schürmann. "We shall all be very interested to try the masks."

I could almost see him thinking they were going to be thoroughly unpleasant.

"And of course we all hope the new weapon will bring us a quick victory," he concluded.

That was the only thing no one could argue with.

We were all given masks and shown how to put them on. It felt like being suffocated and I couldn't wait to get the bloody thing off. And that was standing still.

Fighting in this is not going to be fun – and the thought that I could die if I take it off is even less appealing.

And the whole idea of gas is revolting.

"It's not my idea of war at all," Alfred grumbled later. "I'd far rather have a fair fight. We'll just be walking into trenches full of men who've been poisoned to death. That's not war."

"It's barbaric," I said. "How can anyone fight back against gas?"

"By gassing us as well," Karl replied. "That's the only thing this'll lead to. They'll have to retaliate in kind."

I hadn't thought of that. "Don't you think it's immoral?" I asked him.

He shrugged. "War's immoral. You could argue that every weapon ever invented is barbaric – though I must say this does seem particularly horrible."

"I don't care, if it wins the war," said Müller.

"I don't agree," Tiny said. "Becker's right. It's barbaric, and the Allies will say it's more German frightfulness and that we have to be defeated."

"Yes," agreed Breuning. "There is a limit."

But the next day the newspapers arrived and the front pages screamed that the French had used poison gas against our troops – so it seemed we were the ones who were retaliating. We had no way of knowing if the reports were true, but the neatness of the timing made me suspicious.

Reaction was mixed when we were told that we were to be part of the first line of reserves rather than going in at the beginning. Peter expressed disgust loudly, Kurt and Alfred more quietly. Most of us said nothing.

We might get away with it, I thought. *We might not have to fight at all, especially if the gas works...* I was ashamed of my feelings and kept them to myself. I knew it was a vain hope, that we almost certainly would be needed, but at least it meant that the date of our execution wasn't fixed.

It turned out that no one's execution date was fixed. The wind obstinately refused to blow in the right direction, and the attack was postponed, and postponed again.

Poor sods in the front line, keyed up and waiting to go in – and each time stood down again. That's enough to fray your nerves before you even start.

A few days later our guns opened up thunderously.

It's beginning. It won't be long now before they send for us. I still had the sneaking, half-ashamed hope that we'd get away with it.

Next to our camp was a casualty clearing station, and we

tried to pretend it wasn't there. The graveyard beside it was even less encouraging, especially as a small group of carpenters was busily making coffins and crosses.

"Blessed are the meek, for they shall inherit the earth," Alfred said as we stood watching them.

"Or six feet of it, anyway," Karl replied. "Or a space in a communal pit. No doubt the coffins are for the officers."

"I thought it was the peacemakers who inherited the earth," objected Kurt.

"That rules us out," I said. "No one could call us peacemakers."

"What happens to us, then?" Karl asked.

"You're going to Hell, for a start!" I answered. "They don't let fornicators into Heaven."

He laughed. "Well, then, I'll see you all there! It's probably more fun than Heaven, anyway. All the tarts will be there for a start."

"Ah, yes," said Alfred with a grin. "But you're not allowed to fuck them. The devils fuck you instead."

"Ouch!" Karl wriggled theatrically. "Though I suppose it might be all right if they're pretty devils!"

"No, no – they're big ugly bastards with huge cocks!" Alfred spoke with some relish, and we all burst out laughing. All except Peter, who looked at Alfred as if he stank.

That sounds more like Alfred's idea of Heaven – not that I care. He's a good soldier and a good mate, and that's enough for me.

The only advantage of being near the clearing station was that we'd get some idea of how the battle was going, and so of when we might be needed. For the first couple of days the traffic down our road was light. *Things must be going well,* I thought. *We've not seen that many casualties so far.*

The numbers increased on the third day, and towards

evening a large group of walking wounded appeared. We stood beside the road with cigarettes and flasks of tea and rum. We knew there was little point asking them for information but we couldn't resist.

They accepted what we offered, with weary gratitude.

"Thanks, mate, I'm parched."

"Just what I needed."

"Got a light?" The man was leaning heavily on a makeshift crutch, bent over.

"Yes, of course." Karl lit his cigarette with his silver lighter, and the man straightened up and took a deep drag.

"Good God!" Alfred exclaimed. "Ludorff!"

"Friedemann! I'll be damned!"

They embraced awkwardly.

"Ludorff's one of my corps brothers," Alfred said.

"How's it going?" I asked.

He shrugged. "Some and some. Some of them ran but some of the buggers are putting up a pretty stiff fight."

"The gas worked, then?" Peter asked excitedly.

An odd look came over Ludorff's face. "Yes." He looked at Alfred. "Not my idea of fighting, though."

"Do you need any help?" Karl said.

"No thanks, it's not far now." He embraced Alfred again. "See you in Paris."

"Hey – you lot! Get back here and get ready to move!" Gefreiter Fischer's voice cut through their farewell.

"*Shit!*" we said in unison.

They want us after all, I thought, the last shred of hope dying. *I wonder if I'll come back.*

It was hours before we went anywhere. Eventually we moved off into the night, towards the flashing, thundering horizon.

The ambulances and the walking wounded had to take to the sides of the road to let us pass. It was, of course, more important to get reinforcements to the Front than to get the wounded back, but I was deeply aware of the inhumanity of the machine.

"War," Karl said, shaking his head.

It must feel like forever, waiting for all of us to go by, I thought, praying that I would come back in one piece. I had no desire to see the inside of that clearing station and I had even less desire to be killed.

Dear God, if I have to die then please make it quick. Please don't let me suffer like Anton. I wished I could forget him but he kept coming back in my dreams. Anton, and Hartmann with his wrecked face and missing arm…

We halted in the middle of the night, still with some distance to go to the front line. Kurt asked Krypke what was happening.

"There's no room in the trenches. We'll move up once the attack's begun."

There was nothing to do but wait, and I tried to sleep. It was impossible. I was far too wound up and the bombardment increased in intensity so that I could hardly think.

They must be about to attack… After a while the bombardment ceased, and then the order came to move forward. I could almost feel Death coming closer, for some of us anyway.

We made our way along the newly-dug communications trench and into the front line, where we settled down to wait again.

I realised suddenly that it was past midnight, that it was my twentieth birthday. *What a way to spend it! I wonder if I'll see the end of it, never mind my twenty-first.*

That was far into a very uncertain future.

Funny how I used to be able to plan, and now I'm sitting here wondering if I'll see tomorrow and trying not to think about it.

The noise of battle was terrific and the enemy was obviously putting up a stiff resistance.

"I thought the gas was supposed to kill everyone," said Kurt.

"I think the key word there was 'supposed'," Alfred replied.

After an hour or so things quietened down a little, and then the first bloodied remnants made their way back towards us.

Their response to our challenge was an agonised, "For God's sake, don't shoot! We're German!" in the accent of my native Württemberg.

We helped them into the trench, seeing them clearly only in the flares and the flashes of the artillery.

The flares reminded me of Anton, and here were fresh horrors: a man blinded, his face smashed, clinging to his comrade whose arm hung awkwardly; another dragged between two others, his left leg missing, his belt pulled tight round what remained of his thigh. The trench was so crammed that it was almost impossible to move them along.

"They're fighting like devils, that lot," said one. "We've left God knows how many on their wire."

"It's murder – sheer bloody murder," stammered another. He began to cry, whether from pain or shock I didn't know.

"Shut the fuck up, Willi!" said the man with the broken arm.

Willi sobbed and I turned away. *I must keep my self-control, whatever happens. I have to be as calm as Karl was at Langemarck.*

In the hour before dawn the bombardment was stepped up again. The first cold light showed our strained faces. Peter was shaking and grey with fear, his eyes staring, and I felt sorry for him.

All that bluster, and now it's really about to happen you're shit-scared. At the same time I felt rather contemptuous. The fact that someone else was so obviously frightened made me feel bolder.

I dug some chocolate out of my haversack and offered it to him, my hand quite steady, as if to say, Look, *I'm* not in a state.

He shook his head and I was suddenly ashamed. He had every reason to be afraid and I had no business belittling him.

"Have you got any rum?" I shouted into Karl's ear. He produced the silver hip flask that his aunt had sent him for Christmas.

"Can I give some to Peter?"

He shrugged. "If you like." He looked at Peter and then back at me. "Is he all right?"

"I fucking hope so."

Otherwise I'll have to drag the bugger with me and I'll have better things to do. If he doesn't come with us I'll bash his fucking teeth out.

Peter seemed a little steadier after the rum.

"Don't worry," I said to him. "You'll be fine when we get going."

Krypke made his way along the trench with some difficulty and told us that we were to attack at nine. I had to force myself to listen to the rest of it.

"Another bloody daylight attack," I said to Karl after he'd gone.

"Gongs all round for the survivors!" he replied with a grin.

There were nearly two hours to go. I just wanted it all to be over: not just the battle but the whole bloody war. I wanted to be sitting safely at home in my parents' house, reading by the fire; I wanted to be in a warm bed with a soft, willing girl…

I looked at my watch after an hour and found that five minutes had passed. I took the thing off in disgust and put it in my pocket. *Only the officers need watches. They'll tell us when it's time.*

The bombardment increased to the point where speech was impossible and thought nearly so. I almost pitied the English, having to endure it. *There can't be anyone left alive over there, we'll be able to walk in…*

That's what you thought the first time, Franz… And then I remembered vividly what it was like to stand up when the air was full of flying metal and all you wanted to do was press yourself into the earth.

And now I'm going to have to do it all again.

VI

I lost all track of time. I had no idea whether there were five minutes to go or twenty-five.

"Gas masks on!"

Horrible fucking suffocating thing.

"Fix bayonets!"

My blood curdled. My hands shook and I wondered if Peter had noticed.

"GO!"

Somehow my legs found the strength to propel me over the sandbags, through the wire and forward. The ground was strewn with bodies, rifles and packs. Some of the wounded called out to us in desperation, though they must have known we couldn't stop for them.

I was gasping for breath as I ran over the broken ground. *What fucking idiot thought of this? The Tommies had better all be dead...*

They weren't, but their fire was nothing like as heavy as I'd expected and few of us seemed to fall.

We were lucky. Our dead lay thick in front of the English wire and the sight filled me with murder.

We jumped down into the trench. It was empty apart from the dead and the badly wounded and we pushed on to the next one. That was the same.

"They're running away!" shouted Müller.

We scrambled up the sandbags—

"STAY HERE!" Krypke's voice was like the crack of a whip but it was all he could do to stop us. We had to be content with pouring bullets into them as they ran, and had the satisfaction of seeing dozens go down.

Krypke had taken his gas mask off and was still standing. I removed mine cautiously and sniffed. There was a very slight taint in the air but nothing more, and I filled my lungs and felt the breathlessness ease.

"'Pursue to the last breath of man and horse'," Kurt quoted disgruntledly.

"And run into our own artillery fire, General?" Karl said with a smile.

"They'd broken. We should have gone after them."

You're right, I thought, *we should have gone on*. Then I suddenly realised that we had, finally, taken an enemy position. We were on the move.

The defenders had obviously put up a fight, and German dead lay in the trench as well as English. The gas had done its horrible work and many of the English corpses stared at us, their eyes wide in contorted, livid faces.

"Oh, look," said Alfred, "their buttons have all gone green."

"That's curious," I said, glad of the distraction. "I wonder if that happens first."

We all gazed at the buttons – and saw, appalled, that some of them were still alive, gasping and frothing as they drowned slowly. There was nothing we could do for them. Their agonised faces were too much for us and we turned away.

"Perhaps we should shoot them," Karl said. "Get it over with."

I stared at him. *How can you be so callous?*

"Do you want to die like that?" he asked. He looked at me, his eyes full of horror and pity, and I understood.

"No – but we can't just shoot them. I can't, anyway…

We don't know they're beyond help, do we? The medics have oxygen, don't they?"

Karl shrugged. I could hear him thinking that it was already too late, that treatment would only prolong their agony.

"We treat our own kind worse than animals," he said.

Peter and Alfred had come through safely, and our losses were slight. The brunt had been borne by the previous waves, and Masur and Klose were not short of work.

They started to give the gas casualties oxygen but it was obviously far too late.

"Poor sods," said Klose. "We'd best deal with the wounded."

And there were plenty of those, both our fellows and the Tommies. One of the latter was a sergeant with a smashed leg, and he screamed his head off when he came round to find Germans all round him.

"It's all right," said Masur, pointing to the red cross on his armband. "We just want to help you."

The Tommy yelled something and lashed out wildly.

"Anyone speak English?" Klose called out.

"I do," said Karl.

"Tell this fellow we're not going to hurt him," said Masur.

Karl laughed. "That'd be a black lie, wouldn't it?!" He bent over the Tommy. "It's all right, Sarge," he said in his almost unaccented English. "These are our stretcher-bearers – they'll look after you and we'll get you to hospital as soon as we can, along with our chaps. Cigarette?"

"Oh. Oh, right. Cheers, mate."

"Trying to poison the poor fellow, are you?" I asked as Karl gave the man one of his black fags.

"What the fuck are you doing in the German Army?" the sergeant asked Karl suspiciously.

"Oh, I'm Prussian apart from my English granny."

"Prussian? Oh, fucking hell!"

"But I keep my horns and tail hidden."

"Fucking hell," said the Tommy again, and then he yelled properly and passed out.

"Not going to hurt him?" Karl said to Masur.

"Oh, shut up!"

We were ready to press on and it wasn't long before fresh orders came.

A couple of hours later all the devils of Hell were let loose. I'd never heard such a bombardment. I daren't hope we'd have such an easy time of it again, but we did. They retreated again and this time we were right behind them, making bloody sure they kept running. It was bloody wonderful. We were on our way to Paris at last!

We only halted to avoid running into our own barrage, and took possession of another abandoned trench to reorganise ourselves for what might come next. Peter was flushed with excitement, his eyes shining, and I saw the same look in everyone's faces.

So this is what victory feels like.

"What's the time?" asked Alfred. "I've lost my bloody watch."

I looked at my wrist and was surprised that it was blank. *Oh, of course – I put my watch in my pocket.* I fished it out and stared at it. Both hands were mashed into the face by a shrapnel ball, which was still stuck there.

"Jesus, you were lucky!" said Karl. "There must be a moral in that somewhere."

"Someone up there protecting you," Breuning said.

"Bollocks!"

But all the same the old feeling of invulnerability returned. Nothing could touch me. I was immortal.

The next day we attacked again, with the same result, and found ourselves in a trench near St Julien.

We wanted to press on but Krypke told us to wait for Schürmann, who joined us a couple of hours later.

"We're to stay here, boys," he said, "and hold this trench."

"Don't like the sound of that," Alfred muttered to me. "Why aren't we going any further?"

"God knows – but I don't fancy being stuck here."

The trench was a horrible sight, not from gas but from the sheer heaviness of the bombardment. In places it had been completely blown in and was just a series of shell-holes, littered with sandbags and bodies, some hideously ripped apart.

We dug frantically to repair the position before the inevitable counter-attack, and it seemed every time the spades went in they struck bone or unearthed some ghastly remnant of humanity.

"There's a big gap on our right, sir," Braun said to Schürmann.

Karl and I looked at each other. *That's not good…*

"That's where they'll come from," Kurt said, pointing. "Along that old comms trench."

We worked flat out, piling up sandbags and debris into a barricade. The sweat ran off us as if it were July, but we all knew our lives depended on our work and no one slacked.

Our efforts were completely wasted. Just when we thought our barrier was high enough and wide enough, the bastards began shelling us. At first the shells landed behind us – clearly we'd got further than they realised – but the explosions got closer and closer.

Schürmann fired off flares, calling for artillery support, and I saw red and green lights going up all around.

"I don't like this," Kurt said. "How do our lot know how far we've got? We'll just—"

The earth shook to a direct hit not far away and we pressed ourselves into the ground. One massive concussion followed another and we could barely see or hear or think.

We waited, breathlessly, for the moment when the shelling would stop and the attack would begin. We had to be ready…

Someone screamed, earth rained down on me, there was no

end to the brain-deadening cacophony. I could only endure and wait, sick with apprehension.

And then it stopped. Earth and sandbags and bits of bodies were piled in horrible confusion all around us. This was the position we had to hold against the English.

"Here they come!"

We waited for the order. My heart was pounding, my mouth dry – *Christ, Schürmann, how close do you want them—*

"Fire!" Sauer's voice, not Schürmann's.

For a desperate eternity I thought we wouldn't be able to hold them, thought we'd be overrun – then suddenly there were no more khaki figures running towards us.

"Right, let's get this position sorted out," said Braun, and we began the back-breaking work once again, knowing the next bombardment would undo it all.

This is not good, I thought. *We've got no idea where the fellows on our right or left are, and it's only a matter of time before the Tommies try again.*

"Who was that fellow who had to keep rolling the rock up the hill?" asked Bauer.

"Sisyphus," Tiny replied. "And I know just how he felt!"

But we knew it was our only chance of surviving.

It was already too late for several. Breuning had been quite literally torn in half, the two pieces lying a metre or so apart. Schürmann lay staring at the sky with a look of faint surprise which gave his face a shocking vulnerability.

Karl and I exchanged looks. It was inconceivable that he should be lying there dead, with that expression which made me feel I should be protecting him.

There was a hole in the left breast of his tunic.

"So the Tommies do have snipers," said Alfred.

"So it would appear," Karl said.

"That's a filthy job," I said indignantly.

"No time to be idling, boys," said Braun. He was looking at Schürmann's body with the same odd look on his face as Karl.

I sighed and turned away.

Braun was right, of course, and I could almost hear Schürmann saying, Don't stand there gawping, Becker! Get to work!

I remembered how he'd stayed with us the previous autumn and how he'd come back to us when he didn't have to, and I couldn't rid myself of the idea that he had died not for the Fatherland, but for us.

From all around came groans and cries of "Medics!" and Klose and Masur were working flat out.

I hope I get killed straight out, not mutilated.

There was a horrible, thin howl from the right and I forced myself to look.

Neumann was doubled up in agony, his trousers soaked in blood, his hands clutching his groin.

Oh, Jesus, the poor bastard. Of all the places to get hit.

"Let me have a look," Alfred said, but Neumann's hands were locked tight. As Alfred tried to prise them loose Neumann screamed and screamed.

None of us could stand it.

"Jesus, Franz, if that happens to me put a bullet through my head," Karl said.

"Me too, mate," said Tiny. "I'm buggered if I'm going through life like that."

My sense of immortality disappeared abruptly. I didn't want to live like that either, as… What? A eunuch? Less than a eunuch… The phrase would not leave me but stuck unwanted in my mind. Suddenly losing an arm or a leg didn't seem quite so terrible.

We expected another attack at any moment but none came. *They're just regrouping*, I thought. *They'll be back, tonight or tomorrow.*

The sky clouded over just before sunset and the day finished in a sort of dismal, flat greyness. That was how I felt – flat and grey. I was suddenly extremely tired and rather shaky.

The night brought carrying parties with food, water and ammunition – which we desperately needed – and just after midnight a wiring party turned up. We didn't know whether to be pleased or not. The wire would be very useful, but we didn't want our position to become a new, fixed front line.

The wounded were taken back. Neumann had long since lapsed into unconsciousness and I hoped he would die.

If that happens to me I'll shoot myself. I can't live like that.

Darkness gave us the freedom to move cautiously above ground and we put some of the dead, including Schürmann, into a shell-hole and shovelled earth over them. We knew full well that the next bombardment would disinter them, but it seemed important to make that gesture of respect.

Oberleutnant Sauer had taken over command again. He told us our orders were still to hold the position. There was no mention of a further advance.

"I hope we're not going to get stuck here," I said to Karl.

"That makes two of us."

I was so tired I could hardly stand. *There won't be any sleep tonight or tomorrow*, I thought wearily, *and God, how I need to sleep.* I wanted to close my eyes and not open them until the sun was high in the sky, and wake to the safe, familiar walls of my bedroom at home – or better still to a feather bed with a soft, warm girl beside me…

I woke with a jolt as I nearly fell over, picked up my spade which had fallen from my hands, and continued digging.

The arrival of the rum ration broke the monotony. Its reviving warmth had barely settled in my stomach when the night exploded into thunderous, incandescent violence. It was like being in the middle of a volcanic eruption. I pressed myself into the wet earth again, to endure blindly the clods and hot shards raining down on me and the shattering explosions.

One of the wiring party gave a piercing cry of agony which cut right through the din and straight through my head.

The bombardment went on and on, churning up the earth until the air stank of rotting flesh.

If this goes on much longer we'll all be like that. The Tommies will be able to walk into the graveyard.

The shelling stopped. A host of flares went up and we stared into No Man's Land, waiting. The flares burned out and were replaced. The wounded man in the wiring party groaned and cursed and I wished he would shut up. They daren't try to bring him in – in the ghostly brilliance of the flares some nervous bugger would probably shoot them.

You poor bastards. When they attack you'll be right in the middle of it.

My nerves were jangling. *Why don't they come?* I strained my eyes for the least movement but saw no one.

It must be some new trick. Some clever general's had an idea. They'll wait till we've decided they're not coming, then they'll attack.

It began to rain. The flares lit the falling drops into a swirling silver curtain, almost impossible to see through. Still nothing.

A dirty violet-grey dawn broke. Clouds scudded low overhead, the rain poured down, and I could hardly tell where the earth ended and the sky began. In front of me was a desolate wasteland of wet grey mud, full of shell-holes and scattered with corpses. Nothing moved.

"They're coming!" yelled Peter.

Christ, you've got good eyes, I thought. *I can't see... Jesus, there they are!*

It was Krypke who gave the order, not Sauer. I didn't have time to think what that meant.

We'd had plenty of time to wait for them and we were ready: all of us and the machine-gunners. It was slaughter. That's the only word for it. I'd like to be able to forget it.

I almost felt sorry for them. If they'd come straight after the bombardment it might have been more like a fight. Instead it was like being on the firing range and they didn't stand a chance.

An hour later we stood down and I looked around. All our work had been completely undone, and we faced the soul-destroying task of rebuilding the trench yet again.

Karl wasn't beside me. He was always beside me.

"Where's Karl?" I almost shouted.

"Here, Franz." His voice was strained.

He was sitting in the bottom of the hole, his face white with pain. There was a jagged shard of metal embedded in his right shin, sticking out through his boot.

"Jesus!" I said. "Are you hit anywhere else?"

"I don't think so. I think it's broken."

"Alfred," I said, "Karl's got it in the leg."

I trusted Alfred rather more than the medics, and anyway they were somewhat busy.

"Let's have a look."

Alfred cut Karl's boot open and felt gently around the splinter. Karl gasped, his eyes closed.

"I daren't touch this, Karl," Alfred said. "It's gone into the bone and you know how bone closes on metal. The surgeon'll have to take it out. At least you've stopped bleeding."

When he can get to the surgeon.

"Don't let anyone else try to do it," Alfred added very quietly.

Karl nodded.

"Thanks, Alfred," I said.

"Yes, thanks," said Karl, trying not to let the pain show.

"Franz, can you see my water bottle anywhere? I can only find my hip flask."

"Have mine," I said. "I'll take yours when I find it."

As he took my bottle his fingers brushed mine, leaving a smear of blood. I looked at it and shook my head.

"Karl, this can't be yours," I said. "It's not blue."

"Very funny," he said. Half a minute later he added, "I'm not exalted enough for blue blood. You have to be titled for that."

You must be feeling bad. That was very slow.

We began cleaning up. We'd almost become accustomed to the frightful stench, but each time we unearthed something particularly nasty a fresh wave of it hit us and made us retch.

The stink of death was in my throat and my clothes and my skin, and I felt as if I'd never be rid of it.

You'll be next, said the rotting fragments of the dead. Soon you'll be just like us.

If we stay here much longer I probably will be. So much for Paris. I'll be lucky if I ever see anywhere else again.

I found Karl's water bottle and took a huge swig from it.

"Keep your head down, Franz," said Alfred. "That sniper who shot Schürmann will still be around."

Half of me hardly cared. It would only be hastening the inevitable, and a bullet through the brain would be better than lying in No Man's Land screaming for hours.

Schürmann's corpse had been disinterred and lay face up, his eyes full of dirt. One of his legs had been blown off and his uniform was torn. There wasn't much point burying him again, but it seemed disrespectful to leave him exposed.

The enemy seemed to have run out of ideas and the day was relatively quiet, but it was one of back-breaking work. My hands were blistered and my shoulders ached but as the saying goes, sweat spares blood.

Jesus, but I've had enough of this. More than enough.

Tiny's arm was in a sling and he sat down carefully next to Karl.

"You all right, mate?"

"Not bad." Karl handed Tiny his hip flask.

"Cheers… When we get out of here, come to Hamburg and I'll show you the Reeperbahn."

"What's that?" I asked.

They both laughed.

"Hamburg's red light district, of course!" said Tiny.

"I'll take you up on that!" Karl said, and they started swapping stories about tarts.

Listening to them was a very welcome distraction. *Bloody hell – I have had a sheltered life*, I thought as Tiny told Karl about some oriental girl who could sign her name with a pen held in her fanny.

"Tell you what, she didn't half give you a good squeeze!" Tiny said. "Never felt anything like it!"

"I'll bet!" said Karl, and went on to tell Tiny all about his couple of hours with… well, I guessed she was Anton's mother, though of course he didn't say. Her name was the only thing he left out as he went into explicit detail, using the most basic language.

Anyone who thinks social class matters should listen to you two. One Hamburg docker and one Brandenburg nobleman, and only your accents tell you apart.

When night fell Braun warned Karl that he'd have a long wait to be taken back.

"I'll wait with you," said Tiny.

"Don't be bloody daft," Karl replied. "The sooner you get back the further up the queue you'll be. Bugger off, now!"

Tiny got to his feet and almost fell over. "Bloody 'ell, went all dizzy for a mo."

"Take this," said Rippel, holding out his cane.

"Thank you, sir. D – dunno if you'll get it back, though."

"Doesn't matter – there are plenty going spare."

Schürmann's and Sauer's for a start, I thought, and wondered if Rippel had already crossed them off the list in his mind. Every officer who fell took him closer to getting his epaulettes, after all.

"Right, then – I'll be off," said Tiny. "Bit of luck they'll send me home and I'll see my missus and the kids."

It was nearly four in the morning before the stretcher-bearers came for Karl. He just managed to stop himself crying out when they moved his leg.

Tough bastard, aren't you? You've waited hour after hour with no word of complaint. I wonder if I'd be able to do that. I hope I never find out.

"So much for not leaving me on my tod," I grumbled to him. "I knew that was a load of hot air!"

"I'll kiss the nurses for you!" he said, his voice very strained.

"Jammy fucking bastard!"

He waved cheerfully as they carried him away.

You really are a jammy bastard, I thought – *you'll spend your birthday in hospital, in a nice comfortable bed, not fighting like I had to on mine. And they'll send you home.* Home.

"It's all right for some," I said to Bauer. I was trying not to think that Karl and I might never meet again.

I hope they get that splinter out of his leg all right. I hope they don't have to amputate. That would be dreadful.

I was at home, in our drawing room. I'd lost my right leg and I was sitting in a chair, a depressed, useless wreck, my crutches beside me. Far worse, Germany was losing the war and our town was being shelled.

Our house was hit with a terrific crash and the ceiling began to fall in with ghastly slowness. Johanna screamed, and Papa turned to me with accusing eyes and said, "You were supposed to protect us—"

"Franz, wake up!" Alfred was shaking my shoulder.

Papa's eyes disappeared but the bombardment was real. I didn't know which was worse – that vivid dream of defeat and failure or the reality of cowering in a ditch as the shells rained down.

This time they attacked right after the bombardment and there were hundreds of them. We crouched in the stinking, battered remains of our position among the tumbled sandbags, broken bodies, discarded equipment, waiting for the order…

Oh Christ, we've waited too long, we'll never hold them! You've done it now, Krypke, you stupid cunt, you've got us all killed—

"Fire!"

They fell, but not fast enough, and we fired and fired. My shoulder was bruised and my rifle was hot and still they came on. Alfred was kneeling on what remained of the parapet and the stupid bastard didn't even get down to reload.

Fucking idiot, you'll get killed, and then what use will you be?

Some were less than fifty metres away. We poured lead into them and they wavered to a stop, then turned and ran. We were all standing up, firing at them – and then we cheered because we'd seen them off, we'd been reprieved.

Alfred slid down beside me.

"Alfred, you are a fucking maniac," I said.

He shrugged and grinned at me.

That Tommy sniper must have bought it or you'd be dead.

"Oh, bugger it," he said suddenly, staring at his left arm. It was bloody from elbow to hand. "When did that happen?"

"Didn't you feel it?" I asked as I tore his sleeves off.

"No. I felt a bit of a thump when they were shelling us, but you know how it is – stuff rains down on you all the time, and after that we were a bit busy, weren't we?" He shrugged. "It still doesn't hurt."

It will.

"Just as well this didn't happen to Karl," he said as I patched him up. "It would have ruined his career. Doesn't matter if my fingers are a bit stiff, after all."

"I hadn't thought of that."

I should have done, though. Alfred's forearm was a real mess, torn to the bone in places. *How could you not have felt this?* I wondered, and then I thought, *This is just what I want. Something relatively minor to get me out of this bloody place before I get killed. I don't mind if my fingers are a bit stiff, either.*

Otherwise I won't survive.

The bombardment had taken a frightful toll of us. The bastards had the range almost exactly and we wouldn't be able to take much more of their attentions.

Of our little group only Bauer, Kurt, Peter and I were unscathed. Flechsig was dead, Kienle and Müller both on their way to hospital. Krypke was the only officer in what remained of the Fourth Company, unless you counted Rippel. Braun was still alive and so were Gefreiter Fischer and Unteroffizier Rombach.

I didn't want to know our total numbers. *Whatever the figure might be now, it'll be zero in a couple of days*, I thought, and wondered idly whether I would be killed or mutilated.

That's a stupid way to think, Franz. Just dig.

At around midnight Fischer stood beside me. "We're being relieved tonight."

I looked at him in disbelief. He was telling me that I was going to live, for a few days more.

"So let's hand this trench over in a half-decent state."

Please God, don't let anything happen before the relief gets here. It would be terrible to be killed at the last minute.

The enemy must have been just as exhausted as we were – they left us in peace, and we turned our backs on the Front and trudged gratefully away. I felt the cool night air on my face and drew it deep into my lungs.

Best make the most of it. You'll be back here soon enough.

Our shattered remnants were withdrawn east, into rest, to be reorganised and reinforced. Kurt was promoted to Gefreiter, and Peter and I were astonished by how quickly he opened a gap between himself and us, of just the right width. I was happy for him because I knew how much this first promotion meant to him.

You'll be on your officer's course before long, Kurt. They're going to need you.

Rippel got his epaulettes and actually seemed to grow when he put them on.

We said, "Congratulations, Herr Leutnant," with sincerity, hoping we'd be put in his platoon – but of course we were stuck with Krypke, who did seem to be losing some of his sarcastic edge.

Horn still hated him and swore to shoot him in the back the next time we went over the top.

"Not as if they'll do a fuckin' autopsy," he said.

"And I never heard a word," said Bauer with a grin.

A couple of weeks later we were back in the soup again. We'd thought Ypres would have been taken but it hadn't.

"We're not much further on," Peter said to me.

"No."

We learned why very quickly. The Tommies were fighting like devils. We managed to push the line a bit further forward, but at the cost of being smashed to pieces yet again.

The most savage fighting of all was near a ruined chateau that must once have been very beautiful.

It reminded me of Karl's house: the architecture was similar and there was a terrace overlooking a lake, though a much smaller one. The contrast between the tranquil setting and the barbaric violence of battle was truly shocking, as if the gates of Hell had burst open.

When we finally dislodged the Tommies, we found to our astonishment that they were Canadian.

"Why did you leave your lovely homeland, and come and fight in Europe?" I asked one of the prisoners in the best English I could muster.

"My hometown's a bit small and it's in the middle of nowhere. I wanted to see the world, I fancied a bit of adventure…"

Same as me – a bit of adventure.

"We both have that," I replied.

But yours is over now. You're safe, and when the war ends you'll go home, whereas I – who knows?

Before long we were ruined again, and by the time they'd sorted us out the battle was over. We still weren't in Ypres.

The entire Spring Offensive seemed to have run out of energy, and we were too happy to be reprieved to think what that meant. Or perhaps we didn't want to think about it, because of course it meant the war was nowhere near over and we were going to have to do it all again, and the less we thought about that the better.

So we abandoned thought and enjoyed the relative quiet. The Ypres area was always dodgy, but if you didn't do anything stupid you had a good chance of making it out again.

To my astonishment I too was promoted to Gefreiter.

"And you really should think about going for a commission," said Oberleutnant Waitz, our latest Company Commander.

"Thank you, sir, but I'm more than happy with this," I replied.

"Well, let me know if you change your mind." He stroked his moustache thoughtfully, obviously wondering how to persuade me.

You can forget it. The Devil himself wouldn't convince me.

"Just shows how short they must be getting," I said to Kurt. "Promoting you makes sense but if they've got as far as me they're scraping the bottom of the barrel."

"Bollocks," he replied. "Just look at the difference between you and the new chaps. You know a lot more than you think you do."

"I suppose so," I said, and when I thought about it I realised he was right.

We got sent on the same training course, which got us a nice break from the usual routine, and Kurt's break turned out to be rather longer than mine. On the last day he was told he was going straight onto his officer's course.

"You've lost that bet with Karl," I said. "You'll be commissioned before him."

"You should go for it," he said.

"What, take the Express Ticket to Eternity?" That was what someone had nicknamed a junior officer's commission, and with good reason. "Not fucking likely."

"There are advantages."

"Yes – if they pick your corpse up you get a proper grave!"

He just laughed.

I went back to the Regiment and began to settle into my new role. I didn't find it as easy as Kurt had done. He had a natural feel for the job and never had any difficulty getting his men to obey him, and I envied that. I was obeyed, but there were times when I felt I hadn't handled things quite as well as I might have done.

Alfred came back, with a dramatic jagged scar down his arm.

"So how was Berlin?" I asked him.

"I didn't get that far. They sent me to a hospital in Brussels – very pleasant it was too, especially when I was allowed out."

"Pretty nurses?" asked Bauer.

"Wouldn't you like to know?" Alfred said with a grin.

"Jammy fucking bastard! While we've been stuck here with only the bloody rats for company."

"And there's no end to those fuckin' things," said Horn.

He wasn't joking. Since the Spring Offensive they had multiplied. Their beady eyes, sharp teeth and long scaly tails sent a shiver down my spine, and I always had the feeling they were sizing me up for their next meal.

We all knew what they ate, but as if there wasn't enough food lying out in No Man's Land they came into the trenches all the time and stole anything that wasn't sealed away. They even ran over us while we were sleeping.

"We need a terrier," said Bauer. "If I get leave I'll bring one back with me."

Leave – Karl should be back soon, surely? Tiny's back, though his arm wasn't broken. Let's see – six weeks in plaster, maybe a week or two of leave afterwards?

I missed him far more than I'd imagined I would. Things just weren't the same without him.

"When's Leussow coming back?" Tiny asked me.

"Don't know yet. Must be soon."

"Oh, right."

"How was home?"

"All right, I suppose. The missus is finding things hard going, on her own with the boys – we've got five and I had to take my belt to the oldest one. Thirteen he is now. Gave his Ma a load of lip. I told him he has to behave like a man till I get home for good, not like a fucking brat."

Don't suppose you made it to the Reeperbahn, then...

And that would have been more exciting than being in the trenches. Life had got rather dull.

No one was really sorry about that – except Alfred, who volunteered for every raid and patrol.

"I get bored," he said by way of explanation. The rest of us just shrugged.

'Fucking nutter' was the phrase that came to mind, but it was such a statement of the obvious that no one could be bothered to say it. Most of us went on raids often enough to show willing, but the business was too crudely violent for me to enjoy it.

Shooting men is one thing, but bashing someone's head in with a nailed club is quite another – and once you've got into their trench you have to get everyone out again, and that's easier said than done.

Patrols into the ghostly terrain between the lines were far more to my taste. There was something about creeping along unseen in the darkness... Once we ambushed a Tommy patrol, killed one, injured two more, and sent the rest scurrying back to their wire.

"Serves 'em right," said Horn as he cleaned the blood off his knife.

Just like home, no doubt, I thought but was strangely disinclined to say.

"It's getting bloody difficult to keep any sort of offensive spirit going now it's all gone static," Rombach grumbled to me. "Too many of the fellows just want to keep their heads down and do nothing. We have to show the Tommies that No Man's Land belongs to us, and that they can't get away with nothing."

"Yes, I know," I said. And I knew he was right. We were there to fight, after all.

'Fight' seemed to have been redefined. Among the latest reinforcements were Taschner and Faltermeier, who turned up equipped with telescopic sights and soon got to work shooting Tommies.

I had reservations about that. Yes, we didn't want the Tommies to get too comfortable, but killing them in cold blood struck me as dirty.

Taschner did nothing to change my opinion. He wrote up his notebook diligently and announced his day's score to anyone who would listen.

"At least someone's givin' it to the bastards," said Horn.

"Not sure that's the way it should be done," Bauer said.

"Bloody close to murder, if you ask me," said Wolter, who was in my section.

"What do you think?" I asked Alfred later.

He shrugged. "We're here to kill the enemy, aren't we? Doesn't matter what he's doing at the time – he's still here."

"Does seem rather cold-blooded, though," I said, "and just like the gas, they'll retaliate in kind."

The sniper who'd shot Schürmann seemed to have been a one-off, and as yet we hadn't been troubled by any more of the bastards.

"Well, there is that," he conceded, "but I reckon it's necessary."

If those two are doing that job then with a bit of luck Karl's off the hook, I thought as Taschner chalked up a second lieutenant.

"Don't know what the stupid bastard thought he was doing," he said. "Just stuck his head and shoulders up above the parapet."

"Won't do it again," said Faltermeier with a grin.

"Want to swap round after lunch, Spots?" Taschner asked.

"Yeah, why not." Faltermeier handed Taschner the binoculars and lit a fag.

There was quite a contrast between them – Taschner was a thickset fellow of about thirty, whereas Spots was a skinny little chap and aptly nicknamed.

His face was covered in acne and I felt rather sorry for him. I'd suffered as well, but fortunately mine had disappeared once I'd got to seventeen. Faltermeier was not so lucky and seemed to grow new pimples every day. When he shaved he cut the tops off them, leaving him with a very speckled face.

Imagine trying to get a girl into bed, looking like that, I thought, wondering if he'd ever managed it.

Hardly matters out here – I don't suppose the tarts care.

Kurt returned as Officer Cadet Meyer and, just as we'd predicted, we had to stand to attention and call him 'sir'.

Alfred was green with envy and went off to the Company command post, no doubt to ask Waitz when his course would be. He came back looking much happier.

"So what did he say?" I asked.

"Now that Kurt – or rather Meyer – is back, I'll be next."

"Better go easy on the raids, then," I said, "or you'll end up dead or a prisoner instead."

"Bollocks."

Curiously I had no difficulty remembering to address Kurt correctly, because once again he'd fitted instantly into his new position. I wanted to ask him what his father thought about his promotion but it felt too personal.

Maybe I should go for it after all, I thought as I tried to get the mud off my boots. *Someone else doing this for me would be a vast improvement.*

Yes, and your chances of seeing next Christmas would be zero.

To my surprise I did get promoted, to Unteroffizier. *Maybe they're trying to tell me something – but they're wasting their time. No way am I putting on a set of nice shiny epaulettes.*

Spring had turned to summer. At the beginning of July we were in rest, enjoying a gloriously hot day. I lay half asleep on my back, enjoying the heat, pretending that the war was on another continent. I could almost manage to believe it…

"Hey, look," Alfred said. "It's Karl."

My eyes flew open and I was suddenly wide awake.

"Is it really?" I replied with feigned nonchalance.

I sat up slowly and got to my feet.

"The Devil didn't want you, then?" he said, and threw his arms round me and squeezed so hard I couldn't breathe.

It's so good to have you back.

"How are you?" I asked. "Leg healed?"

He looked fit and healthy. "Oh, I'm all right. You?"

"Still here, as you see. Oddly enough I was just wondering when you'd be back."

There was a short man beside him whose face made me think of a rat or a weasel.

"This is Koch," he said.

They sat down with us and we started talking. Karl seemed relaxed and happy, and I realised how much good the break from the Front had done him.

I could do with a bit of that. I feel better than I did but I'm still pretty tired and stale.

Suddenly I noticed that he had a small oak-leaf badge between the cockades on his cap and a cylindrical leather case hanging from his belt, just like Taschner and Faltermeier.

So did Koch.

"What have you got there?" I asked, as casually as I could.

Karl hesitated.

"Telescopic sight, of course," said Koch. "We brought 'em from 'ome an' the armourers fitted 'em an' zeroed 'em."

There was an awkward silence. I remembered what I'd said when Schürmann was killed, about sniping being a filthy job, and I could see in Karl's face that he remembered too.

"So you're both snipers, then?" asked Tiny.

"That's right," Koch replied. "We gets the chance to do somethin' now it's all gone quiet."

"Good for you," said Bauer. "Though if you ask me it's a risky business."

"Well done," Alfred said to Karl. "Mind you, you deserve it. You're a bloody good shot."

"Thanks," Karl said.

His eyes met mine and there was a hint of disquiet in them. *It doesn't matter – you're still my best mate, no matter what dirty job they give you.*

"How's Friedrich?" I asked neutrally.

There was something like relief in his face at the change of subject.

"He's doing all right now, thanks. Looks like a fucking pirate, though, with a black patch and a scar right down his left cheek." He traced the line on his own face as he spoke, from his forehead to his jaw.

That sounds like quite a mess.

"I said I'd buy him a parrot but he told me to fuck off."

"Are they giving him a glass eye?" Alfred asked.

He nodded. "He's got one – it's a very good match but wearing it's a bit of a fatt and half the time he doesn't bother. He's looking forward to getting back... It was good to see him. He's got a desk job at the War Ministry and his boss gave him a few days off, so he met me at the Stettiner Station in Berlin and we went home together."

I had the feeling he had a lot more to say but didn't want to say it in front of the others.

"So what were the nurses like?" asked Peter.

"Mostly Bavarian," Karl said very seriously. "So I was always the last fellow to get water or food, or a bottle to piss in."

"Quite right too," said Peter.

"That's outrageous!" Alfred burst out.

Karl started laughing. "No, they were lovely – when I came round from the anaesthetic I thought I'd died and gone to Heaven."

"Heaven – you?!" said Bauer. "Now you're really talking shit."

"Did you get your leg over?" asked Horn.

"Not till I was in Berlin – but I made up for it when I got there!"

"Bastard!" we all said together.

Karl turned to Koch. "Well, we'd better report to… Who's the Company Commander these days?"

"Oberleutnant Waitz," said Alfred. "Decent sort of fellow."

"I take it Krypke's still here?"

"Oh, yes," said Horn. "Those useless Tommies missed the fucker."

"And Kurt's an officer cadet now," I said, "so he owes you five marks."

Karl and Koch headed for the Company office.

"Rather him than me," Peter said when they were out of earshot. "That's too bloody dangerous."

"Oh, I don't know," said Alfred. "At least it gives you a chance to do something as an individual."

"Yes, but everyone tries to kill you," Peter replied. "I mean you personally."

I got up. I didn't want to hear any more. I got halfway to the barn and then I saw that Karl had left Koch to go on ahead and was coming back.

"I forgot to congratulate you on your promotion," he said, and again there was that slight awkwardness.

It doesn't matter, I wanted to say, but for some reason the words wouldn't come.

I'll have to show you instead. "Thanks… Shall we go to the Soldiers' Home for a bite to eat this evening?"

He smiled, the old warmth back in his eyes. "Good idea."

"Don't worry if you can't make it… How's it going to work with your duties now? I mean, I take it we're still in the same Company?"

"So far as I know. I'll do my best to be there this evening."

He hesitated as if there were something else he wanted to say, and then left.

I watched him go, full of an emotion that I couldn't quite name.

Peter's right. The enemy will be doing their damnedest to kill him. The idea of it sent a shiver down my back. *They try to kill us all, but somehow that's more personal.*

They came back about half an hour later.

"Good news," Karl said. "We're still part of the Fourth Company."

"Didn't get rid of you that easily, then!" I said.

We found a quiet corner in the Soldiers' Home and he bought me a beer. For a moment I didn't know how to start the conversation.

"Is your leg all right?"

"Yes, fine, healed up no trouble at all. And I got the best part of two weeks off after I left hospital and it was bloody good to get home and to see Friedrich."

"He's been in Berlin some time now, hasn't he? How's he doing, really?"

You only saw each other because you both got whacked. What a business this is.

He sighed and shook his head.

"Not that well... His face is a real mess – gave me quite a shock when I saw him – and the left side's partly paralysed. He said he's sick of being stared at and he just wants to get back here. He was supposed to come back a couple of months ago but it reopened."

"Shit."

"Yes, and it was in public as well. He'd bumped into an old friend from cadet school – he'd caught it as well – and they decided to treat themselves to dinner at the Adlon, and that's when it happened, in front of a dining room full of people.

He's got no feeling in that part of his face and he didn't realise anything was wrong until his friend told him. He – he said he's never been so embarrassed in his life."

"It was hardly his fault – and it doesn't hurt for people to see what war really is. All that shit in the papers about glory!"

"Judging from the number of black armbands and fellows on crutches and so on, they should have some idea. Anyway, he had to have another operation… He keeps touching the left corner of his mouth. I asked him why and he said he can't tell if it's closed or not and he's afraid he might be dribbling."

"Jesus."

Karl sighed again. "The real problem is that he lost most of his company at Nonneboschen. He… well, you know what he's like. Doesn't talk much at the best of times. He asked about Langemarck instead – I tell you, Franz, I've never seen him so angry." He lowered his voice. "He said whoever ordered that should be shot."

"He's got a point."

"Yes… Anyway, I plied him with Pa's best brandy and bit by bit it all came out. It was the finest moment of his life, he said, leading those men against the English. They came under very heavy fire – small arms to begin with, and we know how the Tommies can shoot."

"Don't we just."

"And then their artillery got the range. No one faltered. They were magnificent, he said, he was so proud of them. He said the fighting was savage – they were determined to break through and the Tommies were just as determined they wouldn't."

That must have been quite a fight – two professional armies slugging it out hand to hand.

"At some point he realised he couldn't see out of his left eye but he kept on until he dropped. The next thing he knew someone was bandaging his head. Anyway, the man lying next to him was Feldwebel Roenz, from his company, who said they'd had to retreat but they'd seen him lying there and dragged him along."

"Brave of them."

"Indeed. It turned out almost no one was left. And that's the problem – he had it drilled into him, all his life, that his first duty is to his men, and now he's alive when most of them are dead."

"What more could he have done?"

"Quite. And his colonel agrees with us – visited him in hospital and told him he was recommending him for the Iron Cross, First Class. Friedrich said the colonel's a tough old bastard but he could hardly talk about what had happened to the regiment. He said there were only five junior officers left and about a fifth of the men – then his voice cracked and he got up and left."

That's enough to make anyone weep.

Karl sighed heavily. "He means it when he says he can't wait to get back. God knows I don't want him to get hurt again, but I hope that next time – there'll be a next time, I know there will – I hope it's bad enough to get him out of it, otherwise…" He broke off and stared at his hands.

What a world, where a man's best hope for his brother is that he'll be injured badly enough to be invalided out.

"Maybe they won't send him back at all," I said. "I mean, if it's going to keep reopening they'll have to keep him in Berlin, won't they?"

"True… I hope it heals this time, though. It's a real bastard, having your face wrecked like that. People just stare."

He lit another fag and then went on, "Mind you, he's got a corker of a girl now. We've known the family off and on for years but we met her again at a party and she doesn't seem to mind about his face at all. I tell you, Franz, if I had a girl like that I wouldn't be in a rush to get away."

"Much chance we've got."

"True." He started laughing. "Mind you, Pa won't like it one bit."

"Why not?"

"Because Friedrich's engaged to... Never mind her name."

"What, officially? When did that happen?"

"When he was about five. Pa and her father agreed it between them. I asked Friedrich what he's going to do about it, and he said he's going to say that being as he's damaged goods she's released from the arrangement. Her parents won't like it either but that's their problem."

That's what you get for being born into the nobility – an arranged marriage, even though it's the twentieth century.

"So does his girl know?"

"Not yet. There's no need to say anything unless it gets serious, is there?"

"Suppose not."

"I still managed to lead him astray for a night, though, girl or no girl!"

"So how was Berlin?" *I'll bet you saw those dancers...*

He stretched and grinned widely. "Exhausting! My God, the women! I spent a whole day with those dancers I told you about... I tell you, Franz, there's no point having one woman when you can have two." He started giving me all the details, the bastard.

"Karl, *shut up*, for Christ's sake! I don't want to hear all that! I haven't had a decent fuck for months. Just tell me about the rest of it."

He laughed. "All right, then! Friedrich and I went to stacks of parties – he didn't want to go but I made him – got pissed almost every night. Had to go everywhere in civvies, though, being as I'm still a private… What do I call you these days?"

"Corporal," I said with mock severity, and then grinned at him. "You can call me what you like when there's just the two of us."

"Oh, good… Have they given you leave yet?"

"No. No one's even mentioned it. I'm dying to get home."

"I'll bet. The farm's in a real state, though – there's almost no one left. Friedrich's doing what he can, but his job at the War Ministry's full time and he can't do a lot of physical work – starts feeling dizzy after a couple of hours. He's supposed to be resting and getting fit to come back here, not wearing himself out. I don't know what Pa thinks he's doing. He should be running the farm, not playing soldiers."

"He could say the same about you."

"Hardly."

"He's a staff officer. You're just cannon fodder. You must know enough to run the farm yourself, and the Army could spare you more easily."

I never could get a rise out of him. He just grinned.

"I'm no farmer, Franz – I'm just a labourer. I can plough a straight furrow but I can't tell when to start the harvest. Pa could write a book about it and he'd be better employed growing food. They could find another staff officer tomorrow. If he really wants to do his duty he should help feed the country."

There was a long pause and then he said, "Here I am, banging on about Friedrich and the farm, and I haven't even asked what your news is."

I shrugged. "There isn't any, really, not since my last letter. It's been fairly quiet."

"Enjoying your new lofty status?"

"It's all right, though it was a bit strange at first. The funny thing is, Papa was really complimentary about it. I just don't understand him. He wrote me a really nice letter, saying he's pleased I'm doing well and he hopes I'll get more promotions. It's beyond me... You remember, he was dead against my joining up in the first place."

"Perhaps he's just glad to see you making a success of it—Jesus, is that the time?"

"Shit – we'd better get back."

We only just made it before tattoo. Kurt was waiting for stragglers.

"Good evening, Officer Cadet, sir," Karl said with a smart salute. There was the briefest of pauses and then he added, deadpan, "I believe you owe me five marks."

Kurt laughed. "Not yet, Leussow! You'll have to wait till I get my epaulettes!"

Karl laughed as well. "Yes, sir, I believe you're right. Well done, anyway."

Koch was talking to Taschner and Faltermeier. Karl sat with Bauer, Alfred and me, and when we lay down for the night he curled up beside me. It felt so right, his being there again, and I felt a quite absurd degree of contentment.

Good, I thought as I drifted off. *Nothing's changed.*

I wasn't so sure about that after I'd seen him work a few times. I couldn't actually watch him work as such – there were a number of very well-concealed loopholes set into the parapet and they all had canvas curtains hung round them – but I could see him standing motionless at one position or another, and every time his rifle cracked I was sharply aware that some Tommy was probably dead or dying.

Once, out of curiosity, I asked him if I could have a look.

"Of course – just be bloody careful you don't let any light through. The Tommies are getting better at this game and you never know who's looking."

I was very careful indeed.

The sandbags of the English trench were suddenly clear and

close and I could see the small gap in the parapet. Just then a Tommy appeared and paused, turning to look back the way he'd come. I even saw his lips move as he spoke to someone.

His head was framed perfectly in the sight. *Jesus – if Karl were standing here instead of me you'd have had it. Your lucky day.*

I'd never agree to do that job, I thought as I got down, *not in a thousand years.*

How can you do it, Karl? Shoot some fellow who's walking along their trench, or shaving, or engaged in some other harmless activity?

"Seen enough?"

"Yes… thanks."

He looked at me rather expectantly but I didn't know what to say. I certainly couldn't tell him what I was thinking.

"Interesting," I said. "Much clearer than I thought it would be. How much magnification have you got?"

"Oh, this is that four-power Zeiss sight I told you about before… Fancy some coffee? I could do with a break."

"Good idea. What about Koch?"

He turned. "Thanks, mate. Smoke?"

"Thanks."

I only accepted to be polite. I didn't care for Koch at all. He recorded every hit with seeming relish, whereas Karl wrote up his book with indifference.

How do you feel about it? I wondered. *Or is it like Langemarck? Do you allow yourself to feel anything?*

There was no way I could ask him. I could imagine his eyes turning hard and grey, as they always did when he wanted to hide what he felt. *You can't afford emotion*, I thought, *not doing that. You must have to be as cold as ice.*

I was pretty sure, though, that he didn't like Koch any more than I did. Once or twice I saw him looking at his partner with something like distaste, but the expression was always so fleeting that I could never be sure it was actually there. I had the impression he didn't care for Taschner either – he was always pleasant, but with a degree of reserve.

They probably think it's because he's a toff. It's probably what they expect.

After a couple of weeks there was another, more worrying development. Taschner regularly worked alone from hidden positions in No Man's Land, which most of us thought was insane. To my horror Karl adopted the idea, wandering out in the middle of the night looking for suitable hiding places. It scared the hell out of me.

If you get hit, you're on your own. There's no way we could go and fetch you until dark, even if we knew where you were. You'd just lie there until you died, alone and in pain. It doesn't bear thinking about.

They won't get him, I told myself, *not the way he hides. Even if you knew where he was you still wouldn't be able to see him.*

He'd made a loose, hooded cape from old sandbags and soaked it so thoroughly in Flanders mud that you could hardly see it, even against the sides of the trench. But I still had to make an effort not to worry about him.

Our comrades had other grounds for anxiety.

"It's all very well," grumbled Wolter. "They do their dirty work and then there's always the fucking payback."

"It is war," Alfred reminded him. "And it's only the snipers and the raiders who are still fighting."

"All the same."

Wolter did have a point. One day Taschner had the good fortune to shoot a senior officer who was inspecting the trenches opposite.

"Nice one," said Faltermeier as they stepped down. "No doubt about him."

"What was 'e?" asked Koch.

"Colonel."

"Hey, well done, Taschner. You're at the top of today's list!"

"Well done, Taschner," Karl said warmly. He meant it, I could tell.

So presumably you'd be just as pleased if you'd done it yourself. I just can't fathom you at all these days. I thought I knew you well but now I'm not so sure... but I've had that feeling of grim satisfaction and isn't it really the same thing? Don't I just want to believe there's a difference?

"If you goes on like that you'll get—" The rest of Koch's words were drowned out as the English artillery opened up on us with horrifying accuracy, obviously determined to punish Taschner's impudence.

They shelled the crap out of us and I cursed Taschner to Hell and back.

In the midst of the appalling din I heard the shriek of a shell coming straight for us. I buried myself as far below the parapet as I could and the world disappeared in a thunderous, shattering crash.

My face was resting against something rough. I was very comfortable and rather sleepy. *It would be nice to lie here all day...*

"Jesus Christ!" Krypke's terrified scream cut through the racket and roused me to full consciousness.

I tried to move, but the parapet had collapsed on top of me and I was buried from the waist down beneath a heap of earth and sandbags.

"HELP!"

I managed to turn my head towards him and froze in horror. A great scarlet jet spurted from his groin, and another and another.

"Oh, my God!" I gasped, and then found my voice. "*Medics!* MEDICS! Here, QUICK!"

It was futile. I could hardly hear myself. I couldn't reach him. I tried to free myself, but I couldn't pull the sandbags away.

Krypke tried frantically to grip his severed artery. It was already too late.

"BECKER... *Becker*... Help, Beck... Be..."

I couldn't reach him. All I could do was shout and pull at the sandbags and watch him die.

The shelling ceased as abruptly as it had begun.

"Help!" I shouted. It was too late for Krypke but I was stuck fast. I didn't know if I was injured and I was afraid of what was coming next. No one near me seemed to be alive, and my rifle was somewhere beneath the debris.

If the Tommies get here I'm dead.

After an eternity Karl and Braun arrived on their hands and knees.

"You took your fucking time," I said to Karl.

"Couldn't hear you until that row stopped."

They began to dig me out.

I pointed at Krypke. "I couldn't reach him."

Klose went over to Krypke and shook his head, and he and Masur went to look after the fellows they could help.

"Never mind him," said Karl. "Are you all right? Can you move your legs?"

To my great relief I could. "I think I'm all right."

"We'll get Friedemann to look at you," said Braun.

There was blood everywhere. Krypke's uniform was sodden with it and it had soaked the sandbags. There was a hole at the top of his thigh as big as my fist. I'll never forget his fingers scrabbling hopelessly in that hole, or the look in his eyes, or that horrible fountain of blood.

"Don't waste your sympathy," Karl said.

"I couldn't reach him. All I could do was watch."

"Just be thankful it wasn't you. He was an arsehole. Being dead doesn't make him any less of one."

"But—"

"No buts. Get Alfred to look at you."

I looked at Krypke's body again.

"Go on," said Karl, his hand on my shoulder.

Wolter stood suddenly in front of Karl.

"That's the trouble with you bastards," he blurted out. "Tiny's gone, *just fucking gone!* There's nothing left of him, not a scrap!"

"He was my friend, too," Karl said quietly, and turned away.

"Well, what have you got to say about it?" Wolter persisted.

Leave it out, I thought.

Karl looked at him, his eyes hard and grey.

"What do you expect me to say?" His voice was very calm, but there was something very cold in it that matched his eyes.

Wolter stared at Karl, seemingly lost for words.

"They were shelling us as well," Karl said in the same even tone. "And there'll be times when you'll be bloody glad of what we do."

"Yeah, like when?"

"Get this trench in order, boys," I said. "We don't know what's coming next."

"Like when?" Wolter demanded again.

"Leave it out, Wolter. Get to work," I said.

"Just cos he's your mate—"

"It's got fuck all to do with whose mate anyone is. I gave you an order!"

For a moment I was surprised at the rough edge in my voice, and out of the corner of my eye I saw both Karl and Braun looking at me with approval.

Wolter got to work without another word.

Alfred examined me and said nothing was broken, but as the

day wore on I began to ache and by nightfall I was hobbling like an old man.

Karl sat next to me later. "You all right, Corporal?"

"Yes, thanks."

"Nasty thing to have to watch."

"Yes. I couldn't reach him," I said again.

"I know. There was a hell of a lot of stuff on top of you... Still, at least it was him and not some decent fellow."

"Karl, how can you say that? The poor bastard was petrified."

"That's not what I meant. I wouldn't wish that on anyone – but he was an obnoxious little shit and nothing can change that." He was silent for a few seconds. "But he did sing beautifully and we found a picture of a girl in his wallet, so I suppose someone will miss him... It's a real shame about Tiny."

"Yes. He was a good bloke."

And they missed the ones they were after. None of the snipers had even a scratch.

There was a pause and then he asked very quietly, "Do you agree with Wolter?"

I shook my head. "You've got your job to do. That's all any of us can do, isn't it? Do our jobs."

"Yes. That's how I see it as well," he said expressionlessly. "I just do my job."

He stared into space for a moment, his face impassive. I remembered suddenly what he'd told us in the training camp, how he'd hated hunting and had only become such a good shot to spare the animals suffering.

Perhaps they shouldn't have chosen you for this – and yet, and yet – how can anyone be so good at something and not enjoy it just a bit? And you know yourself how satisfying it is when you hit the target.

No one was sorry about Krypke's demise, though, especially as we got Leutnant Hafner as our new Platoon Commander. He was a vast improvement – thoroughly professional and the sort of fellow you knew you could rely on.

The very next day he gave me the wonderful news that I was going on leave. Ten whole days away from the Front, six of them at home! I couldn't believe it.

I took my leave of Karl rather awkwardly. We were being parted again and I didn't like it, especially when I knew how many risks he took.

"Now who's leaving whom in the soup?" he said, and I laughed.

I hope I see you again. I hope you're still here when I come back.

"Have a good time, Franz," he said. "Give my love to the beautiful women of Germany!"

"For God's sake, Karl, I'm going to my parents'! I'll be lucky to get anything there."

"Franz, if you come back without having had a free fuck I'll... well, I don't know what I'll do to you but I'll think of something, I promise! What else is leave for, for God's sake?"

"Well, seeing my family..."

He shook his head in mock despair.

"Fellow's got water in his veins," he said sadly. "Remember, a free fuck – and I want to hear all about it. I'm starting to run out of fantasies!"

"Oh, you don't need my help! You'll think up plenty more... Don't do anything stupid, Karl, or I won't have anyone to tell about my conquests!"

"You see before you the most intelligent man in the Prussian army—"

"*German* army."

"No, no, I meant what I said. No doubt there are many far more intelligent men from other parts of the Empire, but I am without doubt the most intelligent Prussian."

"That's not difficult!"

"Bugger off or you'll miss your train! And bring me back some chocolate – you know, the dark stuff. None of that milk crap."

That'll be easier than finding a girl in my parents' dull old town – but who cares? No war for ten whole days. No Western Front, no Army food, no lice, no shells... Heaven.

VII

The journey home was bloody slow. I had to change trains in Brussels, then in Cologne, and again in Stuttgart, and each time I had to wait hours for the connection.

Brussels station was so full of soldiers that it was almost impossible to move. I had two hours to kill, and fell into conversation with a Hussar who was on his way to the Front.

"You're going the wrong way!" I joked.

"That's for sure," he agreed. "But with a bit of luck it won't go on much longer."

I wasn't so sure about that when I got to Cologne – it was full of troop trains heading west. *If we need that many reinforcements then maybe we're building up to another offensive... or are they just to replace the losses?*

A hospital train had pulled in, and as it was being unloaded I caught sight of several motionless, blanketed men on stretchers. I turned away.

I do not want to come back like that.

I bought a newspaper and had the usual good laugh at it. The accounts of life at the Front were so far from anything I'd experienced that I wondered where the journalists had been.

It's all lies, I thought as I skimmed over another article about some 'glorious action' or other. *It's just fairy stories for the civilians.*

My parents have been reading this crap. I'll have to put them straight. I owe it to the others to tell the truth.

Eventually I stood on the platform in my home town. The station looked just as it had when I'd left nearly a year before and I looked around, half-expecting to see that eager youth rushing to catch the train.

Would I have gone if I'd known what was coming? I wondered, and knew that I would. *For my friends, for my country – all the time we're under attack, I shall fight on.*

The shops were achingly familiar: the baker's, the shoe-shop, the bookshop where I used to spend my pocket money. The town was peaceful in the morning sunshine and the war could have been on another continent.

I clumped up the stairs to Papa's office, my boots ringing loudly, my pack and rifle awkward and encumbering. I stood for a moment before the glass door.

'Josef Becker', it said in gold letters, as it had ever since I could remember – and yet it was somehow alien, as if I didn't belong.

Nothing has changed here, but I have changed, so much.

I opened the door. Schwaiger, Papa's old clerk, looked up. The polite enquiry in his face changed to disapproval at the sight of a rumpled soldier and then to incredulity.

"Herr Becker! *Herr Becker!*" He leapt to his feet. "Your son is here!" He flung open the door of my father's office. "*Your son is here!*"

Papa ran out.

"Franz, my boy! My dear boy!"

"Papa—"

He'd never hugged me before. There was a sudden lump in my throat and when Papa stepped back I saw that his eyelashes were wet. Neither of us knew what to say.

He turned to Schwaiger. "Make some coffee – and go to Schmidt's and get some cakes."

"Of course, sir. This *is* a happy occasion." He smiled at me warmly. "Welcome home."

"Thank you."

"Franz, come in and sit down," said my father. "I had no idea you were coming."

"I wanted to surprise you."

"We'll surprise your mother and Johanna as well, then – if old Schwaiger hasn't told the whole town by then! But how are you?"

"Fine. And all of you?"

"We're well enough. Your mother's been worried sick about you but it can't be helped. I… er… I'm very proud of you. As you know I didn't approve of your enlisting, but you seem to be making a good job of it and I've come to believe that it was the right thing to do. I'm sure there'll soon be further promotion, and more ribbons to go with that one."

"Oh, I don't know about that."

"You still haven't told us the full story of how you earned it."

"It was just as I wrote in my letter. I was more surprised than anyone when I got it."

"It was very brave of you to go back for him."

I was beginning to feel embarrassed. Fortunately Schwaiger saved me by coming in with the coffee and cakes. He'd bought hazelnut cake for me – my favourite – and I was touched that he'd remembered. It wasn't quite as good as it had been before the war – there wasn't much cream – but it still tasted far better than anything the Army could provide.

My back was itching and I rubbed it against my chair. So much for no lice! I'd been deloused before leaving the Front but it hadn't taken the eggs long to hatch out.

"Papa, I should have told you before – I've got lice."

His face changed and I could see him beginning to itch – or to think he was itching.

"Well… er… there's no reason why we shouldn't put up

with some of your discomforts, is there? Probably do us all good."

"It's just I don't know what Mama will say."

We both knew how she liked everything kept. More than one maid had been sacked for not cleaning thoroughly enough.

"Isn't there anything we can do about it?" he asked.

I shook my head and told him some of the ways we tried to rid ourselves of the bloody things – I didn't mention burning off our pubic hair, though. That would have been a bit much for him.

"They always come back," I finished, "whatever we do."

"I see. Well, it seems we'll just have to accept it. Now, tell me what it's really like out there. Your letters said hardly anything."

The reality of war didn't belong in that quiet office. I was an intruder from a strange, violent world, and I didn't know what to say. I told him about the routine of rest, support and front line, and a bit about the mud and the difficulty of repairing the trenches when it rained.

"Franz, I know you want to spare your mother anything unpleasant, but I'm not a child. This isn't a large town. Many of our young men are dead or injured." He looked at me in an odd, kind way. "Some of your school friends have fallen: Stefan Krüger, Klaus Ullrich, Hans-Jürgen Schmidt."

I looked at the grime that lingered under my fingernails. We'd gone through school together, played together, had boys' adventures that had seemed so big at the time.

"You must understand," he continued, "that we can't place their deaths in any sort of context. It's not as if they died of an illness or in an accident in the street. We know they died for our country, of course, but we can't imagine what happened to them."

You don't want to, I thought, Anton vivid before my eyes, the light of the flare brilliant.

"And the officers' letters don't say much. Bruno Krüger said the letter he received about Stefan said almost nothing."

"Could I have some more coffee, please?"

"Yes, of course."

"Papa, I understand what you're saying, but it all gets very confused. You lose track of people, you don't see what happens to them, and then later you hear they're dead. I'm sure the officers tell the truth as far as they know it."

Like hell they do. No one could write, Dear Frau Döpfner, your son was disembowelled by an English shell and screamed all afternoon...

I wished Papa would change the subject.

"I'm not sure we're told the truth by anyone," he went on. "Certainly not by the newspapers. For example, Langemarck. I read the statement from the High Command—"

"About the French positions which were overrun by our men on 10th November? Yes, I read that too."

And I'd been completely unable to relate it to my own experience. For a start we'd gone in on 23rd October, and our opponents were the English. The High Command could have been telling the truth, but I found it hard to imagine after what had happened to us.

"I've also heard that it was a massacre – and I don't know which to believe. You were there. You can tell me."

That lunatic singing advance, Karl and I pinned down for hours, Anton screaming and screaming until I wished he would just die, the remnants of the Company fighting desperately in the bitter days that followed...

I looked around my father's safe, comfortable office, at the legal books lining the shelves, at the leather-topped desk. The closest he'd ever come to violent death was defending a murderer ten years earlier. It would be like describing colour to a blind man.

The silence lengthened.

"I'm sorry, Papa, I can't tell you what you want to know.

I only saw one small part of it. We certainly didn't take the positions we attacked, not on the first day or on any other, but I don't know what anyone else did."

"But… Franz, you say you didn't take the positions, so what did happen? And were you all singing, as it said in the paper?"

I poured myself another cup of coffee. I didn't want one but neither did I want to answer.

"With us, it wasn't the French. It was the English. They're professional soldiers. We'd had six weeks' training. There was no way we were going to take anything from them."

There was a long pause and I thought I was off the hook.

"It said in the paper that so much blood had been spilled that the fields were steaming," he said.

The curious mist rose into the air.

"Why's it going up?" I asked.

"Because it's warm," Bauer said. "Hot air rises."

I stared at my coffee. A wisp of steam rose gently from it and I felt suddenly sick.

"Franz?"

"Sorry… er… there really isn't any more to say about it. Can we talk about something else?"

So much for telling them the truth. I just can't get the words out. If I survive, I'll write about it, one day, after the war, or maybe my parents will get my diary published – if I can manage to write in the bloody thing.

"Look, Papa, I'm starving, and I'd really like to see Mama and Johanna."

"Yes, of course you would. I'll drive you home now. I can spare a couple of hours today."

It was like being in a triumphal procession. Papa owned one of only four cars in our little town and everyone turned and stared as we passed. I felt like royalty.

The whole town will know I'm home.

He pulled into the drive and I got out of the car, feeling oddly detached. I'd lived in that house most of my life. I dimly remembered us moving there when I was five, and even when I'd gone to Heidelberg it had still been home. Now I stood looking at it, wondering whether I'd ever be at home anywhere again.

Papa opened the door and I followed him inside. The strange, alienated feeling wouldn't leave me. *This isn't how I thought it would feel... Maybe it'll be different when I see Mama and Johanna.*

They weren't in the drawing room.

"I expect they're in the garden," said Papa. "It's such a lovely day."

I followed him through the French windows. My mother and sister were sitting on the bench under the chestnut tree, sewing, the dappled sunlight shining on their pale summer dresses.

The feeling of dislocation choked me. *You're sitting here so peacefully and I've just come from the slaughterhouse of Europe. Men are killing each other and you're sitting here like this—*

"Look who's here!" Papa shouted, the triumph in his voice jarring.

Mama dropped her sewing, and she and Johanna stared at me as if I were a ghost.

"Hello, Mama, Johanna..." My voice sounded odd and flat. *Maybe I am a ghost, only I haven't realised it yet. How do you know if you're dead?*

Johanna recovered first. "Franz! Oh Franz!"

She leapt up, ran across the grass and flung her arms round me. I hugged her back and the strangeness started to fade.

I had a sudden, unwelcome thought and broke out of her embrace.

"Johanna, I'd better tell you – I've got lice."

"You WHAT?! You pig, you did that on purpose! I've got them now, I know I have!"

She burst into tears and ran into the house.

My mother was beside herself.

"Johanna! How *dare* you speak to your brother like that! *Come back here at once!*"

"It's all right, Mama, she can't help it," I said.

It was never discussed, but we all knew she became completely impossible every month.

Just my luck to come home at the wrong time. She'll probably be like that for the entire week.

"You'd better not touch me either," I added.

"Don't be silly," said Mama, and put her arms round me and held me close. For the first time I understood the wounded who called for their mothers.

"It's good to be home," I said.

She took hold of my shoulders and studied my face. I smiled but something she saw put a shadow in her eyes.

Does everything I've done show? I wondered. *Do I have the mark of Cain on my forehead?*

"You must be hungry," she said. "I'll get Klara to make you some food."

"Thanks. I'm starving."

"Go and have a bath and get changed. Leave your uniform in the bath. Klara will boil it later and that should get rid of the vermin."

I went up to my room, wishing I could feel at home. *It's bound to feel strange at first*, I told myself. *You just need to settle in.*

The bath was wonderful. Utterly wonderful. It was hot and I had it all to myself – and yet I missed the laughter and joking of the others. I hadn't been on my own for months.

What are you all doing? Is Karl somewhere in No Man's

Land, carefully hidden, his face smeared with mud? And what about Kurt and Alfred?

Once again I found I missed Karl, to a quite absurd extent. *No point worrying about him – you just have to hope he'll be there when you get back. Now stop thinking about the war.*

I'm going to have to get some new clothes, I thought as I got dressed. The first two shirts I tried were too tight across the chest and shoulders and I realised how much muscle I'd put on. And my trousers were slightly loose at the waist – I'd never been fat but I'd clearly got leaner – and a centimetre or so short in the leg.

I didn't know I was still growing. I'll have to ask Alfred about that.

I looked in the mirror and for a moment I didn't recognise myself. I kept a small mirror in my pack for shaving, but this was the first time I'd really been able to study myself since the training camp, months ago.

Although I'd washed and shaved there still seemed to be a layer of grime on my face, as if it had soaked into my pores. There were lines round my eyes that had never been there before, and my eyes themselves had a hardness that was totally unfamiliar. I tried to remember what I used to look like, but failed. I turned away from the mirror and went downstairs.

Johanna had recovered from her tantrum. "Sorry, Franz," she said awkwardly.

"It doesn't matter," I said.

In the past I would have teased her mercilessly. *How is it that the war's made me more tolerant of her moods? Surely it should be the opposite?*

All three of them bombarded me with questions, most of which I couldn't answer or wanted to avoid.

"Do you get enough to eat?" asked Mama. "And is it good food?"

I wondered what she'd think of the standard Army rations. Infantryman's fodder, Karl called it, which was about right.

"We get plenty of food," I said. "You can see that—"

"Yes," Papa interrupted. "You've filled out very nicely."

"And as for quality, the cooks do their best but it doesn't compare with your cooking. What's for dinner, by the way?"

I was only partly trying to change the subject. I was still starving, in spite of the snack Klara had made me. I seemed to be perpetually ravenous.

"Roast pork... And where do you sleep? Is it clean? And what about washing and... er... hygiene and so on?"

Oh, for God's sake! She's going to want to know what I wipe my arse with next! I answered all her questions as patiently as I could, not suspecting that worse was to come.

"And what's Karl doing now? Is his leg better?"

"Yes, it's fine. He's back with us."

"Has he been promoted as well?" asked Papa.

"No."

"I'm surprised. I'd have thought he'd have been the first to be chosen, with his background."

Oh, God, don't start that. I was trying not to worry about him, and the last thing I wanted to hear was one of Papa's diatribes about class and how the Junkers were thick barbarians, and so on and bloody on.

But hasn't Karl's background led to his becoming a sniper? That was one thing I really didn't want to tell them. I had no idea how they'd take it. *They'll probably see it as cold-blooded murder – after all, it looks that way to some of us.*

"There are some very interesting pictures in today's paper," Papa said. "I'll just find them for you."

I didn't want to look at them. We all laughed at the photos in the papers because it was always glaringly obvious that 'the front line' was at least a kilometre further back. The trenches were always far too neat, and everyone was far too clean and doing things that no one in the real front line would even think of doing in daylight.

"Here we are," he said. "There's a very interesting article about snipers."

He held out the paper to me. I glanced at it and couldn't help smiling at the picture.

"He's never in the front line," I said. "They're really careful, believe me. They hide themselves very well. No one just sticks his head up like that."

"You've seen them, then?" Papa asked.

"Of course. All the time."

"I hope they'll never ask you to do that," said Mama. "It's not very nice."

Not very nice? What does she think war is?

I laughed. "No chance. I don't shoot well enough."

"But you're a very good shot," Papa said.

"Not compared to them I'm not. You should see what Karl can do."

Shit – I didn't mean to say that. It just slipped out.

"You mean Karl's a sniper now?" Johanna asked.

"Yes – but don't worry, there's no chance of me doing it. It's far too bloody dangerous anyway."

"Language, Franz!" Papa was suddenly severe and I wanted to laugh.

"I think it's horrible, just shooting men like that," said my mother. "I don't like to think of you having to shoot anyone."

I almost dropped my glass. I felt a sudden desperate need for a cigarette, and fumbled in my pockets for my case and lighter, trying to buy time to work out what to say.

Johanna came unexpectedly to my rescue.

"I'm sure Franz doesn't want to talk about the war any more," she said. "Why don't we tell him what we've been doing?"

"Yes, do," I said with relief. "You must have lots of news you haven't given me."

They hadn't. It was all unbearably trivial but it was better than being asked questions that I couldn't answer.

I was looking forward to coming home so much. I never imagined it would be so difficult.

Dinner was delicious, anyway, and Papa opened some of his best wine. I began to relax.

It's just a matter of readjusting. I must have changed a lot, and it can't be easy for them either.

After dinner Papa lit a cigar and leaned back in his armchair, blowing smoke at the ceiling. *That smells really good*, I thought.

"I'd like a cigar, please, Papa."

He looked at me as if he was about to refuse. Then he said, "Well, I suppose you're grown up now," and offered me the box.

Grown up? I've experienced parts of life – and death – that you'll never know about. You might be my father but I feel a century older than you. How I envy Karl his family of soldiers.

"Thanks."

"Would you like a brandy to go with it?"

"Yes, please!"

The brandy went down very well but the ration was two small glasses. I wasn't sure whether Papa was putting the brakes on me or whether he was trying to make the bottle last. It seemed rather rude to ask for more and anyway I was more tired than I realised after my long journey. My eyes were almost closing.

"Time for bed, I think, Franz," said Mama.

She was looking at me with such affection that I felt rather uncomfortable, but at the same time I resented being told to go to bed.

I get ordered around all the bloody time in the pissing Army and then I come home and get ordered around here as well. Then I realised how happy it made her to have me at home and to be able to tell me what to do.

"Yes, I think it is," I said, and went dutifully upstairs.

My room was very quiet. I undressed, got into bed and lay staring at the ceiling, suddenly wide awake. My bed was far too soft and I couldn't get comfortable, no matter what I did. And it was far too quiet – no one snored, or muttered in his sleep.

Strange how we adapt. The first couple of nights in the training camp I couldn't sleep because of the racket the others made, and now I can't sleep because they're not here.

I tossed and turned, and in the end took my quilt and pillow and lay on the floor. Even then the pillow was much too soft, but eventually I managed to fall asleep – and then Krypke was bleeding to death in front of me and I woke with a start, covered in sweat, my heart pounding.

At first I didn't know where I was and my heart raced faster, and then I realised I was at home. *I hope I didn't shout out,* I thought when I'd calmed down a bit. *I don't want them to know about the nightmares. Everyone has them, but I don't want to have to explain.*

It was getting light before I managed to get back to sleep, and when I woke the sun was streaming in through the curtains. I stretched lazily. No need to rush, no duties, no dawn stand-to.

I'm safe, I thought suddenly. *All the time I'm here nothing can happen to me. And I'm warm and dry, and I don't itch. All I need now is a nice, soft girl beside me – or preferably underneath me. I wonder if I will get my leg over while I'm here...*

Eventually hunger drove me out of bed and downstairs. It was well past the normal time for breakfast in our house and I wandered into the drawing room, wondering if there was anything to eat.

"Did you sleep well, dear?" asked Mama.

"Yes, fine thanks," I lied. *If I did shout then you didn't hear me. Good.*

"I told Klara not to clear away until you'd had breakfast. Just ring for more coffee."

There was quite a spread in the dining room and I stuffed myself. I'd forgotten what really good fresh food tasted like. But the coffee didn't taste the same as the brews we made and Karl wasn't there to share it.

I hope he's all right. I'd better get that chocolate he wants today, before I forget.

The day passed very slowly. I tried to read but nothing interested me much. Two things filled my mind: the war, which I didn't want to think about, and how I was going to get hold of a girl before I went back.

I had no idea where to start. I'd never been with a girl in my home town.

That evening the phone rang. It was for me.

"Who on earth can that be?" I asked. All my friends were at the Front.

"Hey, Franz! How're you doing?"

"Chris! What the hell are you doing here?"

"Same as you. My old man saw you in your old man's car. How about we meet up?"

"Tomorrow?"

You'll know where I can find a willing girl. You were the first in our class to lose your virginity. My blood practically clotted when you told me about it.

"Deal. I'll call round at six and we can go and have a few beers and some grub."

I don't think my parents were too pleased, but they couldn't really object to my seeing an old school friend, especially as so many of them seemed to be dead.

He was ten minutes late, as always. I'd never known Chris to be on time for anything.

"You'll be late for your own funeral, Sevening!" I said as I opened the door. That was what old Franck used to say each time Chris was late for class.

"That's just what I'm hoping!" he said with a grin. "Keep dodging the old bugger with the scythe! I hope you're thirsty!"

"You bet I am!"

The beer was cool and fresh and went down very well. That was something I'd really missed – good German beer. We didn't get it often enough – or enough of it.

Chris chattered away as he always had, but he had the same look in his eyes that I'd seen in the mirror.

We've all got it – it's just I didn't notice at the Front because we're all the same. It's the look Karl's brother Friedrich had when he spoke to us in the training camp, the look you get when you've only stayed alive by killing the other fellow first, more times than you can count.

I was beginning to understand the sadness in Mama's face. *It can't be helped*, I thought, and put it out of my mind.

When he paused for breath I said quietly, "Chris, where do we find girls round here? I'm dying for a fuck – a proper one, with someone who actually wants it."

He looked at me in mock horror. "My, you have changed! What happened to Mr Pure and Righteous?"

"He learned to wait in a queue for the next available tart… I was never that pure anyway – I just didn't know how to get a girl into bed, and I still don't really… but I tell you, I'm sick of paying. I want it for free before I go back."

"Got to be done… There's a dance hall not far from here. We won't have too much competition these days. Drink up and let's get going."

When we got to the dance hall I recognised the name – it

was a place Papa had warned me against many times, "a hotbed of vice and corruption". I'd been very tempted to go there when I was at school but I'd been too afraid of someone seeing me and telling him. Now I couldn't care less.

There were far more girls than men.

This looks promising.

"Go for one who's by herself," Chris said. "Try that one over there, by the pillar."

The girl was rather plain and slightly plump, wearing a pink dress that didn't really suit her.

"She's not very pretty."

He rolled his eyes.

"You're not going to marry her. You're only going to fuck her. And the plain ones are always really grateful. She probably goes like a rabbit. Go on. I bet you five marks you get your leg over."

"Done."

I walked slowly over to the girl. "Would you like a drink?"

"Ooh, I'd love a beer," she said in a working-class accent.

For God's sake, Franz, don't be such a bloody snob! You're not going to marry her...

I handed her the glass with the best smile I could manage.

"What's your name?"

"Helga. What's yours?"

"Franz."

"Why aren't you in the Army?"

"I am. I'm on leave." She looked sceptical. "No one chooses this haircut, does he?"

"No. No one in 'is right mind, any'ow." She giggled.

The band was playing a waltz.

"Like to dance?"

"Ooh, yes."

She was light on her feet and followed me perfectly, her body moulding itself to mine. I was starting to get hard and wanted to press her close to me, but decided that that would be crude and premature. A couple more dances, then a walk in the park. That should do it.

The park was deserted apart from courting couples. We strolled and then kissed, and then I steered her into the bushes. She hesitated for a moment but I persisted and soon had my hands wherever I wanted them. I started to pull her drawers down.

"You will be careful, won't you?" she said.

Of course I bloody will. You think I want some horrible disease?

"Don't worry. I've got a condom."

Horrible thick bloody rubber thing – but I daren't not use it. God alone knew where she'd been.

"I mean, it being my first time and all."

"Your *what*?"

"I 'ad a fiancé. 'E was killed last August."

I felt as if she'd thrown a bucket of cold water over me. I took my hand out of her drawers and lowered her skirt.

"Helga, this isn't the way to do it."

"Just get on with it. I'm bloody sick of being a virgin."

But I couldn't. Desire had died. In some strange way I felt I was betraying her dead fiancé and I couldn't bring myself to touch her again.

"This isn't right. Not like this, with a stranger in the park. Wait until you find another man you care about."

Her face changed abruptly and a look of contempt came into her eyes.

"'Ark at you. So bleedin' pompous, like some bloody preacher. 'Oo the fuck d'you think you are, anyway?"

I didn't wait to hear any more. *What a waste of a bloody evening*, I thought as I went reluctantly back to the dance hall.

I don't know why I'm bothering. I don't want to try again. I just want to find Chris and get the hell out of here.

I found him easily enough, standing by the wall looking very fed up. His face lit up when he saw me.

"At least one of us got a bit!" he said triumphantly.

"Er… actually I didn't…"

"What?"

I told him what had happened and he stared at me.

"You're off your fucking head. Well, if you won't fuck her I will. Where is she?"

"I left her in the park. She's probably gone home."

"Terrific. Fucking terrific."

"No luck, then?"

"No. Not even your cast-offs. Oh, sod it! Let's go to the whorehouse. That's a certainty, anyway."

I didn't want to pay – it was too much like Belgium – but I did need a fuck and there didn't seem to be any other way I was going to get one.

At least the whorehouse was a lot more civilised than the soldiers' brothels. There wasn't a queue, and I got to choose between three girls who were rather less jaded than the Belgian tarts. I felt rather disgusted with myself afterwards, but I was twenty and had no idea how much longer I might live.

I had to wait for Chris and my self-disgust intensified as I sat there. By the time he appeared all I wanted to do was get completely hammered. And we did, in a grotty little bar, drowning ourselves in beer and schnapps until we could hardly walk.

I wished him all the best and staggered home. I tripped up the steps to the front door and swore, then found that for some strange reason my key refused to go into the lock. Finally I managed to open the door and fell over the threshold.

The hallway was in darkness.

That's a bit off. They could have left the bloody light on for me.

The drawing room door opened and the blaze of light half-blinded me.

"Franz! What time do you call this?" Papa was furious. "Your mother's been worried sick about you!"

I burst out laughing. "Why?" *What on earth could happen to me here?* "Wha's problem?"

"And you're drunk!"

"Course'm bloody drunk. Been drinkin' all evening."

As I walked across the hall the floor swung evilly and I staggered against the wall.

"The state of you! What have you to say for yourself?"

I couldn't say anything. I was laughing so hard that tears were running down my face.

"Chris'n'I had few drinks, thassall." *And I fucked a whore, too.*

"Go to bed!"

"Yes, sir!"

I saluted, tried to climb the stairs, tripped, grabbed the handrail and dragged myself up to my room, still laughing helplessly. I fell onto my bed without bothering to undress, and then I stopped laughing because the room had started spinning.

I lay very still, hoping I wasn't going to be sick. A black wave broke over my head and carried me down and down...

Where the fuck am I? And why is someone burying an axe in my head?

My mouth felt as though a rat had died in it. After a while I remembered the dance hall, and the park, and the tart, but most of what followed was blurred. The only thing that was clear was Papa meeting me in the hall and my being almost incoherent.

"Chris and I had a few drinks and I fucked a whore."

I sat bolt upright. *Oh, Jesus Christ! Did I say that?*

I wasn't afraid of Papa any more, but I knew how upset he'd be if he knew about the tarts. It would ruin my leave completely, probably ruin our relationship for ever, and that would half-kill Mama.

I got up and washed hurriedly. I didn't want any breakfast but I had to know what had happened.

"Good morning, Mama, Papa, Johanna."

"Franz, dear, I was so worried about you last night. I had no idea you were going to be so late."

"I'm sorry, Mama. We didn't intend to be, but one thing led to another."

"You mean one drink led to another," Papa said. His tone wasn't as severe as I'd been expecting. "Well, I suppose you have to let off steam when you can."

Thank Christ for that. He doesn't know about the rest of it. He can't do. There's no way he'd take it so calmly.

"I'm sorry you were worried. It just never occurred to me that you would be. I mean, what can happen to me here?"

Mama looked at me as if she weren't sure what to say.

"There's been a lot of trouble recently," she said rather reluctantly. "Robberies at knifepoint, that sort of thing. Some of the streets aren't safe after dark."

"And the police never seem to catch them," Papa added. "I sometimes wonder what the Government does with my taxes – apart from waging this stupid, unnecessary war, that is."

"Josef, no politics, please. Franz has to go back in four days' time."

Thank you very fucking much. I was trying to forget about that. And there was something she hadn't realised.

I hesitated. *You'd better tell them now, Franz...*

"Mama, er... it's three days' time."

Her face fell. "But you've got ten days!"

"Including travelling. It took me two days to get here and

it'll take me two to get back. And I have to be back on the last day of my leave, so I'm there for the next morning."

"But… I thought…" Her eyes filled with tears. "It's such a short time. We haven't seen you for months and—"

She broke off. I knew what the next words would have been. *And we might never see you again.*

"And it'll be months before they give you leave again," she finished.

"Yes, probably." I didn't know what else to say.

"You've only just got here," Johanna said. "I hate the Army and *I hate this horrible war!*"

She burst into tears and ran out of the room. *Oh shit. I was wondering when she'd lose control again. She was doing rather well till now.*

"Oh, dear," sighed Mama. "I don't know what we're going to do with her. She seems to be getting worse."

"It's just one of those things," I said.

"It's not a fit subject for the drawing room," Papa said. "Your mother and I will talk about Johanna later."

I bet you don't, I thought. I got up, went upstairs and knocked on her door.

"Johanna."

"What?"

"Open the door… Come on, Sis, let me in."

I heard footsteps and then she opened the door slowly, her face streaked with tears. I shut the door behind me and put my arms round her.

"I don't like the war much either," I said quietly. "But it's my duty."

She looked at me.

"It must be horrible," she said. "I don't want to read the paper, because they write about the men who get killed and wounded, and it makes me feel sick. And then when it says how many of the enemy have been killed I just think that they're just men like you are and I get so scared for you."

"So do I, Sis."

"And Mama doesn't want to think about what you have to do. What does she think would happen to you if you didn't shoot them?"

I sighed. "Look, let's not talk about the war any more. There's nothing either of us can do about it, so let's just try to enjoy the next few days. And if you want to help me when I'm there, then keep writing. Even if you've got nothing to say, just send me letters, and tell the parents the same… Wash your face and we'll go downstairs."

The days passed slowly and yet the end of my leave seemed to be hurtling towards me. I tried not to count down but it was impossible. Three more days, two more…

Only two more meals at home now, I thought as we sat round the dinner table that evening. *Only one more full day here, then I'll have to go back, maybe for good.*

So many men had fallen and I could see no reason why I should be spared.

That thought wouldn't leave me for much of the night and I tossed and turned restlessly, unable to sleep for more than a few minutes at a time.

Johanna and I spent a lot of my last day in town, partly because there were things I needed, but more to pass the time. I couldn't face the thought of sitting in the house all day.

I bought Karl's chocolate, and she insisted on buying him a bar as well.

"You don't have to," I said.

"I know that, stupid. But he's your friend and I like him, and he's… Well, you said it's very dangerous, what he's doing now, so… Don't tell the parents, will you?"

"That you're buying presents for my disreputable friend? Don't worry."

"Is he as bad as Papa says?"

"Maybe even worse. Rather depends on *what* Papa says... I think you're sweet on him."

She went scarlet. "Of course I'm not. You really are stupid, Franz."

"Don't I get any chocolate, then?"

"No, you don't. You get a pair of gloves."

"But it's summer."

"No, really nice leather ones."

"They'll be really useful. Thank you."

Most of what I bought was for the others: cigarettes, cigars, sweets – small luxuries that would make life in the trenches a little more pleasant.

I'd thought long and hard about what to buy Karl and had decided to get him what I most wanted for myself. Something to keep with us, just in case the worst happened and we ended up like Anton.

We stopped for coffee and cakes.

"Sis, can I leave you here for a while?" I said when I'd finished. "I just need to go to the pharmacy."

"Yes, of course. Are you feeling ill or something?"

"No. Nothing like that. I won't be long."

The pharmacist seemed to think my request for morphine pills entirely reasonable but looked at me sideways when I asked for a second packet.

"I hope you're not thinking of doing away with yourself."

"They're for my friend," I said.

"Even so." I could hear him thinking he'd heard that one before.

"He's a sniper. He often works alone in No Man's Land. If he gets injured we won't be able to get to him for hours."

"Yes, I see… And your friend's name, for my records?"

"Karl von Leussow. Thank you."

I bought a box of Venus condoms as well, and on impulse got another for Karl.

The pharmacist raised his eyebrows.

"Seems our brave boys keep themselves busy out of the line as well as in it. Well, at least you're not likely to catch anything with one of these."

"I sincerely hope not." *Not that I'm likely to survive long enough to die of syphilis.*

"What did you buy, then?" Johanna asked. I think she'd got a bit impatient waiting for me.

"None of your business… If I'd wanted you to know I wouldn't have gone by myself, would I?"

She poked her tongue out at me. "Secrets, secrets. I'm so sick of grown-ups' secrets. I'm sixteen, you know, not six."

"Yes, well, some things are private. There are things you don't tell me about, aren't there?"

She blushed furiously. "You're not supposed to talk about that."

"So don't ask me questions, then!"

My parents laid on a splendid last evening meal for me, but I couldn't sleep in spite of Papa's fine wine and brandy. All I could think was that my leave was over and that I might never have another. I lay staring at the ceiling, trying not to feel sorry for myself.

At the same time I was impatient to be gone. The hours dragged until morning, and I was up and dressed well before I needed to be.

I looked at myself in the mirror. When I'd first been issued with my uniform it had seemed too big for me, although it was the right size. It was more that my student self had not filled clothes made for a man. Now I saw a soldier looking back at me, a corporal with the ribbon of the Iron Cross, Second Class through his buttonhole. I had aged immeasurably in the space of a few months.

Is that the right way to grow up? I wondered, and turned away from the question because it was pointless.

We all went to the station together and I took my leave of my family with a heavy heart.

Last time, I left in such high spirits, off on my big adventure. Now I know what war is, and I can only pray I'll come back.

No use thinking about that. I'll write up my diary. It's been a while.

I hadn't realised just how long it had been. I'd written hardly anything about the spring fighting – and doing so turned out to be more difficult than I'd expected. *Just make notes*, I told myself, *then you'll be able to flesh them out later.*

Later? When the fuck will that be?

As the train crossed the Rhine the song came into my head: "Fast stands and true the Watch, the Watch on the Rhine," and suddenly we were marching along a Belgian road in the autumn, on our way to meet the enemy for the first time.

Most of those men are dead or mutilated now.

I hope to Christ Karl's all right. All through my leave I'd tried not to worry, but every time I thought about him it was with a level of concern that surprised and slightly disturbed me.

You're not his keeper, I told myself with irritation. *He'll survive or not with or without your fretting.*

As we crossed into Belgium I had a stupid feeling that it was the last time – that I would never make the journey again.

I'll be killed and they'll bury me in some bloody mass grave – if they pick me up at all – and this time next year I'll just be bones...

I brought myself up sharply. *If you start thinking like that it'll come true, you idiot. You'll be careless and get a bullet through your head. You have to believe you'll survive. Think about something else.*

I hope we're in rest. Going straight to that bleak wasteland will be just too bloody depressing.

We weren't in rest. When I reported to Regimental HQ after a long trudge from the station, I was told that the Fourth was in the front line.

Fucking wonderful. Though perhaps it's better just to jump in and swim.

"The First is in support and you can go up with them tonight," said the Adjutant.

"Very good, sir."

One of the telephone operators told me where they were. Hardly anyone was out and about apart from a tall, thin corporal. He told me the comms trench couldn't be used in daylight.

"There's a bit where it's a bit open, see, and some fuckin' Tommy sniper's got it marked. Got two blokes the other day, both stone fuckin' dead. Took the second one 'alf the day to die, mind. Anyway, reckon it's time one of ours dealt with 'im."

I can guess who'll get that job, and it'll be bloody dangerous.

Not good to hear that the Tommies have more snipers now. We'll all have to be twice as bloody careful.

The idea that I could be shot dead at any moment made my back hairs stand on end.

Murdering bastards, I thought – and then remembered that my best mate was one of them.

"Anyway, you can come up with our carryin' party tonight… and bein' as there's fuck all to do right now, I'm goin' to brew up. Want one?"

"Yes, thanks a lot."

"Everyone else is 'avin' a bit of a kip. Waste of daylight 'fyou ask me."

After an hour or so I realised that 'everyone else' was probably in hiding. He rabbited on about his peacetime occupation, bicycle racing.

I heard all about his fears that his muscles were wasting away through lack of riding, about how difficult it was to keep from getting fat with so much inactivity.

"Course my big ambition's always been to win the Tour de France, show those Frenchies a German can ride, but now I'll never do it cos by the time the fuckin' war's over I'll be too fuckin' old and there'll be all those young men with strong legs and no belly –"

If he had a belly then Christ alone knows where he kept it. To my eyes he was in need of a few good meals.

"– and who haven't been mouldering in the trenches, and I won't stand a fuckin' chance."

Then he started talking about bicycles – frames and brakes and God knows what else. I glazed over completely.

If I'd waited for a pause I'd still be listening to him.

"Thanks very much for the coffee," I interrupted, "but I'm really tired after the journey. Is there somewhere I could get a kip?"

"Yeah, course, mate." He looked at me with disappointment. "Didn't 'ave you down as a daylight-waster… Few bike rides, that's what you need. Give you a bit of go."

"I'll try it sometime." *The fuck I will, if it means meeting more like you.*

He pointed me in the direction of a barn. As I went in a number of heads turned towards me and I felt an air of relief, as if everyone had breathed out at once.

"Where's Diehl?"

"Sorry, Sarge, I don't know who Diehl is."

"Tall, thin bloke. Talks about bikes all the time."

I started laughing. "I'd guessed you were all in hiding."

"Shut up, for fuck's sake," said another voice. "He thinks we're asleep!"

"I keep telling him to belt up," the sergeant said, "but he always starts up again."

"Maybe you should put him up for a bike messenger's job."

"We're trying, believe me. Trouble is, he shuts up when the officers are around and they don't believe how bad it is."

I was weary of talking. "Is there somewhere I can get my head down for a bit?"

"Yeah – over there."

I curled up in the corner and the next thing I knew someone was shaking my shoulder.

"Come on, mate! We're setting out soon."

They gave me the rum to carry. *That'll make me popular, if nothing else does*, I thought. The jar was heavy and awkward, and after a couple of hundred metres I remembered why carrying the rum had never been my idea of fun.

I managed to avoid Diehl for the first hour or so, and after that we had to move in silence so even he had to shut up.

I suppose I should feel sorry for him. Poor bugger's dreams are all turning to dust... but at least he's not dust himself yet, unlike so many. I couldn't feel much sympathy for someone who was still in one piece.

The first man I saw when we reached the line was Braun, looking just as solid as ever.

I don't believe they can kill you.

"Welcome back, Becker! Good leave?"

"Yes, thanks, Sergeant Major. What's the news?"

"Bugger all. Been dead quiet. We lost a couple of blokes but no one from your section. Goldblum got a scratch in his arm but didn't have to go back, and your mates are all here as well. So it's just like home."

I looked at the planking and the sandbags, at the mud in the bottom of the trench gleaming in the moonlight.

"Not what my mother would think!"

"No, well, that's women for you... Your section's out working on the wire – not much point you joining them now so you might as well get your head down for a bit. Oh, and we've given the snipers a dugout so they can sleep when they want to. The Tommies have got themselves a bloody sharp one."

"So I heard... The rest of us are still in holes in the wall, then?"

"Same as ever – all the comforts of home!"

I stowed my kit in one of the alcoves below the parapet. It had the usual smell of damp earth and though I could have done with more sleep I decided to leave it till later. I always had to be bloody knackered to sleep in those holes.

Karl might be awake. There are only a couple of hours to dawn.

I hesitated, not wanting to disturb men I knew needed a good rest, then moved the gas blanket carefully aside.

A single candle gave a dim light. Three men lay wrapped in grey blankets, dead to the world.

Karl was sitting propped against the timbered wall, his eyes closed. I stood looking at him, powerfully aware of the fragility of life.

His eyes flew open and he reached for his rifle.

"Karl!" I hissed. "It's me!"

He relaxed and grinned, and then laid his finger across his lips. None of the others had stirred.

He pointed to the entrance and followed me out. When we got outside I saw he had his rifle and cape with him.

It's so good to see you. "Sorry I woke you."

He smiled warmly and it was as if I'd never been away.

"You didn't really. I was just thinking it was time to get

moving and I must have dozed off... How are you, you old bastard? And how are the girls back home?"

He hung the cape round himself and blended almost instantly into the planking. The moon had disappeared, and in the weird light of the flares I could see only his face. That too began to disappear as he smeared it with mud.

"Oh, well... you know..." There was no way I could tell him about Helga.

"What's the time?"

"Three."

"Shit! I didn't realise it was so late. I'll have to get moving. Look, you can tell me all about it when I get back – and I mean *all* about it!"

All I saw were his eyes and his teeth. A second later there was one of those eerie moments of total darkness. When the next flare went up I thought he'd taken advantage of it and gone.

You could have said something – and then I saw his shadow. With his hood up he was more like a wraith than a living man.

He put his foot on the ladder, then paused and turned back towards me.

"Oh, Franz – be careful. The English have found some fellow who's really rather good. We're trying but we haven't found him yet – he's too bloody clever."

It was as if some oracle were speaking to me, a voice from a barely-seen priest in some strange temple, and I shivered.

That's the third warning I've had. Best pay attention.

He climbed over the top and disappeared. I went to the periscope but couldn't see him anywhere.

Very good – but you have to stay hidden when it's full daylight and I hope to Christ you get it right. You'll be out there a bloody long time, with everyone looking for you. And if they see you...

I didn't want to think about that.

I went back to the hole and tried to get some sleep before

the dawn stand-to, but my thoughts followed Karl out into No Man's Land as if I were creeping beside him, searching for a place to spend the day.

How can you do it? Hide out there all day, waiting and watching? Knowing that they'll kill you if they spot you and that no one can help you if you get hit, that you'll die alone?

It's no use, I thought. *There's nothing I can do… You stupid bastard, Franz. You forgot to give him the bloody pills. They're bugger all use to him in your monkey, aren't they?*

By halfway through the day I'd almost forgotten I'd been on leave. Alfred was pleased to see me, and Kurt welcomed me back sincerely but with due reserve.

For some reason my section seemed glad I was back. Wolter had been acting in my absence and I had a strong feeling he hadn't made a very good fist of it.

Horn was nowhere to be seen.

"Where's Horn?" I asked Alfred.

He pulled a face. "Got taken off to the Knights' Castle."

Slang for the hospital for venereal disease.

"Shit." *Poor fellow – he's a bad lot but I wouldn't wish the pox on anyone.*

"Well, that's what you get for fucking whores, isn't it? Fancy a brew?"

"Thanks." *And for the change of subject. I hope those condoms work…* "When's your course?"

"Don't know yet. Probably next month."

"Will you come back to us or will they send you somewhere else?"

"Don't know that, either! Hope I'll be back – keep the old group together."

"I'm still here," said Kurt – or rather Meyer. "So I reckon you've got a good chance… Oh, by the way, I had a letter from Otto."

"How's he doing, sir?" I asked.

He shook his head. "Not too good, really. They don't know why but his leg won't set properly. He's had another operation and they say if it doesn't knit this time they'll have to amputate."

"Shit... You just don't think of that happening."

"Not with a young man, anyway," Alfred said. "It might be something to do with how the bone was broken – sometimes it's hard to get complicated fractures to knit."

"He says one problem is they've been chipping away at his thigh bone," Meyer continued, "and even if it mends all right this time, his right leg's about three centimetres shorter than his left."

"Well, they won't have him back, then, will they?" I said. "He'll be out of it for good."

"That's what I thought until I read the next bit. He says if it heals he'll apply for the Air Service."

"He's insane!" I burst out. "No one in his right mind would go up in one of those bloody things!"

"I agree," said Alfred. "The enemy I can deal with, but when you look at those flimsy contraptions... Not fucking likely! I don't know how the wings stay on."

"Some of the time they don't, do they?" said Meyer. "Like that one we saw a few weeks back."

We'd been watching the aerial combat, betting on the outcome, and had been appalled to see a French aircraft fall in five separate pieces, the fuselage hurtling earthwards, the wings following, turning over and over. I didn't want to imagine the terror of sitting there, waiting for the impact.

"They won't have him there either, anyway," I said. "Surely the same rules apply."

"That's what I thought," said Meyer. "But he's looked into it and apparently quite a few fellows join the fliers because they're not fit to fight on the ground any more. Otto says he'll be going to war sitting down, so it won't matter how long his legs are."

"Well, I'll believe it if it happens."

We were out mending the wire when Karl came back in. I hated wiring. I always managed to cut myself on the bloody stuff. It was vicious and there was no way of holding it that didn't leave you with a sharp edge in your hands.

I felt his presence in the darkness rather than seeing him, and I think he moved unseen and unheard past most of the others. I heard him murmur the password and then he was gone.

"Dracula going back to his coffin," Wolter muttered under his breath.

I decided I hadn't heard.

It was late in the day before Karl emerged blinking into the light.

"You see, Wolter," I said, "he can come out in daylight."

"What's that?" Karl asked.

"Wolter here thinks you look like Dracula in that cape," I said with a laugh. "And maybe he's got a point!"

I could see Wolter thinking that wasn't quite what he'd meant, but there was no way he was going to say any more. Everyone knew what he thought of snipers, anyway.

Karl held his hand out in the sunlight.

"No problem," he said with a shrug.

Then he turned to Wolter.

"Isn't there enough out here to scare you without dreaming up vampires?" he asked cheerfully.

Wolter muttered something and turned away.

"Don't wind him up," I said to Karl. "Oh, by the way, I've got a couple of things for you."

"Don't tell me – you've managed to conceal a busty blonde in your monkey!" he said as we squeezed into my cubbyhole.

"Nothing so exciting... I should have given you these straight off," I said, handing him the packet of pills, "but there wasn't time."

He studied the packet for a moment, and then looked at me with an expression I couldn't quite read.

"Thanks a lot, Franz," he said warmly. "That's a bloody good idea. I just hope I never need them."

"You and me both. I just didn't like the thought of... well, you know."

"Neither do I but—"

There was a sudden groaning from the timbers around us and dirt rained down on our heads. Karl threw me out of the hole so hard that I collided painfully with the wattle lining of the parados.

He wasn't far behind me, but one of the beams landed on his leg and he swore as I tried to pull it aside.

"Just get the weight off my leg, Franz –"

I started to stand up to get a better grip on it. Karl grabbed my belt and pulled me down, and in the same instant I heard the crack as my cap flew off.

"You fucking idiot! How long have you been out here, and you do that, *you stupid fucking cunt*!" Karl's voice was hoarse with anger, and with good reason.

I should have realised, as he had, that the parapet had collapsed. I'd come within millimetres of getting my brains blown out.

Braun and Oberleutnant Waitz came running round the traverse.

"Stop!" Karl and I shouted together. "The parapet's collapsed!"

Braun crawled towards us. "That the leg you broke, Leussow?"

"No, Sergeant Major. Not this time."

Just as well for me. If you hadn't been so quick I'd be dead.

Together we managed to free Karl from beneath the heavy post.

"Anyone hurt?" Waitz asked.

"No, sir," Karl answered. "But that English bastard's got this place marked already. He must have seen what happened, or his spotter did."

"It's going to be a bastard of a job to repair that in daylight," Waitz said. "Braun, get someone to put up a sign and get a working party together. I don't need to tell you to be very careful."

"Very good, sir. Becker, stay here and make sure everyone keeps his head down."

They went back the way they'd come.

I found my cap lying in the mud. There was a pair of holes right through the top of it, just above the cockades. I put my finger through one and spun it round.

Karl looked at me and shook his head.

"Stupid bastard," he said affectionately. "That's two beers you owe me."

"Your other presents are buried under there," I said. "Some of your favourite chocolate and... a box of Venus!"

He laughed. "Now, that's a present worth having! I'll put them to good use next time we're in rest! I'd better get busy, though. If that bugger keeps shooting we might have a chance of spotting him."

He crawled away for a council of war with Koch, Faltermeier and Taschner.

A few minutes later Braun returned with two signs saying 'Watch out! Sniper!' and I put them where I hoped they'd be conspicuous, and then joined the working party.

It was bloody awkward having to work on our hands and knees – the timbers were heavy and we couldn't get much purchase on them. As the new parapet got higher it gave us a bit more cover, but we still had to be bloody careful.

"My back's fucking killing me," said Wolter, and stretched. "*Don't –!*"

He collapsed into the bottom of the trench, face down in the mud. A split second later I heard the thump of the shot.

I bent down and lifted him out of the reddening slime. He gave a sort of grunt and collapsed, dead.

For fuck's sake, he was only working on the bloody parapet! I thought with a surge of rage. *He wasn't doing any harm to anyone, and his life's been extinguished so fucking casually.*

The sandbags behind me were spattered with blood and brains. *What a fucking waste.*

"Poor sod," said Goldblum.

Karl does this to the Tommies all the time… Shoots some poor bastard who's just minding his own business. Once the thought was in my head it wouldn't go away, but repeated itself over and over.

I bumped into him about half an hour later and didn't want to look at him – and when I did my feelings must have shown. There was a brief sadness in his eyes, replaced abruptly by a cold, hard look that said, Fuck you, then, as clearly as if he'd spoken.

I opened my mouth to say, Karl, I didn't mean it like that, but he'd already turned away.

Shit, I thought. *Shit, shit,* shit.

VIII

We managed to get the parapet back up to a reasonable height and then left off until nightfall. It was still a dangerous spot, as Nitschke discovered. He didn't duck quite low enough and went the same way as Wolter.

Two dead in the space of a couple of hours.

The Englishman didn't fire again that day. No doubt he felt it would be reckless to do any more, and given that at least four of ours were looking for him he was probably right.

When the food came up I was careful to sit next to Karl. The last thing I wanted was a rift between us.

"No luck, then," I said.

"No…" His eyes searched mine for a second, with no trace of emotion. "Faltermeier thought he saw him for half a second but I'm buggered if I did. He's got to go, though – he's far too bloody good."

Be careful, Karl. If he sees you first you've had it.

"It would have been poor old Wolter," he added after a moment. "I wonder if he had a premonition."

Alfred looked at him with curiosity. "Do you believe that happens, then?"

"I don't know… It's probably just imagination and coincidence but I can't help wondering."

"I think it's self-fulfilling prophecy," Alfred said. "Someone thinks his number's up so he gets careless."

"You don't have any feelings about what might happen to you, then?" I asked him.

"No. None at all. And if I did I wouldn't pay attention to them. Like I say, that's when you do get hit."

"What about you, Karl?"

He thought for a moment.

"I think Alfred's got a point," he said, which didn't actually answer the question. "And you?"

"No," I said. "But I do have an open mind about it. My grandmother – my father's mother – said two years ago not to buy her any Christmas presents. As far as anyone knew she was fine – but the week before Christmas she had a stroke and died. Completely out of the blue."

"She might have been having symptoms," Alfred said.

"Even so. Even if she'd been getting headaches or something, how could she have known she'd die before Christmas?"

"She probably didn't," Bauer said. "She just knew what a load of skinflints you all are!"

"You cheeky sod! You can give those cigars back!"

I realised Meyer was listening quietly.

"How about you, sir?" I asked.

He smiled. "What about me?"

"Do you believe in premonitions? And do you have any?"

He gave me a very straight look.

I've gone too far, old friend or not.

Then he laughed, rather uneasily. "Do you think I'd be going for the old Express Ticket if I did? I mean, why make it more likely?"

"Just wondered… But if you did have a premonition, would it stop you taking the commission?"

"Of course not. You can't live like that – how would you know if it was really going to happen? You'd never do anything… Bit weird about your granny, though. I have to say I can't account for that at all."

"She must have been feeling unwell," Alfred said again. "Maybe she'd been to the doctor without telling any of you."

"'There are more things in Heaven and Earth, Horatio, than are dreamt of in your philosophy'," Karl said in English.

"I wish you wouldn't do that," Meyer complained.

"Sorry, sir," Karl said, and repeated it in German.

"Hamlet, isn't it?" Alfred asked him.

"Yes. About the ghost."

"Don't tell me you believe in ghosts!" Alfred burst out laughing.

"If you'd grown up in our house, you might too," Karl said cheerfully.

"Is it haunted, then?" Bauer asked.

Meyer was picking dirt from under his fingernails with a very abstracted air. Then he got up and left.

You didn't like this conversation one bit. Maybe we hit a nerve.

"Don't know," Karl said. "But sometimes there's a bit of a strange atmosphere."

"If you ask me it's all rot," Alfred said. "You've all got too much imagination. What do you think, Franz? Ghosts or no ghosts?"

"No idea. Never seen one."

"You've stayed at Karl's, though."

"Yes, and I know what he means… but there's nothing you can really… well, no strange noises or anything like that, just a feeling…" I shrugged. "Probably imagination, like you say."

I'd had enough of the conversation as well. It was pointless and rather weird.

"I think we've all got enough to occupy our minds at present, anyway," I said. "And some of us have to get back to work. Goldblum and I are still homeless."

Some time later I found my monkey, dirty but happily not crushed. The contents were all intact, including Karl's chocolate.

I gave it to him the next morning.

"Thanks, Franz, that's just what I wanted. Would you like some?"

I laughed. "You know you're on safe ground there. I don't know how you can eat that vile black stuff!"

"Because it's not sweet and gooey like that milk crap."

He broke off one square and ate it very slowly, after putting the rest away. I didn't know how he could do that, either. I'd eaten the bar I'd bought for myself within the first hour of the journey back.

"You still haven't told me about the women you had back home!" he said mischievously.

"Oh, I will when we've got a quiet moment," I said.

The hell I will. You wouldn't have left Helga in the park. You'd have relieved her of her virginity without a second thought.

"Hey, boys, it's my birthday!" Faltermeier said. "And my mum's sent me a cake."

It was rather small, and she'd enclosed a note apologising and saying that good ingredients were hard to get.

"Never mind," he said. "There's enough for the four of us."

Taschner got a brew going, and the snipers sat down to coffee and cake. I had a sudden surge of nostalgia for that pleasant morning ritual, for our favourite café in Heidelberg. We'd sat there so often with a pot of good strong coffee and a different cake each time…

"This *is* civilised," said Taschner. "Just think, we could almost be in a café on Unter den Linden."

I had to stop myself laughing. Four filthy, lousy men, sitting in a muddy trench, drinking out of tin mugs and eating cake with their grubby fingers – a smart café on Unter den Linden?

You've got one hell of an imagination, Taschner – pity you don't have a conscience to go with it.

"We're just missing a pretty waitress," Karl said.

"With big tits and an arse this wide," added Faltermeier, almost spilling his coffee as he gestured.

The conversation died as they all stared longingly into space. *Now, that does sound good*, I thought, and was lost in reverie myself. *All that soft, female flesh...*

"This cake's bloody good, Spots," Koch said. "Can I stay with your mum when I get leave?"

"Course you can," Faltermeier replied. "She'd be happy to see you."

She wouldn't if she knew him. I wonder if Faltermeier's told her what he does...

I left them to their incongruous party. Taschner cracked a joke which I didn't catch and they all burst out laughing. I turned round, and saw Karl shaking his head but laughing hard all the same.

You're all sitting there eating cake, drinking coffee and telling jokes – and when you've finished you'll go back to killing. You'll blow some poor bastard's brains out without a second thought.

Later I asked Karl what Taschner had said that was so funny. He looked rather embarrassed.

"I'm not repeating that," he said. "It was in extremely bad taste, even by our standards."

Your standards or mine? I thought but didn't want to say.

"You know Taschner," he added. "What do you think he makes jokes about?"

"You thought it was funny."

He looked at me with a hint of his earlier coldness, mixed with resignation. "What if I did?" There was a pause while he studied his hands. Then his eyes met mine again. "You'll all be happy enough if one of us gets that English fellow."

He'd gone before I could think of a reply. He was right, of course, and I knew it, just as I knew I was being very hard on him. I just wished I could stop thinking about poor Wolter.

The English aren't here to invite us for a beer. And who am I to judge Karl, anyway? But what he does is different...

As it turned out I'd arrived in the front line almost in time to leave it, as we went into support the next day. I had mixed feelings: we were let off the rest of the repair to the parapet, which was bloody hard work, but support was going to be endless carrying parties, which wouldn't be much easier.

Karl and the others wanted to stay and continue hunting their opponent, and Waitz was more than happy to agree, for the honour of the Company.

"Sorry, chaps," he said about ten minutes after the relief arrived. "The Third Company snipers reckon it's their turn and Oberleutnant Wisnewski agrees, so that's the end of that idea."

"Never mind, sir," said Taschner with a grin. "That lot won't be up to catching him!"

"I 'opes you're right," Koch said as we headed for the comms trench.

"Yeah," said Faltermeier, "we've got a score to settle!"

The week in support was every bit as knackering as I'd feared. The snipers were spared carrying duties, and went to the range every day instead.

From what I could gather in the brief intervals when Karl and I were conscious at the same time, they had a competition going – the man with the worst score for the day had to stand the other three beers in the Soldiers' Home.

"Maybe I should work on my marksmanship," Bauer said. "Spending the day on the range and the evenings getting half-cut would be a fucking sight better than being a human packhorse every night."

"Depends how cold your blood runs," said Peter.

262

Bauer pulled a face. "There is that."

The week in rest was very welcome indeed, and at last Karl and I got a chance to talk properly.

"Fancy a walk?" he asked me once I'd surfaced.

"Good idea."

As we wandered along I tried to frame the words to tell him that I didn't think badly of him, but I couldn't work out what to say.

I was still pondering when he said, "Now tell me about your leave."

"There's nothing to tell. My parents haven't the faintest idea what's going on out here and I couldn't tell them. I got drunk with an old friend who was home on leave as well, and that's about it."

"About it? No leg-over?"

"Well, Chris and I went to the knocking shop—"

"You mean *you had to pay*? With the shortage of men in Germany at present?" He shook his head sadly "Franz, you need some lessons. You're a good-looking young chap and you still can't get a girl into bed. I don't know—"

"No, it wasn't like that. I mean, she would, only..." and I found myself telling him all about Helga.

He stopped walking and looked at me. "How could you be such a fucking prig?"

"I knew you wouldn't understand. That's why I wasn't going to tell you."

"No, *you're* the one who doesn't understand. Can't you see how you insulted her? She threw herself at you, and you said 'Not good enough'. How do you think that felt?"

I hadn't thought of it that way. Put like that her anger was entirely reasonable.

"Well, I expect she's got what she wants by now," I said.

"Probably... but Franz, how could you pass up the chance

to fuck a virgin? I mean, men pay over the odds in dodgy whorehouses for supposedly virginal fourteen-year-olds – you get the chance to have it for free and you say no!"

"Do they?" I asked, half in disbelief.

"Yes – didn't you know?"

"No, I didn't… So have you, then?"

"Fucked a virgin?" He laughed. "I should be so bloody lucky. Not even on the farm – their brothers and cousins all got there first!"

"Not even in the dodgy whorehouses?"

He laughed again. "Do you really think there's such a thing as a virgin in a brothel?"

"No, of course not!" I laughed as well, mostly out of relief that things between us were as they had always been.

The next day Waitz told Karl and Koch that they were both to receive the Iron Cross, Second Class.

"What for, sir?" Karl asked, bemused.

"Well, you've been doing rather well, as I'm sure you know."

"I… er… I don't think my efforts are worth a gong," Karl said awkwardly. He looked very uncomfortable.

Koch stared at him as if he'd grown two heads. "Shut up and be grateful, Leussow."

"Yes, quite," Waitz said. "It's not for you to decide."

"No, sir. It's an honour, of course."

"Now you know how I felt," I said to him after Waitz had gone.

"Not really," he replied, and it was plain from his tone that the subject was closed.

You don't want a gong for killing. Neither would I.

It still made a good excuse for a party and we all got nicely mellow.

It's good to have some time with you, I thought as I looked at Karl the next morning. I'd woken before him, and lay on my side studying his face. He looked so young and vulnerable in sleep, as if the war hadn't touched him.

How little it takes to destroy even a strong man like you. I can only hope that peace comes before that happens... especially given the risks of what you're doing these days.

And I want to show you that I don't give a shit about your job.

Some men looked at the snipers with an obvious mixture of admiration of their skill and revulsion at their exercise of it. Taschner and Koch didn't care what anyone thought of them, Faltermeier was very much Taschner's oppo and stuck to him like glue – but I felt that Karl didn't like the looks he sometimes got.

He was my friend, whatever he did, and I still saw the man and not the filthy job.

And yet... We got a pass and went into town, far enough back that there were civilians and a semblance of normal life. We were sitting outside a café in the sun, relaxing and enjoying the warmth and contemplating the prospect of a girl later.

"Shame we'll have to pay," I said.

"Yes, isn't it?"

The waitress was clearing away at the next table. She probably wasn't really as pretty as she seemed, but I was hopelessly sex-starved.

"Shall we have something to eat after?" I asked.

"Good idea."

At that moment the waitress dropped a cup. Before I could blink Karl had caught it and was handing it back to her.

Jesus Christ, that was fast. Poor bastards don't stand a chance, do they?

"Nothing wrong with your reactions," I said, hearing a slightly sour note in my voice.

He saw the look in my eyes and didn't reply, but stared across the square, his face impassive.

Shit. All the effort I've been making and I've just undone it all.

There was a long silence and then he said, "You know the one about stones and glass houses."

"I didn't mean—"

"Yes, you did." His tone was matter-of-fact. "I know perfectly well what you meant, Franz. We know each other well enough."

Well enough for me to try to put into words what I've wanted to say for days?

"Karl... Look, I know you didn't choose to do this—"

"I didn't refuse either," he said flatly.

That set me back a bit. "Could you have done?"

He shrugged and didn't answer. *That means yes.*

"The thing is," I continued, "I've been asking myself why what you do feels different, why it... and I can't find an answer. I mean, they're not here to buy us a beer."

He looked at me steadily for a moment. "All right, Franz – since you raised the subject, ask yourself this: what's the difference between my shooting an enemy when he forgets to duck his head or your shooting him when he's running towards us? He's just as dead either way, and he's a soldier, for fuck's sake. That's what we're all for. Oh, and you're only alive because of my reactions. Try remembering that as well."

There was a long pause while I considered what he'd said.

"And one other thing you seem to have forgotten," he added in a friendlier tone, "is that you owe me two beers."

It seemed I was forgiven.

"Done!" I said. "After the whorehouse?"

"But of course!"

We went back arm in arm at the end of the evening and lay down beside each other as always, with the old feeling of harmony.

I'd go anywhere with you, and to Hell with whether we'd get back again.

The following afternoon the Company had to fall in. It was our last day in rest and we wondered what was going on.

"I hope it's not some fresh bloody offensive," I heard Sommerburg mutter, and decided to ignore it.

"What the fuck do you think you're here for?" Bauer said loudly.

Braun gave them a look and they shut up.

"I have some news for you all," Waitz said. "I'm being transferred to command the Ninth Company with immediate effect, owing to Oberleutnant Zechner having been killed last night. Leutnant Hafner will take over command of the Company in the interim, and Leutnant Rippel will take over his platoon. Leutnant Blume from the Sixth Company will replace Leutnant Rippel."

"Bloody good thing, too, them giving it to Hafner," Karl said as we got ready to move.

"I agree," said Taschner.

"Just cos he thinks the sun shines out of your arses," said Schmidt II.

"Sees the value of snipers, you means," Koch retorted.

"Bollocks," said Peter.

"At least we've got Rippel now," said Bauer. "He's a decent fellow."

No one could argue with that. Rippel was proving himself to be tough, capable, and fair.

"I'm sorry to see Waitz go," I said. "Though Hafner will do a good job."

"If they let him keep it," said Meyer. "He might not be senior enough."

Koch pulled a face. "Just 'as to 'ope, doesn't we?"

"Always!" said Faltermeier with a grin.

When we got back into the line we heard that the Tommy sniper was responsible for Zechner's demise.

"Don't know how he did it," said one of the fellows in the Ninth. "We were working on the wire and the boss came out to inspect it – you could hardly see your hand in front of your face, and that bastard managed to shoot him dead."

"Epaulettes catching what light there was," said Karl.

"That's just why I don't want to wear them!" I said.

The parapet had been repaired and my old cubbyhole had been transformed into a proper dugout. Apparently one of the fellows in the Ninth was a joiner, and he'd produced a very nice little room with solid wooden walls. It was practically luxurious.

Hafner took one look at it and declared it to be the new Company command post. The junior officers moved into the old HQ and so on down, until Rombach and I moved into a hole even more cramped than the last one, which would only hold one of us at a time.

If I see that bloody joiner he's getting a piece of my mind. Why didn't the stupid bastard just put it back as it was?

The snipers were untouched by the mass move. Karl told me it had taken Hafner about half a second to decide they should be left alone.

There was a bit of grumbling but no one really objected. We all knew how important their job had become – their English opponent shot Hochstein through the jaw and made a hell of a mess of him, and killed Wegener the next day.

Our four worked their arses off to try to get rid of the bastard.

Time you had a break, I thought one morning, and got a brew going.

"Coffee's up," I called out. "Freshly brewed, good and strong, just as we like it."

Karl stepped down.

"You must have read my mind," he said. "Come on, Koch."

The two of them sat next to me.

"Thanks, Franz – just what I need," Karl said as I filled his mug.

He stretched, then leaned his head back against the planking and closed his eyes. The lines in his face looked deeper.

You look tired. Very tired. You need a rest – you can't afford to lose concentration.

"How do you take yours, Koch?" I asked.

"Black, thanks, just as it comes."

Our eyes met as I handed him his coffee. *There really is something rather unsavoury about you. It's as if you make me feel even dirtier than I am already.*

"We're doing pretty well so far today," he said to Karl, "even if we 'asn't seen our friend. One definite and one probable. You got that officer spot on, right in the back of 'is 'ead, but 'ow you missed that first one I'm buggered if I know. It couldn't of been easier."

"Crosswind," Karl said without moving or opening his eyes.

"You still 'ad a crosswind for the officer and that was much 'arder, but you got 'im."

"It was the first one of the day. I misjudged it. I'm not fucking perfect," Karl said without emotion. He still hadn't opened his eyes.

Koch opened his mouth, closed it again and handed me the mug back.

"Bit too strong for me, thanks," he said.

I'm glad something is, I thought as he got up and disappeared into their dugout, his boots clumping on the duckboards.

Karl sighed.

"That bugger should work with Taschner," he said quietly. "The fellow he reproached me for missing had his head bandaged and looked half-dead – must have been hit in the shelling this morning. If I'd been out by myself I wouldn't have fired, but with him looking over my shoulder it's not that easy. As it is, he suspects I missed on purpose but he can't prove it, so he can't make trouble for me."

"Do you think he would?"

"Don't know – but the official view could be that I was in dereliction of my duty. They're not words I want to hear. And don't forget that's the Tommies over there, and one or two people can't forget I have English blood."

"No one could really suspect you of disloyalty."

"I'd like to think not… I have to say I can't see the point of shooting someone who's already injured. As far as I'm concerned they can go back in peace."

"Quite." *Good to hear you still have some standards.*

"He'd have shot him, of course, but that's his business… and I wouldn't be so bloody rude as to point out what he misses." He paused and got out his silver cigarette case. "I won't offer you one, Franz. I know you don't like them."

"No, I'll stick to my own, thanks."

Oh, what glorious incongruity – here we are, filthy as anything, sitting on the muddy fire step, and you use that elegant black cigarette holder.

"Light?" he offered.

"Thanks."

He was still using his silver lighter, engraved, like the case, with the Leussow arms. It's good to see someone utterly refusing to give in to his circumstances. I'd have been worried about them being stolen but everyone tended to walk round Karl. They knew how strong he was and no one wanted a fight with him.

"He doesn't like it when you go out, I can tell you," I said. "I think he worries. He sits round with a face as long as your arm."

Karl laughed. "That's not concern for me… No, really,

Franz, it's not. I overheard him talking to Spots about me. He said, 'He shoots very well, but he's a funny bloke. He goes off on his own half the time, and what really pisses me off is that he doesn't keep count properly when he's out there'."

He took a long drag and then went on, "I don't know where he gets that idea. I have to write everything in that bloody little book, don't I? Rounds used, effect, and so on. I don't know how he thinks I can fib. So next time you see him sitting around with a long face, just remember all he gives a fuck about is those lovely points he thinks I'm not chalking up."

He got up and put his mug away. "When he comes back out would you tell him I've moved off to the right?"

Taschner wasn't his usual self the next day, but seemed to be fretting about something. After the evening stand-to he became increasingly impatient, which was most unlike him.

About two hours later he set off towards one of the forward observation posts, and came stumbling back carrying Faltermeier. He laid him down gently but it was plain that he was dead. There was a neat hole in the middle of his forehead and I could guess who'd put it there.

"I'll have that fucker," Taschner snarled. "One day the bugger'll get it wrong and I'll send him to Hell. Poor Spots... Poor little fucker was only sixteen the other day."

"*What?*" Faltermeier had been as tall as me, and I'd thought he was just one of the unlucky blokes whose acne drags on.

"Yeah – lied when he volunteered. That's why his face was such a mess. Don't matter now, though, do it?"

And that's why he had that moment of carelessness. That's what happens when a boy does a man's job.

It made me angry as well. *His mother knew – she sent him that cake. Why didn't she tell them he was underage? They'd have sent him straight home.*

Karl was standing beside me. "Shit," he said sadly.

Taschner turned towards him. "It's my fault," he said. "I shouldn't have let him work out there by himself. He kept saying he was going to go out, and it was getting harder to stop him. I thought if he worked from the OP he might shut up about it."

Karl shook his head. "You did your best – if you hadn't looked out for him this would have happened weeks ago. He didn't think enough."

Couldn't think enough, more like, I thought, remembering some of the idiotic things I'd done at that age. *No bloody brains* – which brought to mind something I'd heard Taschner saying to Faltermeier the week before: "Use your fucking brains while they're still in your fucking head!"

He's got no brains now, poor sod...

"That fucker's mine now," Taschner said.

Karl looked at me and said nothing.

They took Faltermeier's body back and Taschner stomped off to the dugout to write to his mother.

"Koch won't be staying with Faltermeier's mother, then," I said to Karl later.

"Oh, he probably will – he'll write to her and say he wants to give her his stuff back, or whatever. He'll have to think of something."

"Why doesn't he just go home?"

"Because Koch is one of the few men who's in more danger at home than out here," he said very quietly. "If he sets foot in Düsseldorf he's got a very good chance of being killed... You know he's an orphan?"

"Yes."

"Well, he was brought up by his grandfather – and if you think that sounds nice and cosy, Grandpa's a pretty serious criminal, up to his ears in God knows what. Young Koch was one of his enforcers. He went a bit too far and killed one of the opposition, so they're out to get him."

"Jesus. Nice company you're keeping."

He shrugged. "He does the job well – and who am I to comment?"

That was a revealing remark. "So he joined up to get away from them, then?"

"No – that was patriotism. Keep the fucking Frenchies away from the Rhine."

"So where did he learn to shoot?"

"Same as the rest of us – Grandpa has a hunting lodge."

"And Faltermeier's dad's a forester... Did you know how old he was?"

"Yes. That's why we all looked out for him. That's why he was paired with Taschner, because he's the oldest – and didn't you notice he never went out?"

"Koch doesn't either."

"No, well... he just reckons it's a fucking stupid thing to do. Spots wanted to go out, all right, as you heard, but we wouldn't let him – not that it's made any bloody difference."

I could hear the anger in his voice. "Why didn't you say something? They'd have sent him straight home."

"He'd just have volunteered again under a different name. Being as we all knew, we could keep the brakes on him. He was a bloody good shot and he'd have been very good indeed if he'd managed to stay alive." *That's quite a compliment coming from you.* "It really was best for him to be with us."

Faltermeier just got what he was dishing out, I thought – and then wished I hadn't thought it, because that would mean Karl deserved the same treatment and the last thing I wanted was for anything to happen to him.

A couple of days later Karl crept out well before dawn.

Taschner had spent the night out and we were expecting him back before first light, but he didn't appear.

We were standing-to as usual as the dawn came up. Hafner was looking through the periscope, as he always did.

"What in God's name is that?" he exclaimed suddenly.

Koch's head appeared from under the curtain round his position. "It's Taschner and Leussow, sir!"

"What? Let me see!" Hafner ducked under the curtain and I heard a muffled shout of "Jesus fucking Christ!"

He reappeared. "*Covering fire!*"

In the grey light I glimpsed a figure rolling over the lip of a shell-hole and falling limply into the next one, followed a few seconds later by another who pulled himself up and rolled quickly over the sliver of exposed ground... and again, and again.

I daren't look at them but concentrated on the Tommies, who were shooting back.

I hadn't been able to tell which man was Karl.

It all got rather hot for a few minutes and then I realised the English had stopped firing. So did we, and there was an uneasy truce.

It's a trick. They've got us to stop and now they'll shoot them. They've only missed so far because Karl and Taschner know the ground so well... And where's that bastard who killed Faltermeier? What's he doing?

They were at the edge of the wire. The first rays of the sun lit up two figures in filthy field-grey, one crawling towards us on his belly through the mud, dragging the other, who had a grubby bandage round his head and seemed to be unconscious. I could hardly breathe. As they got closer I saw with immense relief that Karl was the uninjured one.

The Tommies haven't realised what Karl and Taschner are, or they'd have shot them for sure.

They made slow progress through the wire, and then they were at the edge of the parapet. Hands reached up to lift Taschner down and Karl tumbled into the trench after him to shouts of "Well done!"

He sank onto the fire step, gasping for breath, sweat pouring down his face.

"God – bugger's heavy!"

"Well done, Leussow!" said Braun, and handed him his hip flask.

"Usual?" Karl asked.

Braun smiled and Karl took a long swig of the spirit.

"Thanks," he said and handed the flask back.

"Very well done," said Hafner.

"Thank you, sir… I left the capes – in a shell-hole."

"Very wise."

"I'll fetch them tonight. I've got Taschner's rifle, though, and his sight… Oh, *shit!* What a fucking mess."

Both rifles and both the cases containing the sights were caked in mud.

"I had to roll right over a few times, sir, but the ground's soft—"

"Won't be anything that can't be sorted out. The main thing is the two of you are back safely." Hafner turned to the medics. "Much damage?"

"No, sir," said Klose. "His scalp's torn – looks like it was a shell fragment – but his skull seems all right. He wouldn't have lasted until dark, though, the way he was bleeding. Is there somewhere we can put him where he'll be out of the way?"

"Put him in the dugout," Karl said. "Koch and I can keep an eye on him."

"That was a damned good job, Leussow," said Hafner. "Damned good. You can come and make your report later, once you've finished cleaning up."

"Thank you, sir."

"*You fucking idiot*," I said after Hafner had gone. "What did you have to do that for, for *Taschner*, for Christ's sake? You don't even like him."

"It wasn't really for Taschner – it was for me."

"Oh, I see. You just fancied playing Russian roulette with the Tommies."

"That could be me tomorrow. I couldn't leave him out there all day."

"If you think I'm doing that for you in broad daylight, you're off your fucking head. Well, you are anyway… Look, give me Taschner's rifle, or you'll be all day."

"Thanks, Franz." He scraped some mud off the stock of one of the rifles, handed it to me, and scowled blackly at the state of his own.

I'd teased him once that he lavished more care on his rifle than some women did on their babies. "About right," he'd said with a grin.

"I'll have to take them both back to the workshop tonight with the sights – though it might be better to keep Taschner's in company stores till he gets back."

The workshop was beside the range where Karl had so impressed the officers, quite some way behind the lines.

"You'll have to ask Hafner to give you tomorrow off."

"I can't work tomorrow anyway – I daren't use this till it's been checked over and the sight re-zeroed."

I was putting off even looking at Taschner's rifle as I wasn't sure how Karl had identified it so quickly. *Knowing Taschner, there's probably a row of tally marks—*

"Oh," I heard myself say. "How beautiful."

Taschner's initials were carved into the wood in a beautiful Art Nouveau monogram. The T was central, with the A and J on either side of it, and the sinuous lines seemed almost to be alive.

"I didn't realise Taschner's an artist."

"He isn't. Spots did it – he did them for all of us. Look."

A gracefully curving L held a smaller K, with a lower case v in the triangle between the K and the L.

"That's lovely," I said. "He was really talented."

Karl nodded. "He was always carving. Made the most beautiful little animals. I've got a really lovely hare he gave me."

"I never realised."

"No – he was very shy about it and only did it in the dugout. We used to tell him off because the light's so poor in there."

So that's why he wanted that lump of wood from the collapsed parapet, I thought, remembering how diffidently he'd asked for it and how he'd studied it, turning it over and over.

"Karl, won't they give you grief over the monograms? I mean, these are Army property."

"What are they going to do to us? Anyway, they're ours until we get killed or move on."

"So what happened?" I asked.

"You know that ruin a bit off to our left – I think it was a cowshed or something? Anyway, that was my plan for today. You get a good view of where one of their comms trenches meets their second line, the sort of spot that's well worth watching. You know, sometimes they're a bit careless, or they don't realise how exposed it is, and I was hoping for an officer, maybe even a senior officer."

You mean you were hoping to kill one as he was just walking along – and you talk about it so casually. I was careful not to look up. I didn't know what my eyes might say.

"The only thing is, it's a bit of a dodgy place."

I looked up sharply. I suspected that Karl's 'a bit dodgy' equated to many men's 'thoroughly dangerous'.

"Dodgy how?"

"Well, it would be just as useful to our friend – you can use

277

it facing either way." *Oh, bloody wonderful.* "And it would make a decent target for the artillery."

"You're barking fucking mad."

"But I hadn't noticed anyone using it for a while so I decided it was worth a go. When I got there I checked it over and there were no signs of life, but it was pretty dark. I'd just got myself nicely settled with an hour or so till dawn, then a really bright flare went up, right overhead, and I got the most God-awful shock because I wasn't alone."

The story was getting worse by the minute. I was almost starting to wish I hadn't asked.

"What looked like a small mound of rubble a metre or so away was another fellow, but he was facing the same way as me, so that was the 'Oh shit' moment over. But I was really pissed off, because I was obviously going to have to find somewhere else. Anyway, he didn't look right – he was just slumped there – and I went over and found he was out cold.

"Another flare went up and I turned him over and saw that it was Taschner and that his head was bleeding, fairly steadily. And I thought, 'Oh fuck, I'm going to have to get him back'. Thing was, I didn't know when he'd copped it or how much blood he'd lost.

"So I patched him up, put the sights in their cases, and loaded myself up with two rifles and one Taschner. I thought I could probably get away with carrying him until first light, but it was bloody hard going – my feet kept sinking in and it was bloody hard work pulling them out again. Taschner's not exactly light, either, and I nearly dropped him a couple of times.

"As soon as the sky got a bit less black I got us both into a shell-hole and took our capes off and left them there. I thought we might get away with it if we looked like a couple of ordinary Fritzes.

"So after that I was doing what you probably saw – rolling

Taschner from one shell-hole to another and rolling after him, zigzagging. It was bloody slow and before long it was broad fucking daylight, but then you lot were covering us so it felt just a bit less unpleasant.

"I could feel our friend watching and I couldn't work out why he'd let us get so far – then I couldn't believe it when it all went quiet. I think that was the first time I thought we had a real chance."

"Karl, for God's sake, why didn't you just patch Taschner up and stay out there until dark?"

"Like I say, I didn't know when he'd been hit – was there much shelling last night?"

Karl could sleep through almost anything.

"A bit, round about midnight, and some mortar fire a bit later."

"I thought I heard something. Anyway, it's just as well I didn't wait or he wouldn't have made it."

"But Karl, it was Taschner," I said quietly. "He's not exactly a credit to Homo sapiens."

"If you ask me, he's a perfectly representative specimen. There really is no hope for our species... Doesn't matter who it is, though, does it? And anyway, he'd saved my bacon, and I couldn't have worked with him there – for one thing he'd been working there, and what if he'd come round and starting yelling his head off?"

"Hang on, Karl – when did Taschner save your bacon?" *What have you not told me?*

"Today, of course. The Tommies must have that place marked. I'd have fired once and they'd have blown me to Kingdom come. Taschner was just lucky they didn't manage a direct hit last night."

"Lucky you found him, too... Don't you lot tell each other where you're going?"

He shrugged. "Sometimes – depends how concrete our plans are. I was asleep when he left, anyway."

"You were about to use the same place he'd just been using. Karl, for fuck's sake, even I know you can't do that."

"No, you're right – we will have to get more organised… There's not just us, though, is there?"

"Does it never occur to you that Koch just might be right?" *Your luck's going to run out one day.*

"Cat's got nine lives, hasn't it?" he said with a grin.

"On that basis, you're long dead!"

Alfred came and joined us. "What the fuck did you do that for, you crazy bastard?"

"Alfred, you calling me crazy is truly the pot calling the kettle black."

"No it bloody isn't! I've never done anything as stupid as that."

"Have a look at your left arm and remember how you got the scar. You were fucking lucky that was all you got."

Alfred couldn't very well argue with that, but he didn't let go.

"And you're fucking lucky they didn't guess what you are," he said, "or it would have been curtains. Just think – they could have got rid of two Hun snipers at once. I don't play for those stakes."

Karl laughed. "Yes you do! We all do."

Alfred shook his head. "Not the way you do… One slip and it's exit stage left. No one's going to take you prisoner."

I was beginning to wish Alfred would shut up about it.

Karl just grinned at him. "You go out on all those patrols… Come on, what happens when you meet the Tommies? You bash each other's heads in with nailed clubs and sharpened spades and blow each other up, and *you* have the sheer fucking nerve to call *me* crazy!"

"Really was your lucky day, though. Even your English oppo left you alone."

"God knows why. I swear I could feel him watching."

"What would you have done?" Alfred asked suddenly. "I mean if it'd been the other way round."

"If I'd been out I'd have let them go," Karl answered without hesitation. He paused for a moment and then added, "If I'd been here... probably the same, but it would depend."

That was good to hear – then I realised how much cold calculation lay behind the first statement. What he'd really meant was that it wouldn't have been worth the risk of giving himself away.

"Though I wouldn't have shot the injured one," he said quietly, and I remembered the fellow he'd deliberately missed a few days before.

"No," said Alfred. "I didn't think you would."

"Depend on what?" I asked.

"How bold they were getting," Karl replied. "We can't have the Tommies thinking they can wander about No Man's Land when they feel like it."

"Absolutely," said Alfred. "Wouldn't do at all."

"You're going to have a bloody long night, aren't you?" I said, changing the subject. "I mean, if you have to find the capes and then get back to the workshop."

"Come out with us if you like," Alfred said. "I'm taking a patrol out at about midnight."

"Thanks – as long as I don't have to carry one of those Neanderthal clubs! Not my idea of fun at all. Far too bloody messy."

"You'll need something," Alfred said.

"Give me a couple of grenades, then. I can give you them back later."

"How in God's name are you going to find the right shell-hole?" I asked.

"It's not as featureless as you think. I'll start at the old cowshed and go in the same direction – like I said, we hadn't got far before I dumped them."

It took him a good bit longer than he'd anticipated, and he only just got away down the comms trench before dawn.

He came back the following night looking much happier.

"Everything in order?" I asked.

"'Tis now, though one of the mounts had had a knock so it's just as well I went. Being as they weren't that busy they got on with it straight off. They said they'd give me a shout when they needed me, so I went and lay in the sun for a bit and watched the clouds going by and did the same again after we'd finished on the range. Very pleasant it was too."

"Jammy bastard." *You were entitled to a quiet day*, I thought but had no intention of saying. "Did they say anything about the monogram?"

"No, not a word... I was thinking, though – if the fellow who gets Spots's rifle adds his own it could be very interesting for some future historian."

I found myself wondering how many owners a sniper's rifle might get through by the end of the war. *So long as Karl's has just the one. That's all that matters.*

The next day I overheard Hafner and Rippel talking.

"We'll need to replace them," said Hafner. "We can't be two down, not now the Tommies are getting in on the act."

"I spoke to the hospital," Rippel said. "They said Taschner should be back in about a month, so I think we'll be all right if we just replace Faltermeier."

"What about Friedemann? He's a pretty good shot."

"Hasn't got the temperament. Prefers the hand-to-hand stuff, happy as Larry out with a bunch of like-minded thugs, and bloody good at it, too."

"True. Becker?"

282

Shit – you can't ask me to do that! I wouldn't touch it with a fucking barge pole.

"No. Doesn't shoot well enough. Don't get me wrong, he's accurate, but he hasn't got that bit extra, what you might call feel. Not instinctive. Hasn't got the temperament either."

That'll teach me to eavesdrop, I thought, slightly offended at Rippel's assessment of my ability. When I thought about it a bit more I realised that every word was true and that he'd put his finger right on the differences between Karl and me.

About half an hour later Alfred was summoned to Hafner and came back grinning from ear to ear.

"I'm off as soon as we're out of the line!" he said jubilantly. "On my officer's course!"

"Congratulations!" said Meyer. "I hope they send you back here."

"So do I – I don't want the Medical Service getting their hands on me. It would be too boring for words. I do my best not to draw attention to myself."

The rest of us started laughing.

"Alfred," I said, "you volunteer for every bloody thing that's going. That's hardly 'not drawing attention to yourself'."

"No, but if I get noticed for things like that, then they might not realise I was halfway to being a doctor."

"You're off your head," Karl said. "You really think they'll never check your record?"

"I hope not, or I'll be stuck in some bloody hospital somewhere, no fun at all. There's plenty of time for that after the war."

"Assuming there is an 'after the war'," Karl replied.

"Well, if there isn't then I certainly don't want to be stuck in a hospital!"

"You know, I really don't know what makes you tick," Meyer said. "Don't you want to help people and cure them?"

"Never really been my motivation – I'm more interested in research. There must be cures for diseases like leprosy and syphilis and TB, not to mention cancer. I've always wanted to work on things like that."

"That's still helping people."

"Yes, but not directly. I mean, I'd be bored to death in a small-town practice. It's the intellectual challenge I want. The hands-on, treating people side of it doesn't really appeal to me. Don't know why – just doesn't."

"You'd have a crap bedside manner, anyway," I said. "You've spent too much time sending men to the next world rather than keeping them in this one!"

"Yes," said Peter. "He'd probably turn up with a sharpened spade and a couple of grenades!"

"Or with the fellow with the scythe in attendance," Karl said.

"Some of the patients would be happy to see him," Alfred replied.

That's for sure.

"We'll be calling you 'sir' soon, then!" I said, to change the subject.

Alfred grinned. "Go for it yourself."

"You know my answer to that!"

"Mine too," said Karl. "No seat on the Express for me!"

Alfred almost didn't make it to 'out of the line' – he and his patrol had a very hot encounter with the Tommies and left Schmidt II dead in No Man's Land.

"We tried to bring him back," he said, "but he died halfway."

"Have to get our own back next time," said Meyer, who'd been leading.

"I'll have to leave that to you, sir," said Alfred.

The evening before his departure Hafner got hold of a couple of barrels of good German beer, and the Company assembled to give Alfred a send-off.

When all our mugs were full Hafner said, "Well, here's to your success, Friedemann. From what I've seen you'll do very well indeed – and I hope we see you back here."

Everyone cheered and raised their mugs to him, even those who didn't know him well. Beer is beer, after all, and any excuse for a party was more than welcome.

The beer was followed by an impromptu and rather merry football match. Halfway through, I forgot that Meyer was on the opposing team and passed to him, and got rolled thoroughly in the mud as a punishment. They won, which was deemed to be my fault, but no one really cared.

Towards the end of the week we heard that Hafner had been confirmed as Company Commander.

"Thank God for that," said Karl. "Now we just need replacements for Taschner and Faltermeier."

"And the sooner the bleeding better," Koch added.

When we got back into the line we found that the English sniper was still in business. We had two dead in no time.

"How do you know it's the same fellow?" I asked Karl.

"Modus operandi – think that's what they call it."

"Yeah, that's right," said Koch unexpectedly. "It's Latin – means method of operation."

I looked at Karl who raised an eyebrow and continued, "He's always very well hidden, very fast and very accurate. Now they might have two like that in this sector – after all, we've got several – but on the form to date I doubt it. And if there were more than one then there'd be more shots. The pattern fits with it being just him. Though that won't be the case for much longer."

"No," said Koch. "We 'as to get the fucker before 'is friends arrive."

"Quite right," Hafner said, and we leapt to our feet. "I want to talk to the pair of you about just that."

285

It was starting to rain.

"Would you like a cup of coffee in our dugout, sir?" Karl suggested.

"That would be very pleasant, thank you."

The three of them disappeared to make their plans.

"Well, that'll do for a start," Hafner said as they emerged a couple of hours later. "We'll go for an early start tomorrow. How do you want to play it, Leussow? Out or in?"

"I think it would be better if I stayed in, sir. If I'm out I'm stuck in one place and the angle might be impossible, but if I stay here I'm free to move along."

"Good thinking."

Before dawn Karl and Koch went to one of their carefully-prepared positions, Koch as spotter. All of them had tried to see the positions from No Man's Land and had reported that they were invisible, even when you knew exactly where to look.

A couple of hours after sunrise Hafner said, "Time for the dummy head, Braun."

"Yes, sir." Goldblum raised the head above the parapet and the pole was knocked instantly from his hands. We looked at each other.

"Bloody hell," he said.

"Hopefully they'll have seen something," Hafner said, and headed back to the bay where Karl and Koch were.

Peter put the periscope up.

"I reckon he must be in that pile of rubble but I can't see anyone. Have a look, Corporal?"

"Thanks."

The pile of rubble showed up clearly. It must once have been a farmhouse or something. It would be a perfect place for a sniper but I could see no sign of life at all.

I handed the periscope to Goldblum, who said, "I see where you mean, but we're never going to see the fucker, are we?"

After an hour or so Hafner came in search of a light.

"What's happening, sir?" Peter asked.

"Not much. Leussow and Koch reckon he's in that heap of rubble. There's a vertical gap between two stones about halfway along the right-hand half of the heap and that's where they think he is. The trouble is they can't be certain. If he is there then it's a bloody good position. The only thing is, it's right opposite Leussow's."

My back hairs prickled.

"What are they going to do, sir?" I asked.

If the camouflage isn't as good as Karl thinks it is, then he's had it.

"Leussow wants to wait. I've suggested another dummy head but he thinks it would be too obvious."

I wish you'd take charge a bit more. We all know how good Karl is but you let him take too many risks.

He finished his cigarette and went back.

"It's just a bloody great shadow in that gap," said Goldblum. "Here, Bauer, you have a look."

Bauer took the periscope from him. After a couple of minutes he said, "I can see the gap but I don't know how they're going to see him. What do you think, Corporal?"

I agreed with them. The vertical gap in the stones showed up clearly, but I couldn't see anyone, or anything, in there.

The sun was very bright and the harsh light bounced off the pale stones, deepening the shadow between them. *We don't have the benefit of magnification*, I thought, *and Karl's got his four-power sight... The glare must be worse for him, surely.*

Karl will have to be certain before he fires. He won't want to betray himself to that English fellow. He's far too dangerous.

An hour later a layer of high cloud began to dim the sun. An hour after that the cloud had got quite a bit thicker and the light had softened considerably. I looked through the periscope again and, while I still couldn't see into the gap, I did notice that the contrast between light and shadow was much less harsh.

The Tommy hadn't fired again. *He's not having much luck today. Everyone's being very careful—*

Karl fired and the shot was so unexpected that I nearly dropped the periscope. Some small stones bounced out to the right from behind the pile, as if someone had kicked them.

I went back round the traverse and saw that Karl had stepped down.

Quite right. If you didn't get him he knows exactly where you were. Your only advantage has just gone.

"I don't know," Karl was saying. "He could be faking. He might just have kicked those stones out so we'd think I'd hit him."

"Well you didn't 'it the rubble, so you must of been spot on through the gap," Koch said.

"I might have been over his head."

"Nah. I swear I saw 'is rifle move."

"Before or after I fired?"

"Both. The movement after was jerky, though, like 'e'd been 'it."

"I thought so too, but I'm not certain."

"I think you got him, Leussow," said Hafner.

"I don't know, sir. I think we'd better all be careful. I'll have to move on now. I can't work from here again today. I suggest you try another dummy head in an hour or so. If he's still alive we'll have to try again – but preferably tomorrow, or better still the day after."

"You're not working any more today anyway. Your time's your own."

"Thank you, sir."

"Well done," I said.

He sat down on the fire step and Bauer and I sat either side of him. He lit a cigarette and inhaled deeply, staring into space.

"It might be a bit early for congratulations," he said. "I'm not sure I hit him…" He stretched his shoulders and rolled his head slowly. "God, I'm stiff."

You must be – apart from being in one position for nearly five hours the tension in you must have been enormous. We were all pretty tense and we were just watching.

"Any chance of a coffee?" he asked.

"Get some coffee going, Bauer," said Braun. "I think we could all do with some."

Bauer put the water on to boil and Karl got up and left us. When he came back the coffee was ready, and after drinking his he stood up, stretched again, picked up his rifle and disappeared into the dugout.

Two hours later we tried the dummy head but without result, and there were no more shots from the English sniper.

Late in the day I borrowed Koch's binoculars and stood at another of their well sandbagged positions. The gap between the stones still looked small.

I can hit a man easily at that range, but no way could I shoot into an opening like that, let alone hit someone hiding there.

That's what Rippel was talking about. That's the difference between me and Karl, between a good shot and an expert marksman. If I could shoot like that I'd be doing his job and I really don't want to. I'd probably get killed anyway – I haven't got that cold focus, and I'm not sorry about that.

IX

A couple of hours before dawn Karl and I were talking in the snipers' dugout, while he smoked a last cigarette before going out. Koch was working, so we had the place to ourselves. I was enjoying a rest between the end of my sentry duty and the dawn stand-to, stretched out very comfortably on the planks of Taschner's bed. Lying down in the front line was a real luxury.

I wasn't sorry I hadn't gone on Braun's patrol. I was bloody tired and it was the last thing I felt like doing.

"That candle's almost done," Karl said. "I'll have to get some more next—"

Braun came into the dugout, his blackened face devilish in the flickering light.

"Souvenir for you, Leussow," he said with a grin, and threw something to Karl. "Bloody good shooting."

Karl had caught the object, and as he looked at it his face went very still and then assumed an expression of casual interest.

"The Englishman?"

"Dead as a doornail, minus half the back of his head. Next time Koch says you could hit a fly at six hundred metres I might even believe him."

He left before Karl could say anything else.

Karl handed the 'souvenir' to me without a word. It was the remains of a telescopic sight. As I turned it over in my hands a fragment of broken glass caught the candlelight.

Jesus. That fellow was looking through this when Karl killed him.

"Do something for me, would you, Franz?"

"Of course."

"Give that to Koch. It's more his style of keepsake than mine."

Our eyes met and held for a few seconds. His were grey in the candlelight and unreadable.

"Well, see you tonight, then," he said.

"See you later," I answered casually.

I hope I do, I thought, looking at what I held in my hand. *I hope no one does this to you.*

Braun couldn't have given Karl a clearer reminder of the danger he'd been in. They must have been lined up exactly opposite each other. If the Tommy had seen Karl first, it would be Karl lying dead.

He must have had a bit of a shock when he realised he was looking straight into the other fellow's rifle – and then he'd stood there for over three hours more, relying on stillness and camouflage, knowing that if his opponent spotted him he was dead.

It made my skin crawl. *That English fellow was good, very good, but his luck ran out. How long before Karl's does?*

I'll give this to Koch as soon as I see him. I don't like looking at the bloody thing. He'll love it, though.

Koch did not disappoint.

"Bleedin' 'ell!" was all he said at first, and he repeated it several times.

Bauer was the first man he saw.

"Hey, look at this! It was that English bastard's!"

"Karl did this?"

"Yup."

"Well," Bauer said, examining the broken sight, "I thought *I* could shoot, but… Has Hafner seen it?"

"Don't know," said Koch. "I'll go and show 'im."

Word spread very quickly that the English bastard was indeed dead.

"Keep your heads down all the same, boys," said Rippel. "There'll be another."

Over the next few days Koch showed that bloody sight to everyone who would look at it, basking in reflected glory and exaggerating the story a little more each time.

I could see Karl getting more and more fed up with being the centre of attention. I could see too that he was fed up with being congratulated by some of the men who usually looked sideways at him.

"You'll all be happy enough if one of us gets that English bastard," he'd said, and how right he'd been.

"You did bloody well," I said to him next time we were in rest. We'd had a few beers and were starting to feel nicely relaxed. "That was a hell of a job, and superb shooting."

"Thanks," he said with a warm smile. "It was a bit more even, as well. Makes a change. Normally it's just like target practice."

His smile faded and there was a fleeting shadow in his eyes, which passed before I was even sure it was there.

"Karl, *even* is the last thing you want. *Even* is fucking dangerous. Firmly weighted in your favour is far preferable."

"And that from you!"

"What do you mean?"

"Franz, I'm well aware you have mixed feelings about what I do… Don't try to deny it, I've seen it in your face often enough."

I couldn't argue.

"One thing I am certain about," I said, "is that I want you to stay alive. You take far too many risks."

"Not as many as you might think. I'm very careful – I want me to stay alive too, you know."

"I still think you're barking fucking mad."

"Taschner won't be pleased," he said, changing the subject slightly. "He wanted revenge for Spots."

He wasn't wrong – when Taschner came back he was highly pissed off. Not only had Karl deprived him of revenge, but he'd done it with a fine demonstration of his own skill and courage.

Taschner heard a splendidly dramatised version of the story from Koch, who produced the Tommy's sight with a flourish at the end.

Karl was obviously embarrassed.

"There's nothing to say it was the same fellow," he said. "You might still get your chance."

"Not sure about that. I reckon it was him, all right," Taschner answered huffily.

"Even if it was, you don't want to believe everything Koch here says about it. You know how he exaggerates."

It was Koch's turn to get huffy. "No I don't."

"You do," said Karl firmly. "I swear the range has doubled and the gap halved in size!"

"So what could you see, then?" Taschner demanded.

"Well, to begin with I thought I could see something like the muzzle of a rifle, but I couldn't be sure. It could have been an old pipe. When the sun got a bit dimmer I could see something where his sight would have been, but he'd disguised it well and I wasn't certain.

"It was a bit nerve-racking – we were lined up pretty well perfectly but the angle would have been impossible from anywhere else. And I couldn't even think of moving – if I was right about what I was seeing then I was stuck till dark.

"All the time the sun was moving round and suddenly there was a gleam of light down through the rubble, from the side, and there was a movement – he must have shifted back into the shadows – and then I knew for sure what I was looking at.

"It was a real surprise when Braun gave me that sight. I

never saw the fellow himself. In fact, I didn't know whether I'd hit him or not. It was a very lucky shot."

You're being a shade too modest. It was, as Braun said, "bloody good shooting", but we both know Taschner likes to believe he's a better shot than you.

"So what happened the night I copped it?" Taschner asked. "I know bugger all about any of it – last thing I remember is leaving here. Next thing I knew I had a fucking horrible headache and couldn't work out why I was in a nice comfy bed with a pretty nurse bending over me."

Koch opened his mouth and Karl said with a grin, "You've had your go at storytelling – it's my turn now!"

He gave Taschner a very straight, factual account of how he'd found him and brought him back.

"Well, bugger me," he said when Karl had finished. "I owe you a beer or two, mate. That was bloody good of you. Broad fucking daylight and all." He shook his head.

Koch rolled his eyes. "You're a fuckin' good marksman, Leussow, and a fuckin' useless storyteller. You've left out the most important part." He turned to Taschner. "What 'e didn't say was that if 'e 'adn't of brought you in, you'd of bled to fuckin' death."

Taschner studied Karl for a moment.

"Cheers, mate," he said quietly. "I owe you big time for that. Tell you what, next time we're in rest I'll stand you dinner and a trip to the whorehouse."

"Thanks very much! I'll look forward to that."

Taschner was as good as his word. The first day we were back down the line the two of them set off early in the evening. They came staggering back after midnight, rather later than they should have been, Taschner with his arm round Karl's shoulders.

They stopped just inside the door of the barn. Taschner turned to Karl and hugged him.

"You're my besh mate fr'ever 'n' ever, y'know tha', don' you?"

"Yeh, coursh I do."

Karl put him down gently next to Koch, and then practically collapsed next to me and started snoring.

"Shut up, you noisy bastard," I said and gave him a shove.

He rolled onto his side and fell silent. Some time later he woke with a loud shout and sat bolt upright.

"Shut the fuck up!" someone called out.

Bit unreasonable, that. We all have nightmares.

"You all right?" I asked him quietly.

"Fine."

He lay down and apparently went back to sleep, but I couldn't and I lay awake thinking until the dawn.

The next morning Rippel appeared.

"Heavy night, was it, Leussow?" he asked with a very straight face.

"Er... yes, it was rather, sir."

"Leutnant Hafner wants to see you in half an hour. Oh, and smarten yourself up a bit. This isn't the front line." The amused gleam in his eyes robbed the words of any severity.

Karl was even filthier than most of us, being as he spent much of his time immersed in the Flanders mud. It was ingrained into his face and hands, and his uniform was never going to be clean again.

"I suppose I'd better wash and shave," he said. "It'd take a lot more than half an hour to get me anywhere near smart."

"Bet you're on a fizzer for being late back," I said.

He shrugged. "Can't be, or they'd want Taschner as well."

You couldn't give a stuff anyway.

He came back shortly afterwards, grinning from ear to ear. "Hey, Taschner! You've stood me rather more than dinner and a tart!"

Taschner looked bemused. "What're you on about?"

"Thanks to you I'm getting the Iron Cross, First Class."

"What?"

"Yes – just for saving your lousy hide! How about that?"

"That's bloody terrific, mate. Just make sure you get the next one for shooting straight! I'm not getting another hole in the head for your benefit."

"Hey, well done!" said Bauer. "Party time!"

"No! I'm not drinking again tonight!" Karl protested.

"Yes you are!" we all shouted.

Hafner was of the same opinion and the party started at five. Before the first barrel was tapped he made a very nice speech, praising Karl's courage and his marksmanship, and saying that he was a credit to the Army and to Brandenburg.

Karl blushed to the roots of his hair.

"Don't know who the fuck he was talking about," he said to me after we'd drunk his health. "Didn't recognise the fellow at all."

Braun had overheard.

"It was all true, Leussow," he said. "You've done bloody well – but then I always thought you would."

"Thank you, Sergeant Major."

"If you ask me you deserve it," I said. "So congratulations."

"Do you really think so? Remember when you got yours? You said that all you'd done was help someone you liked and respected."

"Yes," I said, and added into his ear, "but you saved *Taschner*."

He laughed. "And then had to be hugged by him," he murmured.

A couple of weeks later, to everyone's dismay, Rippel copped it on patrol. Sommerburg and Rombach dragged him back between them and lowered him carefully into the trench, blood pouring from his neck and mouth.

He looked up at Hafner and tried to say something.

"It's all right, sir," Klose said to him. "You'll be fine now."

He died a few minutes later, and I was just relieved because the gurgling had stopped.

I am so sick of seeing men die, especially when they're so fucking young.

"Sorry, sir," Klose said to Hafner. "He'd lost too much blood."

"Hardly surprising," Taschner said quietly, "hole in his neck like that. Only surprise is he made it this far."

"What happened?" Hafner asked Rombach.

"We met the Tommies, sir – you might have heard."

"Yes."

"And one of them chucked a bomb and he was the only one it got."

Hafner sighed. "Can't be helped. Best get his body back before it gets light."

"Yes, sir."

"That's a real shame," Karl said to me.

"Yes – wonder who we'll get instead."

That was answered next time we were in rest. Meyer was summoned to Hafner and reappeared with a nice new set of epaulettes.

Once again we said, "Congratulations, Herr Leutnant," with sincerity.

I hope you don't go the same way as Rippel – but they don't call it the Express Ticket to Eternity for nothing.

"If I were you, sir," Karl said, "I'd rub some dirt into those epaulettes."

"Don't worry, Leussow – that's just what I intend to do! Oh – and here's your five marks."

"Thank you, sir."

At first it amused us greatly to address him as 'Herr

Leutnant', but he settled into his new role so well that Karl and I almost forgot that he'd once sat in lectures and played the fool with us. Command came naturally to him, and he had an easy authority that I rather envied.

He was obviously going to go a very long way, and I reminded Karl that one day we'd be presenting arms to General Meyer.

"If we live that long!" Karl answered cheerfully.

"Speak for yourself," I said. "I intend to manage duration even if you don't!"

"I hope it doesn't go on long enough for Kurt to make general... It'll suit me fine if it finishes this year – in fact, this week would do."

"Fat chance." The subject was too depressing and I changed it. "Have you heard who's replacing Faltermeier?"

"No. I asked Hafner the other day and he said it's going to be a new fellow. Don't know why it's taking so long – or how it'll work out. Koch and Taschner make a very good team, so I suppose I'll get him. Someone has to. I just hope he's got some experience of the front line."

"You can always stick to solo work."

"Solo... You know, that word used to have such a different meaning."

"And it will again. You'll be back on the concert platform again once the war is over."

"If I can remember how to play. When I was at home I played and played – I'd got so fucking rusty. Then just when I was getting some of the notes in the right order I had to stop again.

"Now I just go over as many works as I can in my head, work out the fingering for difficult passages, that sort of thing. That way my brain and fingers might reconnect a bit quicker when I do get back... That's what I think about while I'm waiting."

I'd always wondered about that but not got round to asking.

"But doesn't your concentration wander?"

"No – it's as if my mind's in two parts, half at the piano and half out here. And when I'm out I can only fire twice at the most, and if there is a second one it has to be really worth it and a long time after the first, and then there's the wait before I can come back – so I've always got several hours when all I have to do is watch out for trouble."

"And it's quiet and peaceful without everyone chattering away."

He smiled. "Exactly. Probably wouldn't meet most people's definition of peaceful, but everything's relative, as Professor Einstein says."

"Do you understand that, then?

"Relativity? Good God, no. I'm a thick Junker, not an intellectual."

"Hardly thick."

"Look, I can shoot straight and play the piano, and once upon a time I managed to learn a bit of law, but compared with Albert Einstein I am monumentally thick."

"I'd say that goes for most of us."

I was summoned to Hafner, who told me that I was being made up to Sergeant and who tried, fruitlessly, to persuade me to go for the Express Ticket.

"You can always change your mind, you know," he said. "Just let me know."

"Thank you, sir."

He had news for the rest of us as well – first, that he'd been confirmed as Company Commander and was being promoted to Oberleutnant, and second, that there was to be a Division shooting competition.

"It'll be in two parts," he said. "A general one for the Regiment, with prizes for the top three, and a separate one for the snipers. Just one prize for them. The prize-winners will represent the Regiment, and the snipers will provide instruction to anyone who needs it."

The three of them looked at each other, clearly thinking that the last part didn't fill them with enthusiasm.

"That'll be fun," Koch grumbled later, "trying to teach some prat to shoot straight, when 'e should of learned by now."

"I'm not sure I can teach anyone," Karl said. "I can't remember not being able to shoot."

"Me neither," said Taschner. "I was just a kid when my dad taught me."

The other two nodded and said, "Me too," almost in unison.

"You'll be doing us all a favour," I said. "Let's face it, we don't know anything about the new fellows – we've never seen any of them shoot, and I'd rather be sure I can rely on them."

"That's right," added Peter.

"What're they going to do about our competition?" Koch asked suddenly. "I mean, they'll 'ave to 'ave an 'andicap system or it won't be fair."

"I'm the one who needs to worry about it being fair," Taschner grumbled.

"Oh, 'ere we go!" said Koch gleefully, "get the bleedin' violin out!"

"It's all right for you bastards," he and Karl chorused together.

Taschner bristled. "Look—"

"Just cos you're such a fucking skinflint," Koch said. "You could of brought your own as well, but you're too fucking mean!"

"I had to pay good money for that sight. I didn't get it given me, not like you rich bastards. No way was I giving it to the fucking Army."

Taschner got up and stomped off. Karl and Koch were laughing.

"Every time a winner," Koch said. "Rises to it every bloody time!"

"What are you both on about?" I asked.

"It's like this," Koch said. "When we was asked about being snipers, the Army didn't 'ave enough sights even though they was requisitioning them, so we was asked if we could bring one. Well, Leussow and me did – these are Carl Zeiss's finest – and we can live with not getting them back. Bit like buying War Bonds, I suppose. Anyway, Taschner spun some yarn about 'is being broken or whatever, just cos 'e's too fucking mean to risk losing it."

"We're being unfair, really," Karl said, still amused. "Sights are expensive. Mine was my sixteenth birthday present from Pa, along with a very nice hunting rifle – and I was very careful to leave that at home, so I can sympathise with him."

"So poor old Taschner got what 'e was given," Koch continued, "and every now and then 'e 'as a right old grumble, because 'e's ended up with three-power when we've got four."

"But you'll get yours back when the war's over?" Peter asked. "Or payment anyway?"

"Nice theory," said Karl, "but I'm not counting on it. I just think of it as a donation."

"Won't your father mind?" I asked.

"Being as he gave the entire stud to the cavalry I can't see him making a fuss about one telescopic sight."

"So how are they going to do the handicapping, then?" Peter asked.

"Dunno," Koch replied. "I've got a couple of ideas, though."

It turned out that the staff officer organising the competition had had no idea of the problem until the complaints rolled in. His instant response was that the range should be adjusted so that the target would appear the same size.

"'Asn't the stupid bastard 'eard of wind?" Koch demanded.

"Apparently not," Karl said.

"Not my problem," said Taschner cheerfully.

"It won't do," Koch said. "It won't do at all."

And he went off to protest to Hafner, who'd already lodged a protest of his own.

In the middle of the argument Faltermeier's replacement arrived, a skinny fellow called Dietz. He had, apparently, won a string of competitions before the war and had been working as an instructor back in Hannover.

"I'd had enough of that," he said. "I was bored out of my skull."

"Well, you won't be bored here," Taschner said. "Lots to do, isn't there, boys?"

"That's for sure," Koch confirmed.

Karl nodded. "I'll show you round," he said. "You get Faltermeier's space in the dugout... Teaching recruits, were you?"

"Yes."

Koch and Taschner exchanged glances.

"God, no wonder you were bored," Karl said. "I can't think of anything worse. What was the hunting like round there?"

His tone was casual, but I could see Dietz beginning to feel he was being interrogated.

"Didn't have much time for that," he said, rather brusquely. "Not of late, anyway."

He didn't sound as if he'd missed it. Taschner raised his eyebrows, and Karl was careful not to look at either him or Koch.

"Well, you'll get plenty now. The dugout's this way."

As they turned away Taschner called out, "Hey – did that rifle come from Company stores?"

Dietz turned round. "Yes."

"What power's your sight, then?"

"Three," he replied with a puzzled air.

"*Yes!*" Taschner exclaimed in triumph.

Dietz looked completely baffled.

"Don't mind him," Karl said. "He can't help it – had a bang on the head a few weeks back and he's not been right since."

"Fuck you too, mate!" said Taschner. "Anyway, you can't talk. You never had any marbles to lose."

Dietz followed Karl, shaking his head and clearly wondering what sort of madhouse he was in.

As soon as they were round the traverse Taschner said softly, "Not too sure about him."

"No," Koch answered. "Me neither. Probably be all right after a couple of months."

"A couple of what?" said Taschner, and they both laughed.

"No experience of the front line," Karl said to me later, "and he can damn well get some before I even think of working with him. Which makes it a bit awkward for me – I mean, someone has to show him how things work out here. We can't just leave him to find out."

"I suppose not…"

"Oh, sod it – I'll spend tomorrow in one of the OPs with him. Let's just hope he doesn't get us blown to smithereens."

Dietz sat with us when the rations came up.

"'Ere," Koch said, "you did all those competitions, right?"

"Yeah."

"Well, you're just in time for ours – and you might 'elp solve the problem."

"What's that, then?"

Koch explained. "And they can't sort it out," he finished.

"They could alter the size of the targets," Dietz suggested.

"Hafner tried that," Taschner said. "They said they're Army standard and no one's going to make new ones just for us."

"Yeah, but that wasn't what they said, was it?" Koch said.

"Like I told you, I overheard Hafner complaining to Meyer – wasn't difficult, 'e was practically shouting – and 'e said that twat of a staff officer said they wasn't going to change things for a load of prima donnas."

"A load of *what*?" Dietz said.

"Prima donnas," Koch answered. "It's Italian. It means—"

"I know what it fucking well means," Dietz said indignantly. "Who the fuck does he think he is?"

"That's staff officers for you," said Karl. "Makes you wonder if we're doing the Tommies a favour by shooting theirs."

"When did you last even see a staff officer?" Taschner demanded.

"Must be a couple of months back now," Karl admitted. "He was wandering up the comms trench like a tit in a trance – looked completely bloody lost."

"Saved him trying to find his way back again, though, didn't you?" Taschner said with a grin.

"It did cross my mind to let him go. I mean, it was practically broad fucking daylight and the stupid bastard just stopped and stood there, looking at his map and looking round, and I thought, if you're that thick then maybe they're better off without you."

"Couldn't resist, though, could you?" Taschner said. "I mean, who could? You see the red tabs and that's that: he pays for all the shit ours have stirred up."

"That's about the size of it," Karl agreed.

"You could have shot him in the shoulder or something," Dietz said.

The other three stared at him as if he'd grown a second head.

"You what, mate?" Taschner asked incredulously.

"Where the fuck d'you get that idea?" Koch demanded.

Karl's eyes softened a little.

"In a month or so that won't even occur to you," he said. "And if I'd done that he'd have been back at work in a few weeks. What good would that have been?"

"Listen, mate," said Taschner. "First fact of sniper life – them over there hate our guts and want us dead. And I'm not going to fart-arse about, being nice to bastards who want to kill me, and who fucking near succeeded a few weeks back."

He took off his cap and turned the side of his head towards Dietz.

"See? If it wasn't for Leussow here I'd be dead. So as far as I'm concerned they can all go to Hell – and I'm more than happy to send them on their way."

"You always were," Karl said with a grin. "Even before the bang on the head."

Taschner just grinned back. "I've got scores to settle," he said. "None of my mates made it to the end of last year."

You passed that stage a long time ago. Killing's become habitual and I doubt you ever give it a second thought.

"Second fact of sniper life," Koch said. "Though really it's joint first. Firing's like sayin' 'ere I am – you just 'as to 'ope they wasn't lookin' cos if they was you've fuckin' 'ad your chips. So I make fuckin' sure it counts – sure as I can, that is – just in case it's the last one."

"You don't often get the luxury of choice, anyway," Karl said. "Usually all you see is half a head – and if you do get a better view then you don't waste it."

There was a long pause. Taschner caught Koch's eye and raised his eyebrows. Koch gave a barely perceptible shake of his head in return. Karl looked at me and I could see him wondering what they'd been sent.

I had a degree of sympathy for Dietz. The first time I'd shot someone had been in battle and I still don't know whether I'd have been able to do it cold, as he was going to have to.

They shouldn't give that job to a man who hasn't been at the Front.

"They'll 'ave to adjust the points," said Koch finally. "And God knows 'ow they'll do that."

"I'll get onto some of my mates," Dietz said. "One of them might have an answer."

"I have to say I'm bored with the whole idea," Karl said. "I can think of better ways to spend my time in rest."

"At least you won't catch the pox from a shooting contest," said Taschner. "Not like your usual activities."

Karl grinned at him. "I won't anyway. I never go bare. And you can't talk!"

"Don't know 'ow you feel anything through that bloody thing," Koch said.

"Makes it last longer. You should get one – life insurance!"

"Nah," said Koch. "I won't live long enough to die of the pox anyway."

Karl stretched. "Well, I reckon it's my bedtime," he said. "Early start tomorrow. Though it's not as bad now the mornings are darker." He turned to Dietz. "We can't use the approach to the OP in daylight, so we'll have to be out there by five. Oh – and I don't know what they told you about Tommy snipers, but they're starting to get their act together, so keep them in mind, always."

He wasn't joking. We'd already lost three of the new men. One of them had made the classic mistake of poking his head up for a look at No Man's Land and had been shot before anyone could tell him to get down.

The next morning dragged past.

"Bleedin' 'ell, look at that!" said Sommerburg, pointing at the sky.

One of our two-seater aircraft was being attacked by three English single-seaters. Three of our fighters joined in and we all stared at the sky, riveted by the two-seater crew's desperate attempts to defend themselves and the dogfights that developed as the fighters tried to outmanoeuvre each other.

"Oh, fuck – they got him!" Peter said. "The bastards!"

Our two-seater was heading for home as fast as it could, losing height, with a trail of smoke coming from the engine. One of the English aircraft followed but broke off sharply when he got a burst from the observer's machine-gun. He turned back towards his own lines, flying unsteadily.

"He must have been hit," Peter said.

"That'll be the end of him," said Goldblum. "No one can help him, can they?"

No – he has to get himself down, and land the thing. And how do you do that, anyway?

"Oh, fuck!" shouted Sommerburg.

One of our fighters was falling out of the sky, spinning round and round like a sycamore leaf. It disappeared from view and a moment later a plume of black smoke rose up.

Shit! That's the end of him – I wonder if he was dead already or if he had time to think about what was coming.

It was a quick death, though. Not like lying out in No Man's Land. And you must be less likely to get mutilated…

I was far less bothered about being killed than about those two possibilities. The former filled me with such sick dread that I did my best not to think about it. They wouldn't be able to come and get you, not in broad daylight. You'd just lie there in agony, as I'd heard so many doing.

Shut up, Franz – if you start thinking about that you'll be bugger all use to anyone.

The sky was suddenly empty. In watching those three aircraft I'd lost sight of the others, and they'd all gone.

"Buggered if you'll get me up in one of those," said Bauer.

I wonder what it's like, flying through the air and looking down on the Front?

Karl and Dietz came back after dark and there was an atmosphere between them. They barely spoke to each other, even while we were sitting together eating, and Dietz hardly took part in the usual banter.

In the early hours of the next morning we were out mending the wire when Karl passed us like a phantom.

"Left you on your tod, 'as 'e?" Koch asked Dietz later. "Used to do that to me all the bloody time, used to really piss me off. Mind you, I still get left – Taschner's just as daft about going out, even though 'e got whacked on the 'ead. Beats me why they want to do it – far too fucking dodgy, 'fyou ask me."

"Don't think I'll be doing it, either... I thought I might have pissed him off."

"Why? What d'you say?"

"Nothing really. Hardly anything at all."

Koch scratched his head. "Leussow? Pissed off with you? Don't think that's likely – nothing ever seems to bother 'im – and if you 'ad I reckon you'd know about it." He turned to me. "You ever see Leussow get offended?"

I started laughing. "Once," I said. "Early this year. He bloody near broke Peter's jaw."

Koch's eyes lit up. "Wish I'd seen that."

"It was worth seeing. Peter had it coming – what he'd said was bang out of order."

"Leussow's not the sort of bloke you wants to 'ave a fight with," Koch said. "Far too bloody big and solid. Fucking cold-blooded, too."

Bit rich, you calling Karl cold-blooded. You're right, but you're hardly the one to comment.

"Yes, I saw that yesterday," Dietz said, and I couldn't quite read his expression.

"You 'ave much luck?"

"He did. I didn't."

"Way it goes, sometimes," Koch said consolingly. "They all pops up when you're spotting, and then when you're shooting they all keeps their fucking 'eads down. It'll go the other way next time. Tell you what, though – come with me and I'll show you one of our best positions. Pound to a pinch of shit you'll get lucky there."

"Nothing doing," Dietz said later. "Not my day."

The next day Taschner said, "Dietz, I've got an idea – how's about we all swap round today and tomorrow, so you get to work with each of us? That way you get all our experience. That all right with you, Leussow?"

"Fine," said Karl. "Good idea."

"Why don't you and me start off tomorrow, then?" Taschner said to Dietz.

"Where did you have in mind?" Dietz asked, rather cautiously.

"One of the OPs, I think, or we could stay here. I'll have a think and let you know."

Dietz failed to hide a look of relief.

"Look, mate," Taschner said, "you'd be fucking crazy to even think of going out until you know your way around here. You wouldn't have a clue where to set yourself up. We've been doing this for months and we still have to think about it."

"Quite," said Karl. "I've known someone get killed because he didn't realise the sun would light him up when it moved round – must have chosen his position on a cloudy day."

That was the Tommy sniper you shot, but someone else will have to tell Dietz that story.

"And you can't take two blokes out," Taschner added. "It's hard enough hiding just yourself. And no one's going to think any less of you if you stay in, anyway. Koch always does."

"Too fuckin' right. You two are bonkers. 'Ow you can still go out after what 'appened I just don't know."

"Because we're bonkers, like you said," Karl answered cheerfully.

Dietz's bad luck continued the next day, and the next. He missed twice, to his apparent frustration.

"I think my sight's out," he said.

"I could do with a trip to the range, too," Taschner said.

"Why don't we all go?" Karl suggested. "We go back down the line tomorrow, don't we? We could make a day out of it."

"Yeah, good idea," said Koch.

"I'll go and tell Hafner," Karl said. "Being as there are four of us we might have to book."

He came back about ten minutes later.

"All sorted," he said. "Hafner said he's coming too – said it's been a while and he'd like to get his eye back in."

That'll put a dampener on the day out, the Company Commander joining in.

I was wrong.

"Sounds good to me," Koch said with genuine approval. "'E's a fucking good shot. If 'e 'adn't of been an officer 'e'd of been a fucking good sniper."

"That's for sure," agreed Taschner. "Our good fortune that he is an officer, though. He's always looked out for us, like giving us that dugout."

A couple of days later Hafner and the snipers set off for the range. There was a degree of tension between Dietz and the others, and Hafner was too good an officer not to pick up on it. It occurred to me that he had more than one reason for joining the expedition – he would also get the opportunity to see Dietz shoot and to find out how he was fitting in.

When they came back the tension was still there, but it had changed in a way that I couldn't put my finger on.

"That was a very pleasant afternoon," Hafner said as he left them, and I had the feeling that he hadn't got to the bottom of whatever was going on, but that he didn't like it.

"Fancy a beer?" Karl said to Dietz, quite unexpectedly.

"Er… yes, thanks."

"Trip to the tarts?" Taschner asked Koch.

"Yeah, good idea."

They invited me but I passed.

I'll see if Karl wants to go tomorrow.

He did, and afterwards we went for a meal and a few beers.

"What's going on with Dietz?" I asked. We were sitting together in the corner and everyone else was making so much noise that we could barely hear each other.

He took a long, thoughtful drag on his cigarette, raised an eyebrow and blew out a large cloud of smoke.

"Well, I promised him I wouldn't tell anyone, but you don't count—"

"Cheers, bastard!"

"You know what I mean. Anyway, he's got a problem. That was crap about his sight being out – it wasn't, and we saw yesterday how accurate he is, absolutely first class. No, thing is, first time he saw a Tommy through the sight that was exactly what he saw. A man, not a target."

"That's what I saw, that day you let me have a look."

"Maybe, but you'd be able to do it. It wouldn't be your first time, after all."

"No… It's not a job for someone who hasn't been out here before."

"I agree. You can imagine what Koch and Taschner would think – that's why I took him for a beer last night.

"I told him it was different for the three of us – we'd all had quite a bit of practice before we got the close-up view and none of us gave a shit by then. I also told him straight out to sort himself out and get the first one, otherwise none of us would be working with him. Apart from anything else we can't rely on him. And Hafner saw how well he shoots, and won't put up with him not delivering.

"By the time I'd said all that I needed another beer."

"I'll bet. That was a lot of words for you all in one go!"

He laughed. "True… I just hope he listened."

"He'd probably be all right up against a Tommy sniper – be a bit more even, as you said before."

Karl shook his head. "We can't ask him to do that – it's far too fucking dangerous for a novice. No, he'll just have to learn to see it differently."

"You know," I said, "I hesitated the first time – but they were shooting our fellows so I had to get on with it."

"Yes. Bit more of an incentive."

My sympathy for Dietz had increased – whatever Karl might say I wasn't sure I would be able to look at a man through the sight and just kill him the way they did – but he'd taken the job, the privileges, and the extra pay, and as Karl said, he had to deliver.

He had no luck again on our first day back in the line, and I could see Koch and Taschner becoming impatient. It wouldn't be long before they guessed what the problem was, and they wouldn't be sympathetic.

Karl suggested to Dietz that they work together the next day, and he agreed. He wasn't in any position to argue. Apart from anything else he was depending on Karl to keep his mouth shut.

Dietz has to get on with it today, I thought as they went to their position. At about midday one of them fired, and when they broke for lunch shortly afterwards Dietz's face held a look that I could only describe as relief tinged with guilt.

"Well done," Karl said warmly. "That wasn't an easy shot but you got him, for definite."

Koch and Taschner added their congratulations and I could see Dietz wondering whether it was really something to be proud of.

You'll have to get that idea out of your head. You can't afford it.

"Be three at least by the time we go back down," Taschner said. "You'll pick up fast now."

"You can join our scoring system if you like," Koch added.

"I think I'll get a bit more experience first," replied Dietz. "You three are a long way ahead, anyway."

"Two," Karl said firmly. "I'm not in it."

Koch and Taschner looked at each other and rolled their eyes very obviously.

Karl saw and added with a grin, "Just as well for you – less competition!"

"You what, mate?" Taschner said. "We're going to fucking slaughter you in that contest."

"No chance!"

"'Ere, Dietz, 'as you 'eard from your mates who was going to sort out the 'andicappin'?" Koch asked.

"Yes – I had a letter last week and I passed it on to Hafner. Haven't heard anything yet, though. It was some mathematical way of adjusting the points – can't say I really understood it."

"Wonder when it's going to be," said Taschner.

"Too fucking soon," Karl replied. "I really don't want to know. All I want to do out of the line is sleep, have a fuck, get pissed, and get some decent grub that's not bloody lukewarm. Oh, and not have the bloody rats scurrying about the place… On the other hand the sooner it is, the sooner it'll be over."

"See – you'll get slaughtered with an attitude like that!" Taschner said gleefully. "Just you wait!"

Karl turned to Dietz. "Back to work, I think. You choose the position – you can shoot again, start catching us up."

By the time we went back out of the line Dietz had had more success and there was a subtle change in him.

You've got a choice now – you can either be like Karl, and treat it as a job that has to be done, or you can become like the other two. I wonder which it will be.

On our first day in rest Alfred came back, as Officer Cadet Friedemann.

"That's two of our friends we have to call 'sir'," Karl said.

"Two more of your mates you'll outlive, you mean!" said Taschner.

"Glad you're back, sir?" I asked Alfred.

"Yes – and just in time to go on the big raid."

Meyer was to lead a substantial raid on the English front line – HQ wanted to know who was opposite us and also wanted them roughed up a bit, wanted a 'show of offensive spirit' or some such nice turn of phrase.

"Easy for staff officers to say," Karl said.

"Fucking bloody staff," said Peter.

"Like my brother," Karl said, deadpan.

"Oh – is Friedrich on the staff now?" I asked.

"No. I wish he were. He's back with his company. No, it's Johnny with the carmine collar patches."

Peter muttered something and got up and left. Alfred and I started laughing.

"Looks like he didn't want to insult your other brother!" Alfred said. "Maybe his jaw still aches from the last time!"

"Oh, is that wot 'e did?" asked Koch.

"Oh, yes," said Alfred. "The thump when Karl hit him was quite something."

"Wish I'd seen it," Koch said again.

Alfred was obviously looking forward to the raid.

"Be interesting to see how Meyer handles it," he said to Karl and me. "Braun's going to be second in command so it won't matter too much if Meyer fucks up."

"Do you think he will?" I asked.

Should you really be saying that to us? I thought – but Alfred seemed to have a more relaxed attitude than some.

"Not if it all goes as planned – but when does anything?"

"When indeed."

Meyer did not fuck up. The raid was a resounding success, creating carnage and confusion and bringing back some papers that Hafner sent down the line at once. Two of the raiding party were injured, one quite badly, but that was trivial compared with the casualties they'd inflicted.

Karl had headed out an hour or so before they'd set out.

"If you're going to make the hares run I'll see if I can't pick a couple off," he'd said. He came back in after everything had quietened down again.

"That's one Tommy major the less," he said cheerfully. "The more of them we get rid of the better."

"Ah, that *was* you, then," Alfred said. "I did wonder – I was just about to give him the spade when the bugger just dropped." There was a definite note of complaint in his voice.

"Sorry if I spoiled your fun, sir. He was too good a target to resist – and he was going for his pistol."

"Would've been dead before he could have fired it. Oh sod it, just buy me a beer some time."

"Done."

"Meyer did bloody well," Alfred said to me the next day, sounding impressed and rather surprised. "Really aggressive and right on top of the situation, bloody good leadership. Got everyone out again, too, which is the hard part."

"So you're really looking forward to your commission, then, sir?"

"Too right – and you should go for it too."

"What, me?" I exclaimed. "Why in God's name would I want to wear epaulettes and get shot by some bloody Tommy sniper?"

He laughed. "Maybe you have a point…"

With all that, I'd forgotten about the shooting contest. It had been running for about two weeks, which led to grumbles about differing wind conditions from some of the snipers. And of course they'd all insisted on having their sights re-zeroed before they shot in the competition, which hadn't been allowed for in the original scheduling. We were the last company to shoot.

"I could almost agree with that staff officer who called us prima donnas," Karl said to me. "Unless it's a howling fucking gale everyone should be able to deal with it, at our level anyway. What the fuck do they do in the front line? Wait for flat calm before they go to work?"

The first three in the general competition were men none of us knew. I wasn't unhappy with my own shooting – I was never going to threaten the podium, but I was no less accurate than I'd ever been. And I was very pleased to see that none of my men needed remedial tuition. In fact Scheffel was one of the best in the company.

Karl and a fellow called Schwarz from the Sixth Company tied for the win in the snipers' competition, with Dietz beaten into second, much to his disgust.

"I knew there was something wrong with that fucking handicapping system," he grumbled.

"You can shut the fuck up," Taschner said. "You bloody came out with it, and it's no good moaning cos you lost."

Taschner himself had just got into the top ten and was more than a bit annoyed, but was not the man to be a bad loser.

Karl and Schwarz were offered the chance to shoot again for the win, but both declined and agreed to toss a coin for the privilege of representing the Regiment. Karl lost, to his unconcealed delight.

"That was quite enough of that," he said. "Far too much like work."

"I don't understand you," Dietz said. "Why throw away the chance of representing the Regiment? And you could shoot for

Brandenburg in peacetime. You're more than good enough."

"Not my idea of fun," Karl answered. "Wine, women and song are far more like it."

"But you organised our trip to the range."

"That was survival. You'll be surprised how fast your sight can go out in the front line, and I don't want to find out by missing some bloody Tommy sniper and showing the bastard just where I am."

There was a parade for the prize-giving so we all got a bath and delousing, and clean uniforms.

"I haven't been as clean as this for months," Karl said. "I'd forgotten what it felt like."

"Nah," Taschner said, "you'll never get the Flanders mud out of your face and hands – you can scrub till Doomsday, it'll still be there. And the lice'll be back as soon as the eggs hatch."

As we got ready, Dietz looked at Karl with sudden respect. "How'd you get the gongs, mate?"

"Ah, well… I've been told I'm a – what was it you said, Koch? A fucking useless storyteller?"

"That's it! Totally fuckin' useless."

"So Koch can tell you about the Second Class – that was really a joint effort, anyway – and Taschner can tell you about the First Class. Some time when I'm not around."

"No, I can't," Taschner said. "I still can't remember a bloody thing about it. Koch'll have to tell him."

"Well, the best storyteller gets the job, then!"

"It's not just the gongs I'll tell you about, mate," Koch said. "There was this Tommy sniper—"

"No! Stop right there!" Karl said, laughing. "Dietz, you want to take that story with the whole bloody salt cellar—"

"You can't argue with the evidence, Leussow," Koch said. "That's what Granddad always says."

"What's all this about?" Dietz looked more than a bit confused.

"Don't worry," said Karl. "It'll all make sense later. Just don't ask me about any of it."

"And don't ask 'im 'is score, neither," Koch said. "The daft bugger don't know – won't add it up. God knows why not."

"Because the Devil can tot 'em up as they arrive in Hell," Karl replied. "So I spare myself the effort."

"But you write your book up," Dietz said. "I've watched you."

"Of course. I just don't add the pages together."

"See what I mean?" Koch said. "Bloody daft. Now Taschner and I can tell you *exactly* 'ow many – like I said before, we're running our own competition, and I'm leading by ten points."

"Yeah," said Taschner, "but don't forget I had four weeks out, so I'm leading on daily average."

"Don't ask about their scoring system," Karl said. "You really don't want to know."

"It's like this," Koch said. "You gets one point for a private, two for an NCO—"

"What if you couldn't tell?" Dietz broke in. "I mean, with the Tommies wearing stripes on their arms. What do you do then?"

"Does it fucking matter?" asked Karl. "Dead is dead."

"It's just one point unless you're sure of the rank," Taschner said. "And you can't talk, mate – I reckon you've shot more officers than either of us."

"Because that does the most damage, not to score bloody points. And where do you get that idea, anyway?"

"Something Hafner said."

Karl pulled a face.

"And you trust each other not to fib?" asked Dietz.

"You bet we fucking do," Koch said indignantly.

"Too right," added Taschner. "What do you take us for?"

The conversation was interrupted by our having to fall in. The band played and Oberst Schröder made a boring but mercifully short speech about the importance of good shooting and then did a nice job of the prize-giving, handing a bottle of champagne to the winner of each contest. The more important business was the party that followed.

The also-rans had to make do with beer. I looked enviously at Karl and Schwarz, who were rapidly demolishing their bottle of fizz.

Taschner followed my gaze.

"Have some more good German beer," he said. "Better make the most of it before it runs out and we're back to that Belgian stuff."

"Some of it's pretty good," I said. "Have you tried those Trappist beers?"

"Have I! Tell you what, let's see if we can get hold of some, and then we'll celebrate Karl's victory properly."

A couple of days later he came back with thirty bottles. I was careful not to ask where he'd got them.

"Koch's organising some grub to go with it," he said, "and being as you're Leussow's mate you're invited too."

"Cheers."

It was a bloody good party, much better than the official one, at which the beer had been rationed. The Colonel's idea of a party was clearly not quite the same as ours, or Hafner's for that matter. There was always a decent amount of beer when he organised a do. We weren't sure whether the big boss was keen on sobriety or just plain mean.

Six bottles of Trappist beer each had us all feeling nicely relaxed, and Koch had managed to get hold of a generous amount of bread, cheese and sausage, so we were all happily well-fed. I decided not to ask the provenance of any of it. They weren't likely to tell me, anyway.

Late in the evening a rather drunken Dietz put his arm round Karl's shoulders.

"Know what, mate? I'm no' sorry I lost to you af'er all. Koch showed me tha' English bloke's sight an' I reckon you're shit-hot."

"You don't want to believe all that story," Karl said, sounding considerably more sober than I felt. "Bet he told you it was four hun'red metres. No Man's Land's no' that wide."

"Don't matter," Dietz said. "Can't argue wi' th'evidence. An' he tol' me how you got your Firs' Class. An' b'sides, I owe you."

"No, you don't. You don't owe me fuck all."

Karl was becoming embarrassed. Taschner saw it and rescued him.

"Hey, Dietz, you gonna join our system?" he asked.

"Dunno yet. Still no' sure 'f I wanna carry on."

"You what?" Taschner sounded as if he couldn't believe his ears. "This is the bes' fucking job on the Wes'ern Fron'. Wha' you mean?"

Koch was shocked into semi-sobriety. "Did 'e say what I thought 'e said?"

"No," Karl said. "Don' take any notice. He's pisseder than we are."

"I'm no' pissed," Dietz said.

"Well, you should be," Karl told him. "Jus' drink your beer." He squinted at his watch. "We'd best get back – we don' want trouble, 'specially with all that stuff we lib'rated."

"Tha's for sure," Taschner agreed. "Tha' beer was for th'officers' mess."

I put my hands over my ears. "I didn't hear that," I said. "An' I don' wanna hear any more."

We struggled to our feet and made our way unsteadily back towards the barn. Halfway there Koch started singing and Taschner clamped a hand firmly over his mouth.

"Shu' the fuckup!" he hissed.

I suddenly remembered the sergeant's braid on my collar, and realised I was likely to get into far more trouble than they were.

"Le's jus' get in th'fucking barn," I said. "No more noise."

We made it without attracting the attention of the military police, and were soon asleep in our corner.

There was a bit of a fuss the next day about thirty bottles of beer that the officers were missing, plus a quantity of bread and so on that had apparently grown legs. A small pile of bottles and some cheese rinds were found in a ruined house, but the trail was stone cold.

The five of us were careful to hide our hangovers. *No wonder Trappists are a silent order*, I thought – *their beer's so fucking strong I don't suppose any of them can speak.*

Fortunately for the snipers the day scheduled for remedial tuition was the last day in rest, so they had time to get rid of their headaches.

"That was without question the most boring day of my life," Karl said in the evening. "One of the fellows they gave me was completely fucking hopeless – I think he needed glasses."

"Now you understand why I wanted out," said Dietz. "After a year of that I was climbing the walls."

"Be a relief to get back to proper work," Taschner said.

"Get rid of some of those fuckin' Tommy snipers," added Koch. "Need puttin' in their place, that lot do."

"I think I spotted another of their loopholes last time up," Karl said. "It was well buried in the sandbags and didn't seem to be in use, so I thought I'd leave it till one of the bastards is there, then maybe have a go with steel core, just for a change."

"Works a treat, that does," Taschner said. "I blasted one of the fuckers out a couple of weeks back with a round of that."

"Yes… I'd rather put one through the hole, though," Karl replied.

"Yeah, but if you blast through the plate then they have to rebuild the position."

"And they'll put it somewhere different, and then we have to find it again."

"You just like to make things difficult!" Taschner said. "They have to move the position anyway after we've got one, don't they? And your idea's crap, anyway. If you miss the hole then you're dead."

"So don't miss!"

"Do they have steel core as well?" asked Dietz.

"Similar stuff," Karl said. "And Schwarz told me he's got a mate who's a sniper in France, and one of his oppos got killed when his position was blasted in with some sort of oversized round. Just smashed straight through the plate, made a hell of a hole, took off most of his head."

"Sounds like an elephant gun," Dietz said. "One of my mates back home's got one. Didn't realise the Tommies had them out here."

"I don't think they're in general use – just some enterprising fellow's brought one along."

"Well, let's hope they don't bring one here," Taschner said.

"'Ere," said Koch suddenly, "'ow many points is we awardin' for Tommy snipers, then? Bein' as there's more of 'em now we needs to sort it out."

"Suit your bloody selves," Karl said. He turned to me. "Fancy a walk?"

"Why not?"

When we were out of earshot he said, "That fucking competition!"

I thought he was going to say more but he didn't.

"Pretty macabre," I said.

"That's one way of putting it. I wonder how long it'll be before Dietz joins in."

"Do you think he will? He still seems a bit doubtful about the whole business."

"Five marks says he's in by the end of the month."

"Done." *That's one safe bet.*

On our second day back in the line Karl and Taschner had both gone out, and to my intense anger one of the Tommy snipers killed Silke as he brought the post up. There was a dodgy spot in the comms trench and he must have forgotten about it.

Unfortunately for the Tommy, Koch and Dietz had been watching and had seen exactly where he was. A few minutes later Dietz blasted him out, to everyone's great satisfaction.

"Nice job," I said to him later.

"Thanks, Sarge. Taschner was right – that stuff works a treat."

Scheffel retrieved the post after dark and put up a warning sign at the bad spot. There didn't seem to be much mail which led to a great deal of grumbling, especially from those who were hoping to hear from a wife or a sweetheart.

I'd given up hope of ever having a girl of my own – how on Earth was I likely to even meet a girl, let alone have time to get to know her?

It's cheap tarts all the way to the grave for me. No one's ever going to go to bed with me because she wants to – but that was far too much like self-pity, and I told myself firmly to be thankful I was still in one piece.

There'll be plenty of girls after the war, more than enough to go round. Best thing's to focus on staying alive so I'll be there to enjoy them.

Taschner came back in about an hour after dark, and Karl turned up about half an hour later.

"Hafner wants to see you," Koch said to Karl.

"Oh, right. What about?"

"Like 'e would tell me!"

"Just wondered whether I need to clean myself up first."

"'E didn't say."

Karl shrugged and headed for Company HQ. He came back about twenty minutes later with a very thoughtful look in his face.

"What was that about, then?" I asked.

"I need to have a word with the others," he said.

The other three were sitting on the fire step. Dietz was talking about the tarts in Hannover.

"What did Hafner want?" Taschner asked, seemingly glad of a change of subject.

"Old Schröder's decided we're to have two more colleagues—"

"'Bout bloody time too," Koch said. "The Tommies are getting better at this game."

"And Hafner told me that being as there'll be six of us I'm going to be promoted."

"What – you mean you'll be in charge of us?" Taschner looked as if he'd bitten on a lemon.

"That's about the size of it," Karl said quietly.

"You've only got it cos you're a bleedin' 'von'," Taschner said sourly.

"Yes, I agree," Karl replied calmly. "You'd do a much better job than me and that's what I told Hafner."

Taschner's jaw dropped. "You *what*?"

"'Ang on, did you really say that?" Koch demanded. "To *Hafner*?"

"What did he say?" asked Dietz.

"Told me very firmly to shut up and not question his decisions, said if I didn't wind my bloody neck in I'd find myself instructing back in Germany. He meant it, too."

"Christ, mate, I admire your fucking nerve," Taschner said. "What did you say to that?"

"What do you think I bloody said? You think I want to spend my life teaching like last week? I said I was very sorry if I'd given offence, it wasn't my intention, blah, blah. You've never seen a man eat a bigger plate of humble pie, I can tell you."

"You're staying, then," Koch said.

"Yes."

"Good job. Well, I'm pleased for you, mate. And if we 'as to 'ave a bleedin' NCO at least it's someone wot knows the job."

"Thanks."

"Yeah, I'll go with that." There was just a touch of warmth in Taschner's voice.

"I'd be happy with either of you," Dietz said diplomatically.

"Congratulations," I said.

Braun was not surprised. "Well done, Leussow," he said. "You deserve it and you'll do a good job."

"Well, I'll do my best, Sergeant Major. That's all I can promise."

"Do you know when your course is?" I asked Karl later.

"Not yet."

"You'll be an officer if this goes on much longer."

"Fuck that! Franz, if I'm ever stupid enough to take the Express Ticket, I'll pay you whatever forfeit you choose – just make sure you collect before the bastards shoot me."

X

Almost without us noticing, the summer had passed. It was September, the days were noticeably shorter and the evenings were cool. There had been no appreciable movement in either direction – we were all stuck just where we had been in the spring.

And so some bloody staff officer decided that the meanderings of the front line were too untidy and should be straightened out. Apparently a stretch of about a kilometre around our position had too many small salients. And the same bloody fool and his equally brainless colleagues decided the attack would be carried out in daylight, after a short bombardment. In their unconsidered opinion that would give us the advantage of surprise.

Hafner looked thoroughly uncomfortable when he gave us the news. We could all see what he was thinking, though of course he couldn't admit it.

Meyer had a similar expression when he went over our orders with us.

None of us had any questions. The only one worth asking was the one that was totally pointless: "Why the fuck are we being asked to do this?"

Few of us old hands felt like discussing it with each other either.

It's going to be absolute fucking slaughter. I'll be lucky to come out of it alive. Why haven't those stupid bastards learned anything?

"At last we're going to see some action!" said Schwartz.

"'Bout bloody time too," added Gruber.

Both of them had arrived in the summer.

"When we go over the top you'll wish you were back home," Bauer said. "You won't believe the amount of stuff the Tommies can chuck at you."

"Bloody right – you're both talking out of your arses." Peter's expression made his opinion of them perfectly clear. "You'll just be praying you don't end up pulped."

"That's enough, boys," I said firmly. "We're here to fight and we'll do it to the best of our ability. Go in hard and give them hell – that's the best way."

If we ever get there, that is.

"That's right," Alfred agreed. "That's what *I've* always done and I'm still in one piece."

Karl avoided the subject completely, as did Koch, Taschner and Dietz. They weren't coming with us – fortunately Schröder realised what a waste of their skill that would be. Their orders were to support us from our front line, and the machine-gunners would do likewise.

Training kept us occupied but the time dragged until the appointed day.

I was trying not to think of it as my last day. I tried to convince myself that I'd survive and without being mutilated, but I had great difficulty believing it. Karl spent all our free time with me, and I couldn't help feeling that he was deeply aware that it might be the last time we would be together.

On the day itself we were all wide awake long before dawn.

Karl came over to me before he went to his position, wrapped his arms round me and squeezed so tight I could hardly breathe.

"Good luck," he murmured in my ear.

"See you later," I said nonchalantly when he released me.

Your turn to stay in while I go out to God knows what – but you get a nice little hide while I'm going to be out in the open...

The thought chilled my blood and I pushed it aside.

"I'm counting on it!" he said. "And when we go back down the line we'll have the best dinner we can find and get totally pissed."

"You're on."

The clouds were so thick that the dawn seemed reluctant, and just after the bombardment began the heavens opened. The rain was so heavy that we were all soaked through in two minutes.

"Fucking wonderful," Goldblum said. "It'll be a fucking swamp."

"That'll do, Goldblum," I said.

He'd given voice to all our thoughts but I couldn't have anyone talking like that.

The bombardment was to lift just before we went in at eleven. Of all the fucking stupid times.

I took my watch off and put it in my pocket. Meyer would give us the signal and I had no desire to count down what would probably be my last minutes.

Don't think like that, Franz, or it'll come true. Just do your duty, as you've done before. Go in hard and give them hell.

It was worse, far worse, than anything I could have imagined. My boots sank into the mud, like one of those nightmares of trying to run through treacle, and the air sang with so much flying metal that it was almost solid. The English cut us to pieces, as we'd known they would.

We'd got barely fifty metres and hardly anyone was still on his feet. Meyer was beside me one moment and then suddenly he too was lying in the mud. I grabbed him, dragged him to the edge of a shell-hole, pushed him in and fell in myself.

His tunic was ripped and soaked with blood. I unfastened it, pulled his shirt up and sat back appalled. There was a triangular hole in his stomach, with blood and something foul-smelling running from it.

Shit, that looks really nasty, I thought, *and it's bleeding freely*. Bandaging him was bloody awkward as I had to sit him up and balance his limp, dead weight against me. His back was wet and I thought it was just water, but then I saw to my horror that the shell splinter had gone right through him. I had to use all four of our field dressings, and they got so wet with the rain that I wondered how much use they would be.

At least he was unconscious. I propped him against the side of the shell-hole and fastened his tunic again in a vain attempt to keep him warm. The rain poured down on us without letting up.

How can the sky hold so much water?

I knew what I was supposed to do – gather together what might remain of my men and continue towards the English lines – but it was impossible. To my shame I stayed with him, but how far would I have got before getting hit myself? And what use would that have been?

The frightful din eased and I half-wished it hadn't, because I could hear the screams and cries for help all around.

Come on, Franz – stop being such a fucking coward. I steeled myself to get up, but the English fire stepped back up to fever pitch. Our second wave must have gone over the top.

I raised my helmet above the lip of the hole and it was torn from my hand. Their artillery fire stepped up, shrapnel mixing with the high explosive. No one out there stood a bloody chance.

A bit later I looked at Meyer again and realised there was a steady trickle of blood running down his trousers. I unfastened his tunic again and saw that the bandages were soaked through with it.

He was bleeding somewhere internally. I put pressure on but the blood still trickled through, not fast but with no signs of stopping. Nothing I did made any difference and all I could do was hope he would last until dark.

He came round and started screaming. *The pills, Franz, give him some of the bloody pills, for fuck's sake.*

I put my hand in my pocket and it went straight through into air. There was a scorched hole in the fabric, and the packet of pills and my watch had both gone.

I couldn't stand listening to him and I covered my ears. There was nothing I could do for him, nothing at all. I couldn't even get him out of the rain. We were stranded and the rain poured and poured. The whole world was grey – the sky, the rain, the mud…

Everything was grey except his blood as it ran down into the puddle in the bottom of the shell-hole.

He screamed and writhed until I thought I would go mad. After God knows how long he was exhausted and lay still, whimpering.

I put my arm round him, his head resting on my right shoulder.

"I'm here, Kurt," I said uselessly. "You'll be fine. As soon as it's dark I'll get you back."

Instead of 'Herr Leutnant' I'd said 'Kurt' and 'du' without realising it. *You were my friend long before you were my superior, and none of that matters now anyway.*

The rain battered down on us, drumming on my bare head, plastering his blond hair to his scalp and running down his face. He was dying and I couldn't even shelter him from the rain. All I could do was hold him and listen to him and wait.

It didn't take much longer.

After darkness fell I climbed cautiously out of the hole. The rain had stopped. The air was empty and I stood up.

Nothing happened.

There was no point taking Kurt's body back, not when there

were so many who needed help. I'd gone about five metres when I found Gruber, his left leg broken.

I couldn't carry him by myself. I managed to get him over my shoulder, but my feet sank into the mud and I couldn't get them out again. Luckily Sommerburg materialised out of the ground and we carried Gruber back between us.

At the edge of the wire we handed him over to the medics. We were turning to head back out again when Hafner appeared at my elbow and said, "Becker, you speak English, don't you?"

"A bit, sir."

"Come with me." He was carrying a white handkerchief, and out in No Man's Land I saw an English officer and a sergeant, also with a white flag, brightly lit by a parachute flare. "I want to see what that's about and I want you to interpret."

"If I can, sir."

The English Major was very smart, as was his sergeant. Oberleutnant Hafner and I were bloodstained, filthy, and outranked. The Tommies were keeping us well-lit and our utter defeat was all too obvious.

"Bradshaw," said the Major in clipped tones.

"Hafner, sir."

They shook hands, and Bradshaw said, "You have until dawn to collect your wounded. I give you my word that we shall not fire."

There was more but I didn't understand it – something to do with how far we were allowed to go? I asked him to repeat it slowly.

"Your men must not pass my men," he said simply.

"Thank you, sir," said Hafner. "That is very generous of you."

They shook hands again and we turned and walked away from each other.

What a contrast. A few hours ago it was death to stand out here.

"Where's Leutnant Meyer?" Hafner asked me.

"Dead, sir." That was all I could say.

He shook his head. *I don't envy you one bit*, I thought suddenly. *You knew what would happen, but you had to take us in just the same.*

It was a long and dreadful night. The heavy physical work of carrying men through the mud was the least of it – far worse were the appalling injuries that some of them had received, and the fact that we couldn't help hurting them. We wanted to leave the worst cases for the stretcher-bearers but there wasn't time. All too often we were obviously inflicting frightful agony on men who were going to die anyway.

I lost track of how many I helped to fetch in. All I knew was that we had to hurry if we were to rescue them all before the truce expired.

As the first gleam of light touched the eastern sky there was a warning shot from the English lines and we made our way back through our wire. We'd managed to bring in everyone we thought was alive.

I dropped down into the trench.

"Ah, Becker," said Braun. "Good to see you in one piece. There's tea and rum over that way – don't think it's hot any more, though."

He wrote my name down, and in the early morning light I saw how few names he'd written.

"Leutnant Meyer's dead, Sergeant Major," I said flatly.

"Sure?"

I nodded, shivering with exhaustion and reaction and unable to say another word.

"Go and get some tea and rum down you," he said quietly.

As I rounded the traverse Karl came the other way. His face lit with joy when he saw me, joy that mixed rapidly with concern at my appearance.

"Franz – thank God." He flung his arms round me, and the comforting strength of his embrace almost finished me.

"Kurt –" I managed to say, my voice catching.

I hid my face against his shoulder, afraid I'd break down.

His arms tightened. "Tell me later," he said gently.

As the morning passed the horrific extent of our casualties became apparent. Leutnants Voigt and Meyer were dead, Leutnant Blume seriously wounded. Alfred was wounded though not badly. Schwartz was dead, Goldblum and Bauer were missing, as were many others. The list of dead and wounded went on and on.

Half my fellows had gone, and those who were left stared at me with blank, shocked eyes. I tried to find some words of encouragement, but could think of nothing that wasn't trite and inappropriate.

"You did very well, boys," was all I managed to say.

"Fucking hell," said Sommerburg, which rather summed it up.

I sat on the fire step, completely drained and beyond feeling anything. I woke with a jolt, unable to understand why I was covered in blood, and then I remembered and wished I hadn't.

Karl was sitting beside me, just as bloodied as I was.

"Look at the state of us," he said. "Fancy a smoke?"

"I'll stick to mine, thanks," I said. "Those black things of yours are bloody horrible."

I realised he had his rifle with him.

"You're not working today, surely?" I asked.

"Good God, no. None of us are. Not after they were so decent last night… We've given our dugout to the medics."

We sat in silence. There was nothing to say, nothing that could be said.

Towards midday there was a long drawn-out howl of agony from No Man's Land.

"Fuck," Karl said. "I thought we'd got them all."

"Becker," said Hafner. "What did you reckon to Major Bradshaw? I wonder if they'd let us go and get him?"

"I don't know, sir... He was very definite about the dawn, and they did fire that warning shot."

"Hm. Put up a board with our request and we'll see what they say."

I asked Karl what to write – his English was so much better than mine. He thought for a moment, then picked up the brush and wrote: PLEASE MAY WE FETCH OUR COMRADE?

The two of us held it up above the parapet. After a couple of minutes Hafner said, "Leussow, what does that say?"

Karl took the binoculars and shook his head. "It says, 'Sorry, not in daylight', sir."

Hafner sighed. "They've got their orders."

We had to listen to him howling intermittently for the rest of the day. He would stop for an hour or two and then, just when we thought he must have died, he would start again. It was the most horrible, spine-chilling sound, and I wished I were deaf.

"Fucking hell, the poor bastard," said Peter.

"Don't bear thinking about," Koch agreed.

Once darkness had fallen we went out to look for him. He'd fallen silent and there was no clue as to where he was lying. It was a very slow business checking all the fresh bodies for signs of life, and once I felt for a pulse in the neck of what I thought was a recent casualty, only for my fingers to sink straight into rotting flesh.

I was almost sick on the spot. The smell was so all-pervasive that I hadn't realised some of it was coming from him.

We found three men still alive including Goldblum, lying unconscious with his right arm and leg broken. His pulse was weak and irregular and we hoped he'd make it.

"I hope to God we found him," I said to Karl.

"So do I."

To everyone's colossal relief there was silence the next day, but we never knew whether we'd fetched him in or whether he'd died.

We were pulled out of the line and – unusually – given two weeks in rest, and reinforced yet again. The new men were mostly recruits, green as summer leaves, with no idea what awaited them. I was becoming sick of bright young faces that would probably never grow old.

We got a new Platoon Commander, Leutnant Gross from the Tenth Company. He'd been transferred from a Regular regiment at the start of the year and seemed to be a solid, dependable fellow, the sort you could rely on in a bad situation.

That was more than I could say about myself. I felt I'd failed – failed Kurt and failed to do my duty – and the mingled grief and shame consumed me.

Sleep was impossible. Every time I closed my eyes I was back in that shell-hole with the rain pouring down, holding Kurt while he died. If I did manage to get to sleep then I dreamed about it and woke up after what felt like a few minutes. And then I lay awake, waiting for the dawn and trying not to think.

I couldn't talk about Kurt, couldn't tell Karl what had happened. I knew Kurt had been his friend as well, but I couldn't find the words. He knew I had nightmares, but so did everyone.

Several times I saw him looking at me with concern, but he didn't raise the subject until about halfway through the fortnight. He'd bought me several beers and topped them off with some brandy his father had sent him, and I was starting to feel very well pissed. I didn't notice that he was drinking a good deal less than me.

"That was the most fucking appalling cock-up I've ever

seen," he said. "Someone in HQ should be shot. Even the rats could have told them what would happen."

I didn't answer, couldn't answer.

"We were fuck all use to you," he said bitterly. "The rain was so fucking heavy when you went over, I could barely make out their front line. I thought I got a machine-gunner before it got completely torrential but after that it was fucking hopeless – I couldn't keep the rain off the sight, couldn't see fuck all.

"I tried the conventional sight but with the rain and the smoke I couldn't see their line. It was just like fucking fog. I could see what was happening to all of you, though – far too bloody clearly. All I could do was fucking well watch. They might as well have sent us with you."

"I'm glad they didn't – that might have been you I was with." The words came out before I could stop them.

"You were with him?"

"Shit, Karl, it was… it was…" I had to break off. Then I took a deep breath and told him everything, somehow managing to keep my voice fairly steady.

"Jesus." He shook his head.

"It was the rain, that was the worst thing. I couldn't get him out of the bloody rain. And I should have gone on, not stayed there with him—"

"Franz, that's insane. You wouldn't have got another five metres. I saw the whole fucking mess, remember? The only men who came back were the ones who'd taken cover. There was so much stuff flying about, I don't know how any of you stayed upright more than a few seconds."

"Do you think so?"

"No. I *know* so. Don't blame yourself for anything. The blame lies with the fucking idiots who ordered it. There should be a special circle of Hell just for them."

"But I—"

"You'd just have got killed, and for absolutely nothing. You're no fucking use dead, are you? Dead men can't fight."

"I could have tried to bring him back. You got Taschner back in."

"That was completely different. They weren't chucking shitloads of crap at us. How far do you think you'd have got?"

"Well…"

"It would have been the same result. One dead Franz Becker."

"What would *you* have done?"

"The same as you. There wasn't anything else you could do. Did I pull you to your feet and try to take you forward at Langemarck?"

I stared at my hands. "No… but it's just… I should have done my duty."

"You did. You did far more than anyone should have asked you to do. And for what it's worth, I can't think of anyone I'd rather have with me when it all goes wrong."

I met his eyes and saw that he meant every word.

"And at least he had you with him, and if he'd still been alive when it got dark you'd have brought him back. He wouldn't have had to lie out there like that other poor sod. I don't want to imagine what that was like."

"No. Neither do I."

There was a long pause and then he said quietly, "I'm just bloody glad *you* came back. I saw someone I thought was you go down like a sack of potatoes and not move again, and then when I didn't see you all night I thought you must be dead – so shut up and drink up and be happy you're alive!"

It wasn't quite that simple, but he knew that – and what else could he have said? In my head I knew he was right, but the feeling of impotent failure remained.

A couple of days later he got a letter from Alfred, who said he'd been knocked over in the first few minutes by a bullet through his left thigh. He'd crawled back after dark and was recovering well.

"'No real damage, no bone or major blood vessels, could have been a lot worse'," Karl read out. "'Probably be a bit stiff for a while after it heals'. Oh, he says he might not be coming back to us. He's put in for a new type of unit, storm troops, he says they're called."

"Never heard of them," I said.

"Nor have I… Hang on, he says they're 'fast-moving and aggressive'. Now who does that remind you of?"

I started laughing. "What Rippel described as 'a bunch of like-minded thugs'. He'll feel right at home."

Karl laughed. "That's for sure! He's hoping his Express Ticket will come through soon, as well."

I wonder how long he'll last… Now there are only two of us, and I'm the only one who's still unscathed.

I sat down to write to Otto, to tell him that his closest friend from our university days was dead, and I hadn't a clue what to say. I'd put it off for far too long, but I didn't have it in me to tell the entire story again, and how could I tell Otto that I'd failed to save Kurt's life, that he'd bled to death in such wretched circumstances?

I sat there with the blank sheet in front of me and all I could see was the grey mud and sky, and Kurt's blood running red into the water. I could almost feel the rain hammering on my head. I shook myself but the image was slow to fade.

The letter was almost impossible. I began by asking about his leg, putting off the worst part.

'I'm very sorry but I have some very bad news', I wrote eventually. 'Last week we made a daylight attack on the English trenches. Kurt – or rather Leutnant Meyer – was one of those who didn't come back. As you know, it's not long since he was commissioned but he was a very good officer and Karl and I were certain he'd go a long way. Neither of us can quite get used to him being gone.

Alfred got hit in the leg but not badly, but is hoping to go to the storm troops and get his Express Ticket. Karl's still just the same – luckily he didn't get sent with us.'

The wording was clumsy and inadequate, but it would have to do.

A couple of weeks later I got a reply. We were back in the line, in exactly the same place. It was more than a bit depressing.

'Thanks for telling me about Kurt', Otto wrote. 'If you can find out any more about what happened then please tell me, however bad it is. It's so hard to believe that of all of us only you and Karl are still there. I shan't be rejoining you – my leg has finally healed but it's much shorter than the other one and so the infantry won't have me.

I told Kurt before that I was going to apply to the Air Service instead – and I've got it!! I'm going to be a pilot! And I shall look down on all of you in the mud and smile.'

"He's insane!" I burst out.

"Who is?" Karl asked with an amused smile.

"Otto. Read that."

"Bloody hell, I didn't realise he meant it. Don't ever call me mad again – compared to friend Otto I'm the picture of sanity."

"That's going a bit far…"

He hit my arm playfully. "Everything's relative, remember?"

"You – picture of sanity?" Taschner demanded. "Off your fucking rocker, more like."

"Shut up and get back to work!" Karl retorted.

"Just when I've got a brew going," said Dietz.

"Oh, all right then," Karl said. "I'm anyone's for a decent mug of coffee."

"Don't fancy you," said Koch.

"You going to tell Otto the full story?" Karl asked me.

"When I can."

"Just don't leave it too long," said Peter.

"Didn't ask you, did I?" I replied, the words 'mind your own fucking business' clear in my tone.

"Sorry, Sarge."

He had a point, of course, and I forced myself to write a full account before it was too late. I wrote it hastily and sealed it without re-reading it. I didn't want to see the words on the paper.

The next post brought letters from home for me, and two for Karl.

"Will you look after these for him?" Braun said to me. "I don't want the snipers disturbed."

Taschner was out somewhere and the other three were in their dugout, presumably asleep.

"Yes, of course."

I gave Karl his letters after second breakfast. One was from Alfred and I couldn't help noticing that the other was from his father.

That's unusual, I thought, *he hardly ever gets letters from his father or brothers, but then he hardly ever writes to them. And of course Elisabeth's in England and they can only write via the Red Cross.*

"Thanks, Sarge," Karl said. He looked at his father's letter, put it in his pocket, and opened Alfred's.

"How's Alfred doing?" I asked.

"Says his leg's healing well and as soon as they discharge him from hospital he'll be off on his training course – he's got into the storm troops."

"He's completely fucking mad," I said. "How many of his nine lives do you reckon he's used up?"

"The whole lot – but then the Devil looks after his own!"

"True... Don't know about you, but I rather miss him."

"I do too," Karl answered. "You can't be bored with him around... Not the man to be in a tight corner with, though. Far too bloody reckless."

"Yes... though I'm glad he's on our side – especially when he's wielding his spade!"

"God, yes – you'd have your brains to play with... If you ask me, that spade business is decidedly dodgy – it's one thing burying the bloody thing in some fellow's skull, but then you have to pull it out again and how do you defend yourself while you're doing that? You're quite likely to get your own head split open."

"Messy, too." Wearing someone else's brains was not my idea of amusement.

"I agree," Dietz said. "Buggered if you'd catch me doing that."

"Doesn't care, though," Karl said. "Not when he's in full swing."

"No." *I wonder if it hits him afterwards – not that he'd ever say.*

I got my own letters out of my pocket and opened Johanna's first, thinking it would probably be more entertaining than Mama's.

I was right. It was mostly about school and what her friends were doing, but I could almost hear her giggling and the feeling of home was so poignant, so bittersweet. She was knitting me a scarf for the winter, she said.

It'll be a miracle if it ever gets finished. Johanna's useless at things like knitting and sewing, however much Mama nags her.

I was about to open Mama's letter when I glanced at Karl.

He was staring into space, the Major's letter in his hand. His black cigarette holder was clamped between his teeth, the cigarette smouldering forgotten. He was deathly pale and his face was frozen, his eyes grey and bleak.

Shit. It must be about one of his brothers.

Better wait for him to tell me.

He put the letter away in silence, stubbed out his fag and went to work. He stood at his position most of the day and fired once.

"They're far too bloody cautious these days," he said to me later. "I'll go out tomorrow, get myself a better view."

I wish you wouldn't. You need to concentrate and not have that letter weighing on your mind.

He left an hour or two before dawn. It was an unusually quiet night, the sort of quiet that makes you wonder what's coming.

He didn't make a sound as he climbed the ladder and began to make his way through the wire. For some reason he seemed even more sinister than usual in his hooded cape, and he vanished into the thin mist like the ghost of some long-dead monk.

It's only Karl, I thought, and was suddenly, sharply aware how lethal 'only Karl' was. *You're lethal yourself, Franz – glass houses, remember?*

The temperature kept falling and an east wind brought the first breath of winter.

Karl must be frozen.

The day was quiet as well and passed very slowly. In the late afternoon there was a sudden outbreak of firing by both sides. Nothing came of it but I was afraid for him, somewhere out there in the cross-fire.

If he gets hit he's on his own. There's no one to help him. We don't even know where he is… No need to worry, Franz. He'll be well hidden, he always is. He's probably laughing at them.

He came back in an hour or so after dark, reported to Hafner and then came and sat with us. I was very relieved to see him.

"Aren't you bloody frozen?" I asked casually.

He shrugged. "Not really. Is there rum in that tea?"

"Certainly is. I think you're only just in time, though. There's not much left." I turned to Schulze. "Leussow hasn't had his tea yet. He's only just come back."

"Oh, right, Sarge. Here you are, mate."

"Thanks," Karl said. "Just what I need."

It must taste even better to you, being as it's the first hot thing you've had since before dawn.

"I don't know how you can lie out there all day in this weather," I said. "It's bloody freezing."

I wasn't exaggerating. Frost was starting to form on the parapet.

"Winter's coming, all right."

Wolff was staring at Karl with a measure of awe.

"How many did you get today?" he asked in his reedy voice. It was his first time in the front line and he didn't know how much Karl disliked that question.

Karl said flatly, "Ask one of the others. They'll give you book, chapter and sodding verse."

Wolff got up and wandered off, looking rather squashed. When I saw the hard look in Karl's eyes I understood why.

Karl and I sat in silence, broken a few minutes later by Dietz.

"Want to work in one of the OPs tomorrow?"

Karl was staring at the bottom of the trench, lost in thought.

"Leussow?"

"What?"

"Do you want to work in one of the OPs tomorrow?"

"Yes, why not."

The following evening Dietz asked me quietly, "What's up with Leussow, Sarge?"

"I don't know. Why d'you ask?"

"He's just not quite himself. I mean, he's shooting as well as ever and he's not being unfriendly, but I reckon there's something on his mind. I thought he'd be happy about his promotion, but he's gone dead quiet."

I had to think carefully what to say. I couldn't tell anyone about the letter – Karl would have to do that – but then Dietz had to work closely with him and had some right to know if things weren't in order.

"You might be right," I said, "but we'll have to wait for him to tell us – if he wants to, that is."

"Yes. I'll try to keep a bit of an eye on him."

To my relief Dietz persuaded Karl to work from the trench the next day. Taschner had crept out into the night, passing us quietly as we worked on the wire.

At about noon we heard two rifle shots in quick succession, followed by a piercing scream and a lot of shouting. The English machine-guns opened up in rage and we blasted back at them.

Those must have been Taschner's shots, surely – but who screamed?

In the evening a fine, soaking rain set in, bringing a thick, damp mist with it. The rest of the day had been very quiet.

"What do you reckon?" I asked Karl. I didn't like the thought of Taschner lying out there injured.

"Two shots is always taking a hell of a chance – but they were close together, so let's hope he got away with it."

It was raining even harder some hours later when Taschner came back, soaking wet.

"Still raining, I see," I said.

"Bloody pissing down."

"See – that's what you gets for going out," Koch said gleefully. "You looks like a drownded rat."

"A muddy drownded rat," said Karl. "And now he's going to drip all over the dugout."

"He can drip all he likes on his own bed," Dietz said.

"Cheers, mate," said Taschner. "I love you too!"

He sat down opposite Karl and me and started cleaning his rifle.

"Where were you?" Karl asked.

"Broken Trees. Good place, that."

"Where?" I asked.

"In what's left of that wood off to our left. Fucking hell, I'm wet."

"That's what you gets…" Koch said, not bothering to finish.

Taschner laughed. "Nearly got found out, though. Six of 'em came through the wood. I don't know if they were looking for me, or what. They went by about ten metres away."

Karl raised an eyebrow. "Why'd you let them get so close?"

"See?" said Koch at the same time. "Off 'is fuckin' 'ead."

"Didn't think anyone'd come that way. I just kept still and waited, and one of the buggers looked right at me but he never saw me."

"Fucking bonkers," Dietz agreed.

"Gave 'em a surprise when they set off home, though." Taschner laughed again.

"Pushing your luck a bit, weren't you?" Karl said.

"Get them both?" asked Dietz.

"Yeah… I reckoned that was enough. They're up to something there, like I told Hafner."

"That'll be what the patrol's for tonight," I said.

"Are you going?" Karl asked.

"No. Not this time."

I realised Taschner had enjoyed hiding there invisible,

watching the Tommies pass by and then picking the moment to shoot them.

You're crazy. Stark raving bloody mad. Anyone in his right mind would have been scared to death.

The patrol found the wood to be full of Tommies, stealthily extending their line. Our party livened up their evening with a few bombs, but there were too many of them to do any more.

Hafner told the snipers not to go out, because the artillery was going to shell the place and he didn't know exactly when.

In the morning Karl handed me his father's letter. "Would you read it, please?"

"Yes, of course."

The Major's writing was very neat and precise.

'My dear Karl,

It grieves me deeply to have to tell you that Friedrich is dead. His colonel tells me that Friedrich was seriously wounded on 8th October while leading his company in a counter-attack in the area of Loos and died the following day, without regaining consciousness. He also tells me that Friedrich was "one of my best officers, a young man whose courage and devotion to duty set an example to us all".

Friedrich lived and died in the service of Prussia and the Empire. We shall all remember him with pride and we shall strive to honour his memory.

Yours, Pa.'

I was appalled. "Karl, I'm so sorry."

"Thanks… What I don't like is that it doesn't say anything about his injuries, or how he died or where."

"It says he died without regaining consciousness." The words sounded very hollow.

"Yes, but they would say that, wouldn't they? They probably say that about everyone."

"It does sometimes happen that way."

"True… I'll have to ask Pa if he knows any more, though."

He doesn't, or he'd have told you.

Very stark, that letter, very unemotional – then I remembered the Major's expression when he'd looked at Friedrich, and I realised it was the only way he could deal with losing him.

I didn't want to imagine how it must feel to lose your son. *You hold the tiny baby in your arms, you watch the boy grow into a man – and then some bastard kills him.*

I can't afford to think like that…

"Friedrich always wanted to be a soldier," Karl said. "He knew he'd probably get killed, and as far as Pa's concerned, he's done what he was brought up to do. The first time he came home from cadet school, he told Johnny and me what the Commandant said to them on their first day: 'Gentlemen, you are here in order to learn how to die'."

Jesus. "How old was he?"

"Ten." His tone was matter-of-fact, as if that were a normal thing to say to a young boy.

No doubt it is for Prussians. It is an army with a state, after all.

Suddenly I understood that Karl felt as his father did, that he too would set aside his own survival and that of those he loved, without hesitation.

You meant it quite literally when you said, "Let's go and sign ourselves away". And if you get killed, the Major will remember with pride another son who died for King and Fatherland.

"That's what we're for," he said quietly.

I thought of the portraits in his house and found I couldn't argue.

"Shall I tell Taschner and co?" I asked.

"No, I'll do it, next time I see them."

He told them, very simply, "My oldest brother got hit and didn't make it."

Taschner put his arm round Karl's shoulders and said, "Anything I can do, mate, just tell me."

He obviously meant it.

"Thanks."

"I'm really sorry," said Dietz.

"Tommies, was it?" asked Koch. "Well, we knows the answer to that."

"He was a professional soldier," Karl said.

"Don't you want to get your own back, then?"

"He wasn't here to offer them a beer."

Koch shrugged and I could see he didn't quite follow.

The following week Karl got a letter from Johnny.

'I can't believe Fritze's dead,' he wrote. 'It feels so unreal. I know we half-expected it, but it's still so hard to take in.'

Karl wrote back to him the same day and also wrote to Elisabeth.

"God knows when she'll get it," he said. "I think the letters all go via Switzerland or somewhere."

"What's this about Leussow's brother?" Braun asked me later.

"Died of wounds. That's all he knows."

"No where and how?"

"No."

Braun pulled a very eloquent face. "Never good, that. Has anyone told Hafner?"

"I don't know."

"Hm. Leave it with me."

The same post brought me a letter from Otto, who had *actually been flying.*

'It's amazing, Franz. The wind's so strong you can't put your head out – if you put your hand out it just gets blown backwards. The engine makes the most terrific noise and the whole machine vibrates with it. When you start the take-off run you bump over the grass, faster and faster until you think the aircraft's going to shake itself to bits, and then suddenly the ground drops away and it's all so smooth, and you're flying! Really flying!

And you look down at the ground and everything gets smaller and smaller, all the men and the aircraft on the airfield and the hangars. And when you turn it feels really strange. Learning to land's really tricky as well but my instructor's a good sort. It's brilliant fun – the best ever!

My instructor said that even at the Front they live in huts on the airfield and have proper beds with sheets, and good hot food every day. I tell you, wild horses wouldn't drag me back to the infantry.'

I showed Karl the letter.

"Feast for the condemned," he said. "He's off his fucking head, going up in those bloody things. Give me mud and lice any day."

The more I thought about it the more tempting it sounded. A real bed instead of a cubbyhole in the side of the trench or a heap of straw in a barn…

I've forgotten what that's like. And I bet airmen get a full night's sleep every night, instead of being woken every couple of hours for some duty or other.

The nocturnal trench life was getting very wearing. Support just meant endless night-time carrying parties and trying to sleep during the day. The only time we got any decent kip was in rest, and I would have paid a lot for a whole month of good sound sleep.

Later that day we were watching a dogfight and I thought of Otto's words. *What do they see when they look down at the Front? A sea of mud and shell-holes, between trenches inhabited by cave-dwellers?* I had a sudden, powerful desire to find out, to fly through the air and look down at the Earth.

And then they go back to warm, dry huts and have good food, not like us—

One of the enemy aircraft fell out of the sky in flames, like some ghastly torch.

I imagined the pilot being incinerated, and shuddered. All thoughts of transferring to the Air Service flew straight out of my head.

Karl's right. Otto's fucking crazy. I'll stick with the trenches.

Later that day Karl was summoned to Hafner, and came back with the news that his NCO's course was scheduled for the following week.

"Bloody hell, that was quick," I said.

I remembered the look in Braun's face when he'd heard about Friedrich, and wondered if they'd taken the opportunity to get Karl away from the Front for a while.

Having regard to the extra dangers of his job, that would make sense. One careless mistake's enough to get him killed and I doubt they want to lose him. His score must be very respectable, even if he doesn't want to know what it is.

The anniversary of Langemarck fell the day before his departure. We decided that the rum would have to do for a commemorative drink.

"I can't believe it's a whole year," I said.

A whole year since we walked, singing, towards the English. *You poor bloody young fools*, I thought, almost unable to believe that we'd been so stupid.

"No, neither can I. And who's left with us who was there that day?"

"Braun. And…"

I couldn't think of anyone. None of the officers, for a start. They'd all been killed or wounded badly enough to be out of it, as had all the other NCOs. Anton and Kurt were dead; Otto and Alfred had left us.

"Apart from him there's just you and me," Karl said. "And where are we? Just about exactly where we were then."

With no end in sight, I didn't want to say. *And a year ago Friedrich was alive and still had both eyes.*

"Karl, I… I don't think I've ever said just how sorry I am about Friedrich. I was so impressed with him when I met him – there was something about him, he had such a presence. I thought he was going to go a really long way."

He looked at me, his eyes bright.

"Really?" he asked quietly.

"Yes. You know me – I wouldn't just say things like that. I'd have followed him anywhere."

"Thanks. He was far too brave for his own good— No, that's probably not quite right. Reckless is probably a better word – he might still be alive if he'd got a bit more scared. I knew this was going to happen."

"Have you found out any more?"

"No. I asked Pa but he said that there wasn't any more to know. He'd tried to find out – wrote to Friedrich's CO and got on to a couple of other sources – but didn't get anywhere. I just hope… Well, you know, that it really was as we've been told."

"So do I, Karl."

"I wish they'd kept him in Berlin after he lost his eye. Trouble was, he was too good at his job, and with the rate we've been losing officers…" His voice trailed off, then he picked himself up with an effort that he tried to hide. "Drink up, Franz. Let's drink to their memory and be glad we're alive."

I raised my mug. "To the fallen."

"To the fallen."

Once again we were parted, and I was surprised at how much I missed him.

"Well," said Taschner, "we'll have to get as far ahead as we can before the bugger gets back!"

"That's for sure," Dietz agreed. "How does that competition of yours work, again?"

Koch grinned. "Ah, wants to join now, does you? It's like this…"

I'm not listening to that, I thought, and got up and left. No doubt the Tommy snipers do the same thing, and I'd rather not think about that.

The first thing I said to Karl when he came back was, "Congratulations, Corporal," followed by, "I owe you five marks."

"Dietz?"

"Yes. What made you so sure? I mean, was it something he said while you were working together?"

"No… no, it was when Koch started telling him about it. You remember, the first thing he asked was what if you couldn't tell a Tommy private from an NCO. And then he asked if they trusted each other to tell the truth. He sounded far more interested than I've ever been. And he'd got over his initial difficulty by then – so I guessed it was only a matter of time."

"Well, you were right," I said, and handed over the money.

"Thanks… Can't say it pleases me, though. It's not going to be pleasant watching him turn into… Well, you know what I mean."

A cold-blooded bastard, I thought but didn't say. Karl didn't need to hear those words, certainly not from me.

A couple of days later Karl was out, and Dietz and Koch were talking over coffee.

"You're doing well on daily average, now," Koch said. "Picking up nicely."

"Pity we don't know Leussow's score," Dietz said. "I could get hold of his book and we could give him the points, just between ourselves."

"No way, mate. 'E'd be livid if 'e found out."

"Maybe, but at least we'd know the real scores."

"Be a shame to lose your good looks," Koch said.

"How d'you mean?"

"You do that to Leussow, 'e'll rearrange your face for you, an' you won't look nothing like as good as you does now. Remember what Becker said about the last bloke 'e 'it?"

"He'd be demoted if he did that."

"You think 'e'd give a fuck about that? You knows 'e didn't want it anyway. Nah, mate, you wants to 'ave a bit of respect. Leussow's one of the best marksmen on the Western Front—"

"You're not wrong there! We were in the OP yesterday and I spotted another of their loopholes – you know how easy they are to find, with their sandbags being so fucking regular, and the bloke'd just fired from it – and I suggested he load steel core, but he just said, 'What for?' and shot straight through the hole. Beautifully done, made it look dead easy. Didn't hear any more from that one."

"Yeah, don't surprise me. Anyway, like I was saying, 'e's fucking good, and we just 'as to respect 'im being a bit odd. Look, 'e's not like us. It's just duty for 'im. They made 'im a sniper cos 'e's a fucking good shot an' 'e just gets on an' does the job – don't care about gongs, numbers, nothing like that. An' that's fine by me an' it should be fine by you too. So leave 'im alone."

"Koch's right," I said. "If you piss Leussow off you'll really wish you hadn't. You'll have your teeth for dinner."

Dietz looked at me as if he wanted to say something, but thought better of it. It gave me the opportunity to look straight into his eyes and I didn't like what I saw.

That didn't take long. You're already getting that flat hard look the others have – though there is that shadow that I sometimes think I see flitting across Karl's eyes.

It seemed to me that Karl recognised exactly what he was doing, and that he was trying to keep the inner part of himself separate from it, as if he could make the job what he did rather than what he was.

Not possible. You can't do a dirty job without getting dirty.

I didn't know whether to tell him about the conversation or not. He wasn't likely to take it well, but on the other hand I didn't want Dietz to borrow Karl's book and drag him into their competition. The consequences would not be pretty.

Best leave well alone, I decided. Telling Karl would cause a shit-load of trouble and hopefully Dietz would heed the advice he'd been given. And if he didn't then he'd regret it. There was no need for me to stir things up.

The next day Karl said, "Well, I'd better go and have a chat with Hafner. There are a couple of things we need to sort out – like the sleeping arrangements for six of us."

"And who your new colleagues will be."

"Quite."

He came back an hour or so later, laughing.

"Tell me, Franz," he asked, "have I got a black eye?"

"No – why, did you piss Hafner off even more this time?"

"No, but…" He was laughing so much that he could hardly speak, then he managed to get a grip on himself and continued, "I was about to knock on the board by the gas blanket when I heard a shot inside the dugout and Hafner shouted, 'Got you at last, you bastard!'

"I was wondering what the hell was going on, then the curtain got whisked aside and a fucking great rat flew out and whacked me right in the face! It wasn't quite dead, either."

I started laughing.

"So then Hafner said, 'Sorry, Leussow, saw you just too late' and we were both almost doubled up laughing. He said he'd been trying to get that bloody rat every time up for the last two months, and it was the first time he'd managed to get a decent shot at it. So I finished it off and chucked it over the parapet, where no doubt its friends are feeding on it."

"So did you have a useful meeting after that tremendous start?"

"Yes. We went through the results of the shooting competition. We both feel we should offer it to men we know, fellows who've seen some action—"

"Avoid any more stage fright."

"Exactly. Though I have to say our latest prima donna is exceeding all expectations... Anyway, we decided on Scheffel and Brandt. They didn't get the highest scores but we think they'd be best at the job."

"Do you want me to find Scheffel for you? I think he'd go for it – he's always seemed a bit more enterprising than some of the others and I reckon he'd be happy with the extra money as well."

"If you tell me where he is I'll go – it'll be less like a summons."

He told me later that Scheffel was very pleased with the offer and snapped it up, which didn't surprise me at all. Brandt, on the other hand, seemed rather reluctant and Karl went back to Hafner.

"We don't want anyone who has to think about it," he said to me. "It's not a job for someone who's lukewarm."

"No, quite."

In the evening he and the others sat down and had a long discussion about how things would work with six of them.

"One thing we are going to do," Karl said, "is keep a diary of where we're working. We don't want another situation like the one Taschner and I had a few weeks back. So it all goes in this book. Before you go out, you write down where you're planning to go. You get back in, you write down where you really were, doesn't matter if it's an OP or right out."

"Good idea," Dietz said.

Taschner looked a bit glum. "No offence, Corporal, but if we'd done that before you'd never have found me. You wouldn't have gone anywhere near that cowshed. And by the time anyone realised I hadn't come back it would have been too late."

"Good point – but that's always going to be the risk we take when we go out. The point of the book is that no one falls into the trap of using a position that someone else has just used – like I nearly did that day. And any of us can see how long it is since we used a position."

"But what about the other buggers?" Taschner asked. "We can't legislate for them."

Karl could have pulled rank and said, that's the way it is, but instead he replied patiently, "True. But I want the odds as stacked in our favour as we can get them."

"See your point," Taschner said after a thoughtful pause. "Yeah, makes sense."

Nicely done – you've got his agreement, and the book wouldn't have worked otherwise.

"Now, about the dugout – can we squeeze two more beds in, or are we going to have to take it in turns to sleep?"

Koch scratched his head. "Well, I reckon we could make a couple of bunks."

"Nah," Taschner said, "they'd be too near the ceiling, be far too stuffy up there."

"Let's go and have a look," Karl said, "so we can see what we're talking about."

I was rather surprised – I'd expected someone from his background to be more dictatorial, but instead he was doing his best to find solutions that the others accepted.

When I commented later he said, "They're expected to use their initiative – it'd be daft to lay down the law all the time. I don't expect to have to give direct orders often. I'd far rather they did something because they saw the value of it, and if they've got ideas I want to hear them."

Your job's going to be easier than mine, I thought. *You'll have five intelligent, committed men to supervise, rather than the random crowd I have to deal with.*

They were far better trained than we'd been, and well-disciplined, but there were one or two who would shirk given half a chance, and a couple more who were, frankly, thick and had to have almost everything explained to them, sometimes twice over.

That night I was in the middle of assembling a wiring party when Koch suddenly ducked out from under the sacking round his position and shouted, "The Tommies are coming!"

A second later the sentry sounded the alarm. Everyone was on his feet in a flash.

I'd never heard Koch fire so fast.

I ran to the snipers' dugout and pulled the gas curtain aside. *"Get out! Raid!"*

Taschner sat up, blinking at me blearily.

"RAID!" I shouted.

I turned back into the trench and grabbed an entrenching tool from one of the cubbyholes. A second later there was a series of violent, brilliant explosions in the next bay. Showers of splinters hurtled high into the air, followed by shouts and screams.

As I ran round the traverse I collided with a Tommy coming the other way. He was backlit by more grenades and I saw him raise the spiked club in his hand. The entrenching tool wasn't sharpened and I daren't try to drive it into his head. I swung it into his stomach as hard as I could and he almost collapsed on top of it. I let go of the shaft, grabbed his club and joined the fray.

It was total fucking chaos, hard to tell who was who. I almost fell over a man lying in the bottom of the trench, saw a Tommy with a spade in his hand and hit him with the club. He went down and stayed down.

Someone sent up a flare, lighting the scene to daylight. Koch was in the grip of another raider, who doubled up as a grey figure beside me thrust a knife into him. There were gunshots round the next traverse, and I pressed myself into a cubbyhole as another bomb went off, half-stunning me.

I staggered back out in time to see two Englishmen trying to pull Lafer up the parapet. He was limp between them and I was just about to hit one of them when Leutnant Gross shot him. The other lost his grip and Lafer fell back into the trench.

Suddenly the raiders scrambled up the ladders and back over the top. We grabbed rifles and leapt onto the fire step, and shot as many as we could as they ran through the gap in our wire. Far too many of the bastards escaped into the darkness – we would gladly have shot the whole damn lot of them. We jeered as they ran and cheered each one we hit.

"Bit fucking rude, that," Karl said as we stepped down. "Spoiled my beauty sleep."

He started cleaning the blood off a large double-bladed knife, rather bigger than standard issue.

"Where the fuck did you get that thing?" I asked. It was an evil-looking bit of kit, with a blade a good twenty centimetres long.

"Bought it when I was on leave – thought it might come in handy one day."

He inspected it and stuck it into a sheath in his boot.

"Well, you was right," said Koch. "Cheers for that… Cor, that was just like back 'ome, fucking good fight till one of the bastards 'it me on the 'ead."

"You're lucky it wasn't one of these," I said, brandishing the Englishman's spiked club.

He looked at it with respect. "Too fucking right. I'd be a goner."

"Well, that gave us all something to think about," said Hafner. "What's the situation?"

Lafer was concussed but slowly coming round. We had five dead including Brandt whose skull was smashed in. Strassmann and Vogel had both been badly injured by the bombs, and several others had slight injuries.

Set against that we'd acquired three dead Tommies and seven wounded ones, including the Lieutenant in charge of the raid, who seemed to have collected a load of fragments from one of their own bombs. Sad, that.

The man I'd whacked with the entrenching tool was lying groaning in the bottom of the trench. The fellow I'd hit with the club was dead, as was the one Karl had stabbed, and the man Gross had shot was unconscious.

Serves them all bloody well right.

Unfortunately Greiner was missing and we realised the Tommies must have taken him with them, so they'd achieved one of their objectives.

"They won't get much from him," Braun said. "He's only been here five minutes, knows absolutely bugger all."

And now he's a prisoner. He's done fuck all, and now he gets to spend the rest of the war in a prison camp somewhere in perfect safety, while the rest of us risk getting our bollocks shot off.

It's not really anything to envy, though. I'd far rather be here with Karl and the others.

Hafner took the English officer into his dugout, his face and hands bandaged. Gross followed them – he'd lived in Tommy-land for several years and spoke English fluently, though with a fairly strong accent.

"I wonder what they'll get out of him," Dietz said.

"Fuck all," said Karl. "Keeps him away from us lot, though – someone might give the fellow a whack or two, *accidentally* of course."

By the time of the dawn stand-to all the prisoners and our wounded had gone back down the line, and the dead had been removed. The Tommy officer had seemed slightly unsteady on his feet – he could have been feeling the effects of his injuries, or they might have been passing the bottle round. It was hard to tell.

Broad daylight showed us what a fucking mess the trench was in, and there was a lot of grousing. It was going to take most of the day to repair the damage and get it back in good order.

Some of the new fellows were looking rather dazed – I don't think they'd realised how suddenly death and destruction could arrive. I set them to work, to occupy their minds as much as their bodies.

Karl's tunic was covered in blood, and his face wrinkled in disgust as he looked at it.

"Don't know what Alfred sees in that hand-to-hand business," he said. "Look what a mess the bugger's made, just when I was a bit less filthy."

"Less filthy?" I retorted. "You? You got soaked in Flanders mud our first day back up."

"I don't mind mud. Blood's another matter."

Yes – it's usually a nice long way off, spattered over someone else.

"You must of cut an artery," Koch said. "An' I'm bloody glad you did, or 'e'd of done the same to me."

"All the same."

Karl emptied his pockets, took his tunic off and rinsed it thoroughly in the water in the bottom of the trench. There was a nail sticking out of the timber outside the snipers' dugout, and he hung it there to dry. Koch and I looked at each other, not wanting to point out that the water was not only muddy but had already had a definite red tinge to it.

Karl intercepted our look.

"What?" he said. "Yes, I saw the colour of the water, but at least it's dilute. And yes, I know what's in Flanders mud – but that's dilute as well."

"Aren't you cold?" I asked. The temperature was close to freezing and he was standing there in his shirt-sleeves.

"No," he answered with a puzzled expression. "Why would I be...? Oh, you've never been in our house in the winter. It's always bloody freezing."

"Oh well, back to work," I said.

"Sounds about right to me." Karl turned to Dietz. "You up for a bit of payback for our disturbed night?"

"You bet I am."

"Come on," Koch said to Taschner. "I've got a score to settle. Mind you, I got a couple before they got 'ere. Never shot so fast in me bleedin' life."

"We'll have to dismantle that position and put it somewhere else," Karl said.

"Too fucking right," said Taschner, "after he got so fucking trigger-happy. How many?"

"Got four off, 'it two of the buggers, then by the time I'd reloaded they was 'ere. Used one earlier, see, or it'd of been three."

"What – you mean you missed two?! Hey, that must put me up a bit!" Taschner said gleefully.

"They was running," Koch replied, "and it was dark apart from the bangs. You wouldn't of done no better. And where was you anyway? Fucking sleeping!"

"Yeah, well, at least I had some rest, so watch out today cos I'll be breathing down your neck. Your average is shot to buggery, mate!"

Koch patted his rifle. "I'll let this do the fucking talking – you're all mouth!"

"Books at sundown!" Taschner retorted.

"Ideas for the new position at sundown as well," Karl said. "Then we can start on it tonight."

XI

The new position provoked a lively debate, among three of them anyway. Koch was rather quiet, almost subdued, which was not like him at all. He'd had a kip in the afternoon but it didn't seem to have done him much good.

"What's up, mate?" Taschner asked. "You've gone awful quiet."

"Got a bit of an 'eadache," Koch said. "That Tommy must of 'it me 'arder than I realised."

Karl stood in front of him. "Look at me," he said. "Straight at me… How many fingers?"

He held up four and Koch answered correctly.

"Let me know if it gets worse," Karl said.

Koch turned in early. "I'll be all right in the morning," he said.

The next day Karl and Taschner were both out, and Koch and Dietz tried out the new position. Koch still didn't seem to be quite himself, and Dietz ribbed him mercilessly about a couple of easy shots he'd missed.

Karl took it rather more seriously when he came back in.

"I want someone to have a look at you," he said. "Taschner, take Koch back to the aid post and get a doctor to give him the once-over."

Koch tried to protest. "I'm fine, Corporal, just need a good kip."

"No arguing," Karl said firmly.

"Come on." Taschner took Koch's arm and led him into the comms trench.

"What do you think's the matter?" Dietz asked Karl.

"I don't know... I'm just not happy about him. Something doesn't feel right."

The doctor didn't agree, but sent them both straight back up.

"Didn't reckon much to him," Taschner said. "If you ask me he was only a medical student, seemed to know fuck all. All respect to your mate Friedemann, mind, but we'd have had to go all the way back to the clearing station to find a proper doc."

"We'd best keep an eye on him," said Karl. "All of us. If he gets worse then the clearing station's exactly where he's going."

The next day Koch slept in, and when he emerged seemed to be slightly pissed. He was rather unsteady on his feet and sounded slurred.

"Has he been at the booze?" I asked Karl.

"Shouldn't think so, doesn't smell of it... Think I'll work with him today, keep an eye on him."

Early in the afternoon there was an almighty clang from their position.

"Medics!" Karl shouted. "*Medics!*"

I ran round the traverse to see Koch lying unconscious on the fire step, with Karl bending over him.

"What happened?"

"He collapsed – just passed out."

The medics arrived.

"Where's he hit?" asked Masur.

"He isn't," Karl said. "He just passed out."

"What – just like that?" asked Klose.

"Yes – he'd been acting a bit oddly, had a bang on the head a couple of nights ago."

"But what about that fucking great noise?" I asked Karl. "Wasn't that your loophole being hit?"

"Yes, but that was after – he pulled the sacking down when he fell, and let the light through. One of those Tommy bastards must have been watching."

The loophole had a hole bored right through it.

"Lucky your head wasn't in the way," I said. "Is that what that steel core stuff does?"

"Yup. Knife through butter."

Shit.

The medics had not managed to revive Koch – he was out cold.

"Don't like this," said Masur. "My brother was a boxer before the war, and his sparring partner dropped dead a couple of days after being KO'd. We'd best take him back now."

"I'll come with you," Karl said. "There's a couple of places where the comms trench isn't safe in daylight."

"Yeah, we know where those are."

Taschner looked at Karl and raised his eyebrows.

"I'm coming with you," Karl repeated.

"Dietz and me'll carry on, then," Taschner said. "Shall I pack up Koch's stuff?"

"Good idea. See you later."

Taschner retrieved Koch's rifle from the bottom of the trench.

"Oh, fuck! Look at that – bloody well buggered."

Koch must have fallen heavily, and even I could see that the sight was damaged.

"Beautiful four-power sight, totally fucked," Taschner went on.

For a moment I wondered which he cared more about, Koch or the sight.

He saw my expression.

"Look, Sarge, he's my best mate, but I can't do fuck all for him, can I? It's up to the bloody medics now. And this would have been bloody useful."

"See your point."

I never could read Taschner. Most of the time he was totally cold-blooded, but he'd been really broken up over Faltermeier and I wasn't sure whether the coldness was due to his nature or to the job. *Probably a bit of both*, I decided – *a sniper can't afford a conscience.*

It was dark before Karl got back.

"How is he?" Taschner asked.

"Don't really know," Karl answered. "The doc at the clearing station said it's probably bleeding on the brain and they whisked him off to operate – said they'll send a message to Hafner when they know the outcome."

"That doesn't sound good," said Dietz. "My uncle had a stroke and died a few days later."

"We'll just have to keep our fingers crossed," Karl said. "In the meantime we've got another position to replace."

"They're getting too fucking good and too fucking numerous," Taschner grumbled. "It's not like it used to be."

"We need to get something done about that comms trench as well," Karl added. "If I hadn't been with them they'd have got their brains blown out. As it was the bugger only just missed."

Taschner shook his head. "I couldn't believe it when they didn't want to listen to you," he said. "Fucking stupid."

A few days later we heard that Koch had survived the operation but was on his way back to Germany, partly paralysed.

"I could kill that fucking useless cunt at the aid post," Taschner said.

We all agreed. I'd never liked Koch much but no one wants to end up like that – and if his condition had been taken seriously in the first place then it might not have happened.

And now he'll have to go back to Düsseldorf, where the other gang will be waiting for him.

Karl went to talk to Hafner, to discuss Koch's replacement.

"This is really going to reduce our effectiveness," he said to me later. "Dietz is getting pretty good but he's not been here that long, so it's only Taschner and me who really know our way around now. We're going to have to show the other three the ropes and that's going to eat into our time. Plus we can't expect them to score well till they've had a bit of practice."

"When are you taking Scheffel and the other fellow for training?"

"Week after next. Ranke's the other one."

"Don't know him. And who've you chosen to replace Koch?"

"Fellow called Frantz – doubt you know him either."

"No… Does that mean you won't be going out so much?"

He laughed and hit my arm. "Now, Mother, don't fret about me!"

"Oh, piss off!" I said and hit him back.

I couldn't help being relieved that his life might become slightly less hazardous – then I remembered the punctured loophole.

It's fucking dangerous whichever way you look at it. All anyone wants to do with enemy snipers is kill them and, really, what else can you do? Taschner got it the wrong way round – the reason the bastards want to kill him is because he kills them.

"Have I done enough for one of those monograms yet?" Dietz asked the next day.

Taschner's face darkened.

"It don't work like that," he said, and there was something in his tone that should have stopped Dietz from saying any more.

"Well, how does it work, then?"

"The bloke that did them's dead," Taschner said shortly. "You want one, you'll have to do it your fucking self."

Dietz looked a bit taken aback. "I just thought—"

"Well, don't." Taschner turned and walked away.

"I hit a nerve there, all right," Dietz said to me.

"Yes, with a sledgehammer." I told him about Faltermeier.

"*How* old?"

"You heard right. He was a bloody good bloke, too, and Taschner blames himself for not keeping him alive – so if you've got any sense you won't raise the subject again."

"Shit," he said, shaking his head, and headed after Taschner.

Otto wrote to say that he'd passed his pilot's course and been sent to a two-seater squadron way off to the south of us.

'The airfield's plenty big enough that we don't have to worry about the wind too much,' he wrote. 'We're quartered in a chateau – the officers have the best rooms but ours are still pretty good.'

Pretty good? Even if it's the servants' quarters it's a fucking sight better than anything I ever see.

'My observer's a really good fellow, used to be a Hussar officer, got a brilliant sense of humour. The cook's excellent and we have wine every night and sit round listening to the gramophone and playing cards. When the weather's bad we can't fly so we play cards or go into town…' and on he went.

"Listen to this," I said to Karl later, and read it out.

"Yes, very nice – and how long do you think he's going to last? Five marks says he's dead by the end of the year."

"I'm not taking that bet – it's like wishing ill on him."

Karl shrugged. "It wouldn't make any bloody difference. Otto's signed his own death warrant, going in for the Air Service."

"Yes, but look – he gets a nice warm room with a proper bed, no one wakes him for this duty or that—"

"They don't wake me, either."

"No – and I could say the same about what you're doing. You get extra money and privileges because of the danger, don't you?"

"More because of the skill, I'd say," he said modestly. "If everyone shot like us then there'd be no extras, would there?"

I couldn't really argue with that. I'd never be able to shoot like Karl in a thousand years.

"Flying sounds amazing," I said. "Listen to this: 'Yesterday we took off just as the sun was rising. There was a layer of cloud above us, and as the sun lit it up it went pink and then the most fantastic gold. It was so beautiful I almost forgot where we were supposed to go, and Behnke (my observer) had to give me a rap on the head. We got our photographs all right, though'."

"See – he'll get killed, daydreaming like that," Karl said. "Do you really think the Frenchies are just going to let them take pictures of their gun emplacements and what have you? I'll bet their casualty rates are massive."

"Well, maybe, but at least he won't be stuck out in No Man's Land—"

"No, he'll fry instead. A lot of them burn, don't they?"

"They can't all get killed."

"No? Look, if we get hit we roll into a shell-hole and we're likely to get picked up at some point. If Otto gets hit he has to land the bloody thing. If he passes out, or can't fly the thing, then he's had it – and I'll bet that happens a lot."

"All right, but how likely are we to get to the end of this, anyway? So why not live like men instead of pigs in the meantime?"

"Why throw away any chance of surviving the war? Franz, you're not thinking what I think you're thinking, are you?"

"Christ, that was complicated! If you meant, am I thinking of applying for a transfer, the answer's yes, I am."

He stared at me.

"You're off your fucking head," he said, very seriously. "Right off it. So far off that you've forgotten where you left it."

"Why not come with me?"

"Because I still retain some small measure of sanity. Franz, please don't do it. Stay here where at least you've got a chance. Those things are fucking death-traps – the only reason they give the airmen such a good life is because it's so fucking short."

"So you don't fancy flying?"

"No."

"Not even to look at the clouds and down at the people on the ground? And feel the wind rushing past?"

"*No*. Well, maybe in a few years' time, when the science is a bit more advanced – and when no one's going to try to kill me."

"They try to kill you every day now."

"That's not the same thing."

"Of course it's the same thing," I said, rather impatiently. "As you once said, dead is dead."

"Franz, you're not going to convince me. I just hope I can convince you to stay here."

He had a point – several points, in fact – but I was beginning to fall in love with the idea of flight, was starting to feel a compulsion to leave the ground.

If I'm going to be killed then it'll happen whatever I'm doing. You can't cheat Fate.

The idea of flying began to occupy most of my waking hours. I kept staring at the sky, wondering what it would be like.

If I can get leave, I could go and visit Otto and he could take me up… Just a few days would be enough.

I didn't know how feasible it would be. *Otto's probably not allowed to go on jollies*, I thought. *Taking a mate for a flight's probably not allowed – but I could write and ask him.*

The reply I got wasn't exactly positive.

'It would be really brilliant to see you', Otto wrote, 'but there's no way I'd be allowed to take you flying. I'm in the doghouse with Bolz (our CO) at the mo. Thing is, the airfield's rather muddy and I stood our bus on her nose after landing the other day – hit a squishy patch. Luckily there wasn't much damage but I'm not really persona grata. Have to wait a few weeks for things to settle down, then I can ask.'

I had to laugh at Otto's swift adoption of what I took to be airmen's slang.

Karl laughed at it as well when I passed him the letter, but then he gave me a very serious look.

"Franz, you mean you wrote to Otto and asked him to take you *flying*? You mean it, don't you? You really are thinking about transferring."

"Yes, I am. Don't look at me like that. I'm sick to death of this bloody life. It's not as bad for you – no, it's not. You get somewhere to sleep, even in the line, you don't get woken up all the bloody time—"

"Must remember how comfy my bed of roses is," he said, laughing, "next time the thorns are digging in! You're clean compared to me, aren't you?"

"Only because you insist on going out. Koch was never as filthy as you and Dietz isn't either."

"I'd go crazy if I had to stay here all the fucking time."

"You think I don't?"

"So become a sniper, then."

"You know I can't."

He grinned at me. "Course you can – just go to confession afterwards!"

I grinned back. "I gave up on that a long time back... You

know why I can't – I'm not good enough. 'Not instinctive' was what Rippel said about my shooting."

"Ah. 'Fraid I can't argue with that. Though if you asked me what you could do about it I'd have to say that you probably couldn't. I mean, you're accurate but—"

"Not like you or the others."

"That's it. And I can't give you any better explanation than Rippel's. Sorry."

"Don't worry about it – I don't want to do your job anyway."

The shadow flitted over his eyes again, so quickly that I wasn't sure I'd actually seen it.

"Do you really imagine the war in the air's any cleaner?" he asked quietly. "It's still about death and mutilation."

"It's not that," I answered. "I just want to fly. I keep thinking about it, wondering what it's like, and one day I'm going to have to find out. And I like the thought of a proper bed in a dry room, and decent food and wine—"

"And plummeting down in flames to an early grave."

We were going round in circles, just like the aircraft did.

"Franz, please think very, very carefully before you apply for that transfer," he said. "What if you hate it?"

"That's the thing – I don't think I will. But I will think about it, I promise. I won't rush."

I didn't rush and I did think about it. And the more I thought, the more I realised how much I did want the transfer.

I'd have dithered for weeks if not months, except that Braun told me Hafner wanted to see me.

What on earth is this about? I hope they haven't found out about the pilfered beer and so on – but surely I'd have heard about that by now?

I knocked on the board.

"Come in!" Hafner called out, and I entered the dugout with

a slight feeling of trepidation. Stupid, really – what would they be likely to do to me?

"Ah, Becker – just the fellow. Have a seat."

Have a seat? That was really strange. Leutnant Leicht nodded, puffing on his pipe, a cheerful look on his long face, and I sat on the edge of one of the hard chairs.

Hafner looked cheerful as well, and the atmosphere was relaxed. *Not in trouble, then.*

"Well, Becker – you really should go for a commission," Hafner said. "I know you've turned it down before, but you really should think again."

"What, me, sir?"

Hafner made a show of looking round the dugout.

"Who else could I mean?" he asked rhetorically. "You're intelligent and well educated, you've got plenty of experience of the Front. You'd do very well."

"Maybe, sir, but I'm a war volunteer and I didn't go to cadet school, and so on."

"No one's worried about that any more," he said quietly. "We need men who can do the job – and you can. I'd be very happy to support your application."

I didn't want a commission, that much I did know. The only reason they were offering commissions to men like me was because most of the Regular officers had been killed.

"You can choose whether you go down the officers' career path and take a Regular commission, or just go for a Reserve commission," he went on. "It's entirely up to you. You'd get the Reserve one a lot quicker but there's a limit on how far you'd be promoted."

I took a deep breath.

"Well, thank you very much, sir, but I've been thinking of something else – that is, I'd like to apply for a transfer to the Air Service."

Hafner's jaw dropped. Leicht looked as if the Virgin Mary had emerged from the planking, accompanied by Jesus Christ and an escort of angels.

"Becker, did I hear you right?" Hafner asked slowly.

"Yes, sir. I've been thinking for some time about becoming a pilot."

"You want to go up in one of those bloody contraptions? Are you out of your mind? Look, take a week and think about the offer. I know what everyone says about the Express Ticket, but the fliers get there a damn sight quicker."

"My mind's been made up for longer than that, sir. I would like to put that application in."

They looked at each other and then at me.

"Well, you seem sure of what you want, so I'll put your name forward," Hafner said. "But if you ask me, you're barking mad."

I couldn't really argue with that, so I thanked him and was duly dismissed, leaving a rather stunned silence behind me.

"I've done it," I told Karl in the evening. "I told Hafner I want to apply for pilot training."

"Oh, Franz, what have you done?"

"It was either that or the Express Ticket," I said, "and I didn't fancy being a target for your Tommy counterparts."

He looked at me in dismay. "I thought you were just talking about it – you know, just an idle idea. I didn't believe you actually meant it."

"You can't argue that I'd last longer as a junior officer."

"No, that's true, but can't you just stay as you are?"

I told him about the conversation with Hafner. "So, you see, they'll just keep on asking until I say yes."

He looked very thoughtful. "Yes, I see what you mean. Well, I'll have to think what I want to do now."

"Why?"

"Because I don't feel like staying here after you've gone.

Think about it – you're the only other one left. Once you've gone that's that."

"There's Braun."

"And of course he and I are best mates – I can just see us going to the tarts, or for a piss-up. No, it just won't be the same without you. If you're leaving then I'm going too."

"So come to the fliers with me."

He shook his head. "You know I said I'd be happy to be stuck in a tight corner with you? Well, there is a limit!"

"It's no more dangerous than standing eyeball to eyeball with a Tommy sniper like you did in the summer."

"Completely different. He didn't know I was there – as witness the fact that I'm still alive. Everyone for miles around will be able to see you in your flying machine – and you can't even count on the damn thing staying in one piece. Fucked if I'm going anywhere near them – ever."

There was no way I was going to convince him. Flight hadn't cast its spell on him.

A couple of days later he asked, "So what exactly did Hafner say to you about the Express Ticket?"

"Well, basically he said we need officers, and they're not too bothered about the traditional requirements. For some reason he seemed to think that I'm 'intelligent and well educated'—"

"Fooled him, then!"

"God knows how! And that with my experience I'd be able to do it."

He looked very thoughtful.

"Makes sense," he said after a pause. "There can't be that many of the original Regular officers left – and there'll only be so many coming through Lichterfelde."

"Yes – he said I could go for Regular or Reserve, and he'd back up my application if I put it in."

He raised his eyebrows.

"Yes, I know," I said. "They must be fucking desperate!"

It was my turn to be concerned.

"Hang on, Karl – you're not thinking what I think you're thinking, are you?"

He burst out laughing. "Tell me what you think I'm thinking and I'll tell you if I think you're thinking right!"

"You're not thinking about the Express Ticket, are you?"

"I think you're thinking right about what I'm thinking!"

"Karl, for God's sake stop talking rot!" Then I realised what he'd said. "You can't be serious. You just can't. That's completely insane."

"You're in no position to comment!"

"But the Express Ticket, after what you've been doing… I mean, how can you even think about it?"

He looked at me and this time the shadow was definitely there.

"It's time for a change," he said.

"Oh." *You mean it's starting to get to you.* "What about that instructor's job Hafner mentioned to you?"

"Threatened me with, you mean. Can't think of anything worse. I joined up to fight, not to sit somewhere safe, teaching. It would drive me completely crazy."

"Well, come with me, then. It'll be fun."

"Fun?! Going up in one of those fucking things? Not fucking likely!"

"It's got to be a better bet than wearing epaulettes. Look, your reaction to seeing an enemy officer is to put a bullet in the bugger. Come on, how many have you shot?"

"I've got no idea – you know that."

"Well, go through your little book and add them up, and then work out what percentage they make up of the total. Everyone over there is going to want to kill you."

"They do anyway," he said with a grin.

"Yes, but you won't be hidden away – you'll be out in front when you go over the top, a fucking prime target. For fuck's sake, Karl, you're even more barking fucking mad than I thought you were."

"At least I shall be on terra firma, not sitting there wondering whether the wings will stay on… And what happens if you get hit? It's a fucking long way down, and no one's going to help you. All I'll have to do is roll into the nearest hole and wait to be picked up."

"No, you won't – because your skull will be even emptier than it is already."

He grinned at me again. "Franz, it's no use – there's no way I'm going to follow you, not to the Air Service. And I don't really want to come back here – as I said, it won't be the same without you. So I've been thinking some more—"

"Is that what you call it?"

"Ha bloody ha. What I've been *thinking* is that I'm going to apply for a Brandenburg regiment. If you're going to the fliers then I'll go to my own people."

"Do you think you'll get it? I mean the Brandenburgers, not being a Regular? They're elite, aren't they?"

"Well, yes, but I'm not going for the Guards. And in view of what Hafner said I don't think they'll be as fussy these days, and I have spent a year at the Front."

"And you're from the right sort of background."

He shrugged. "Yes, that might help…"

"And your father knows just about everyone."

"I am not bringing Pa into this. Either I get it for myself or I don't want it."

I was taken aback by the vehemence of his tone.

"Hafner will probably recommend you, anyway," I said. "But I still don't understand how you can even contemplate it."

He sighed. "Duration seems to be a bloody sight longer than

any of us imagined. I don't know about you, but I thought I'd be home by now. We've been stuck here for months, there's no sign of it ending – so I've decided that I'd better make the best of it, and that means going for promotion."

"Duration will be bloody short if you get it. Karl, please don't do this."

"Where have I heard that phrase before? And did you listen to me? Did you fuck!"

The next day he went to see Hafner, and came back looking even more dangerously thoughtful.

"What did he say?"

"Said it was about bloody time I showed a bit of ambition and that he'll put in a good word for me. He did try to talk me out of going to the Brandenburg regiment, though – wanted me to come back. Not that it did much good."

"So where's the regiment at present?"

"Serbia."

"Why in God's name do you want to go there?"

"Frankly, I don't. You can keep the Balkans. Bloody place is nothing but trouble. But I've had enough of Flanders – and don't pretend you haven't."

He was right, of course.

What stunned me was how quickly Karl's application went through. Less than a fortnight later Hafner summoned him and told him that he would be leaving us at the beginning of December, and that after his Reserve officer's course he would be going to the Brandenburg regiment that he'd requested.

"See?" I said. "They must be desperate—"

"Cheers, bastard!"

"Otherwise it wouldn't have come through so fast. You're being a complete fucking idiot – can't you see that?"

"No more than you can! Anyway, there's a bit more to it than that – the speed of it, I mean."

"How d'you mean?"

"Well, I didn't pull strings, approach anyone or anything, but we have got a long connection with that regiment. I'd be pushed to tell you how many of us have served in it. So my name probably helped."

"I thought you all went in for the Guards?"

"No, that's just Pa and Friedrich – recent development, really. So I'm back in the old family tradition after all… Seems I can't quite escape my fate."

That evening he told Taschner and Dietz. They both looked at him as if he'd taken complete leave of his senses.

"You *what*?" Taschner asked incredulously. "What the fuck do you want to do that for? Officers are there to be shot. You know that – *they* know that. One glimpse of those epaulettes and you'll be totally fucking brainless. Nah, mate, 'snot worth it. Stay here with us."

Taschner hadn't called Karl 'mate' since his promotion.

"I never knew you cared!" Karl said with a grin. "Anyway, you should be happy – you'll probably get my job."

"Oh well – in that case you can bugger off as soon as you like!"

"Congratulations," said Dietz. "But really, I agree with Taschner. I don't know how you can even think about becoming an officer – not when they're your favourite game."

"Not quite how I'd put it," Karl said quietly. There was a pause and then he added, "Well, at least I know how snipers think, don't I? Should give me a bit of an advantage."

The other two shook their heads.

"Don't work like that," Taschner said. "As you know. You'll be leading some bloody attack or other, they'll be waiting and you'll be the first to buy it – won't matter how much you know about our nasty little habits. There'll be nowhere to hide. Look – I don't give a fuck about promotion – just go and tell Hafner you've changed your mind."

Karl shook his head. "Too late – I've got my course date."

"So you'll be back as Herr Leutnant?" Dietz said. "That'll be strange."

"No," Karl answered. "I'm off to the Brandenburgers."

"That makes sense," Dietz said. "I've always wondered why you weren't with them anyway."

"I was trying to do something different," Karl said with a note of resignation.

"Well, mate, it was good knowing you," said Taschner. "And at least you won't get killed in front of us. That would just be depressing... Oh, and can I have that nice four-power Zeiss sight of yours? After all, you won't be needing it. You'll just have some poxy little pop-gun. You won't hit anything at four hundred metres with one of those."

"Consider it yours – don't know what you're going to do about the monograms, though. I doubt the workshop will want to faff about with your rifle."

"Maybe if I slip them a few marks... Worth a try, isn't it?"

"And they'd have to change the serial numbers on the sight and the case. Probably easier just to carve your initials on my rifle, even if you can't copy Faltermeier's work."

"There must be another woodcarver here somewhere."

"You're right – we'll have to ask around. And then he can do one for Dietz, and for the others."

Dietz's face lit up. "That would be dead good," he said.

"And for your replacement!" Taschner said cheerfully to Karl.

"Oh, Christ, good point. I'll have to go and see Hafner again. Look, why don't you come with me? It's a dead cert you'll get my job, so you should have a say in who gets chosen."

"And then I'll be deciding who gets which weapon, won't I? So I can palm this old three-power off onto one of the new blokes."

"Exactly – but I'll give you mine anyway before I go."

Taschner paused theatrically. "I was about to ask if you'll be wanting it back later – but of course you won't! Not where you're going!"

Karl grinned at him. "Doesn't it occur to you that you might go first?"

"Nah, mate, no chance. You won't last a fortnight with epaulettes on! I'll take your precious Zeiss home after the war, give it a good home."

"Bollocks! You'll have the wooden cross long before the end. Just leave it back to me in your will – then Oberst Leussow will be able to take it home."

"And who the fuck's he?"

"Me in ten years' time when this mess ends!"

Taschner laughed. "You? Colonel? That happens, I'll have the fucking thing gold-plated and set with diamonds – and pay with my big lottery win! Believe me, mate, I've got a better chance of winning the big prize than you have of seeing the end of the war, never mind making colonel."

"Not when you never buy a ticket, you haven't!"

They disappeared off to see Hafner, still joshing each other as they went.

Dietz looked at me. "Is he serious, Sarge?"

"As serious as he ever is. I know, I know – I've tried to talk him out of it. I think just the same as you do – how he can even *think* about becoming an officer… Well, it's just beyond me, it really is."

"Especially when… Look, Sarge, I've worked with him. I've seen him wait all day for an officer to turn up, wasn't interested in any of the others, said they weren't worth the risk. Believe me, he's bagged more junior officers than you or I've had hot dinners."

"Not difficult when most of the grub's barely warm. How d'you know that, anyway? You didn't look at his book?"

"No. You were right and I thought better of it. Taschner told me he'd overheard Leicht and Hafner talking, saying Leussow'd be in line for another gong the way he was going. So I just don't understand why he wants to make himself into a target."

I sighed. "Neither do I."

As if to underline the point, Leutnant Adler was shot dead the next day.

"See what I mean?" Taschner said to Karl.

"He'd only been here five minutes," Karl replied. "And frankly, he asked for it. What kind of moron ignores the sign saying 'Watch out! Sniper!'?"

"A dead one."

"Exactly. Not the sort of mistake I'm likely to make, now, am I? I see a sign like that, I'm on my hands and knees – not showing off the fancy red underside of my collar. Not that I'd wear a coat like that anyway. Far too fucking showy."

"You see a sign like that, you're planning how to shoot the fucker," I retorted.

"What else am I for? Talking of which – come on, boys, let's make some plans."

The three of them sat together and I left them to it.

Taschner was right about the Tommies getting their sniping act together – someone had clearly got them organised and they were becoming a real pest. It was not good that Karl was leaving before Taschner's NCO's course.

Once again Hafner joined the snipers in their dugout for a conference.

"The timing's a real bastard," Karl said to me later. "Hafner tried to get them to delay taking me, but they won't. He can't get Taschner's course brought forward, either. Scheffel and Ranke will still be novices, so Dietz will be the most experienced until Taschner gets back."

"So who'll be acting?"

"No one. Hafner said they don't need an NCO with just three and I agree – it worked fine before when there were four of us."

"Fate's trying to tell you something," I said. "Stay here where you're needed."

He looked at me half-seriously. "All right, Franz – here's a deal: I'll turn it down and stay here if you do. That means you turn down the Air Service and take the Express Ticket. I'll even call you 'Herr Leutnant' with total sincerity."

"Not fucking likely!"

"Exactly!"

"But how are Dietz and the two new ones going to cope?" I asked.

"They'll just have to. Frantz and my replacement will be trained up soon, and Taschner will be back before you know it. Look, they're all first-class shots, or we wouldn't have chosen them. And they've all got several months out here, so they're not going to do anything stupid. None of us had an expert guide when we started out."

"No, but the Tommies didn't have proper snipers, not like now."

"There'll be, what, about three weeks with rather thin cover, that's all, and you'll spend one of those out of the line. And Hafner's going to try to borrow someone from another company. It'll work out."

"I suppose so. I'll be gone soon, anyway." *And it can't happen soon enough. I've had a gutful of the fucking trenches.*

Scheffel and Ranke both opened their accounts on their first day in the line with their new weapons.

"Not surprised," Karl said to me later. "They both impressed me on the range – not just how well they shoot but their attitude and the way they think. I pretty well bombarded them with questions, you know, 'what would you do if' – and they've both got their heads well screwed on, asked me some pretty good questions too. They should do all right, both of them."

All the same, at the end of that first day Scheffel had a thoughtful look on his face. So did Dietz, who'd been working with him, but in his case it was combined with something I couldn't quite read. He seemed to be slightly downcast for some reason.

"You both did well," Karl said. "Carry on like that but for fuck's sake don't get too confident. Never forget they're waiting to get you. Any questions, comments?"

Scheffel looked as if he wanted to say something but wasn't sure if he should.

"Well…" he began rather hesitantly, "it was… I mean… a bit, sort of… different from before. Did give me pause for thought for a moment or two."

Dietz looked at him. "Different how?" he asked, and I suddenly remembered his initial difficulty.

"Well, it's hard to put my finger on. I mean, in the past they were coming at us with fixed bayonets and I looked at those fucking things and I thought, no way do I want one of those stuck in me, so I shot as many as I could, just to stop them. This was… Well, the bloke was minding his own business and I had plenty of time to look at him – he was just standing where he didn't realise he shouldn't."

"And you thought, should I really be doing this?" Karl said, being careful not to look at Dietz.

"Something like that," Scheffel said. "Did you think that, then?"

Karl shook his head.

"No," he replied quietly, "by then I didn't give a fuck. Look, it's still a case of do unto others before they do unto you – the only difference between what you did today and shooting him tomorrow when they're attacking us is the timing."

"Yeah, that's what I thought."

"I thought what you've just said, Scheffel," Dietz said, quite unexpectedly. "In fact, I had a real problem with it."

"Bugger me!" said Taschner. "That's why it took you so long to get the first one. I couldn't work out what was going on." He looked at Dietz with curiosity. "Never occurred to me anyone would think like that."

"It was the very first time," Dietz said. "I'd never been in the line before, remember?"

Taschner laughed. "Well, you've more than made up for it! You're breathing down my neck so hard I'm starting to get worried!" He turned to Scheffel and Ranke. "Do you two want to join our competition?"

Karl got up.

"That's between the four of you," he said. "Just don't get so caught up in your scores that you slip up – I don't want to have to replace you just yet!"

He turned to me. "Smoke?"

We went into the next bay and he lit our cigarettes. He took a long drag on his and leaned his head against the planking.

"Fucking hell, this business is shit," he said flatly. "Dietz was a decent fellow who never wanted to kill anyone and had to really force himself to do it, and now he happily gives himself points for every Tommy he shoots… I ask you, what kind of civilised Europe are we in?"

I didn't have an answer.

"Koch was a different matter," he continued. "He was a murderer already, as you know – I don't suppose a few more made any difference to him – and Taschner was absent when consciences were being handed out, which is probably the best way to be."

"Probably…" *And what about you?* I thought but didn't want to ask.

"I tell you, Franz, there are times when all I want to do is go home to Brandenburg, take the boat out on the lake, and forget everything I've done here."

"You know what Taschner would say to that," I replied.

"'Don't work like that!'" we said in unison, and burst out laughing.

"No, it don't," Karl said. "Sometimes I wish to God that it did."

"So do I… You really think it's going to be better once you've taken the Express Ticket?"

"You know, I've asked myself that and I really don't know. I'm just letting myself in for more of that close-up shit, after all, aren't I, and you know what I think of that. No escape really, is there?"

"No."

He sighed and put his cigarette holder away.

"You know," he said, "the men who really want shooting are the fucking arsehole politicians who got us into this mess."

I started laughing. "Now that's something to hear – a Junker revolutionary! Who'll you put against the wall first?"

"I'll have to think about that! Don't suppose I'll ever get the chance, though."

"What – you mean you really would…"

He'd sounded so serious that I was quite taken aback.

"Well, I am an experienced assassin," he said half-flippantly.

"Yes, but – Karl, that would be murder."

"And shooting some Tommy who doesn't keep his head down isn't? Who decides where the line goes?"

"But the Tommies are armed, they're here to kill us. Politicians are civilians."

"Civilians who send other men to do their dirty work. If you pay someone to kill your enemy, you're just as guilty as he is, aren't you? Or were you asleep in that lecture?"

"No…"

"Well, they pay us to dispose of the Tommies and the Frenchies, so the blood's on their hands too, if you ask me, and it could be argued that they richly deserve to pay for it."

"But…"

He burst out laughing. "Franz, your face! I really believe I've shocked you."

"Well, it's just… I never thought I'd hear you… I mean… Anyway, we're not doing it for the money, are we? We're not mercenaries. It's for…" I wanted to say "for Germany", but the words were too trite and sentimental, and stuck in my throat.

"King and Fatherland?" There was a mocking note in his voice.

"Well, yes. We have to be here, don't we? The Russians and the French had us surrounded – and anyway, they mobilised before us."

"Did they? That's what we were told, but was it true? Was there really no other way but war?"

"But why would they make up something like that?"

"Oh, let's give them the benefit of the doubt and say they believed it – but I'm buggered if *I* know what to believe any more. Now it's started we have to finish it. That's all I really know."

He stared at his hands, and after a long pause he added, "To be honest, I never thought I'd think like that either. Maybe I've been here too long."

"We all have."

The next day we went into support but the snipers stayed in the line. I had the feeling that Hafner, though he recognised the necessity, wasn't entirely happy about it. I shared his reservations: it simply wasn't possible for Karl and Taschner to pass on several months' worth of experience in a few days, and the more they worked the greater was the chance that it would all go horribly wrong.

By the end of that week Karl was looking more tired than I'd ever seen him, and when we went into rest the five of them came with us.

"Well, that's that," Karl said quietly as we settled into a cosy corner of the barn. "I just hope they're fast learners."

"They've got Taschner for a bit yet," I replied.

"Yes..."

"Did you get any grief from the Second Company snipers? I mean, hanging about on their watch?"

"Not really... Well, there was a bit at the beginning. Schmidt – their NCO – was a bit sour about us being there until I explained, and then he couldn't have been more helpful. That was after he'd finished calling me a stupid cunt."

"Well, you are a stupid cunt – the sniper who took the Express Ticket! You've raised stupid cuntishness to heights no one ever dreamed of."

"Oh, shut up! So he said he'll lend us – oh, fuck it, what was the bugger's name? – anyway, he said the fellow's shit-hot, and he's been here almost as long as me, so that should help to fill the gap."

"That's good. Be useful for Scheffel and Ranke as well."

"Hopefully. Tell you what, being spare parts made me realise how bloody good it's been having that dugout. We just had to squeeze in where we could and it was fucking hard to get any sleep."

"Welcome to the real world!"

"Anyway, I'm knackered."

He turned his back on me and was asleep in an instant. I lay staring into the darkness, unable to adjust from the nocturnal existence of the past two weeks. It would settle just in time to be reversed again, I knew that. There were times when my idea of Heaven was just to sleep for a whole day...

But when I get to the Air Service it will all be different. We'll fly in the daytime and sleep at night, like civilised men – and won't that be good!

When I woke I was suddenly aware that it was my last week with Karl, maybe for ever. It was a very strange feeling and I pushed it to the back of my mind. I didn't want it to overshadow the time that remained.

"I don't know about any of you," he said halfway through our rest, "but I was hoping for a bath and a clean uniform."

"And whose fault is it that you're so filthy?" I demanded. "Is anyone else as mucky as you and Taschner?"

"It's not all my fault," he retorted. "Remember that Tommy I skewered when they raided us? Look, you can still see the blood – and I've had enough of wearing it."

"A bath would have been good, though," said Dietz, "and no lice."

"Yeah, well, that don't last, do it?" Taschner said. "Takes about five minutes for the next lot of fuckers to hatch out. Might as well just stay as we are."

"I'm just fed up with being encrusted with grime," Dietz replied.

"Me too," I said. "I've forgotten what soap is… Maybe next time."

"You can't grumble, anyway," Taschner said to Karl. "You'll have a nice new uniform soon, epaulettes and all, shining in the sun. Perfect target! And once they've blown your brains out, you won't care about dirt or lice."

"No one's blown my brains out so far!"

"Only because they've never seen you! Nah, mate, you're going to stick out like a fucking sore thumb. Won't last five minutes!"

I'd had enough of Taschner telling Karl that he was going to be killed, mostly because he was very likely to be right. Karl, on the other hand, seemed to find it genuinely funny.

"What was it Schmidt called you?" Taschner was pushing his luck now, and knew it.

Karl just grinned at him. "You can call me whatever you like when I'm out of earshot," he said. "But you want that promotion and I don't want to hear you!"

Taschner grinned back. "Fine by me, Corporal! You won't hear a dicky bird."

On Karl's last evening we decided to wander into the nearby village and celebrate his escape from Flanders, if not the war. It was a sad dump, blown half to pieces over the months, but there was a small café where the food wasn't bad.

Dusk was falling early, brought on by the rain and thick cloud. We wandered idly along the main street, peering inside the empty houses as we passed. Suddenly Karl gave a cry of glee and disappeared into one of them.

Scheffel and I looked at each other

"What the fuck's that about?" he asked.

"God knows," Taschner said. "Bugger's never been quite right in the head."

I should probably have said something, but I couldn't be bothered and it wasn't really a statement I could argue with.

I shrugged and the five of us followed Karl in, to see him seating himself at a battered old upright. It was damaged and out of tune but it was still a piano. He played one of Chopin's waltzes – wistful, melancholy music that floated out into the dusk and lingered around the broken houses and the muddy street.

We listened, hushed. *Music written by a dying man, played for those who have so far been reprieved, a requiem for those already dead…* My throat tightened.

"I didn't realise you could play like that," Ranke said when it finished.

"I can't," Karl replied.

Ranke gave him a bemused look and he added, "I can play a bloody sight better than that but I'm so out of practice."

"You a professional, then?" asked Scheffel.

"I was on my way to being, yes. All feels a long way away now, though."

"Play something a bit more cheerful, for fuck's sake," said Taschner. "You might be collecting the Express Ticket but I'm buggered if the rest of us are!"

"Well, let's see..." Karl said with mock thoughtfulness. After a theatrical pause he started to play a song that was very familiar to us all, and whose obscene words we roared out into the twilight.

That's more like it – I'd rather not think about death when you're off on the Eternity Express. The thought that I might never see Karl again was disturbing me far more than I'd expected it to. Now that the separation was almost upon us I was forced to recognise what it really meant.

Karl and I had hardly been out of each other's company since we'd rented that flat in Heidelberg. The summer holiday had barely begun when war was declared, and apart from the weeks when one of us had been away from the Front we'd been together constantly. Shared danger had forged a bond between us that was stronger than anything I'd ever experienced – and now we were going in different directions, each to face his fate without the other.

It felt completely wrong, but it was too late to try to undo it. Somehow we'd arrived at this point without either of us intending it to happen.

"I don't know about any of you," Karl said, breaking into my thoughts, "but all those rude songs have put me into the mood for a trip to the tarts."

"Good idea," said Taschner.

This is the last time, maybe for ever, I thought as we stood in the queue, and again when we finally got to the café. I wished I could turn the clock back and reverse both our decisions.

Karl and I squeezed into a corner table and the others got one a short distance away. It wasn't quite the celebration we'd had in mind, but it gave the two of us a chance to talk without constant interruption.

"Penny for them, Franz?"

"Not sure they're worth that much," I said.

"Try me and see!"

"I was thinking it's going to be odd not seeing your ugly mug every day."

"You started it," he replied with a grin. "I was perfectly happy lurking in various unsavoury holes, bumping off the odd Tommy, and you had to mess it all up!"

"Rather more than the odd Tommy," I said. "Rumour has it you were on your way to another gong."

He pulled a face. "Looks like I made the right decision, then... Taschner can collect instead of me, be much more his style."

There was a long pause.

He lit another cigarette, and then added, "For what it's worth, I'll... Well, it'll be odd without your ugly mug as well. You will write, won't you? And maybe we can get leave at the same time. If you come to Berlin I'll fix us up with those dancers – be a bloody sight better than what we've just had."

"You'll be going to the officers' brothels," I said with more than a touch of envy.

"You turned it down, remember? No good being jealous now! And God alone knows what Serbian tarts are like."

"Long black hair, high cheekbones, almond-shaped eyes... Can the Serbs shoot straight?"

"Well, they kicked the shit out of the Austrians, didn't they?"

There was no answer to that. I didn't know which would

be worse – his being killed in front of me or far away among strangers.

"Let's get another bottle," he said. "Be a while before we have another piss-up."

If we ever do... I pushed that idea away. *We're both on borrowed time anyway. Who knows how much longer we'd last if we stayed here?*

"Another couple of bottles?" Karl called to Taschner.

"Yeah, cheers, mate." Just then the table next to them became vacant and we moved across. By throwing-out time we were all well pissed.

We staggered back through the darkness, Karl and I with our arms round each other's shoulders. I had the sudden, absurd feeling that I didn't want to let go of him, as if I wanted time to stop.

You're pissed, Franz, thinking daft things like that.

That was certainly true and I fell asleep the second my head touched the straw.

I woke in the middle of the night, the feeling of Karl's warm back against mine familiar and comforting. And then I remembered that he was leaving in the morning, and that I'd have my blanket to myself from now on.

That won't feel right at all. We promised not to leave each other, and look what's happened.

The next morning Karl handed his equipment to Taschner with mock solemnity. He couldn't suppress a look of regret as he parted with his rifle.

"Too late now!" Taschner said. "That'll be the last time you get your hands on a proper weapon."

"Not quite," Karl replied. "After all, I've got this for the time being, haven't I?"

He regarded the standard-issue rifle he'd just been given with complete indifference.

"Yeah, but that's just any old anybody's, isn't it? I mean, it's not *yours*. Look, it's even got a straight bolt handle! And you won't have it for long, will you?"

"No, well... Anyway, I might just pick up a rifle every now and then..."

"Nah, don't bother – you'll be so out of practice you won't hit a bloody thing."

"Bollocks! It'll be just like riding a bike. Hafner still shoots well, doesn't he?"

"At targets on the range? How fucking boring's that?"

Karl's eyes met mine briefly and it was as if he'd said, thank God I'm getting out before I end up like him.

Taschner took Karl's sight out of the case and looked through it.

"Nice," he said. "Very nice. Guess where I'm going tomorrow."

"I'll come with you," Dietz said. "I could do with a re-zero. Shall we ask Hafner if he wants to come too?"

"Yeah, why not? He'll be up for it, always is. He can have first go with Leussow's old gear, before they set it up for me."

At lunchtime Hafner tapped a barrel of good German beer and made a very nice short speech, wishing Karl success and praising his professionalism and dedication to duty.

"I have to say that the Brandenburgers' gain is our loss," he concluded. "Leussow, you've been a credit to the Company and you'll make a very good officer."

Karl was, as before, very uncomfortable being praised in public.

"Applause is different," he'd said to me once. "It's words that feel wrong – it's always as if they're talking about someone else."

Hafner proposed the toast and we all drank to Karl's future success. Silently I wished him long life and good health as well – *that should cover all possible forms of harm*, I thought.

By the end of the afternoon everyone was nicely lubricated.

"I'm sorry to see you go," Dietz said to Karl. "I really owe you."

"No, you don't," Karl said. "You don't owe me fuck all. Look in the mirror some time and ask yourself if I really did you a favour."

Dietz looked at him.

"I know what you're saying," he said, "but I'd never have been able to look in the mirror again if I'd failed here. It's a long story – I won't bore you with it – but when I was instructing, someone said that I was only doing it to keep away from the Front and that I'd never be able to shoot anyone, that I didn't have the guts for it."

"Well, he got that wrong, then, didn't he?" Karl replied.

"She, actually."

"Ah. Well, *she* got that wrong, then. When you get leave you can show her your book – that should convince her – and maybe you'll have a nice black and white ribbon to underline the point. Anyway, it's got bugger all to do with me – you'd have managed quite well by yourself."

"Maybe."

Karl looked at his watch. "I'd better go or I'll miss my train."

Shit. Already.

It took Karl several minutes to escape from all the well-wishers. Taschner hugged him with what seemed like genuine affection.

"Look after yourself, mate," he said, suddenly sentimental. "I want to be able to give that nice sight back to you, over a beer in Berlin."

"Beer'll be on you, then, and we'll call it payment!"

Karl and I walked some of the way together, until I had to turn back.

He wrapped his arms round me and held me so tight I could hardly breathe.

"Don't forget to write, you old bastard," he said. "And for fuck's sake remember which way is up in those fucking contraptions."

"Good luck, Karl," I said. "May all the Serbs be cross-eyed!"

He laughed and released me, looked me in the eyes for a moment, then turned and walked away. I stood watching him go, a tall, well-built man whose easy, almost graceful bearing contrasted starkly with his worn, mud-stained uniform.

You'll look a bloody sight smarter in a week or so – no more lying in Flanders filth all day...

At the bend in the road he turned and waved, and then he was gone.

XII

I made my way back to the party. It was almost over, which suited me fine. I felt flat and empty, and couldn't get rid of the thought that I would never see him again.

I got a refill and sat on the grass. Braun came and sat beside me and handed me his flask.

"Chaser," he said.

"Thanks."

"Well, Becker, there's just you and me now."

"Yes." *Sobering thought, that.*

"He's a bloody good soldier and he'll make a bloody good officer. Not sure about you making a bloody good pilot, though!"

"Me neither."

"Why the fuck are you doing it?"

I shrugged. "Just want to fly, that's all. And I didn't want to take the Express Ticket."

"Can't blame you for that. Wouldn't hold any attraction for me either. Look, what he's been doing's every bit as fucking dangerous. He's got just as much chance of making it through either way. And officers get taken prisoner, which is more than happens to snipers."

"True… if the Serbs take prisoners."

"Well, if they don't he's no worse off. If you ask me, you're the one who needs to worry, going up in those fucking things."

"You're probably right."

And I wish that fucking transfer would come through, especially now Karl's gone.

Being without him was even stranger than I'd imagined, and I felt as if part of me were missing. I lost count of the number of times I turned to say something to him before remembering, just too late, that he wasn't there. It annoyed me because I felt such an idiot, and because it was as if he'd died and that seemed somehow to be a bad omen.

The day before we were due to go back into the line a small fellow with a rather round face appeared.

"Steckel, Second Company sniper, Sarge," he said, with a touch of self-importance. "I'm looking for Taschner and co."

"Come with me," I said. "They'll be pleased to see you – we're a bit short-handed just now, as you probably know."

Taschner and the others were indeed happy with the new arrival.

"You're here just in time, mate," Taschner said. "I'll be off in about a week, which leaves Dietz here as the most experienced, and Scheffel and Ranke are new to this game, though not to the Front. And you've been doing the job since…?"

"July."

"Great. How long have we got you for?"

I left them to talk – I had surprise kit inspections planned. Some of the fellows were inclined to get a bit sloppy given half a chance, and I wanted everything in order before we went back up the line.

Steckel turned out to be shit-hot, as promised, but there was something about him that I didn't like. He had a sarcastic turn of phrase and seemed to like putting others down. There was friction between him and Dietz almost from the start, and it was all of his making.

I hadn't realised that Dietz had a lingering sense of insecurity. Steckel picked up on it very quickly and started needling him. He was clever enough to make it subtle. Karl wouldn't have stood for it, and Taschner wouldn't have done either if he'd realised what was happening. Subtlety wasn't his strong point and Steckel's remarks went straight past him.

I wondered whether to intervene but decided I might just make matters worse, especially as I wasn't with them all the time. Dietz was a grown man who could be expected to look after himself, after all, and I was sure he'd tell Steckel to fuck off at some point.

The one time Taschner responded was when Steckel expressed surprise that Dietz didn't go out.

"I'd have thought someone with your record would be out regular," he said. "You don't know what you're missing."

Dietz stiffened slightly, enough for Steckel to see that the remark had gone home. For once Taschner noticed as well.

"Dietz does bloody well for himself from here," Taschner said. "Going out doesn't suit everyone. And it don't necessarily work out, anyway."

Steckel smiled – or rather smirked, with just the slightest hint of condescension.

"You should try it, mate," he said to Dietz with false sincerity. "You'd be amazed what you get to see."

"I'd like a mark for every time I've wondered why I bothered," Taschner said.

"Really?"

"Yeah," Taschner went on, oblivious to Steckel's tone. "Especially when I've got back in and found that the others have all scored and I got fuck all."

Dietz laughed, and I thought I heard a note of relief that he was no longer on the receiving end.

"You were pretty pissed off," he said, "especially when you heard I'd got two!"

"See," Taschner said to Steckel, "he works much better from here."

You shouldn't have said that. You'd made your point and now you've gone and underlined it, and brought the focus back onto Dietz.

"Oh well, each to his own," Steckel said, and again there was that slight hint of superiority.

The sooner you go back the better – you're only going to cause trouble. Maybe we should have been suspicious of Schmidt's eagerness to loan out someone with such a good score – he was probably glad to be rid of you for a few weeks.

As the day of Taschner's departure approached, I realised – with a touch of dismay – that he was the nearest thing I still had to a friend. *Wonderful*, I thought, but at the same time I knew he would die rather than leave anyone in the lurch.

He's a good man to have on your side, whatever you think of him. That coldness would be just the thing in a tight spot.

After Taschner left I felt even lonelier. I'd still heard nothing about my transfer and was getting bloody fed up waiting for it. I considered asking Hafner what was happening but knew there was no point. He'd have told me if he'd heard anything.

Dietz was now the man I knew best, and the two of us weren't exactly close. Once or twice I noticed that he seemed a bit downcast, but I didn't know why. He was just as effective as ever and was proving a good mentor to Scheffel and Ranke, who were both scoring well. Something was bothering him, though, and we weren't friends enough for him to confide in me.

When the Second Company relieved us I sought out Schmidt.

"Your fellow Steckel," I began.

He gave me a cautious look. "What about him? Not causing trouble, I hope?"

Now that was an interesting question. "Why do you ask?"

400

"It was you who asked me," he replied, bluntly but in a friendly tone.

"How does he get on with the others?"

Schmidt sighed. "Well, to be honest, he's a bit of a stirrer – two of the blokes had a major falling-out a month or so back, a real punch-up, and I'd put money that he was behind it but I couldn't prove anything. Is he up to the same trick?"

"Something like it, I think, but I can't put my finger on what's going on. I'm not with them that much."

"Not much point my having a word?"

"No – I mean, what about? I just wanted a bit of background."

"Well, you've got it."

It might be better if we sent him back. Maybe I should see Hafner... but again, what about?

All I had to go on were a few semi-pointed remarks he'd made to Dietz, and the fact that Dietz was clearly uncomfortable about something – which could equally well be news from home. And Steckel's proficiency meant I'd have needed very good reason to complain about him.

A couple of days later Hafner told me there was to be a large raid on the English trenches, led by Leutnant Gross with me as second in command, and that my Air Service medical would be the week after.

Wonderful. Bloody wonderful. At last something's happening about my transfer, and I've got to go on some bloody tomfoolery that's quite likely to get me killed. Shit. Fucking shit.

The raid was to be a major one – a replica of the relevant section of trench had been constructed a few kilometres behind the lines, and there we went to rehearse until we were bloody sick of it.

No plan survives first contact, I couldn't help reminding myself. *There'll be something we haven't thought of, some nasty surprise just waiting for us.*

It was very hard to be positive about the business, but I had to put my misgivings aside. If I didn't believe it was going to work then how would I lead those under me?

My misgivings grew as the rehearsals progressed. On the second day an English two-seater aircraft appeared overhead and circled for a few minutes before one of our single-seaters chased it away.

They had a good look at us. They probably took photographs, and the Tommies will know exactly what we're planning.

There was another aircraft the next day.

"I don't like that, sir," I said to Gross. "That's two days running. The Tommies are far too interested in us."

"Yes, Becker, I think you're right," he said. "They'll have pictures – Hafner needs to know."

So he reported what we'd seen, and Hafner summoned us both the following morning.

"The raid goes ahead as planned," he told us. "As you can expect a reception committee I'm doubling the numbers, and there'll be a brief bombardment before you go over."

He didn't look happy about it, and Leicht, for once, was looking grave rather than cheerful.

"May we have an extra day's preparation in view of the extra numbers, sir?" asked Gross.

"As I said, it goes ahead as planned. Don't blame you for asking, though."

Hafner had clearly banged his head against the brick wall good and hard, without any result.

I wasn't convinced that a 'brief bombardment' was a good idea. It would remove any element of surprise, with no guarantee that many of the bastards would be killed.

"Well, that's one plan buggered even before first contact," Gross said to me. "We're going to have to do a bit of re-thinking, just when we thought we had it all planned out. What do you reckon to the bombardment?"

"Not convinced, sir. The Tommies know which bit of trench we're going to raid, they just don't know when. They'll know as soon as the shelling starts, though, and they'll be ready for us."

"My thoughts exactly. So what do you think we should do?"

"Depends how much we trust the artillery. I'd be inclined to get right up to their wire before the shelling begins, then as soon as it stops we can rush through the gap, throw in some grenades and jump in, before the machine-gunners have time to get their arses into gear. *If* we don't get shorts we'll be all right."

"Quite a big if. They always seem to drop some short."

"Yes… but how many will we lose to a couple of shorts, compared to how many if the Tommies are ready for us?"

"We'll still be bloody close to where they're bursting even without shorts."

"True – but I'd rather take my chances with random crap falling than with aimed shots."

"Good point."

My respect for Gross had increased. It was one thing to ask my opinion but quite another to actually listen to it. I didn't envy him his job or his decision – it was likely to be a bad business whatever we did.

"We could leave half the chaps a bit back in No Man's Land," he said, "then they could join us after about five minutes. That could be the best of both worlds – we'll be near enough to jump straight in, and they'll be further away from shorts and splinters."

And so we had a revised plan, and the only thing we could do was cram in as much training as possible.

The results were not good. Those who had been training and thought they knew what they were supposed to do now had to learn the new plan, and those who had just joined us had to start from scratch. I wasn't sure which group had the harder task. The first rehearsal was chaos. The second was rather better, but by then dawn was breaking and everyone was in need of sleep.

And that was it. The raid was scheduled for the following midnight.

I tried to sleep during the day but it was bloody difficult. I couldn't help going over my part in the raid. After I'd been over it for the fourth time I made a huge effort to put it aside.

It'll be Christmas next week – but I didn't want to think about that either, as there was absolutely no guarantee that I'd be there to celebrate it.

As darkness fell I found I was far more keyed up than I'd expected to be. I had a bad feeling about the whole business. The patrol reported that they'd cut the Tommies' wire without being disturbed, but something felt wrong.

It's because of that bloody aeroplane, I thought, longing even more fervently to be up there looking down, rather than down here being watched.

Hafner made bloody sure we got our rum before we set off, promised tea with the same on our return, and wished us success.

Gross reminded us of the objectives and we crept up the ladders after him, as fine a bunch of ruffians as you would not wish to meet on a dark night, with blackened faces and a very unsavoury collection of weapons.

I should have asked Karl to give me that knife of his – but it's far too useful a thing to give away.

We made our way through the wire and out into the darkness. The mud clutched at our boots and more than once I stumbled over some pathetic remains that still lay out there.

A flare went up and we dropped to the ground. There was a skull right beside me, picked clean by the rats, the empty sockets gazing straight into my eyes. *How in God's name could Karl spend so much time out here? It's nothing but a fucking boneyard.*

It's not the dead we need to be wary of…

The flare burned out and we moved cautiously toward the English wire. Gross and I were leading the first group, and Unteroffizier Rombach was in charge of the second party. They hung back as we continued on, and after we'd gone about another twenty metres the night exploded as the bombardment began.

We pressed ourselves into the mud. Clods of earth rained down on us, together with shards of metal and things I didn't want to recognise. The shells weren't falling short, thank God, but they were bursting only a short distance ahead. We edged towards the wire on our stomachs.

"*Fuck!*" Gross was right beside me but I barely heard him.

He was clutching his left arm.

"Let me see, sir."

I took hold of his elbow and realised his upper arm was broken.

"At least it's the left one. I can still use my right arm."

For a moment I thought I'd misheard, partly because of the noise and partly because what he'd said was completely insane.

"You can't go in there with a broken arm, sir," I shouted into his ear. "They'll kill you. Stay here and we'll pick you up on our way back."

He looked at me and for a moment I thought he was about to argue, but then he said, "No, I'll go back now. You'll have enough problems."

I patched him up as best I could and he started crawling back. Thank God he'd had the sense to realise I was right.

As far as I was concerned his incapacitation put me in command, and arguing about who was in charge was a useless and potentially dangerous distraction.

Half a minute later the shelling stopped. We heaved ourselves out of the mud and lumbered through the gaps in their wire as fast as we could. We reached the lip of the trench before they could open fire, dropped grenades in, and sank down low.

The explosions were deafening and again we were showered with earth and splinters.

We leapt down into the trench and found it full of dust and smoke, and Tommies lying dead or groaning, or staggering about trying to gather their wits – which was just how we wanted them. We laid out as many as we could and then split according to the plan.

I set out with Janßen, Fischer and Buhl to fight our way to their company HQ to get the papers Hafner wanted, while Sommerburg led a group to disable the machine-gun before the others joined us.

I'll bet the fuckers have moved their HQ. I would have done if I knew they were coming – and I hope to Christ I can keep track of where the fuck we are.

There were plenty of Tommies still in one piece, and they weren't about to stand back and let us do what we wanted. It was a bloody, vicious slog, made even worse when some bastard lobbed a jam-tin bomb over the traverse at us. Janßen took the full force of it, the poor bugger, and the rest of us were pelted with chunks of metal and flesh.

Fischer threw a short-fuse bomb over in return and no one challenged us as we ran into the next bay. Three men lay unmoving in the bottom of the trench, half-blocking it, so we had to clamber over them. One was missing half his head.

We reached their HQ dugout just as their captain came out, revolver in hand. I smashed the spiked club into his head so hard that I had to put my foot on his chest to pull it out, and for a moment I thought it was completely stuck.

I tore the gas curtain aside and we rushed in. It was a tiny, cramped space, occupied by one lieutenant. *You'll do for our prisoner*, I thought, and slammed the club into his right arm just as he tried to take aim at me.

There was a crunch as the bones broke, and he screamed as I wrenched the pistol from his hand.

"You go with them," I said, pointing at Fischer and Buhl. He looked at my club, and at the sharpened spades in their hands, and had more sense than to resist. God alone knows what we all looked like.

There was a small desk covered in papers. Hafner had told me that the Tommies were said to be preparing an offensive and that he wanted any relevant information. I hardly knew where to start, and my schoolboy English was inadequate for most of the documents.

The racket outside was getting louder. I grabbed a handful of papers and stuffed them into the canvas bag. I hung it across my body, and went back out and rejoined the fray.

It was an appalling bloody free-for-all, augmented by the second instalment of our force and increasing numbers of fresh Tommies. There was a seemingly endless supply of them, coming at us from left and right and up the comms trench, and we were horribly outnumbered. They'd been ready for us, all right.

I had one grenade left. It was time to get out.

We had to leave the trench where we'd entered it in order to be sure of finding the gap in the wire. I must have used up three of my lives just getting there.

Sommerburg had got there first and had already got two ladders against the parapet. We tried to keep count as we shoved our blokes up the ladders, but there were too many distractions—

I was looking up at a huge Tommy armed with a knife like Karl's. I whacked the club into his stomach and he went down, but there was another behind him, and another.

Rombach arrived with his lot.

"All of them?" I asked.

"Two dead." The rest of them scrambled up the ladders and disappeared.

Two of our fellows were supporting a third, half-conscious with blood running down his face. Somehow they pulled and pushed him up the ladder and out into the darkness. Another staggered towards me, clutching his stomach, blood pouring from his mouth. He collapsed into my arms and I still don't know how we got him out.

I had lost count. Sommerburg and I shouted as loud as we could but no one answered. We clambered up the ladders and kicked them back into the trench. I dropped in my last grenade, then we grabbed the unconscious man between us and set off through the wire.

They'll be picking up their rifles and climbing onto the fire step...

We ran as fast as we could, dragging the dead weight of our comrade, the mud sucking at our boots. Behind us the Tommies opened fire but it was a fucking dark night and we could only hope they'd keep missing.

"Did you – knock out – the machine-gun?" I gasped.

"Yes, Sarge – smashed it – proper."

A flare went up and we sank to the ground. I was glad of the rest – my legs and lungs were burning. It also gave us the chance to have a look at our friend.

"It's Ludwig," Sommerburg said, indicating the scar on his face.

"So it is."

He had a nasty hole in his stomach, and there wasn't much we could do except pack it with his field dressing and tighten his belt over the top, in the hope that the pressure would slow the bleeding.

The flare burned out and we were just about to get up when another lit the darkness. When that one went out we waited for a couple of minutes and then set off again.

The Tommies seemed to have lost interest in us.

There'll be some bastard sniper watching, we're probably

framed in his sight. My skin crawled in a moment of pure, gut-wrenching terror before I got a grip on myself. There are worse ways to die.

The last few metres to our wire took forever. It felt as if Ludwig had gained about fifty kilos and Sommerburg and I were staggering, close to the end of our strength. Pulling our feet out of the mud was becoming almost impossible.

"Password!"

"You can stick your – fucking password – up your – fucking arse!" Sommerburg growled. "What the fuck – do you think – we are – you fucking moron?"

The sentry grinned at us. "Pass, friends!" he said cheerfully.

We handed Ludwig down to willing hands and practically fell into the trench, gasping for breath.

"Jesus fucking Christ," Sommerburg said. "I didn't think I'd see this place again."

Me neither... We emptied two water bottles each, suddenly horribly thirsty.

"Right," I said, getting to my feet. "Who's here, then?"

I called the roll of those who had been on the raid. Blumenthal, Dressler and Ernst were reported as dead, as I knew Janßen was. Sapolsky and Schaub were missing. There were thirteen wounded, including Ludwig. I felt very uncomfortable about Sapolsky and Schaub because I should have got them out of there, and I cursed myself for losing count.

I was just about to go and report to Hafner when he and Leicht appeared. Hafner was pleased with the captured officer, but rather less so with the bloodstained papers I handed him. He gave them to Leicht, who looked through them and shook his head.

"Not what we were after, sir," he said.

Hafner looked at me. "Where's Leutnant Gross?"

"I don't know, sir—"

"You *don't know*?!"

I almost said, isn't he here? and then realised how stupid that would be. Of course he wasn't.

"His arm got broken in the shelling, sir," I replied. "I said we'd pick him up on our way back, but he said he'd make his own way back."

"Well, he's not here."

"We didn't see him after that – but then, we weren't looking for him. He was fine apart from the arm… In fact, he wanted to carry on."

"Are you sure he didn't?"

"Yes, sir. Quite sure."

"Well, there are still a couple of hours to dawn, so you'd better go back out and see if you can find him."

"And Sapolsky and Schaub."

"Indeed."

As the officers left a voice called out, "Sarge! Did you say Sapolsky and Schaub?"

I turned round. Bach was sitting on the fire step, his head bandaged. "Yes."

"They was with me when I got this," he said. "I saw them both go down – it was a bomb, see? But I don't know what happened after that – except I didn't see them get up. I might have passed out, see? And then there was so many bodies lying everywhere I couldn't tell if any of them was them or not."

"I see. Why didn't you say when I called the roll?"

"Sorry, Sarge, I must have been out cold. I keep going dizzy and losing where I am, see?"

And you never were the sharpest knife in the drawer.

"Fair enough. You've told me now."

So we still don't really know what happened to them. Presumably they're either dead or prisoners. I did feel a trifle less guilty, though – finding them in a heap of bodies and getting them out would have been nigh on impossible, and if they were still alive the Tommies would look after them.

The last thing I wanted to do was go back out, but Hafner was right – we had to look for all three of them. No one wanted to be left out there.

It would be like looking for a needle in a haystack, but if we followed our earlier route as closely as possible we might just have a chance of finding them.

I made sure the men had their tea and rum, then crept out into the darkness with four volunteers. Once again I had the hair-raising certainty that we were being watched, that some Tommy sniper was calmly considering whether or not to shoot us, and once again I had to exert all my self-control to put the idea aside.

We found no trace of any of them. It might have helped if we'd been able to call their names but we had to be as quiet as the rats – the Tommies would be very nervous after the entertainment we'd given them and I didn't want to lose anyone else.

We got back in about an hour and a half before dawn. About ten minutes later Steckel appeared – he'd been out as well, not that we'd known.

"No luck, I see," Hafner said to me.

I shook my head. "No, sir. No sign of him. Or the other two. But from what Bach said, they were in the English trench, either dead or unconscious, so that's not surprising."

"Who were you looking for, Sarge?" asked Steckel.

"Leutnant Gross. He got hit in the arm in the shelling and set off back, but never got here."

He nodded. "That must have been him, then."

"What happened?" Hafner asked.

"He got sniped, sir. At least I think it was him – the raid was going on behind him, so I didn't see his face. I was watching him carefully, cos he was coming this way and at first I thought he must be a Tommy. But he wasn't heading for us purposeful, like, but a bit uncertain, and he was on his own, and I started thinking he must be one of yours that had copped it. When he got a bit closer I could see he was a German officer, and he was holding his left arm under the elbow, taking the weight of it, like."

"That fits with Leutnant Gross, sir," I interrupted. "His left upper arm was broken."

"Yeah, that's right – it was bandaged. He looked to be doing all right, though. Then he went down and never got up again."

Shit. I was right to be afraid. Maybe some sixth sense told me he was watching – bollocks, Franz. Total fucking bollocks. These days there's always some bastard fucking sniper at work.

"Did you hear the shot?" asked Hafner.

"No, sir, not with the racket they were making. But I'd put money on it, from the way he went down."

"Fucking bastard!" I burst out before I could stop myself. "Shooting a wounded man's right out of order."

Steckel gave me one of his slightly superior looks.

"It's always open season on officers," he said with that hint of condescension.

"That will do," Hafner said, distaste evident in his face and voice.

Steckel noticed it and stiffened.

"You did well, Becker," Hafner said to me. "Shame you're going to the fliers."

"Thank you, sir."

Made the best of a bad job, was what he really meant. Yes, we'd got a prisoner, but I hadn't found the papers they'd wanted and we'd lost Gross, who was a good man, not to mention the other casualties. Hardly a good result.

"What's his problem, Sarge?" Steckel demanded as we went to get our belated tea and rum.

"Don't know what you mean," I answered shortly.

You should be used to getting looks like that by now and I've no great desire to talk to you. It's your problem.

All the same, I was rather surprised by Hafner's reaction, given how protective he'd always been of the Company snipers and how much he enjoyed his trips to the range with them. He was, surely, well aware of what they were and how they thought. Maybe he just disliked being referred to quite so frankly as game, and I couldn't say I blamed him for that.

Or maybe he just didn't like Steckel, and I couldn't blame him for that, either.

"Your good fortune that he shot Gross, anyway," Steckel said to me. "Otherwise he'd have got you instead. My guess is he was out and didn't want to risk a second shot – not after he'd got the main prize."

I rounded on him. "Officers are not fucking game, just to be shot when you bloody well feel like it."

I was wrong, of course. That was *exactly* what they were. But in true Steckel fashion, he'd hit a nerve. Karl would soon be just that sort of game and I couldn't forget it.

"How many Tommies' heads have you just bashed in, Sarge?" he said with that slight smirk. "I'll bet you went for the officers first."

"They could fight back. Poor Gross was just trying to get back here."

"Yeah – and after healing up he'd have been leading you lot against the Tommies again. That sniper was well within his rights and any of us would do just the same."

Karl never did. He would have let him go.

"Just cos your mate's taking the Express Ticket—"

This time he was taking a sledgehammer to the nerve and he knew it.

"You can leave it there," I said. "I'll have no more impertinence from you."

413

He opened his mouth.

Go on. Step further out of line and give me the opportunity to make you regret it.

To my intense disappointment he closed his mouth without uttering another word and headed for the snipers' dugout.

Little shit. The sooner we see the back of you the better.

The tea was cold, but the rum still warmed. I needed it – the adrenaline had washed out of my system and I felt cold and shaky. I squeezed myself into one of the cubbyholes and tried in vain to get comfortable.

Best try to get some sleep – but it was impossible. I was exhausted and keyed up at the same time, and every time my eyelids closed I saw the huge Tommy with the knife looming over me and I started awake as I slammed the club into his stomach...

In the end I sat there in a kind of trance, staring blankly across the trench as it got light. My right arm was aching horribly from wielding the heavy club, practically throbbing from shoulder to wrist, especially my forearm. It was most unpleasant. All the raiding party had been excused from the dawn stand-to, so I had nothing to do and I wasn't sorry. I felt completely fucked.

"Here you are, Sarge."

I jumped, astonished that I had, after all, managed to fall asleep. Dietz was handing me black bread and cheese, and a steaming mug of coffee.

"Cheers, Dietz – that's really good of you," I said with genuine appreciation.

"Thought you might be hungry after your party night."

I realised I was ravenous. The food went down without touching the sides. Dietz grinned and handed me another chunk of cheese.

"Catering's improved, I see."

414

"Oh, it's from my girl – she sent me a parcel… She's a real cracker – look."

He handed me a small picture of a young woman who was undeniably lovely.

"Very pretty," I said, handing it back.

"She's the reason I'm here."

Oh – so that's the bitch who said you'd never have the guts to shoot anyone. Why on earth do you want to be with someone who belittles you?

Dietz was gazing longingly at the photograph.

"Fancy some chocolate?" I asked.

"Oh, yes, please! That's one thing she didn't send."

I trudged off to find my rucksack. There was still half a bar of milk chocolate in it, and we shared it.

"That was bloody good," he said. "Thanks."

I suddenly noticed that my hands were caked in mud and blood, as was my tunic. I picked what looked like a lump of mud from my sleeve, realised it was flesh and threw it away in disgust. *Poor Janßen…*

"I'd better clean myself up a bit," I said.

"Your face is still black as well, Sarge – in fact, you're quite a sight."

There seemed to be something he wasn't saying, and I wondered what it was. He was being rather more friendly than usual and I didn't know why.

"Shame about Gross," he said.

"Yes, it is."

I wasn't sure I wanted to discuss Gross with a sniper. He probably had exactly the same view as Steckel: open season on officers, regardless of the circumstances.

"Well, better get to work," he said, and got up. It seemed I was not going to find out what was on his mind.

The water in the bottom of the trench was muddy, but it

would do to get the bits of Janßen off my tunic. I took it off, found a sweater in my rucksack and was just about to put that on when Dietz came back.

"I don't know what you said to Steckel, Sarge," he said with a glint in his eye, "but he's dead pissed off. The rest of us are really enjoying it."

"Is that so?" I said neutrally.

"Just thought you might like to know."

I wasn't about to answer that, and to be fair he didn't expect me to.

"That your blood?" he asked, pointing at my right forearm.

My shirtsleeve was torn and bloodstained, and I found I had a cut about five centimetres long. It wasn't deep and the blood had clotted long ago.

Well, bugger me. No wonder it was throbbing so much.

"You'd better get that cleaned and sewn up," he said. "All that mud and stuff's pretty filthy."

"Yes, you're right… I'll leave it till after dark. They'll be busy and I don't fancy the comms trench in daylight."

"That makes two of us." He set off with rather more purpose this time.

I inspected my arm and decided I'd been bloody lucky to escape with such a small scratch.

As I cleaned myself up I had to smile at what he'd told me. Clearly everyone had much the same opinion of Steckel, and it was his own damn fault.

I wondered what he'd said to the other snipers to piss them off so much. Scheffel was such an easy-going fellow that it was hard to imagine anything getting under his skin, but Steckel was a past master at shit-stirring. Well, maybe the boot would be on the other foot now he'd had a warning shot.

In the afternoon I went to get Hafner's permission to go back to the aid post.

"It's only a small cut, sir—"

"Let's have a look… That needs cleaning out before it gets infected, sooner rather than later."

"I prefer the comms trench at night."

"Hm, so do I. See what you can find out about the others while you're there."

"Will do, sir."

By the time it got dark I was so tired that I almost couldn't be bothered going anywhere – but Hafner had told me to go, so I had no option.

My tunic was still soggy from the 'wash' and I shivered as I put it on.

It'll dry out, and life will be easier if I'm properly dressed. In my sweater I'd look like some fellow on a skive, and being challenged at every turn would be a real pain in the arse.

I wasn't in the mood for aggravation – and quite apart from that, the sweater was pale and the comms trench still had a few dodgy places. Getting shot was not part of my plan for the evening.

It wasn't far to the aid post, where an obliging medic sorted out my arm. I was embarrassed at being there with such a trivial injury.

"No, you're right to come," he said. "Infection can kill and it would be stupid to die from a small cut for want of getting it cleaned… This is going to hurt."

He opened the cut right up and poured iodine into it.

"*Fucking hell!*" I gasped.

"Don't say I didn't warn you."

He began stitching. To begin with I barely felt it as the pain from the iodine was so intense, but by the end I had my teeth gritted hard.

"Last one."

Thank fuck for that.

417

When I'd recovered my powers of speech I asked after the men injured in the raid.

"I'll get the doc to tell you, Sarge."

Assistant Doctor Krüger was barely older than me. *You must be the bastard who reckoned Koch was all right*, I thought, and tried to keep it out of my face.

"Let's see," he said. "Right – Ludwig was dead when he got here, I'm afraid, blood loss, but a major vein had been severed so there wasn't anything you could have done for him."

That's hardly a surprise. Pity he had to die in such an abortion of a job.

"And there's the head wound, Bach – not too sure what the outcome will be there. You can never tell with these things."

I bit my tongue hard – but then maybe he'd learned something.

"And the rest of them are on their way to hospital. Oh – and that Tommy Lieutenant had a smashed elbow. Someone did a proper job there – had to be amputated."

I didn't admit I was the culprit – but what choice did I have? I had to disable him or he'd have shot me – and if I hadn't decided to take him prisoner I'd have smashed his skull.

As it is he'll see the end of the war, and who knows if I will?

And all for what? I asked myself as I made my way back up the line. *Nothing we did is going to make the least difference to this fucking mess.*

I reported to Hafner as soon as I got back. He was alone in the HQ dugout.

"No surprise about Ludwig," he said. "Bringing him back in that state can't have been easy."

"It's bad about Sapolsky and Schaub, though," I said. "I should have got them out."

He looked at me, and after quite a pause he said, "Yes, you should – but there's often a gap between what should happen and what does happen and, quite frankly, you shouldn't have been there at all. And I never said that."

"No, sir."

You could have knocked me down with a feather. Hafner was never one to hide behind higher authority – it was always "These are my orders", even when we knew perfectly well they weren't.

He's probably had enough of his men being killed because those higher up are too obstinate to listen to reason, and so have I, but what can either of us do?

"Get some rest," he said kindly. "You look all in."

I was so tired that I fell into a deep sleep in spite of the discomfort of the cubbyhole, and I was so far down when I was woken for the dawn stand-to that I didn't know where I was.

No sooner were we on the fire step than all hell broke loose as they shelled the crap out of us. And then they didn't attack. It was revenge for the raid, and it left us with a hell of a clear-up job and several casualties. More pointless fucking mayhem, more death and mutilation that achieved absolutely nothing.

I was heartily sick of the entire business.

The year was nearly done, and there was only a week until Christmas. According to the usual routine we'd be spending it in rest.

I thought back to the previous year, remembered the Christmas trees on the parapet, their candles flickering in the freezing air, and that extraordinary meeting with the Tommies, and I wondered whether anything like that would happen again.

Probably not – there's been too much bloodshed. Surely there's too much ill-feeling on both sides now. And the Tommies opposite must be dead pissed off with us after that raid. They'll hardly be in the mood for a football match.

Whatever might happen in the front line, we won't see it.

We'll probably be in that crappy village – but at least we should get a proper Christmas party.

As soon as we got into rest I set off for my pilot's medical. Hafner gave me three days, just to be on the safe side.

"Well, Becker," he said as he handed me the pass, "I suppose I should wish you luck!"

"Thank you, sir," I replied.

I hope I don't fail the bloody thing – that really would be crap – but to my relief I passed. Now all I need is to be released from the Regiment…

I wrote to Karl to tell him and to wish him a Merry Christmas and a Happy New Year.

'I bet you'll have a bloody decent bash in the mess in Döberitz,' I wrote. 'At least we're in rest this time, so we're hoping for one ourselves.'

The bash was very decent indeed. Hafner provided two barrels of beer, there was wine and rum as well, and the cooks managed a good spread. And the post had arrived.

I had a huge parcel from home. My family had sent me warm socks, chocolate (probably on the black market, but so what?), a thick brown sweater with a note from Mama saying she thought the colour might be a bit more practical than the last one, and the scarf that Johanna had actually finished. Her knitting was a bit ragged in places but I didn't care – it was warm and that was all that mattered.

There was also a box full of all sorts of things: gingerbread, packet of nuts and dried fruit, and so on, with a note saying it was for me to share with my friends.

I called all my blokes round and held the box above my head as a lucky dip. There were a few things left over, so I took them to the snipers and we sat and stuffed ourselves. Dietz had two parcels, one from his parents and another one from his girl (who might have been a bitch but was certainly generous), so he had plenty to share as well. It turned into quite a feast.

There was also a small package from Karl, with a long letter in which he said he was bored to death.

'Franz, you would not believe some of the things I've been told here. They should get rid of every instructor who hasn't been in the front line. There was a lecture about snipers. It was months out of date and frankly I'd have made a much better job of it – but then I do know what I'm talking about. At the end I went up to the instructor and offered, politely, the benefit of my recent experience as a sniper on the Western Front.

Well, that was a mistake. He was not best pleased, to put it mildly, and turned out to be an appalling snob who didn't like men being commissioned from the ranks (yes, even with a "von"), and berated me for not "doing things properly" by going to cadet school. He certainly didn't want to hear anything I had to say.

Anyway, some of the other fellows approached me a bit later and asked me what I thought about the lecture. I ended up giving them a talk in a corner of the mess – which suited me fine as I didn't buy a drink all evening! And the next day there was another group wanting to pick my brains, and another the day after that. My mess bill is almost non-existent.

It'll be good to have Christmas away from the Front – though I'll be with you in spirit.'

The package contained a box of cigars.
Very nice. I shall enjoy these.
Spirit's probably the best way to be here, I thought, and couldn't help envying Karl. *There's probably champagne, and better food than we're ever likely to see, and maybe a trip to Berlin, and even girls...*

I'd forgotten what it was like to go to bed with a girl who

actually wanted me, rather than spending a few minutes with a tired tart. It would be so good to have all afternoon with some pretty, willing creature.

I drifted off into a very pleasant reverie.

"Sarge?"

I realised Scheffel was holding out a mug of coffee.

"Thanks." Coffee was a poor substitute for soft, warm flesh, but it would have to do.

"Thought it might offset some of the alcohol. You were miles away – that was the second time I spoke to you."

"Girls."

"Oh. Sorry I interrupted. Have you got leave coming up?"

"No chance – it's Belgian tarts all the way."

"Never mind, eh?"

There was a Christmas tree in what remained of the village square, and we gathered round it as midnight approached. The Catholic and Lutheran padres held a joint service, which left me completely unmoved. The story seemed too improbable after over a year of war, and I rather envied the Jewish fellows not having to listen to it.

But they're asked to believe all sorts of improbable stuff as well, and the poor sods aren't supposed to have roast pork, or bacon... Pretty grim, that.

I was relieved when the service ended and the party resumed. 'Silent Night' had gone right through me. So few of the men who'd sung it the year before were still with us.

We spent Christmas Day semi-comatose – the festivities had continued until dawn and we'd all eaten and drunk rather too much.

The next day we went back into the line. Those we relieved were thoroughly jealous of our good fortune as they'd had a rather thin time of it. There'd been no fraternisation and the snipers on both sides had continued working – though ours said they'd aimed off, and as we'd taken no casualties it seemed the Tommies had as well.

Apparently orders from on high had stated that hostilities were to be maintained, but it seemed nobody had actually wanted to kill anyone – for that one day, anyway.

Dietz seemed to have rather attached himself to me, and I often had lunch with him, Scheffel and Ranke. It was usually a convivial meal, washed down with Scheffel's excellent coffee and accompanied by cheerful banter.

When Steckel joined us the atmosphere was always a bit strained, and it was clear that he was tolerated but not liked. Fortunately he went out a lot. There was no doubting his dedication or his skill – it was just a shame he was such a little shit.

On our third day in the line I joined Scheffel, Ranke and Steckel, and couldn't help noticing the tension in the air. *Steckel's been up to his usual tricks*, I thought, trying to remember when Taschner was due back.

Dietz wasn't there.

Probably gone for a piss – but the time ticked by and there was still no sign of him.

"Where's Dietz?" I asked.

Scheffel and Ranke looked at each other.

"Somewhere out there," Steckel said, waving his hand in the direction of No Man's Land.

"What, you mean he's out?"

"That's right."

"That's not like him," I said.

"Well, he realised it was time to give it a go," Steckel said with that irritating smirk of his.

Scheffel and Ranke exchanged another look, and then Scheffel looked at me and raised his eyebrows slightly.

I was beginning to get the picture. I remembered Steckel

needling Dietz previously about going out, and suspected that he'd done it again, to greater effect this time.

"He can tell you about it when he gets back in," Steckel said, and again there was that self-satisfaction in his voice.

He knew better than to push his luck with me again, but there was nothing to stop him being a prick and he knew that, too.

Dietz shouldn't let Steckel get to him, but then Steckel gets to me as well. I didn't have to live with him and I'd been able to pull rank to shut him up. I didn't envy the others one bit.

When Dietz gets back I'll have a word with him, remind him that how he does his job is up to him, and that it's not Steckel's place to tell him what to do.

But Dietz didn't come back. Midnight came and went, it had been dark since about five, and there was still no sign of him.

"Where was he working?" I asked Steckel.

"I don't know – he didn't tell me."

"Well, what did he put in the book?"

Scheffel got the book, turned to the current page and handed it to Steckel.

"Ah, yes," he said. "Broken Trees."

"You can find it in the dark?"

"Oh, yes. Dead easy."

"Right," I said. "You and I are going out there now. Scheffel, Ranke, I need one more."

They volunteered simultaneously.

"Toss a coin or something," I said.

Steckel looked at me. "We don't really need another man, do we, Sarge?"

"Yes – we might have to carry him back, and that'll be fucking nigh impossible with only two of us."

Added to which I don't trust you not to leave me in the lurch if there's trouble.

424

Scheffel won the toss.

"Lead on," I said to Steckel, and we followed him out.

Here I am, back in fucking No Man's Land in the bloody dark. Where the fuck's my bloody transfer got to?

"This is it," Steckel whispered after what felt like an age.

We'd reached the remains of a copse – there were several splintered trunks, mostly sheared off close to ground level, surrounded by shattered branches of every possible size.

"In here."

We followed him through a gap in the timber, into a tunnel of broken wood. It opened out into a space best described as a small cave, partly open to the sky, surrounded by fragments of branches lying in tumbled confusion. It would be very difficult indeed to see into, even in broad daylight, and there was quite a bit of wriggle room.

Bloody hell – a snipers' palace.

There was a glimmer of a crescent moon appearing occasionally between thick clouds – that and the light from the occasional flares cast strange, disorientating shadows and made it very hard to see what was there.

Scheffel beckoned to us – and there at his feet lay Dietz, stone dead, his empty eye sockets gazing at the sky, part of his forehead chewed away.

Didn't take the rats long to get to him. Nasty little bastards.

The lower half of his face was a right mess and there was black, congealed blood everywhere.

"What the fuck did they get him with?" Scheffel muttered.

"Ricochet off the tree would be my guess," Steckel replied. "So what now?"

Good question. If we take him back he'll get a proper burial. If we leave him here we can cover him with branches and he'll be another of the thousands rotting into the Flanders mud.

The real question was how much of a risk we would be

taking carrying him back. It would be hard, slow work and we would be very conspicuous.

Not worth it for a corpse, and anyway this is a good sort of resting place. Damn sight better than a communal grave.

"Let's put some branches over him," I whispered. "We can take his tag and effects back."

"His things will all be in the dugout," answered Steckel.

"Get his tag, then."

Steckel looked at me and at Dietz, and I could see him thinking it was going to be an unpleasant job.

Get on with it. It's your needling and insinuations that put him here.

"We haven't got all night," I murmured.

Steckel grimaced as he retrieved the tag from Dietz's neck.

Serves you bloody well right.

Dietz's rifle lay beside his body, also covered in blood.

"You can deal with that, as well," I said.

He picked it up with obvious reluctance.

"You'd better find the case," I added, turning the screw. "Company stores will want the full matched set, not to mention all those nice little tools."

He looked at me in surprise. *Didn't realise I knew all that, did you?*

The case was still attached to Dietz's belt and, unsurprisingly, was also bloody.

Steckel's hands really have got Dietz's blood on them now.

We piled branches over Dietz and stood for a moment.

I hope it was quick. I hope you weren't lying there bleeding to death in agony. I should say an Ave for him – even if I can't believe any more, it might still all be true.

"Ave Maria, gratia plena…"

The others didn't join in. Not Catholics, then – I didn't know whether Dietz had been or not but it didn't matter. They understood "Amen" and whispered that, a bit late.

We turned to leave.

Scheffel glared at Steckel. "This is all your fault," he whispered with venom.

I put my hand on his arm.

"Let's get back," I murmured. "Everything else can wait."

I was so angry myself that I could cheerfully have murdered Steckel and left him out there as well, and I could see in Scheffel's eyes that he felt the same.

We could kill him and no one would ever know. Whack him on the head and make up some story about bumping into a Tommy patrol...

The temptation was almost irresistible. Almost, but not quite.

When we got back I made Steckel clean the tag and come with me to report Dietz dead.

"You can go in and tell Hafner," I said. "And I'll be listening."

He pulled a face.

"And you can drop that expression."

When he came out I said, "And now you can clean Dietz's gear."

He had more sense than to pull another face. Fortunately for him most of the blood had soaked into the sacking they all used to camouflage their weapons, but there was still quite a lot to clean up.

I was really enjoying making the bastard's life as unpleasant as possible, and I went and had a little chat with Braun.

"Believe me, Becker," he said, "if there's one speck of blood left he'll be cleaning that kit till Doomsday."

And Braun told me later that he did indeed reject Dietz's gear when Steckel tried to hand it in.

"Not very pleasant for the next fellow, last owner's blood lurking in the stitching of the lid, is it? Unhygienic, too. Better give it a bloody good scrub, hadn't you?"

By the end of all that Steckel was getting the point and had lost some of his smug self-satisfaction.

Two days later Taschner came back, proudly wearing his corporal's buttons on his collar, and was greeted with enthusiasm and palpable relief.

"Where's Dietz?" he asked after a few minutes.

I looked at Steckel. "You tell him," I said.

"He's dead, Corporal. Out in Broken Trees."

"*You what*?" Taschner's face darkened. "What the fuck was he doing out there?"

"Well, he—"

"Steckel talked him into it," Ranke said. "Kept on needling him, asking him why he didn't go out. He tried the same thing with us but we told him to fuck off. We told Dietz not to take any notice, that it was bollocks and he shouldn't give a shit what Steckel thought, but it was drip, drip, drip, wasn't it, Scheffel? All the bloody time. And he knew it was all going home."

"Bloody right." There was pure hatred in Scheffel's eyes.

"So what happened?" Taschner's voice vibrated with anger.

"It looked like a ricochet – made a mess of his face." Steckel actually sounded uncomfortable.

"So the poor bastard died alone, out there, just the way no one wants to go."

"Well, there was a lot of blood so I reckon it hit an artery."

"Oh, you do, do you? You're finished here. I'm off to see Hafner now, before I wring your fucking neck."

Taschner had spoken so viciously that Steckel actually flinched.

"Well, look," he stammered, "he was a grown man. It was up to him what he did."

I had never seen Taschner so angry. For a moment I thought his self-control had deserted him. He stepped forward, his face almost touching Steckel's, then after several long seconds he took a deep breath, stepped back and walked away.

An hour or so later Braun said, "Becker, Hafner wants to see you."

Hafner was looking very serious and so, unusually, was Leicht. For the second time I was invited to take a seat.

"I've just had Taschner in here with some peculiar story about Steckel goading Dietz into going out," Hafner said. "Being as you're friendly with the snipers I wondered if you could shed any light on it."

"Yes, sir, I think I can."

There was surprise in Hafner's eyes. I think he'd been expecting the usual reluctance to drop someone in the shit. As far as I was concerned, Steckel was going in deep, with my boot on his head.

"It's all a bit strange… Steckel's been a pain in the arse since he got here. I don't know why, but he seems to enjoy winding people up, and he's got a knack of finding a weak spot and playing on it. He tried it with me – frankly he was rather impertinent and I put him in his place."

Hafner's look changed to approval and there was a hint of a crinkle at his eye corners.

"The thing is, sir, that Dietz was – well, a bit insecure, I suppose. Not as a sniper – he was bloody good, as you know – but more as a man, if you see what I mean."

"Felt he had to prove himself, you mean," Leicht suggested.

"Yes – that's exactly it. His girl in Hannover persuaded him to transfer out here, and yes, Steckel did insinuate that Dietz should be going out. I didn't realise how much effect it was having or I'd have tried to put a stop to it."

"Easier said than done," Hafner said. "Tell Scheffel I want to see him."

It was really Dietz's insecurity that killed him, I thought as I left. *If he'd been happier in his skin he'd have told Steckel to fuck off – which doesn't excuse Steckel's behaviour. He knew the effect he was having and he turned the screw quite deliberately.*

He left us that night and no one was sorry to see him go.

Taschner sat next to me the following morning.

"Did you know it was happening, Sarge?"

"I had an idea," I said, "but I only heard him once – you remember, before you left. I didn't realise he'd been saying it almost constantly."

He shook his head. "What I don't understand is *why*."

No, you wouldn't, I thought. Taschner was an uncomplicated fellow – he killed with disturbing casualness and I doubt he ever gave his victims a second thought, but as a comrade he was the most loyal, solid bloke imaginable and he had no hidden depths. It would never have occurred to him to play games like Steckel's.

"Me neither," I replied. After a pause I added, "I wish I'd known how bad it was – I'd have done more to stop it."

"Nah," Taschner said. "Nice thought – but you weren't in the dugout with them." There was a pause and then he added, "Good that you left him in Broken Trees, though – better than being shoved into the ground with a load of other blokes. You know, Red Indians put their dead in trees, and proper Indians put them on towers for the vultures to eat – well, some of 'em do, anyway."

I looked at him in surprise.

"Yeah," he said, "fascinating the customs people have."

That wasn't why I was surprised, but I didn't want to admit that I'd always thought him less than intellectual. It would sound insulting, however I phrased it, and I respected him too much for that.

"Broken Trees was one of the best places," he said. "Shame we can't use it any more... God knows what he did to get caught out there."

"Maybe the Tommies were on to it – I mean, we hadn't been

in the line long when it happened, so maybe one of the Fourth Company blokes had used it a couple of days earlier."

"Yeah, maybe. There's always that. Maybe we should keep the book in Company HQ, now the Tommy snipers are so much better. If someone else uses that place it'll be curtains for him too."

I'm glad I'm not doing that job. It's too cold-blooded for me and way too dangerous. I had to laugh at myself. *Going on that raid was hardly safe, and everyone knows how risky flying is.*

I suppose it's more a case of what sort of danger you find acceptable – hiding in No Man's Land knowing that a single slip will bring death is not my idea of amusement.

"Did he have anything over his face – like a scarf or something?" he asked.

I shook my head. "Sorry, mate, we couldn't tell. It was all a bit of a mess."

I didn't want to tell him that Dietz's lower jaw had been smashed and almost completely severed. He was angry enough about the whole business and that level of detail wouldn't help.

"You have to be really careful your breath don't show in this weather," he said. "And piss steams even worse. It's best just to do it in your trousers and dunk yourself in a shell-hole on the way back so it don't smell."

"We all smell pretty bad anyway, and that water really stinks."

"Yeah, but no one wants to stink of stale piss like some old drunk."

"What if you need a crap – I mean really need one?" I was pretty sure I knew the answer but I couldn't resist asking.

He grinned at me. "Well, if you can't hang on it's a proper shell-hole bath, and the water's fucking freezing!"

Rather you than me – so far I've managed not to shit myself and I want to keep it that way.

We spent New Year's Eve in the line and it wasn't the party we would have liked. There was far too much tension in the air, and no one was exactly thrilled that we were starting another year of war.

It was all supposed to be over by that first Christmas, and now we're starting 1916 and there's no sign of it ending.

Peace must come soon, surely.

XIII

The New Year held a surprise for me. I was summoned to Company HQ, where Hafner and Leicht regarded me with very mixed expressions.

"This will probably make your day, Becker," Hafner began.

I tried to damp down my rising excitement – there was only one thing I thought he could mean, and I didn't want to get my hopes up just in case it was something else.

"Your transfer's come through. You're to leave us a week from now – that's if you still want to go. You can change your mind, you know."

Not fucking likely.

"Thank you very much, sir – and yes, I do still want it."

"Well, Becker, if you ask me you're barking mad, but I'll just wish you the very best of luck."

Because you're going to need it, hung unspoken in the air.

"And from me, too," Leicht added.

"*And* – you've got two weeks' leave before your pilot training," Hafner added. "So a very Happy New Year to you."

"And to you both."

I almost skipped out of there.

I'm escaping! I'm going to be a flier, no more grovelling in holes in the mud. I shall be up in the sky, looking down on the poor sods in the trenches. And I've got two whole weeks away from the sodding Army!

I wrote to Karl at once, with all the dates – there had to be some way of meeting up. And I wrote in great excitement to Otto and Alfred.

I also told Karl that Dietz was dead, but left out the details. I wanted to tell him face to face – the whole thing would sound just too odd otherwise.

Karl replied very quickly. After lamenting the loss of what had remained of my sanity, he went on to say that he also had leave after his course and that it partly overlapped with mine. *Berlin*, I thought, *dancers*! But then I read,

'And the thing is, carmine-collared Johnny's got leave too, and he and I had arranged to borrow a villa in Villingen in the Black Forest – do a bit of walking and maybe cross-country skiing, and a lot of chasing girls and boozing – but the bugger's decided to go to Uncle Detlev's house party in his barn of a place in the wilds of East Prussia.

It's Auntie Monika's birthday and we'd made up our minds to avoid it (long way to go and very boring), but – this is where it gets complicated – Uncle's cousin's brother-in-law (warned you) will be there with his brood, including the beautiful Alexandra, and guess what? Johnny prefers her company to mine, the rotten bastard!

He's wasting his time – the lady is a model of virtue and his chances of getting his leg over are pretty well nil. I've a horrible feeling he just wants to gaze adoringly into her eyes and murmur nauseating sentimental crap into her ears, when he could have come on holiday with me and had glorious rumpy-pumpy. Fellow clearly has no sense at all.

What's more, he can't even think about getting involved with Alexandra – Pa's told him he has to go through with the match arranged for Friedrich, so that's him firmly engaged.

So, long story (not very) short, I'm going to Villingen anyway, so why not join me? It's not Berlin but there will be girls (there always are, after all), and it's very beautiful, so will be good for the soul after all the ugliness.

I was very sorry indeed to hear of Dietz's demise, though have to say that I'm not entirely surprised.

Regards to all who know me, and see you in Villingen,

Yours, Karl.'

No, it isn't Berlin – but the more I thought about the idea the more I liked it. The Black Forest would be the perfect antidote to Flanders, and he was right – there are always girls. You just have to find them.

Poor Johnny, stuck with the arranged marriage regardless of what he wants. I'm so glad I'm not a 'von'.

The week in support dragged by, every day seeming to last as long as two normal ones. I was as careful as possible, but even so there was an unpleasantly loud crack one night as we were going up the comms trench.

Not what I want to hear, I thought as I hit the mud, *but then hearing it's far better than the alternative.*

The drama an hour or so later was highly entertaining: two grenades exploded in No Man's Land, followed by four rifle shots in rapid succession, a scream, then another explosion, a pause of a few seconds, one more shot, another grenade, then drawn-out cries of pain that ended some minutes later in a horrible gurgling sound. And then silence.

It was only too easy to imagine the end of the Tommy sniper.

Serves the fucker right, I thought, truly thankful that Karl had escaped such a fate.

When we went up the following evening two of the fellows told us the story with glee, right up to the point when they cut his throat.

"Well, 'e was yellin' 'is fuckin' 'ead off, and we couldn't

stand the row," the first one said, laughing. "And 'oo was going to bother givin' 'im first aid an' luggin' 'im in? 'Specially bein' as 'e'd just shot Schramm and poor old Röser – stone dead, 'e is. Three kids back 'ome an' all."

"Just what his sort deserve," said the other. "Fucking murdering bastards."

Two casualties to get rid of him as well, though that was probably nothing compared to the damage he'd been inflicting.

"There'll be another, boys," I said as we started back down the comms trench. "So keep your heads down at the dodgy places."

Taschner just shrugged when I told him the story.

"'Bout what we expect," he said. "I found one of ours out in No Man's Land once – his throat had been cut as well, and his face was all smashed up. Looked like they'd kicked the crap out of him before they killed him."

By the end of the week I was knackered from the back-breaking labour of carrying endless supplies up to the front line, and I just wanted to be on my way.

I did take advantage of the coming and going to drop into the aid post and get my stitches taken out.

"You've healed up fast." It was the same medic who'd sewn me up. "You're not going to like this."

He was right. The stitches were quite well embedded in my flesh and the process was sickeningly painful. I only just managed to stop myself yelling at one particularly bad one, and I was left with two rows of little holes either side of the scar, seeping blood. Inevitably he dosed them with iodine.

God alone knows what it must be like to collect a real injury – I hope I never find out.

Finally the last night arrived. *That's it*, I thought as we arrived back at the barn. *From now on I work in the day and sleep at night – and in a real bed. No more cubbyholes, no more filth, no more lice, no more rotten, stinking No Man's Land. Halle-fucking-lujah.*

It was my turn for a Hafner send-off.

Once the barrel had been tapped and everyone had a full mug, he said, "For those of you who don't know, Sergeant Becker has become a man of an extra dimension to the rest of us – quite literally. He's off to the Air Service to become a pilot."

There was a murmur and I saw incredulity on several faces.

"For some reason he appears to believe that flying is a slower route to Eternity than the famous Express Ticket." Laughter. "And given that aircraft are struggling to overtake locomotives he may well be right. In any event, the fliers' gain is most definitely our loss."

It was my turn to blush to the roots of my hair as Hafner praised me as an NCO and as a comrade. Fortunately he kept it short.

"And so, let us all drink to Becker's future success."

"Success!"

All the mugs were raised to me.

I never want to be the centre of attention like this again.

An hour or so later Schmolke came over to me. "Sarge, the boys have got something to say."

And there they all were. There was a bit of conferring and then Sommerburg said, "We just wanted to wish you the best of luck, Sarge, and to give you this."

'This' was a cigarette lighter, beautifully made from an old cartridge case, with my initials engraved on it. I was touched to the point of embarrassment. It hadn't occurred to me that they would think so highly of me.

"Thank you, boys. It's really good of you – excellent workmanship, too."

I drank their health, and was in the middle of saying

goodbye to each of them when someone put his arm round my shoulders.

"You're not getting away from us that easily," Taschner said.

"Be with you in a sec," I said, finished my farewells and turned to him.

"Come and have a drink with us," he said. "We want to say goodbye properly – and we've got my Iron Cross to celebrate."

"True." *You've got no qualms about being decorated for your score.* "May you soon have the First Class to go with it," I added, raising my mug.

"Cheers, Sarge," he said. "It won't be the same round here after you've gone."

I realised that I was probably the man who knew him best, and the nearest to being his friend.

"Oh, you'll be too busy to notice," I said, "especially when you're training Thingy." Karl's replacement was from another platoon and I just couldn't remember his name.

"We need to replace Dietz as well," he said, which cast a bit of a shadow over the party.

"He was a good bloke," Scheffel said. "Always had time to answer questions, never made you feel stupid."

"To the fallen," Taschner said, and we all drank.

And then, quite suddenly, it was time for me to leave. It was my turn to be hugged by Taschner, which I couldn't avoid and which left me feeling vaguely grubby.

He just does his job, I told myself, but the problem was the way he did it, and the total absence of anything resembling a conscience. *It's not only that,* I thought as he released me. *His job is different. I've only ever killed when I had to, in order to survive. He has a choice.*

"Look after yourself, mate, up in those bloody things," he said, and for a horrible moment I thought he was about to get sentimental. Luckily he wasn't pissed enough for that. "And say hello to that crazy bastard Leussow from me."

"Will do – maybe we can all get together in Berlin, after the war."

His eyes lit up. "Yeah, that would be great. Have a proper piss-up."

I took my leave of Hafner, with some regret. He was a bloody good company commander, but of course I couldn't tell him that. I could only wish him luck.

As I left I was utterly astonished to find that I had mixed feelings. I was ecstatic about escaping from the trenches but the life had become familiar and, although my close friends had all gone, I was leaving plenty of good comrades behind.

But I never was one for looking back.

To my joy there was a bath and a clean uniform before I set off home, so I was able to get rid of my very tired and still bloodstained tunic.

That was a relief – I'd been certain Mama would notice the blood and I'd had no idea how to explain it to her. Even saying I'd been giving someone first aid would only have made her worry more.

There was another problem – I'd written to tell my parents that I had leave, because I thought Mama might need some warning of having to cater for me, but I certainly hadn't told them *why* I had leave. After much thought I'd decided it would be best to tell them face to face that I was going for pilot training. That way they wouldn't have time to wind themselves up.

The real difficulty was when to tell them – they were so pleased to see me that I felt it would spoil the first day. That had already had a shadow cast over it.

"But I thought you had two weeks," Mama said.

Not again. I'd set out the arithmetic in my letter. Two days to get home from the Front, one day to travel to the flying school – flying school! – leaving eleven, of which six would be spent at home and five with Karl. Mama had failed to read it properly, just like last time.

"Yes, I do, but I'm meeting Karl. I did tell you. He's borrowed a villa in the Black Forest."

"And what are you going to do there?" Papa asked with a note of disapproval.

I could see his dislike of Karl beginning to surface.

"Depends on the weather," I said. "Either hiking or cross-country skiing."

"And in the evenings?"

For God's sake – I'm twenty. I've spent over a year on the Western Front.

"We've got a lot of catching up to do."

"I think it sounds lovely," Johanna said. "I'd love to come with you."

"That is completely out of the question," Papa said sternly. "You cannot possibly spend a week in a villa with two young men, even if one of them is your brother."

"No, dear," Mama added. "Think of the scandal. You'd be completely unmarriageable after that."

"But I don't understand—"

"Sorry, Sis," I said, "but they're right. Anyway, you'd be bored."

"I would not! And I like Karl."

"Look, we'll be talking about all sorts of boring stuff and about people you don't know. And Karl's probably not quite as you remember him anyway."

There was a vast gulf between the student and the sniper, one that would be only too obvious to someone who hadn't watched him change.

"What do you mean?"

440

"Am I the same?" As the words left my mouth I realised I shouldn't have said them.

Mama looked at me sadly.

"You've grown," was all she said, and I could see in her eyes that it was a long way from being the only change.

For one awful moment I wondered whether everything I'd seen and done was engraved on my face, for everyone to see.

She was right about my having grown, though – I was going to have to buy new clothes again. Even the shirts I'd bought on my last leave were too tight. It surprised me as I thought I'd stopped growing, but I seemed to have put on another couple of centimetres and quite a lot more muscle.

"You're taller than I am," Papa said with pride. "And broader. They must have been feeding you well."

"I wouldn't say that!"

To my relief the mood had lightened.

This will be as good a moment as any.

"I've got something to tell you," I said.

They all looked at me with curiosity.

"The reason I've got leave is that I'm transferring to the Air Service. I'm going to be a pilot."

There was a stunned silence.

"You can't!" Mama burst out. "You just can't! It's far too dangerous." She looked to be on the verge of tears. She turned to my father. "Tell him he can't do it!"

Papa seemed quite unable to speak.

Johanna recovered her voice first. "That's amazing!" she said. "I've been reading about the pilots in the illustrated papers – I'd love to do that! It must be wonderful to be up in the sky among the clouds."

"That's what I think too," I said. "And I've had enough of the trenches, so I put in for a transfer some time ago."

"But you're our only son!" Mama said.

"Look," I said, "where I've been isn't exactly safe, as you should know. You just have to look at the casualty lists. And my Company Commander wanted me to apply for a commission—"

"That would have made far more sense," Papa said. "It's about time you got promoted."

"But it's far more dangerous. Everyone always tries to shoot the officers first."

"Karl's being commissioned, though, isn't he?" Papa asked.

"Yes – and we all think he's off his head, especially having been a sniper. Look, aircraft don't often get shot down. They're really hard to hit."

I'd made that up – I had no idea how often it actually happened, just that we hadn't seen it much. They did seem to crash quite a lot but I didn't want to mention that.

"If I'm going to buy it then I'll buy it, no matter where I am or what I'm doing," I said. "I'm sick of living in mud and having lice."

"My friends will all be so jealous," said Johanna. "They'll all want to meet you next time you're on leave."

Now that *was a thought. Maybe a pilot's badge would bring unexpected benefits...*

"That's not important," Mama almost wailed at her. "How can you be so selfish as to think of that?"

"My friend Otto Kramer's been flying for months," I said, "and nothing's happened to him. I've lost count of the number of junior officers we've lost in that time. You've got a far better chance of my surviving if I'm flying."

False logic, but hopefully they would buy it.

Papa didn't, of course.

"Franz, as you are well aware, that is a complete misuse of argument. But it's obviously too late for you to change your mind so we shall just have to pray for you. We are all in the hands of God."

If you say so, I thought, wondering what kind of God would permit any war, let alone a war like this one.

"But, Franz, can't you tell them you've changed your mind?" Mama pleaded.

"Even if I wanted to, it's far too late," I said. "The Company's released me, my replacement will be there by now, and I'm expected at the flying school. Anyway, as I said, I've had enough of the trenches."

"Where's the flying school?" Johanna asked.

"Near Potsdam."

Papa did not look happy. Yes, right next to the spiritual heart of Prussia and close to Berlin, the Capital of Sin which I intend to visit at every opportunity.

Someone change the subject, please.

"What sort of aircraft are you going to fly?" Johanna asked. "After your training, I mean. Are you going to fly Fokkers like Immelmann and Boelcke?"

"I don't know yet." I was astonished that she knew the names of the two aces and that they flew Fokker monoplanes.

She looked at my face and laughed.

"See – I told you I read the illustrated papers! Boelcke's so handsome – I want to put his picture on my bedroom wall but Mama won't let me."

"You shouldn't be thinking about men," Mama said. "You should attend to your schoolwork and your prayers."

Johanna and I daren't look at each other.

"How is school?" I asked, grateful that Mama had provided a different topic.

Johanna prattled on, and I sat back and let it all wash past me.

My parents did not refer to flying again. Johanna and I had a long chat about it in a café in town, over weak coffee and what passed for cakes.

She really did read the papers and knew almost as much about flying as I did. She'd practically squealed that morning when she'd seen the newspaper.

"The Kaiser's given Boelcke and Immelmann the Pour le Mérite!" she'd exclaimed excitedly. "Isn't it fantastic?!"

"That's amazing," I'd replied, and indeed it was.

That the two pilots had been awarded Prussia's – and thus the Empire's – highest military award was a tremendous honour not just for them but for the whole Air Service.

"If I were a man I'd join the Air Service," she said in the café. "It's so boring that women aren't allowed to do so many things."

"You don't want to fight," I said. "Believe me, Sis, you really don't."

She thought for a moment.

"Maybe not," she conceded, "but there are loads of other things that I'm not allowed to do – like vote, or go on holiday with whoever I like. It's just not fair."

I'd never seen it that way. "Maybe things will change after the war."

"Maybe."

"Maybe you'll have to have a women's revolution – you know, like the French revolution, but guillotining men instead of aristocrats! Just give Karl and me time to leave the country."

She threw a large cake crumb at me. It missed and she started giggling.

"What?" I asked.

"Shut up. Let's just pay and leave." She could hardly speak. *What the fuck's this about?*

I had to wait until we got outside to find out.

"There was a really elegant woman behind you with her hair in a big bun," she said, "and the crumb got stuck in it!"

I found I was laughing helplessly at the image of a smart

woman with a bit of cake lodged in her immaculate coiffure. It really wasn't all that funny – it was just that I had months of tension stored up and it was good to laugh at something trivial and harmless.

White humour instead of black? I wondered, and for some reason that also struck me as inordinately funny.

Eventually we stopped laughing and wandered home. Our parents were out and we had the living room to ourselves.

"Sis, about the holiday—"

"Oh, don't worry. I know I can't come, and anyway I'd probably get in your way. It's just so boring. I'd really like to see Karl some time, though – he's the only person who's ever treated me like a grown-up instead of a child."

I hadn't thought of that.

"The thing is, Sis, that, well, he…" I didn't know how to put it.

"Look, I'm not stupid," she said. "I read about Boelcke and Immelmann and their eight victories each, and I think about the men they shot down, and how awful it must be to be shot and then fall out of the sky and crash, and I read the news from the Front and I understand – well, no, I don't, do I – but I do realise that it's all about men being killed and wounded, and I see men in town on crutches or with an arm missing.

"And Karl was a sniper, so I know what he's been doing. I mean, I know as a sort of idea. Obviously I don't know about the reality of it."

I was surprised and rather impressed. I hadn't expected my sister to have become so serious.

"It's not just all of that," I said. "Papa thinks Karl leads me into bad ways."

She giggled. "And does he?"

"I'm not answering that! Look, Karl likes girls—"

"I should think he does!"

"No, I mean he likes them a lot. And lots of them."

"And don't you?"

I could feel myself blushing. "I'm not answering that either! But you really don't want to fall for him."

It was her turn to blush. "Rot! I'm not falling for him. I just want to be friends, that's all."

Like fuck you do. I see the look in your eyes every time you mention his name. You are not meeting him again.

Karl was the best friend I was ever likely to have, but I didn't want my sister's heart broken. She had a schoolgirl crush on him and I couldn't imagine him returning her affection. And even if he did it was unlikely to end well.

Luckily Mama arrived back and saved me from having to say any more.

On the Sunday it was clear that I was expected to go to Mass.

What a bloody farce.

"I think I'll give it a miss," I said quietly.

Mama was horrified. "But, Franz, you have to go to confession! If you don't, and *Something Happens*, you'll go straight to Hell."

"I went to confession a week ago," I lied. One sin.

"But you must have sinned since then! It's a whole week!"

Oh, the endless obsession with sin, and the utter hypocrisy that said that killing in battle somehow didn't count. And how were the dead supposed to rise again when they were blown to fragments?

"Even an impure thought is displeasing to God," Papa said severely.

Oh yes – I've had plenty of those… There was that girl on the station platform in Cologne, for a start. She'd kept my mind happily occupied for a good two hours, not to mention joining me in my bed on my first night home. Another sin.

I couldn't tell them I didn't believe any more. It would have really distressed them, and for nothing. *Go to bloody Mass, Franz, and then if you do get killed at least they won't be worrying about your soul.*

So I dutifully went to confession, said my penance, and let my mind wander during the service. It was abruptly refocused as the priest intoned, "Hoc est corpus…"

The body of Christ. The blood of Christ. Body, blood – suddenly I remembered the disgusting state of my tunic after the raid, covered with blood and scraps of flesh. And now I was expected to eat flesh and drink blood.

It's only figurative. It's just a dry wafer and a sip of red wine – even so, the symbolism revolted me completely and I sat there sweating, wondering how I could get out of it.

I could mutter that I wasn't feeling well, but my exit would disturb everyone and upset my parents. *It's just a dry wafer and a sip of wine,* I repeated over and over – *but that's not true, because consecration turns the bread and wine into flesh and blood.*

Superstitious crap. Of course one thing can't change into another, whatever the priests might claim.

I forced myself to the altar rail, and when my turn came I somehow managed to keep down what I was given. Throwing up the Eucharist would have been even worse than walking out, and some in the congregation would have seen it as evidence of terrible sin or even of possession. My parents would never have heard the end of it.

I am never doing that again, I thought as I left – and part of me did indeed wonder whether I was so immersed in sin as to be unredeemable.

Nonsense, Franz. It's all nonsense. You felt sick because it reminded you.

"Are you all right, Franz?" Mama asked when we got home. "You're looking a bit pale."

"Yes, fine," I lied.

I managed to eat my lunch and slumped in a chair afterwards, hoping I wasn't going to be sick. I tried reading to take my mind off the persistent nausea but it didn't work.

"I'm going for a walk," I said.

"Oh, what a good idea," Mama said. "We'll come with you."

I shook my head.

"I'm very sorry," I said, "but I'd really prefer to be on my own."

Her face fell and then she tried to smile. "Well, don't be too long, then."

I wandered through the freezing streets and into the park. The trees were bare and there was a hint of snow in the air, and it was quiet and peaceful.

The fresh air did settle my stomach but not my mind, and I couldn't get to sleep that night…

Janßen disintegrated in front of me as the jam-tin bomb exploded, showering me with blood and bits of his body, and a chunk of flesh went into my mouth and stuck in my throat.

I woke screaming.

"Franz, are you all right?" Papa opened my bedroom door and put the light on.

I turned away from him, embarrassed because I was shaking like a leaf.

"P-put the l-light out," I stammered.

His footsteps approached me in the darkness.

"I'm all right," I said as levelly as I could. "Please go back to bed."

To my immense relief he retreated and I heard the door close. I lay awake staring into the darkness, sick and shaking. I was far too scared to go back to sleep and after a while I sat up in bed, put the bedside light on, and sat smoking and waiting for morning.

The atmosphere over breakfast was rather tense. No one wanted to mention the incident in the night but it lingered in the air. Once or twice Papa looked at me as if he wanted to say something, but he had the sense to keep his mouth shut. Johanna gave me a sympathetic look, which I rewarded with a scowl. It was bad enough that I'd made such a racket, and the last thing I wanted was some misguided attempt at understanding.

You'll never understand in a thousand years, and you should be grateful for that.

I realised suddenly that it was my last full day at home and that I'd better make a bit more effort. God alone knew when – if – I would be home again.

It actually turned into quite a pleasant day, but by evening I was exhausted from pretending everything was all right when it wasn't. I was really looking forward to being with Karl, because of course he would understand. I wondered what sort of nightmares he had.

By bedtime I could hardly keep my eyes open. Papa – unusually – allowed me a third small brandy. Maybe he was hoping that it would send me to sleep and that I wouldn't wake them up again. It must have been disturbing for them, after all.

I had a broken night and lay awake for what felt like hours, but fortunately I didn't have any more bad dreams.

Mama put on her bravest face the next morning. I could see her trying not to think that I was certain to be killed and that she'd never see me again. Papa looked resigned and Johanna said she was green with envy that I was actually going to learn to fly.

"I'll be back," I said as I got on the train. "They won't get rid of me that easily! I'll send a photo as soon as I've got my pilot's badge – and, Sis, don't forget to show it to all your friends!"

"Franz, really!" said Papa.

"Be careful," Mama said. "Those machines are dangerous."

It's all bloody dangerous.

"It's going to be the most wonderful fun," I said, "so just remember how much I'll be enjoying myself."

All the same I leaned out of the window until the train rounded the curve and my family disappeared from view. Just in case.

XIV

It was quite late in the afternoon by the time I got to Villingen and the light was fading badly, not helped by a heavy snowfall.

There, standing on the platform, looking very smart in a new greatcoat, was Feldwebel Karl von Leussow.

I saluted as smartly as I could. "Congratulations, Sergeant Major!"

"Thank you, Sergeant!" he said, returning the salute, and then he threw his arms round me, laughing. "Franz, I am so pleased you're here!"

"So am I!" Which was all I could say while he was practically squeezing the breath out of me.

He looked fresh and rested, the crow's feet much less apparent than when I'd seen him last. The hard, flat look was still in his eyes, but it was overlaid with genuine warmth.

"You survived the last weeks in the good old trenches, I see!"

"It was a bit touch and go with that bloody raid – I don't know how I got out of it in one piece. It was the last thing I wanted to do, I can tell you."

"I believe you."

"It is sergeant major and not officer cadet, isn't it?"

"Oh yes. I didn't change my mind. Reserve Officer will be quite enough."

"So when do you get the commission?"

"When they're happy with me – there's no way a regiment

like that's going to have a Leutnant straight from corporal, even a Reserve one."

We fell into step as we left the station, our boots crunching through the fresh snow.

"How are your family?"

"Fine."

"And how did they take your news?"

I sighed. "Well, you know…"

That was stupid. He didn't. Karl's family life was so uncomplicated that I envied him, and that too was stupid because losing your mother at seventeen isn't exactly fun, and I knew that Friedrich's death had affected him far more than he'd ever admitted.

"I don't envy you," he said. "Even when Mama was alive she was an officer's daughter, wife, mother… I can't imagine having to explain things to civilians."

"You mean not explain them."

"Quite."

"The parents were pretty horrified about the flying but Johanna's all for it. Said if she were a man she'd join the Air Service."

"Insanity runs in the family, then!"

"While I was there it was in the paper about Boelcke and Immelmann getting the Pour le Mérite – even the parents thawed a bit towards the idea then. You could almost see them imagining me with one."

He laughed. "You should be so lucky."

"That's what I tried to tell them – for one thing, there's nothing to say I'll be flying Fokkers and, for another, shooting down an enemy aircraft must be bloody difficult. I mean, they don't hand out the top award for nothing."

"With both of you moving in three dimensions, yes, the deflection could be very tricky indeed. You'd be best off cutting down the relative movement as far as possible – which is probably what they do. If you were going in the same direction and you attacked from behind and below, there'd be almost no relative movement and they wouldn't see you. Be dead easy, that – the tricky part would be getting into position."

I started laughing. "See – I've got you interested after all! Your marksman's brain just couldn't resist! And now you've started thinking about it…"

"Oh, shut up! I'm not going up in one of those bloody things and that's that."

The villa was far more splendid than I'd imagined, set in a large garden.

"Karl, how on earth did you get hold of this place?"

"It belongs to a family friend. They'll be coming in a couple of weeks so we'd better not mess it up."

"What about servants?"

"There's a caretaker, and a cook and a maid who come in, but no one living in. It's very private – nice and restful."

My room was luxurious, with a huge carved French bed piled with pillows. At least I'd brought my smart new trousers and a couple of new shirts, so once I'd changed I didn't feel too shabby – apart from my old sweater, which had always been rather baggy and now fitted perfectly.

Karl had changed as well and looked incongruously scruffy in the opulently furnished drawing room.

"Karl, did you find your clothes don't fit?"

"Yes – these are all Friedrich's. You remember, he was always bigger than me."

You've caught him up now, and you obviously have no problem wearing a dead man's clothes. I wondered how I'd feel about doing that.

"Makes you think, though, doesn't it?" he said. "I mean, all the fellows who are dead. If we're still growing…"

It wasn't a thought I wanted to have, that our late comrades – and our late enemies – weren't even fully grown men, that the war was being fought by adolescents. And if our bodies were still growing, what about our minds?

"He was a grown man," Steckel had said of Dietz – but he wasn't really, was he? How much of his insecurity was due to youth?

"So what happened to Dietz?" Karl asked, and I started because it was as if he'd read my mind.

I told him the whole story, from Steckel's arrival to his departure.

"What a fucking little shit," he said, anger in his voice. "Dietz was a good bloke – he didn't deserve that."

"It wouldn't have happened if you'd been there. You'd have told Steckel to shut up. Taschner didn't realise what was going on, and anyway he had to go on his course."

"No, he wouldn't have seen it. It would've been far too subtle for him."

"You said in your letter that you weren't surprised Dietz had bought it."

"No…" he paused thoughtfully. "It's not easy to put into words, but he… well, he wasn't really confident enough. That's why I never encouraged him to go out – because to do that you really have to *know* you can do it, but at the same time you can't be overconfident. And you need a level of detachment that Dietz never quite managed."

"You mean he wasn't quite cold enough."

He looked at me steadily for a moment. I realised that I had, in effect, just called him cold-blooded, and that he had no answer.

"Yes," he said calmly, "that's exactly it. Because every decision you take has to be weighed carefully, without emotion. That's something you just can't afford – and with Dietz it was always there. There was always that need for approval."

"It looked quick, though," I said. "There was a massive amount of blood and we hadn't heard anyone crying out."

"That's something, anyway. And at least the bastards didn't get their hands on him."

"No..." I told him about the Tommy sniper getting his throat cut and the fellow Taschner had found with his face bashed about. He knew about that one, of course.

You played for such high stakes in that job. No wonder the Express Ticket doesn't seem such a big deal – but as Taschner said, as a junior officer you'll be out in the open...

By then it was time for dinner, and to my dismay my appetite died as soon as I saw the stew. It was delicious but the chunks of meat turned my stomach right over, and I had to leave most of it.

Karl noticed and I saw the concern in his eyes. I could almost see him deciding to be tactful, and he didn't say anything until we were back in the drawing room with a couple of large brandies inside us.

"Any preference for dinner tomorrow?" he asked casually.

"No – whatever the cook wants to give us."

"I thought we'd go for a long walk, maybe have lunch in a village pub somewhere."

"Good idea."

There was a long pause.

"The food was fine, Karl," I said. "I've just lost my appetite."

I really couldn't say any more.

He smiled. "Well, a good walk in the cold should bring it back!"

He knew there was more to it, and he knew too that I might tell him in my own time and that there was no point asking me.

"Oh," I said, "I've still got two of those cigars you sent me. Would you like one?"

"Yes, thanks."

I fetched them and lit his with my new lighter.

"Is that new?" he asked. I handed it to him and he turned it over in his hands. "Beautiful workmanship... The engraving's very finely done."

"Yes, isn't it? It was a leaving present from the boys. It was really good of them to go to so much trouble."

"Well, you always looked out for them and it showed. Actually – I wasn't going to say this – but I was very impressed with how well you did your job."

"Really?"

"Yes. You know me, Franz. I wouldn't bullshit you."

"No, I know... I feel bad about the two I left with the English, though."

He shook his head. "From the sounds of things you did bloody well. Why in God's name didn't they cancel it, or put it off till the Tommies had forgotten about it?"

"Hafner told me we shouldn't have been there at all."

He raised his eyebrows. "Hafner said *that?!* Jesus, he must have meant it. Hafner never says that sort of thing."

"No."

"Shame about Gross, though. Especially with him already being injured."

"Steckel's comment was 'it's always open season on officers'."

Karl pulled a face. "That's up to him – but it wasn't my style, as you know."

I suddenly realised what I'd said. "Sorry, Karl, that was really stupid of me."

"What was?"

"Repeating what Steckel said."

He started laughing. "Don't be bloody daft! You think I'm not well aware that I'll be everyone's favourite game? Believe me, Franz, when we attack I'll be sure to wear a rumpled, grubby tunic, cover my epaulettes in mud and carry a rifle. And any sniper who imagines he'll see one hair of my head at any other time is living in fairyland. I've had plenty of practice at not looking like what I am, after all."

"True…"

That night I dreamt about poor Janßen again. Karl shook me awake and I sat in bed, trying not to be sick.

"Shove over," he said. "The room's freezing."

There was plenty of room for two and I moved across. He dropped his dressing gown on the floor, got in beside me, fluffed up a couple of pillows and pulled the duvet up to his chin.

"That's better… I'll stay if you like."

"Thanks."

"Strange, sleeping on your own, isn't it," he said, "when you're so used to having the other fellows around? You have one of those vile dreams and you wake up and it's so quiet – there's no one snoring, just silence and your own thoughts. Makes it very hard to steady yourself down, and even then you don't want to go back to sleep."

"You have them too."

"Everyone does – you know that."

"I hadn't thought of that – the being on my own bit."

But he was right – the only times I'd slept alone since the war began were on leave, and it did feel strange.

"It's something I really noticed when I was back home, just before my course started," he went on. "The house was so quiet, with my being the only one of the family there – and I had a nightmare, a real shocker, and being alone seemed to make it worse."

"What was it about?" I asked, before I thought what I was doing.

"All right – I'll tell you mine if you'll tell me yours! I was out in No Man's Land, and the Tommies had worked out where I was and six of them were sneaking out to dispose of me.

"I shot three of them and then I had to reload – the whole thing was my own damn fault for going for a second shot. I got one more and then one of them threw a jam-tin bomb and it went off right beside me, but it wasn't strong enough to kill me, just left me all cut about and like a bloody pincushion with nails and so on sticking out all over.

"And then the last two didn't come to finish me off. They just disappeared and left me there, and I knew there was no point calling for help, that no one would be able to come out, and I was bleeding but not fast enough, and the pain was getting worse – and that's when I woke up."

Nice.

"That was always my worst fear – it was always in the back of my mind that they might do that to me. You know how some fellows hate snipers."

"Yes." And giving one a lingering, agonised death was exactly what some sick bastard would think of doing.

"Your turn."

So I told him about Janßen and the state of my uniform after the raid, and that led on to communion and my difficulty eating. I was surprised I managed to say so much – I think it was because the atmosphere was so intimate and yet we weren't facing each other, so I didn't have to look him in the eye.

"Nasty. But it was just in the dream that it went in your mouth?"

"Yes."

"You have to stop that sort of thing from getting a hold on you. Tell you what – we'll go for a bloody long walk, and have schnitzel or chops or something else that's not in lumps. It won't remind you so much and after a bit you'll get used to eating without thinking... Mind you, it's all cultural, isn't it, these taboos? Some tribes make a ceremony of eating their late comrades and enemies, especially those who fought bravely. I think they believe they'll absorb the dead man's courage."

"What is it about snipers and anthropology?" I asked, laughing in spite of myself.

He turned his head and looked at me, amused and curious. "What do you mean?"

"I had all sorts of stuff about burial rites from Taschner, and now you're talking about cannibalism."

It was his turn to laugh. "Oh, I see… Well, I had some very interesting conversations in the dugout. It's amazing what other fellows know, when you get the chance to find out. Koch used to talk about art, would you believe."

"Art?!"

"Yes – apparently Grandpa's quite a collector. Mind you, he can afford it."

For some reason I struggled with the idea of a gangster collecting pictures.

"What sort of art?"

"Impressionist. Apparently he's got a whole gallery full of…"

The next thing I knew it was morning and for a moment I wondered why Karl was sound asleep in my bed… Then I remembered, and was astonished that I'd not only got back to sleep but had slept without dreaming. His being there had been more of a comfort than I'd realised and I felt rather less troubled.

The walk was glorious – we tramped through snow sprinkled with diamonds by the low winter sun, the trees towering over us in majestic indifference. The air was pure and pine-scented, and the only sound was our footsteps.

Karl was right – the place was good for the soul after the shattering ugliness of the Front. Being able to walk upright wherever we wanted, without having to think who might be watching, was nothing short of miraculous in itself.

I have a few days of guaranteed life and I'm going to make the most of them.

By the time we found a village pub I was starving, but I still had an almost overwhelming feeling of nausea when I actually started eating. I'd followed Karl's suggestion and chosen schnitzel, and I tried not to look at the pieces I was cutting off it.

He kept up such a stream of trivial chatter that I wanted to tell him to shut up – and then I realised I'd been so distracted that my plate was almost empty.

The hike back was not quite such fun as quite a lot of it was uphill, and the sun was going down and the temperature with it.

"A nice large brandy when we get back, I think!" he said cheerfully. "And I've still got some Stollen left over."

"How did you manage to save that?"

Stollen was always the first thing to be finished at Christmas in our house.

"Sheer willpower! No, I put it away and took care to forget about it."

Karl had always been good at saving things. He was the only man I knew who could make a bar of chocolate last a fortnight.

"So, what about these girls you promised?" I asked as we sat by the fire. Brandy and Stollen was an excellent combination and unthreatening in appearance, and I ate about three slices.

"Well, I did a bit of a recce on my first night here. I found a pub in town and got talking to the barman, who's a couple of years older than us."

"What's he doing here, then?"

"Lost a foot last summer, somewhere in the East. Said the Austrians were completely fucking useless, no help at all, but that's another story. Anyway, I asked him where people go for a bit of fun and he started telling me about the tarts – so I said, no, no, my friend and I have been on the Western Front since autumn '14 and we're sick of paying."

"Too right!"

"And he gave me this."

Karl handed me a pink card.

"Free Love Club," I read out. "What the hell's that?"

"Don't you have one at home?" he asked with a note of puzzlement. "They're very popular – there are loads in Berlin."

"Maybe – but where I come from we have proper morality, not the Prussian variety!"

"Ha bloody ha. So the next evening I investigated."

"And?"

"Well, this is the sort of town where they lock up their daughters, so all the women were a bit older – married women or widows."

"How much older?"

"Thirties. Young enough to still be attractive but old enough to know what they're doing. And how old do you think most of those Belgian tarts are, anyway?"

"You said married women."

"Yes – but their husbands know about it. Some of them go on the same night, they probably tell each other all about it later. There's a sauna and steam area where you meet people, and private rooms where you go once you've paired up. I had a bloody good evening, I can tell you."

"So tell me, then."

And he did. By the time he'd got to the third woman I was practically drooling and almost painfully hard. And then a bit later he'd had a threesome. He gave me every last detail.

"What time does it start?" I asked.

"Not tonight."

"Why not? Karl, you bastard, I've got a stonker like a bloody iron bar after your stories, and now you tell me there's no chance of a fuck tonight!"

"It's not a mixed night – that's tomorrow. So you'll have to wait – unless you fancy men's night!"

"They don't have that?!"

"Certainly do – and women's night. No, you'll just have to wait till tomorrow and resort to the usual measures in the meantime!"

"Oh, for God's sake! I really could go off some people!"

He laughed. "You won't say that tomorrow!"

The following day dragged interminably. We went for another walk but all I could think about was the evening. Finally it arrived, and it did not disappoint.

There were, unsurprisingly, more women than men at the club. At first I was uneasy at being naked in front of a group of women, especially as some of them were rather attractive – then I saw the way they looked at us, and realised that arousal would be taken as a compliment.

We'd only been there a couple of minutes when a plump but pretty woman took me by the hand.

"Would you like to come and play?" she asked, brushing her nipples against my chest.

My response was rapid. She glanced downwards and murmured, "That looks like a yes to me!" and led me to one of the private rooms.

She wasn't quite what I'd had in mind, but any misgivings evaporated the moment her mouth closed on my cock. I had to stop her doing that as she was too good at it and I was getting too excited. She turned out to be bloody good at everything else as well.

I wanted her again but she wanted to move on, which seemed to be the etiquette. No one wanted emotional contact, just that of flesh.

I lost all track of time. At some point one of the women said, "Bring your friend as well," gesturing at Karl.

That was a step too far. I was trying to think of an excuse when I was saved by his disappearing with a woman with large, pendulous breasts.

"Maybe next time," I said to my companion, and closed the door behind us before she could suggest someone else.

Some time later my body had had enough, even if my mind would have liked to continue. I had another shower and lay on one of the loungers, sated and on the verge of going to sleep.

"What did you think of that?" asked a familiar voice.

"Bloody fantastic!"

"Ready for home? Or do you have another session in mind?"

"I don't think I can!"

"Nor can I," he said happily. "I am completely fucked out – for now, at any rate."

"I'd never have believed a place like that could exist in such a sleepy little town," I said as we walked home arm in arm.

"Just goes to show," he said. "Seek and ye shall find, and all that."

I fell asleep the second my head hit the pillow, and by the time I woke the sun was pouring through the curtains. I hadn't felt so relaxed for a very long time.

Karl was reading the paper over breakfast. I was ravenous and piled my plate with ham and bread.

He grinned at me. "Hungry work, that! Should last us a day or two, anyway."

"When's the next mixed night?"

"Our last night here, according to the poster in the foyer."

"Oh, good."

"Indeed. Who knows what the future will bring?"

"You'll be investigating the Serbian tarts."

"Ah. No, as it happens, I won't. They'll be French. The Brandenburg Corps is in France now."

Part of me was very relieved – there always seemed to

be something barbaric about the Balkans and I was glad he wouldn't be going there. But at the same time I knew the French could fight.

"Where?"

He looked at me for a moment. "Somewhere near Rheims. But that's between you and me."

"Of course."

"And what about you?" he asked. "Do you have any idea what you'll be flying and where?"

I shook my head. "No idea. Johanna asked me the same thing – as I said, she's really interested in flying and the aces. Took me by surprise, that did. And she said all her friends will want to meet me when I've got my pilot's badge."

"Is that so? Well, I suppose it is rather glamorous. I'd never thought about the effect on girls, though." He actually sounded quite interested.

"So become a flier and have them flocking round you!"

"Become a flier and you won't need a funeral," he said. "They can just fill in the hole."

I poured us another cup of coffee and he went back to the paper.

"Good God! Listen to this!" he exclaimed. "'Notorious gangster murdered. Albrecht Koch, long known in the Düsseldorf underworld, was found last night stabbed to death on the doorstep of a villa belonging to Friedrich Bremer, his grandfather. It seems that he had been killed in a different location and his body placed there as a warning. Koch would have been an easy target for the family's rivals as he was partly paralysed due to a head wound received on the Western Front, where he served with distinction as a sniper'."

"Bloody hell! He was right to be worried about going home, then."

"So it would appear."

"Poor old Koch – rotten way to go."

"I'm not sure I have much sympathy," he said. "He was a murderer, after all – they wanted to kill him because he'd killed one of theirs."

"True… I'm surprised the police didn't pick him up first."

"I don't think there was ever much question of that," he replied. "Koch told me there weren't any witnesses – and he hinted at corruption, as well."

"It's still one more whom we used to know," I said. "I never liked him much but I'm still sorry he's dead. And if you ask me, all those gangland types are much the same – who knows what the man he killed had done?"

"We can't have violence on the streets, though… Shall we see if we can hire some skis today?"

"Yes, good idea."

It was pure joy gliding through the silent countryside, along gently undulating trails. I tried to store up as much of the peace and beauty as I could, only too aware that my leave was running out fast.

After we handed the skis back we stopped at a café for a snack. There was a poster on one of the walls advertising a 'Charity Ball to benefit the Wounded', phrased in rather purple prose that made me want to both laugh and throw up.

"Oh, look," Karl said. "A dance. Tomorrow."

"In aid of 'our glorious heroes'," I said.

"Well, we must allow people their illusions. God alone knows what's 'glorious' about having your bollocks blown off… Dance could be fun, though. Girls."

"Shortage of men."

"Quite." And before I could say another word he'd bought two tickets from the waitress. "All we have to do now is find Baroness Greding's place, which can't be exactly difficult."

"Karl, you're forgetting something," I said as we walked back

465

to the villa. "What the hell are we going to wear? I mean, it's going to be smart, isn't it, and the Baroness's flunkies won't let NCOs in."

"Oh, shit. You're right – they won't. Sorry, I just didn't think of that. Tell you what, we'll have a look in the wardrobes – there's bound to be evening dress that'll fit, and if there isn't then we'll have to find a hire place."

Some chance. How likely is it that the owners of this villa are the same size and shape as either of us, or that there's a tailor hiring out evening wear in a small town like this?

To my astonishment I struck lucky in the first wardrobe we tried.

"Cinders, you *shall* go to the ball!" Karl cried triumphantly as I stood in front of the mirror. "Very dashing – the girls will be eating out of your hand!"

"Let's see if there's something for you."

And there was.

"Well, that's us both sorted," he said.

"Apart from the remarks about not being in uniform," I said.

"Just tell the truth – you're on leave before pilot training. If fliers really are glamorous then that should give you added appeal!"

"So long as they don't think I'm shirking."

"Franz, for God's sake – who cares what they bloody well think? You know the truth and that's all that matters. And even if you don't strike lucky, there's the Club the night after, and when you're at the flying school you'll be able to get to Berlin – they'll have to let you out now and again."

"And you can give me the address of those dancers!" I said mischievously, knowing full well that he would do nothing of the kind.

"Sorry, Franz – but you know me. I never give anyone's address without asking them first."

"I know. Just teasing."

That night Karl woke me from another horrible nightmare. "Not the same one, I hope?" he asked as he got into my bed.

"No. It followed from the one you told me about – I was in the front line, you were out, we heard the mayhem when they got you, and then I had to listen to you screaming, and I couldn't do anything to help you."

"Sorry. Maybe I shouldn't have told you."

"No, it's fine – if you hadn't then I wouldn't have told you about my dream about Janßen, and you wouldn't have been able to help."

"Is it getting easier – eating, I mean?"

"Yes. I mean, I'm not back to normal but I don't feel I'm going to be sick any more."

"That's something." He sounded relieved.

"How did you know? What I should do, I mean?"

He sighed. "Friedrich wasn't too clever after Nonneboschen – you remember, he lost his eye there and most of his men. He was in quite a bad way mentally – nightmares, insomnia, couldn't eat. So I tried a few things and it turns out that what worked for him seems to be working for you."

"There's an alternative occupation for you after the war," I said. "You can train as an alienist."

"Not fucking likely. Dealing with mad people all the time? Bugger that."

"Mad people?" I repeated uneasily. "What, like me and Friedrich?"

"You are not mad and neither was he," he said firmly. "You both had an entirely reasonable response to extreme circumstances... No, it's the piano for me and only the piano, as you know. That's if there is an 'after the war'."

That was the first time I'd heard him say anything like that. It was a thought he'd always kept locked away.

"We can only hope," he added after a long pause.

"That's what I tell myself."

"Oh, you'll be all right," he said confidently, "but war has never been kind to my family. We've always been left in the field. After the Seven Years' War there were only three male Leussows left – two old men and a boy of six who'd never seen his father."

"History doesn't have to repeat itself... Karl, how can you be sure I'll be all right?"

"You will. Just wait and see."

I laughed. "You sound like a fortune-teller at a fair! And what about yourself?"

He put on a quavering, old-crone voice. "The crystal ball is dark..."

"Oh, bollocks! You do talk the most perfect rot."

"In a way I do," he said thoughtfully. "Because the Seven Years' War saved our bacon. Up till then we'd always divided on inheritance, so we'd been getting poorer and poorer, but everything came into that one boy's hands. He decided it was best kept that way, and set up the entail. Add in the rich widow he married and we were set up nicely."

"And there are still three of you now."

"True. And I should be spared inheriting, which..."

I woke slowly into a state of very pleasant languor, lying slightly curled on my left side. Someone's knees and feet were touching mine, an arm lay across my ribs, and my arm rested on the other's waist. The bed was wonderfully snug, especially with the extra warmth from the other body.

For a moment I couldn't remember where I was, or with whom, and I opened my eyes to a strange bedroom and an initial feeling of complete disorientation.

Karl was still asleep and I didn't want to wake him by moving.

It's like sharing a blanket in the barns, I thought. We'd often woken to find that one of us had draped an arm or a leg across the other, and the comfort was psychological as well as physical, especially when things had been messy and our nerves were frayed.

The only difference was that now we were naked, in bed, but as the contact wasn't intimate that didn't bother me and I doubted he would mind either.

His face looked so young and innocent in sleep.

There's a deceptive appearance. Innocence is long gone, and we're both so very old in experience.

I didn't want to think about all that.

He blinked, and his eyes opened slowly and looked at me. He blinked again, then smiled at me sleepily. Suddenly I realised the situation could be misunderstood – I didn't want him to think I'd set it up on purpose.

"Morning," I said.

"Is it?"

"Broad fucking daylight!"

"Mm, so it is." His eyes looked straight into mine.

"Karl, I didn't… I mean, I've just woken up too, like this—"

"Don't let's talk. It's too early."

His eyes still held mine and he didn't move. There was a warmth in his gaze that I hadn't seen for a long time.

Neither of us moved, or spoke, or looked away. Time slowed, seemed almost to stop. Nothing else existed.

Eventually he stretched. "Very nice, lying here, but I need a pee and I'm getting very hungry!"

The spell was broken and a couple of minutes later we got up. By the time I was washed, shaved and dressed it was almost as if it had never been.

The morning sun poured into the dining room, harsh and bright, not at all like the soft light that had filtered through my bedroom curtains.

I couldn't quite read Karl's eyes as he passed me coffee and rolls. The warmth had gone, replaced by something that could almost have been regret or sadness. I didn't understand that at all.

Maybe he's just aware that his leave is running out, and that soon he'll be back at the Front.

"Walk or ski?" he asked.

"Ski again, I think. We've both done plenty of walking, after all!"

He laughed. "That's for sure! Probably been to the Moon and back."

We got back just in time to get ready for the dance.

I wasn't sure if I really wanted to go. The whole idea felt strange and artificial. Reality was the Front, not swirling pastel silks and tailcoats.

I hope I can remember how to dance. It's been so long I'll probably tread on the poor girls' toes.

"Quite a contrast to how we looked in Flanders," he said as we got ready. "Still worried they'll think we're shirkers?"

"Couldn't give a fuck."

"Me neither."

No one will think you're a shirker when they see your eyes, Karl, I thought but was careful not to say. *I wonder if that look's permanent or if it'll fade once the war's over.*

Baroness Greding's was just outside the old town walls. We walked there through the crisp winter night, the snow crunching beneath our feet.

"I hope it's not full of blushing virgins," he said.

"As you said before, they probably keep their daughters under lock and key. You won't have any luck tonight, Don Giovanni!"

"Bet you I do!"

"How much?"

"Ten marks."

"Done."

The Baroness's house was a blaze of light and colour. Everyone was dressed up to the nines and clearly determined to forget the war. One glance showed, however, that the women far outnumbered the men.

This could just be a happy hunting-ground...

The major-domo asked our names and announced us in booming tones.

"Herr von Leussow! Herr Becker!"

"Must have been a sergeant major," I muttered to Karl.

"Indeed."

The Baroness was small and plump and glittering with diamonds. The Baron was absent. At the Front? Dead?

Karl bowed gracefully over her hand and I followed in his wake. That he took precedence over me on social occasions always made me smile to myself. It was something he simply accepted, just as he accepted that the Baroness and her husband took precedence over him. I don't think he ever gave it a second thought – it was just how things were.

There were more girls than a man could do justice to, many of them young and pretty, and the tables groaned with food from Switzerland.

This must be costing a fortune. Still, she looks as if she can afford it.

Eat, drink and be merry, for tomorrow we die... or in a few weeks' time, anyway.

After dancing almost non-stop for an hour I paused for breath. The girls were pretty enough, but rather insipid and tediously virtuous. I'd seen Karl a few times, with a succession of girls, but never with the same one twice.

My ten marks seemed quite safe.

I took another glass of champagne.

"Hello, Franz. What are you doing here?"

I hadn't heard that voice for years but it still made my spine tingle.

It can't be Sophie.

I turned round. "Countess – how lovely to see you."

I held onto her hand a moment longer than necessary, thinking how chaste that kiss was compared to those my adolescent imagination had given her.

"Franz, really! Don't be so formal!"

"How are you, Sophie? I'd almost forgotten how lovely you are."

That was a lie. Not in a million years would I forget how lovely she was. When I'd been sixteen and spotty I'd lusted after her desperately. One glimpse had been enough to make me sweaty, rock-hard, and scarlet with embarrassment. She'd been so remote at twenty-one, so cool and polished, so different from my clumsy awkwardness. My dreams were full of her, and my fantasies.

She was plain Sophie Morsch in those days. Her father owned a large paper mill just outside town and had been a school friend of Papa's. My dreams were shattered when she married. Ernst, Graf Schönwald was rich, suave, and sickeningly handsome.

"I'm very well, Franz. How are you?"

"Fine, thanks. Enjoying my leave."

"You're in the Army," she said flatly.

"Isn't everyone? How's the Count?"

"I had a letter from him yesterday. He's in France somewhere, with the artillery. He was wounded last year, not badly, thank God, but they sent him back there so quickly. I do wish it were all over and that he were home."

She hadn't changed at all. She looked so delicate, so vulnerable, her big blue eyes looking up at me. I wanted to hold her and kiss the worry away...

God, she was beautiful! Such a sweet little face, pale, clear skin, golden hair piled on her head and that wonderful figure. *If I'd been older she'd have been mine – no, she wouldn't, you idiot. You wouldn't have stood a chance against the Count and his money.*

"But you haven't told me what you're doing here, Franz."

"I'm here with a friend. He's borrowed a villa on the edge of the town and we're here for a few days. I don't know where he's got to… Oh, there he is."

I waved to Karl and he joined us.

"Sophie, this is my friend Karl von Leussow. Karl, this is Sophie, Gräfin Schönwald."

Karl's manners were beautiful. Very polished, very correct, but with no trace of stiffness. Sometimes I was very aware that I was a bourgeois – a rich bourgeois, but middle-class all the same.

I'd intended to ask Sophie to dance, but the next waltz began while they were talking and she accepted his invitation at once.

Bugger the nobility! That's the second time one of them has snatched Sophie away.

I watched them rather sourly. They were both good dancers and they moved together easily, as if they'd known each other for years. I could cheerfully have throttled him.

They stayed together for the next dance and the one after that. I was damned if I was going to wait for her to get tired of him, and there were several pretty, shy young things obviously dying to be asked to dance.

Even while I was dancing I couldn't help watching the two of them. When they weren't dancing they were drinking champagne together. Both of them had lost interest in anyone else, me included.

I was so full of jealous petulance that it took me a while to see what was happening. I'd never seen him look at a woman like that before. I'd seen him flirting with girls more times than I could count, but this was different.

They passed close by me and I was shocked by the intent look he was giving her, as if no one else existed. His eyes were almost blue and softer than I could have imagined, and his face was alight as he listened to something she was saying.

Does he know she's married? I wondered. *Her title could come from her father, and she's wearing gloves.*

He wouldn't care – but should I tell him?

Not your business, Franz. We might both be dead in a month, and anyway they're only dancing.

Suddenly the orchestra was playing the national anthem and the dance was over. Sophie left with her sister-in-law, who could hardly have been pleased that she'd devoted most of the evening to one young man.

Karl and I walked back to the villa. It was a bitter, crisply cold night and the snow lay thick on the pavements. Above us the sky was clear and black and the stars were bright. Our breath clouded in the freezing air.

"Ah, Franz! What an evening! What a woman!"

I'd never seen him so happy. He flung out his arms and waltzed down the street, singing.

"Karl, for God's sake be quiet! You'll wake everyone!"

He lost his footing and fell into a snowbank and lay there laughing. I went over to help him up and he pulled me down into the snow.

"You bastard!" I grabbed a handful of snow and stuffed it down his collar.

"Get off, you sod!" Snow straight in my face. All right, we were a bit drunk. So what?

Suddenly we were brightly lit. *Shit – no fucking cover—*

"What's going on out there? Clear off, you louts, or I'll call the police!"

An angry, bearded man was leaning out of an upstairs window. *Thank fuck for that.*

"Try the trenches if you think we're noisy!" Karl shouted back.

"Clear off back to Berlin! We don't want your sort here!"

"Come on, Karl. We don't want trouble."

"Christian, come back to bed!" A woman's voice, muffled and sleepy.

The window closed abruptly and the curtain shut off the light. We got up and leaned on each other, laughing.

The next day Karl called on Sophie and she accepted his invitation to dinner that night. I was more than a bit peeved.

"I thought we were going to the Free Love Club," I complained.

"Oh, sorry, Franz – I'd completely forgotten… Look, you'll be all right going by yourself, won't you? Now you've seen how it works."

"Well, yes…"

He was right, of course. All I wanted was another bloody good fuck before my very uncertain future. All the same, I couldn't resist teasing him.

"What was it you wrote about Johnny?" I said. "Ah, yes, that was it – 'I've a horrible suspicion he wants to gaze adoringly into her eyes and murmur sentimental crap into her ears'!"

"Bollocks! I don't want to do anything of the kind. I'm just having dinner with a rather attractive woman, that's all."

"I saw the look you were giving her!"

"I do believe you're jealous!"

That hit the spot and I very nearly told him she was married, but I knew it wouldn't make any difference.

Karl had no scruples about adultery. When we'd been at Heidelberg he'd gone to a weekend house party and had come home looking like the cat that had eaten the entire dish of cream.

"That was exhausting!" he'd said happily. "Just between you and me, my hostess wanted me for one purpose only – and I was very happy to oblige!"

"But she's married!"

"No one owns someone else, do they? He should pay her more attention, instead of spending the summer sailing and the winter shooting."

At the time I'd been far too innocent to understand why a thirty-five year old woman would want a nineteen year old fellow to fuck her stupid all weekend.

And anyway he was only having dinner with Sophie.

We headed into town together.

"Have fun," he said, "and don't do anything I wouldn't do!"

"That gives me plenty of scope!" I retorted, wondering what Karl wouldn't do sexually.

Anything goes between consenting adults, he'd said once, and I'd never been too sure what "anything" actually meant.

There must be a line somewhere but God alone knows where it is.

I had another excellent evening, but once I was satisfied an uneasy niggle crept into my mind. Every woman I'd been with had somehow been transformed into Sophie. I couldn't stop thinking about her, and the fact that she was having dinner with Karl instead of with me began to rankle.

I knew her first, I thought in a sudden fit of jealousy. *It should have been me looking into her eyes.*

It'll be all right when I get back to the villa. He'll be sitting there, we can have a brandy together and I'll know nothing's happened between them. I'll tell him all about my evening and he'll wish he'd joined me instead of wasting his time gazing at Sophie.

But the villa was in silent darkness. I let myself in quietly and went upstairs to my bedroom. The bedside clock said two in the morning – so where was Karl? If we'd been in Berlin I wouldn't have thought twice about it, but I couldn't imagine anywhere in Villingen staying open all night.

Surely he can't be in Sophie's bed? The thought made me go hot and cold.

A few minutes later I heard footsteps, two sets, creeping down the stairs, then the front door closed quietly. I hurried into the next room and looked down into the street.

The bright moon lit their hair to silver and threw their shadows black on the snow. His arm was round her and his hand lay on her waist in a gesture partly protective, partly sensual. She leaned her head on his shoulder and he kissed her hair. It was hanging loose down to her waist, shining against her dark coat. She hadn't bothered to fasten it up again.

He'd been fucking the woman I wanted.

I had a sudden vision of her naked, on her back, her thighs spread to receive him. And that would have been just the beginning. Maybe he'd knelt behind her, or had her against the wall. I could see her legs around his waist, his hands under her bottom, see the lust in their faces. My face burned and my head throbbed with rage.

They must have been in bed when I got back. Sophie's bed was too difficult, of course – she lived in a house full of people. The villa was easy. So easy, too, to take advantage of a lonely, worried woman.

I was too angry to go back to sleep and I went downstairs to wait for him and confront him. Time passed and he didn't return – *obviously taking a very slow stroll to Sophie's*, I thought sourly.

I shivered, suddenly aware that the room was freezing and that my borrowed dressing gown wasn't much help. My anger was also starting to cool, and suddenly I realised that I didn't want to encounter Karl after all, that maybe the whole thing was better slept on.

Sleep proved elusive. I heard Karl let himself in, and anger flared again.

You bastard. You amoral fucking bastard.

And yet… a thought entered my head. I pushed it out, and it crept back in again. *I should have told him she's married. It's partly my fault. Maybe,* I countered, *but what difference would it have made? Karl doesn't give a shit, you know that.*

But what about you, Franz? How many of those women at the Free Love Club were married?

That's different. Their husbands knew what they were doing – they weren't sneaking off committing adultery behind their backs.

So what about Sophie? What sort of loving wife is she? She jumped into Karl's bed when she'd only known him five minutes. And was her concern for her husband genuine or was she playing for my sympathy?

Dawn was breaking, the first faint light creeping through the curtains.

God alone knows what's waiting for Karl in France. They must be planning something big if they've brought the Brandenburg Corps back. Is it really so bad for him to have gone to bed with a woman he actually wanted, instead of having yet another casual fuck?

I remembered the look on his face while they'd been dancing, and realised he'd been completely captivated by her. Having her in his bed must have meant something.

I was wise not to confront him last night. It all looks different in the daylight.

All the same, the atmosphere at breakfast became strained very quickly.

"Morning, Franz," he said, unsurprisingly in very good spirits.

"Morning," I said sulkily.

"How was the Free Love Club?"

"Good, but it probably didn't compare with fucking the Countess," I said. "Have fun, did you?"

I hadn't intended to say anything but the words slipped out before I could stop them.

He looked at me, surprised.

"I saw the two of you leaving."

"Oh. Well, yes, we came back here after dinner and yes, we went to bed…" His face was alight. "I've never met anyone like her… We're going to write and I'm hoping to see her again next time I get leave."

"If her husband isn't home."

"What?"

"Her husband. Wasn't she wearing a wedding ring, or were you so overcome with lust that you didn't bother to look?"

He looked at me in confusion and dismay. "She's a widow."

I almost choked on my coffee. "Is that what she told you?"

His good humour had vanished and the last hint of warmth left his eyes.

"Well, I suppose she hinted rather than telling… Franz, I have the feeling there's a lot you haven't told me."

"Yes, there is. Karl, I'm sorry. I should have told you she's married and I don't know why I didn't – I suppose because it never occurred to me that anything would happen between you, with the time being so short. Anyway, I've known her since we were children. I had a crush on her when I was a teenager but she married the Count. He's an artillery officer – she told me he's in France somewhere. Very much alive, as far as she knows."

There was a very long pause and then he said coldly, "What a fucking idiot I am."

"Hardly," I said. "How were you to know she was lying? I

479

doubt you're the first or the last. She made a real play for my sympathy as well – in fact, I'd have been in with a chance if you hadn't turned up."

I was beginning to realise that Sophie was something of a bitch. She must have realised how Karl was starting to feel about her, and she'd just played with him.

"So all she wanted was a fuck." He laughed. "Well, I suppose that's the biter bit, so I can't complain."

There was a pause and then he added, "So that's why you were so pissed off with me just now? Because you wanted her?"

"Yes, but I think I was better off without her," I said slowly. "I just hope you had a good time."

"It was all right... I wanted to see her again because she actually seemed to be interested in me... I thought maybe... but clearly I was wrong. Oh, what the hell! I got a fuck and you owe me ten marks!"

I'd completely forgotten about our bet.

"Oh, shit, so I do! We'll have to go to the bank – I haven't got enough on me."

"Tell you what, give me half now and the rest next time we meet."

"Fine by me – but what if one of us doesn't make it?"

He laughed. "Then it gets written off. I'm happy with that if you are."

I handed over five marks. "You can spend it on French tarts," I said.

"I'll need some more Venus first," he said. "And I'll bet you do too, after the Free Love Club! Now tell me all about it... No, hang on, that's not fair, because I don't want to tell you about Sophie and you don't want to hear it anyway."

"Stuff that," I said. "Listen to my story and you'll wish you'd had the sense to come with me!"

And I told him most of it – I was never able to go into quite the level of detail that he did, but I still told him enough to make him shift in his chair.

"We made the most of our leave, anyway," he said.

"Yes… Shame it's over."

When will this business end? When will we be able to enjoy life without the thought that it could be finished at any moment?

"Franz, whatever happens, remember –" He broke off.

I looked at him, waiting for him to continue, but he didn't.

"Remember what?" I prompted as his silence continued.

He smiled warmly. "Remember which way is up!" he said flippantly.

That wasn't what you wanted to say, but whatever it was you've obviously changed your mind.

"And you remember everything you've ever learned," I said. "I want that weekend in Berlin!"

"It shall be yours next time we get leave together, I promise."

His train was due to go about an hour before mine. I had to post my civilian clothes back to my parents, so we went to the station first, where I left him with his bags. We reckoned there'd be plenty of time for me to get back to see him off.

The queue was ridiculous, mostly women sending parcels to their sons. I attracted a few curious stares, as if no one could understand what a soldier could be sending to anyone.

By the time I was first in the queue time was getting very tight. And the bloody woman at the counter had made a mistake of some sort with the address, and had a long and increasingly emotional altercation with the postmistress.

Oh, for fuck's sake! Why couldn't the stupid cow have got it right? I'll be lucky to get there in time to say goodbye at this rate.

For a moment I wondered why it was so important – neither of us had ever set much store by farewells, but for some reason this felt different.

Finally I got my parcel sent, looked at the clock and somehow remembered to mind my language. I ran, as fast as I could, through the snowy streets, into the station and onto the platform.

Karl's train was pulling out, the last carriage leaving the station.

Too late.

He's gone, I thought miserably. *I'll never see him again.*

I slumped onto a bench, surprised at the strength of my feelings. *You're being melodramatic, Franz* – but then I realised it was the first time we'd been separated with such uncertainty ahead of us. Every time previously, the one leaving had been going to greater safety: on a course, on leave, or to hospital.

This time neither of us knew what awaited him and I could only hope that we would meet again.

It's no use, Franz, I told myself as my train chugged towards Berlin. *There's nothing you can do to help him – and you're going to have enough to think about yourself.*

I'm actually going to fly. I looked out of the window at the clouds drifting across the sky. *I'm actually going to climb up among the clouds, and look down at the Earth.*

It was so exciting that I could hardly wait to get to the airfield.